Francis William Lauderdale Adams

**A child of the age**

Francis William Lauderdale Adams

**A child of the age**

ISBN/EAN: 9783337215507

Printed in Europe, USA, Canada, Australia, Japan

Cover: Foto ©Andreas Hilbeck / pixelio.de

More available books at **www.hansebooks.com**

# A CHILD OF THE AGE

# A CHILD OF THE AGE
# BY FRANCIS ADAMS

*Stirb und werde!*
*Denn so lang du das nicht hast,*
*Bist du nur ein trüber Gast*
*Auf der dunkeln Erde.*

GOETHE.

LONDON : JOHN LANE, VIGO ST.

BOSTON : ROBERTS BROS., 1894

[NOTE.—This novel is the first of a series which Francis Adams intended, had he lived, to complete. In a letter, dated March 23rd, 1892, he says: 'It was my modest little scheme to draw types of all the social life of the day. "A Child of the Age," is the first of a series of novels and tales. Oh, I was going to do as big as Balzac that way! Fancy what a pretty scheme for a jackanapes of eighteen, and to have sweated at it all these years! I finished the last but one of the novels (chronologically) on my way back from Australia [1890]. There are three novels to do yet and about eight short tales.' He also intended to work through the same cycle of characters in his Verse. The early chapters of the 'Poetical Works' correspond to and illustrate this novel.

In 1879, at the age of seventeen, Adams left Shrewsbury School—the Glastonbury of this novel—and spent the next two years chiefly in Paris. In 1880 he wrote the first draft of the book, and during the two years following, latterly in London and Ventnor, he recast and corrected his work. Under the title 'Leicester, an Autobiography' it was published in 1884, while the author was in Australia. Some time after, on reading his novel critically as the work of another writer, he was surprised to find how truly he had depicted experiences which at the time of writing he had still to undergo. In another letter [1885] he says: 'I see its faults clearly, but entirely fail to reproduce its excellences. It is a remarkable book and it came to me to write it in a quite spontaneous and inspired way.' He said on another occasion: 'It was an honest attempt to give a candid revelation, but it was crude and morbid and not quite candid. Beware,' he adds, 'of taking "my [characters] for [myself. [I] [am] terribly objective; even when I wrote "Leicester," I wrote of one entirely unlike myself.'

The book is now published in its final form as revised and to a great extent rewritten by its author a year or two before his death.]

# A. L. A.

*Vita janua mortis.*

*Let me think of you, O pure and radiant Spirit, as you were to me once, and as you are to me now.*

*I thought of you as noble, great, god-like. I saw only the serene beauty of what was best in you, and it transfigured all your Work, and gave it a divine significance. Now I notify faults in you and in it, grave faults and limitations as grave. My worship of you is over, and I discriminate in my very admiration. My worship is over, but I sometimes feel as if my love were scarcely begun. And I perceive also that, even in my boyhood's doting blindness, I yet saw clearly; for, to me as I was then, you were indeed wonderfully significant, noble, great, god-like. You were the father of my soul no less than of my body, and the yearning to achieve Works not altogether unworthy of the simple grandeur of truth and contemplation found its well-spring in the light and limpidity of your heavenly-brooding eyes.*

*You never knew this, and now you will never know it.*

*When I passed from the blinding midsummer light that lay deep upon the green strange earth and the blue and winding sea-gulf, and entered that shadowy room—when I closed the door, and, in all the fulness of my solitary anguish, bent and kissed you on the eyes and lips (You could not withdraw yourself from my embrace, O my love, O my god, for all your transcendant beauty of perfected life!), it was as if some unloved and unregarded Lazarus had kissed the dead lips and* eyes of Christ. You were my Christ. You raised me from the dead, from the hell of the departed, and my faith was to accomplish the equal miracle of your own resurrection.

But the disillusionment of the evolution of time, for all true Spirits, though it is grievous and implacable, has the most precious consolations. As I have lost Christ the Son of God, but have gained Jesus the Son of Man, and count my loss for gain: so, O pure and radiant Spirit, I have but changed the impassioned idolisation my boyhood lavished upon you for a chaster affection, an everlasting regard.

1886.

*' Die and live again! For so long as thou*
*hast not done so, thou art nought but a be-*
*wildered stranger upon the darksome earth.'*

# A CHILD OF THE AGE

# I

## I

AT some time in my earliest childhood I must, I think, have lived near a wind-mill: for I have, every now and then, ever since I can remember, seen one in the middle of a tender yellowy-golden band of sunset on a sandy elevation. Somewhere, perhaps below in the house in which I am, a canary, cageless, with upward-throbbing throat, sings.

And then I know a darker vision: a darker vision of a slanting planked floor, with an uncertain atmosphere therein, and a sound from thereout, as of a ship on the sea. A dim-rayed lamp oscillates in the middle. A woman is up in one of the berths, soothing and giving suck to a baby fractious with sleep and misery. In the far corner is a huddled tartan-petticoated lump-round, with two protruding bare knees—a child unkempt, dirty, miserable, afraid of some heavy coming footstep. I know in some way that I am the child.

And then comes yet another vision, but lighter, and in a broader scene. A red-cheeked woman rolls a perambulator and a quiet little boy down a cindery path in the shine of a moist sunset. They stop by a grey, sweating, barred gate. (There are four or five bars: not less.) In a little, the boy struggles out from the tarpaulin of the perambulator on to the clammy earth: crosses the tall wet rank grasses: climbs on to the gate, and looks at a band of tender yellowy-gold down by the horizon, which is to him a new revelation of his earliest dreams. For on that day that tender yellowy-gold band and far sky of light seem to him to contain

A

faint outlines of great white-winged angels: beyond, a chasm of clearer purer light; and beyond, God.

Now everything changes. My next recollection of a certain fixed occasion brings with it an acquaintance, often strangely minute and distinct, of myself and of the life that was around me. Thus:—

From standing with some wistfulness in the twilight road, I turn slowly away, shoulders rounded, collar awry, hands deep in my pockets: slouch to the right, along the second side (at right angles to the road) of the wall, and there stop—thinking.

A white duck hurries waddling, filled with anxious-ness, across the grass farther on, and paddles her bill in the edge of the stream. And I walk with big strides till I am parallel to her: reach the wooden bridge (duck the while paddling her bill in the stream's border of watery mud):—give one look at a hole in the bank from which trickles the thick inky, sluggish drain-fluid; and enter the porch.

No one in the kitchen. The clock tick-tacking with big silent swing: the plates, with their ruddy flickering fire-light, in rows: the lamp not lit yet.

Then I hear a motion as of some one shoving a jar on to a shelf in the pantry: cross quickly through the kitchen: down the red-tiled passage (up come two or three loose tiles with a collapsed fall), catching a semi-earthy smell from under the cellar door (some one's in the pantry: Anne, I think): run upstairs two steps at a time: turn down the dark passage: reach the ladder foot: climb up: shove open the door: enter the dim garret: go on to the window: look out over the grave-yard, and then turn and begin to take in, half-uncon-sciously, the red-painted lines on the card over the washing-stand: '*I love them that love* ME, *and those that seek* ME *early shall find* ME.'

At that I turn again: go back to the window, and, with a knee on the white-painted window-sill, look out into the twilight sky, in which I see vaguely the tall dark wild rook-trees with their black broad tops, the many gravestones, and the small church to the right.

Then:

'*Ber-tie!*'

The word, rising a note, startles me, half-thrills me.
Anne is at the foot of the ladder.

Up she steps: shoves the door open altogether, and
at once begins:

'Lor', Master Bertie, why you look as if you'd bin
seein' a ghost out in the graveyard, you do.   Gracious
alive, the eyes of him !   Did you ever now ? . . .'

'What do you want ?' I ask.   'If you want me for tea,
I'm not coming.   Tell Mrs. Purchis so.'

Anne urges that Mrs. Purchis is in such a bad temper
this evening.   And it being his last night too, eh?   And
it isn't good for him to drop off his victuals like that,
and *he* going away to school to-morrow, and hasn't eat
anything to speak of this week,—considerin'.

I take to my old attitude, with my knee upon the
white-painted window-sill, now faint and dim, and look
through the dark rook-trees into the darkening fields.
Anne continues: 'Which she does hope he doesn't bear
any malice, Master Bertie, and him going away to-
morrow, to school, and might never see her again, but
they both be dead and buried before then ; and, if it
wasn't that . . . (Then, sharply): But she always *did*
say, and we'd see who was right or not, that that boy
would come to no——'

I leap to her.

'I will throw you down the ladder,' I say, catching
her by the arm, 'if you don't go . . .'

She, rather frightened, goes.

All that evening I sat on the sill, looking out across
the churchyard to the hedge and the rook-trees.   The
black shadows grew broader and deeper.   There was
no moon.   A light wind was singing through a crack in
the lead-work, close by my ear.   And at last Timothy
Goodwin, the sexton, came limping along the London
Road with a lantern : unlocked the gates, locked them
again, carefully, after him : limped to old Mr. Atkin's
grave, and began cutting the grass on it with a clink-
ing shears, having put down the lantern by him.

I watched him and thought about things.

Presently he lifted up his light: put it down again
and began on another patch.   Then he took up his

light and stood for a moment, brushing the knees of his corduroys with his hand : then turned, and limped towards the gates.  I smiled through the tears that were in my eyes and on my cheeks.  If I had been there with old Timothy, I would have put my arms round his neck and kissed him.

On he limped over the grass, through the tombs, over the sanded walk, the lantern-light passing before him ; till now, he reached the gates : unlocked them : has gone out : re-locked them.—And there he goes, jogging over furrows and hollows like a Will-o'-the-wisp, up the London Road.

The clock in the square dark church-tower struck out the hour.

An impulse came to me.  I went to the bed and down onto my knees; but then, remembering that He —God—was up above in the sky, I clasped my two hands together, and looked up to Him, and said :

'Dear God, You are a long, long way away from me : right up in the deep, blue sky, higher than all the darkness, and farther away than even the sun, and the moon, and the stars.—But I love You ! oh, I love You ! because You know everything I think about, and everything that I want to do.  And I pray that You won't let me die till I am very old and have done all the things I want to do.  But please help me to be a great man.  Through Jesus Christ our blessèd Lord, Amen.'

Then I got up, and undressed, and slipping into bed, was soon asleep.

The next morning Mr. Purchis and I came up by train to some large station, where we got out and crossed to another platform.  As we were going, he, having me by the hand, told me to tie my white woollen comforter round my arm, so that 'the Colonel's man ' might know me at the other end.  I was put into a third-class compartment : Mr. Purchis gave me a shake by the hand, and turned and went away down the platform.  I did not care to watch him more than a few yards or so.  I did not care to look at the other passengers.  It all seemed like a sort of dream, and I did not think I was going anywhere in particular.

There were a good many other people in the carriage. Some got in: some got out: I didn't notice them much.

After a long time (it was growing darker now) an old lady next me, who'd been asleep, awoke and took a basket from under the seat and put it upon her knees, and, in a little, said to me that we were 'close to London now, my dear.' I said: 'Thank you!' and looked out of the window.

Then the train stopped by a long planked platform, and the people (three now) all rose up. A clergyman got out first and pulled a glazed bag along the floor down to him. Then the old lady got out, and her daughter (as I thought) handed her down the basket and got out too.

After a little I went up to the other window and pressed my face against the pane and looked for 'the Colonel's man.' Then I thought that he mightn't be able to know me without the white-comfortered arm, so I put it out through the door, and waited.

All at once a man with thin legs in brown trousers came out from between two old ladies with band-boxes right up to me. He touched his hat. This was 'the Colonel's man.'

We took a cab and went across London, and stopped in a square before another large station, but not so large a one as the first. A porter undid the door, and we got out, and the box was taken down, and put on to a trolly, and we followed it into the station. There it was tilted beside two others onto its head (the trolly I mean), and we had ten minutes to wait before the train-gate was open.

'The Colonel's man' began talking to the porter about something. I went on a little and stood and looked at some pictures hung up by a newspaper stall. One was of a great ship in the docks, going to be launched. As I was looking—

'Come along,' said 'the Colonel's man,' taking me by the hand, 'the gate's open.'

We went along the platform together and got into a carriage pretty far up. I sat silent: and every now and then my eyelids drooped, and my head moved forward, and I nearly fell.   I should very much like to have lain down and gone to sleep in a cool clean white bed.

At last we came, after many short stops, to a stop, and 'the Colonel's man' put his hand on my arm : and then I was lifted down, and we went out, I just behind him, a porter carrying the box.   At the door in the cool evening wind, 'the Colonel's man' agreed with a boy to take the box up to Park Road for sixpence.   And we all set off.

After a little 'the Colonel's man' and I wore ahead. It was a steep hill, and I felt rather tired but not so sleepy now.   We went on slowly, till he stopped and said :

'Give us a hand.   It *is* a bit of a pull up this hill, young 'un, ain't it—eh ?'

I gave him my hand and we went on again till, passing through the light of a tall lamp-post and through an open gate, we stood on the flagstone before a low doorway.   'The Colonel's man' pulled at the bell-handle.   A bell rang.   Then, in a little, we heard steps and the door was opened by a maid with a white apron and cap.

'Well, good-bye, my lad,' said 'the Colonel's man,' turning to me, 'I'm about at the end of *my* part o' the business, I reckon.   Good luck to ye, sir, good luck to ye !'

He put his hand on my shoulder, and passed out through the gate and into the darkness.   I looked after him slowly.   The maid stamped her feet on the ground.

'Where's your box ?' said she.

At that moment the boy with the wheel-barrow and the box appeared under the lamp-post at the corner, some little way off.   She must have seen him.

'Oh, that's it,' said she, 'I suppose he's paid all right?'

'Yes : "the Colonel's man" paid him,' I said.

'Then you'd better go into the dining-room.   Give us your keys first.'   (I found and gave her the key of my box)—'That's it.'   She pointed to the door in the left side of the hall.

I crossed the oil-cloth carpet : opened the door, and went in.

A large fire was burning with a flickering light.   It flickered on the black glazy table-cloth of a long thin

table in the middle of the room, and on another
running at right angles to it across the right side of
the room, in a broad half-bay window.    Outside there
was a veranda, and the dark evening.

I went to the bench and, half upon it, leant my face
in my arms on the cool table-cloth.    The things around
me were all in a sort of noise above my ears.    I could
not weep soft tears: the tears were dried behind my
eyes.    But, after a little, I seemed to grow dreary:
and could have wished to sleep. . . .

I took to no one.    One or two fellows made up to
me a little at first; but I just answered them and
turned away, neither caring to talk to them or let
them talk to me.    It was not that I was homesick: I
had no home.    I did not know what it was.

I like Wallace better than any of the others.
Neither of us ever have jam or cake: he has not even
3d. a week like me.    He loves his little belly.    He'll
always go to Harris's, the grub shop, for anyone who'll
give him a good big bit of the stuff they're getting.
(Of course you're licked if you're caught going, except
on Saturdays and Wednesdays from two to three.)
And I have often told him that I think it is beastly
of him to do it; but he doesn't care, so long as he
gets the grub.    That's one reason why I don't care to
talk to him about some things I know of.    I tell him
tales, and all that; but that's different.

Whittaker is an old beast.    He's fond of caning
us I'm sure.    When you go into the library on Saturdays after school, to get three strokes if you've had
more than twelve mistakes in dictation, he won't let
you kneel down loose, as if you were praying, but he
makes you bend up over till you're quite tight.    It's
very nasty going tight again after the first one.

Mrs. Whittaker is a humbug.    She says ''umble'
and ''otel' and ''ospital,' and says it's right to say
them that way.    She listens to what the fellows say,
and then tells the Reverend, and they catch it.    Like-
wise she reads fellows' letters.    She corrects fellows'
letters home, and makes them say that Mr. and Mrs.
Whittaker are very kind to them, and other things.

Besides, she tells lies.   She has two babies, little brats
that squawl.   I hate her.

I don't mind the work much, especially the history.
Latin's rather rot, and so is geography and arithmetic.
I like poetry best: we have a book full of it.   The
first poem is called 'The Universal Prayer,' by A. Pope.
The one I like best is called 'A Psalm of Life,' by
H. W. Longfellow.

One Saturday night when Cookie was bathing me—
you see, that particular night I was rather funny,
having been out on the Heath alone—(of course I
should have been punished, perhaps licked, if I'd
been caught; we were never allowed out except we
got leave, in twos)—and thinking about all sorts of
things, and particularly that I should die before I was
twenty.   So, as Cookie was bathing me, I asked her
if she knew what

> ' For the soul is dead that slumbers
> And things are not what they seem,'

meant.   She didn't.—Then I asked her about the
other things in it, one by one; but she didn't seem
to understand them much either.

Well, after I'd gone up to the dormitory (I was
first that night), while the others were up at prayers,
*she* came in quite quietly as I was lying looking at the
white ceiling, and sat down on the bed by me and
took out a little round hot pasty, and said I was to eat
it while she was cutting my nails.   So she drew back
the cubicle curtain, and I got out of the clothes, and
she began to cut my nails.   And while I was sitting
in that way, eating the hot pasty, I thought I'd like
to tell her the 'Psalm of Life': so I asked her if she'd
care to hear it.   She said ' Yes.'   So I began to tell it
her.   She'd finished cutting by the time I'd got about
half through, and sat with my foot in her lap, looking
at me, till I'd done it.   Then we heard them coming
down from prayers: so she told me to jump into bed,
and tucked me up and gave me a kiss, and said:

'I hope it won't make you conceited, Master Leicester,
but you're the best-looking of the boarders.   And I
hope you'll be happy.'

I didn't think of this till Wallace told me on Monday
night that Cookie had left. And afterwards Mrs.
Whittaker said Cookie was a thief and had stolen a lot
of her things, but I didn't believe it.

At the end of the term we were examined by a
gentleman who came from Glastonbury School, where
Whittaker was when he was a kid. Blake was his name.
I liked him. We were all examined together in English
and Scripture, and he said that I was the brightest boy
of the lot, and he said it to the Reverend too, when he
came in at one o'clock and they were standing talking
together at the door.

The next day was Speech-day. We most of us had
pieces of poetry, Shakespeare or out of the poetry-book,
to say. We were supposed to choose our own pieces.
I was just head of my form by the term marks (there
were only five in it, Black, Campbell, Morris, Wallace,
and I), and I chose the 'Psalm of Life.' Currie (the
undermaster) didn't mind; and so I learnt it again, a
little excited: I mean, I read it over with the book,
and repeated it again and again, to make sure I hadn't
forgotten any of it.

I sat in my place, waiting for my turn, with my lips
rather dry, and every now and then I shivered as if a
draught came upon me through an opened door: but I
wasn't really afraid. I was a little excited, I say; and
yet it seemed somehow like a dream and I couldn't
notice anyone's face.

At last my turn came. It was after Whitman's. I
got up shivering, and I thought I shouldn't have breath
to say it all with. But when I got up on to the green-
baize platform, and stood in the middle, and looked
down over them, the ladies in their white and coloured
dresses, and the men, and the boys—all at once the
shivering went away from me altogether, and I turned
my head straight to Mr. Blake at the table at the side,
and smiled to him. He smiled too, but only in his
eyes. And I began :—

> 'Tell me not in mournful numbers,
>   " Life is but an empty dream ! "
> For the soul is dead that slumbers,
>   And things are not what they seem.'

And my voice rose, growing stronger and clearer, and at last I did not see anything there at all, not even the coloured mass of the dresses, but only a warm gold air all round me, and something singing softly all round me like far-off sunshiny water.

Then all at once I laughed, and, though the tears were quite full in my eyes, I could have shouted out, I felt so bold and brave and ready for it all, even for when I should have to die and be buried in the cold dark earth.   And my voice rang as I said:

> ' Lives of great men all remind us
>   We can make our lives sublime,
> And, departing, leave behind us
>   Footprints in the sands of time ;
>
> Footprints that perhaps another,
>   Sailing o'er life's solemn main,
> Some forlorn and shipwrecked brother,
>   Seeing shall take heart again.
>
> —Let us, then, be up and doing,
>   With a heart for any fate ;
> Still achieving, still pursuing,
>   Learn to labour and to wait.'

Towards the end I had grown sadder a little, and, now it was all said and over, I stood there for a moment with my head bent down looking at the ground of the room below the green-baize platform.   It seemed some time, but I dare say it was only a moment, but when they all began to clap, and I looked up quickly and saw them all round me, I hated them all in my heart and could have seen them die and not stirred.—*Not all !* All but one: Mr. Blake.   I seemed to love him a little.

And he nodded and smiled to me again with his eyes, and I smiled back to him as I went down.   And after that I did not hate the others any more; for I did not think of them.

The next thing I remember was that I heard the Reverend saying :

'This prize is adjudged by Mr. Blake to Leicester, but, as he is only a new boy this term, he retires in favour of Whitman (whose recitation of Marc Antony's speech over the body of Cæsar is highly creditable to him) and *he* receives the certificate.'

I cared neither for the prize nor for the certificate. I do not quite know what I was thinking about : but it was about something very far away, by the tops of blue misty mountains, and down the middle trickled a black stream from bowl to bowl. It was very sweet. So that when the prize-giving was over, and they went out crowding, I still sat in my place for a little, puzzled because the mountain and the black stream had gone away with a trail of mist.

Then, as I sat like that, thinking about the trail of mist that went away with the mountain and the stream, Mr. Blake came, bending his head, in through the far doorway. I looked at him.

Seeing me, he stepped down the passage between the chairs, and came to me on the form, and put his hand on to my shoulder lightly, and smiled with his lips. But I couldn't smile back again ; for the mountain and the stream had gone away from me.

'You did well, little man,' he said at last. 'Where did you learn to recite poetry like that ? '

'Yes, but I did not understand it all,' I said, 'the two first verses, I mean, and I don't care for the rest, till the last bit. But that is grand !' I looked up into his eyes.

He patted my shoulder twice gently :

'You go too quick, you go too quick, child ! What can't you understand in the first two verses ? '

' " And the soul is dead that slumbers." '

' Well ? '

' What does it mean ? '

' And that the soul, which only slumbers, is dead.'

' But what does *that* mean ? '

' Dead : that is, that there is an end of it. Some people (such foolish people !) say that when you die, there is an end of you. That is, that you *have* no soul. No such place as heaven ! no such person as God ! Longfellow says : Do not tell me that man's soul, which when we die only slumbers and will awake, perhaps soon, perhaps late, perhaps never at all, in a perfected state of beauty in heaven—is *dead*, finished, ended, over, when a man dies and his body corrupts and turns into dust. . . . Do you see?'

'Yes,' I said, 'I see.'

There was a pause for a moment.  Then:

'Would you like to go to Glastonbury when you are older?' he said.

'Is Glastonbury a big school?  How many fellows are there?' I asked.

'Not so big as many others: *my* old school, for instance, Winchester.  But there are quite enough: two hundred.  What do you think?'

'Would *you* be there?' I asked.

'Yes,' he said, '*I* should be there.'  He did not seem to be thinking about me then.

I looked at him.  My look seemed to recall him from somewhere.

'Listen!' he said suddenly, brightening and bending down; 'don't brood so much, little man.  You hear me, don't you?  Don't go thinking about things till they grow hateful to you.  Try to be bright and merry.  Be with the other fellows more. . . . I was right, there?  You aren't much?  *"They're such fools!"* hey?'  (He laughed.)  'Well, you mustn't mind that.  *You*'re not *always* wise, are you? . . . You don't think I'm sermoning you?'

'No,' I said, 'I see.'

A pause.

He smiled again.

'At any rate,' he said, and pinched my cheek gently, 'Mr. Whittaker has given me permission to write to your guardian, Colonel James, as well as promised to write himself, about your going to Glastonbury.  You *would* like to go?'

'Yes,' said I, 'I should—if *you* would be there.'

'In all probability, I should,' he said.

'I,' I began, 'I . . .' but did not go on.

And it was somehow with this that we parted.

I watched him go up along the passage between the chairs and, bending, through the far door.  And then I felt that I wished I had said something to him, but I did not know what.

In the holidays we (Wallace and I) had breakfast and dinner with the Reverend and Mrs. W., but had our tea alone. I liked that: but Wallace talked too much. And we might go out as we liked on to the Heath or into Greenwich Park, but not down into the town. Three or four times I chanced it, and went to the Painted Chamber, which Campbell had told me of, saying that there were fine pictures of sea-fights there and some of Nelson. I liked to be there: I liked most of all to look at the picture of Nelson being taken up into heaven, for I thought I too should be taken up into heaven some day, when I had done great things and was dead. Then there was the picture of him all bloody and wounded, as he ran up on deck in the middle of the fight: and the relics. I liked the holidays.

Next term wasn't much different from last; except that some of the fellows were allowed, in June and July, to go down to the Greenwich baths early on two mornings in the week to bathe. I tried to get the Reverend to let me go, but he wouldn't.

In the next holidays he, and Mrs. W., and the brats, and Jane (the new cook), went to the sea-side, leaving Alice (the maid) to look after us two. (Thomas, the page-boy, didn't stay in the house then. I don't know why.) I liked that better still. I was out almost all day long, on the Heath, in the Park, down by the river. Once I went up the river as far as Westminster in a boat. That was rare sport. Some men played on a harp and a clarionet, and the music almost made me cry. Wallace hadn't the pluck to come, though Alice offered to lend him the money.

The next term was very bad. I had chilblains: only on the feet though. Wallace had them on his hands and ears. And it was so cold and dull in the Christmas holidays, that I was almost glad when the term began again.

A week after it had begun, I had a letter from Colonel James, and Mrs. W. said I must answer it. So I had to write an answer in prep. one night and show it to Mrs. W. after prayers in the drawing-room. She said it was 'so *peculiar*,' and scratched out most of it, and told me what else to write. So next day I made a fair copy, and, having shown it her, it was put in an envelope which I directed as she read out and spelled to me, and then she put a stamp on it, and I went out and posted it.

Mr. Blake didn't come to examine us this term: another gentleman did, Mr. Saunders, a friend of the Reverend's, who'd been at Oxford with him. But the first day of the holidays I had a letter from Mr. Blake, and he said that he was sorry he hadn't written to me before; he had often thought about it, but he had such a great deal to do that he found it very hard to write to anyone. Perhaps when I had grown up, and had a great deal to do, I should find it the same. But what he was sorriest about was, that he was going away from Glastonbury to another school, Penhurst, and so we should not see one another there as he had hoped, and he hoped *I* had hoped, we should; but I would perhaps find when I got there that I was not *quite* a stranger, but that there was at least one fellow who would take an interest in me and help me, as much as it was good that I should be helped. And I was to be sure and write to him whenever I liked, for he would always be glad to hear from me. I thought it was a very kind letter and it almost made me cry, that about being sure to write to him whenever I liked, for he would always be glad to hear from me. I hadn't known till then that I *was* going to Glastonbury, but, when I asked the Reverend if I was, he said, Yes, in another two years or so, perhaps.—But I didn't write to Mr. Blake: I didn't like to, somehow.

In the midsummer term I was allowed to go to the Greenwich baths in the early mornings twice a week with the fellows that went. Langholm, a big fellow of eighteen who'd been at a public school, promised the Reverend he'd look after me and teach me to swim. So he did. And I soon learnt. And he said I was the pluckiest little devil he ever saw in his life. I liked him to say that.

In the middle of the next midsummer term I had a letter from Colonel James. (He used only to write to me once a year, about Christmas.)—He told me that I was going to Glastonbury next term, and a lot of stuff

about industriously pursuing my studies, and that 'a
good knowledge of the classics, more especially of
Cicero, was the foundation of all that was worth
knowing in the *humaniora*': which I didn't understand,
and didn't want to.   Cicero was rather a fool, I think.
—Mrs. Whittaker, he said, would see that my clothes,
etc., were in a fit condition, and she had also been informed that I might have two shillings over and above
my usual pocket-money.   I felt rather older after that.
I didn't tell anyone about it though.

The Whittakers went away to the seaside, as usual,
leaving Wallace and me with Margaret, the new maid.
(There were always new maids.)   I enjoyed these
holidays.   I bought a pipe and some tobacco, and
smoked it one day in Greenwich Park, but I was very
nearly ill and very dizzy, and thought I would never do
it again.   I did though, not liking to be beaten by it;
but at last I found the tobacco and matches came ex-
pensive, and so left off.

The Whittakers came back early in September, and
then I had a new suit bought, and a lot of shirts and
drawers and things, so as to be ready to go to Glastonbury.

---

## II

At Glastonbury I first kept a diary.   Here is an
extract from it :
' I don't like any of the fellows here.   The fellows
in my study are fools, all in the third form, and so
of course we are always having our study windows
catapulted, and then get it stopped out of allowance.
(Pocket-money.)   I haven't had a penny since I came,
and that's a month !   Then look at the big fellows !
They none of them care a bit about fairness !—I was
sitting on the table in the hall yesterday evening after
call-over when Leslie, a big bully in the Remove, shoved
me off as he was going by, for nothing at all !   I fell
on to the form, and the form went over and I hit my
head against one of the iron posts.   I got up and ran
after him up the stairs and caught him up in the passage
just before the door of his bedroom.   Then I said to

him, "I beg your pardon, Leslie; but why did you
shove me off the table? I did nothing to you." In a
moment he said, "What damned cheek!" (All the
fellows say "damn" here. No one thinks anything of
it.) And caught me a kick would have sent me over, if
it hadn't been for the wall. As it was, I got my coat all
whited and humped my head again on the other side.'

I kept this diary for the first month I was at Glastonbury. After that, repetitions became more frequent,
and at last one half-holiday late in October, more than
a week behind, I in a pet gave it up, and put the book
containing it at the back of my locker in the hall.

The term dragged on wearily.

It grew colder and colder. I got chilblains, first on
my feet and then on my hands, at last suffering torments
with them. And the bread and meat were often quite
uneatable, and what else was there to live on?

It was a somewhat strange feeling of pleasure, I
remember, that which came over me after I had eaten
my first dinner in the holidays in the house of Mr.
Jones, the solicitor. I suppose Colonel James paid for
me. I didn't care for them. Mr. Jones was only at
home in the evenings, and didn't speak to me much
then. But I was happy enough; for I could just go
where I liked and Mrs. Jones didn't bother if I didn't
come in to lunch in the middle of the day so long as I
told her I wasn't going to. At first I felt rather odd going
'out of bounds'; but that wore off. Mrs. Jones is a fat
lady, good-humoured and, altogether, not bad; but she's
always asking me questions about myself and Craven
and Mrs. Craven and the other masters and the ladies
they're married to. As if *I* knew anything about them!

The snow was down then everywhere; it was cold
too; but I had some new thick red woollen gloves, and
my chilblains were much better, and I didn't mind it.
One day I asked Eliza the cook (I liked her pretty
well: she reminded me of Cookie) to give me some
bread and butter and an apple; for the sun was shining
and I wanted to go out for a long walk into the country. I like walking along the roads like that, looking
at the snow all glistening, and now and then a little
bird hopping about or, out by Raymond wood, even a

rabbit loppeting along over the white under the trees. Well, after I'd been walking some way, a big man cracking a whip in front of a horse and a manure-cart caught me up, and I walked beside him a little, for he had a nice face, till he spoke to me.   And then we got on so well together that I told him a great many things that I had read in books about lions, and tigers, and rhinoceroses,   and   boa-constrictors   and   many   other animals; and, at last, that I myself was writing a book, in which a good many of these things I had been tell-ing him were to be introduced; but more especially I told him about the snakes, some of which were to try to stop Jugurtha in a secret passage as he was coming to kill his brother.   For Jugurtha was the name of the hero.   He was an illegitimate son of Mastanabal, king of Numidia : that meant that his father and mother weren't   married;   but   in   those   days (many,   many hundreds of years before our blessèd Lord came) people sometimes *did* have children without being married.   I had read about some others like that, in the Classical Dictionary.

But the carter kept silence and I, fearing from this and a look I had taken at his face, that there was some weakness in this early stage of my book, hastened to add that I knew it *was* a little funny, that part, but as it happened hundreds of years before our blessèd Lord came or any of us were born, perhaps it wouldn't matter so much, after all?   The carter agreed that ' it was odd, too;—at they early times!'   Which rather relieved me.

It couldn't have been much further on than that, that I said good-bye to him and turned back to get home again.   But I lost my way.

It was colder now, and darker.   The sunlight had gone away from everything but a few clouds behind overhead, and, after a little, when I turned to look, it had gone away from all of them but two.   I trudged on again.   After another little, I began to feel my legs tired, and turned back again to see about the sunlight.   It was all gone now.   Then I wished I was at home.   But the shadows were all coming down thicker and thicker, and the road was so slippery, and

my legs more tired and more tired, and I couldn't hold
my shoulders up.   Then I saw a man coming along on
the left side of the road under the trees and was afraid :
then forgot that and went on up to him, but, when I
saw him nearer and, at last, what an old man he was,
with bleared eyes and a red neck-cloth tied round his
throat, although I was almost sure I'd lost the way, I
was afraid he was going to catch hold of me : so how
dare I stop and say to him : ' Can you tell me, please,
which is the road to Glastonbury ? '   He went on by
me, and I went on by him, and under the trees, and on
along the road, and he did nothing.

It was almost dark, black I mean, when I came to a
farm.   I had met no one else but the old man with the
bleared eyes and the red neck-cloth.   I was very tired.

I stopped at a gate and looked into the farm-yard,
where the pond was frozen over and a light shone in one
of the small farm windows.   I did not like to go in and
ask anyone to tell me the way : besides, I had begun to
think about some of the fellows and what they had done
to me till I hated almost everybody, and could have
lain down in the snow and gone to sleep and died and
been carried up by angels past the moon into heaven.

All at once a woman ran out with a flutter in her
dress, across the yard into a dark outhouse.   I did not
stir : I stood thinking about dying and being buried.—
And so, in a little, coming back more slowly, she saw
me standing there with bent head looking through the
second gate-bar.

She stopped.   Then came and asked me what I
wanted ?   And then, somehow, she had the gate open,
and was trying to get me in by the hand and I pulling
back a little.

Well, the end of it was that we went together up
the yard to the door by the small window with the
light in it, and in, into the light warm kitchen : and
she sat me down in a chair by the fire, and, when I
wouldn't answer anything to her but turned away my
head, I don't know quite why (but I still wished I were
dead and buried and no one knew anything about me),
she got up again, and cut a thick piece of bread, and
put a lot of butter upon it and then sugar, and went

with a glass and brought it back full of warm milk, and came and knelt down by me again and began to coax me. And now there was a big lump in my throat, and I kept swallowing it, but it kept coming back again. And at last, when I wouldn't look at her she put down the bread and butter and sugar and the milk on the piece of carpet, and lifted up my face with her hand under my chin, and laughed into my face with hers, her lips and her eyes, and then called me 'a saucy boy' and gave me a kiss (and how fresh and red and soft her lips were!).—Why, I just threw my arms round her neck and began crying and laughing and laughing and crying and wondering where I'd been to all this time, and in the end gave *her* a kiss on the lips, and we were great friends. I don't know how it happened, but somehow or other I told her all about Robinson Crusoe, and ever so many other things besides. And, then her husband, John, came in.—And, when I was going away with John, she put two great apples, one into each of my trouser pockets, and said I must be sure and come and see her again and tell her some more about ' all they fine things in the pictur' books.' And so John and I set off together, turning every now and then to wave our hands to Mary at the door in the middle of the light and she waving hers; till the road wound round and we went by it and couldn't see her any more. Then I began to be tired again and, in a little, John lifted me up on to his back, and I fell asleep, I suppose, and didn't wake up till he put me down on Mr. Jones's door-step.

And so we parted. For the term began two days after that, and, as they were both snow-stormy, Mrs. Jones wouldn't let me go out to see Mary and John. And I did not know how to write to them, for they hadn't told me where to. I had quite forgotten about its being so near the end of the holidays.

We had a new monitor in the bedroom this term— Bruce. (Martin, the old one, had left.) Everyone called him a surly devil, but I didn't mind him so much. This was how my liking for him began. One day, early in the term, he was taking Lower Round. Football is compulsory. There are three Rounds, Upper, Lower

and Middle.   One or two fellows in the Team, or pretty
high up in the Second Fifteen, always 'take' Middle
and Lower Round, that is, they see the small boys play
up, kicking them, etc.—Well, one day he was 'taking'
Lower Round, when Leslie, who's in the Team too,
took to playing back on the other side, so as to show
off.   Then I thought I'd like to see if I couldn't charge
him and, when a chance came and Leslie had the ball
and was dribbling past a lot of us small boys, I ran at
him with all my might, and we both went over.   But
*I* got the cramp.   *He* was up and off again pretty
quickly; but, of course, *I* couldn't do much but sprawl
about.   But Bruce, who must have been close behind,
came up and put his hands under my armpits and lifted
me up like a child (I remember how I somehow liked
to be lifted up in that way by *him*) and asked, was I
hurt?   The game had swept off to the other side of
the field.

'No,' I said, looking up into his face, 'it's only the
cramp in my calf.   It'll go in a moment.   I've had it
before like that.'

He made me play three-quarters back for the rest of
the game and, once or twice, as he passed me asked if
I was all right now?   To which I answered, 'Thank
you, yes.'   I liked him after that in a different way to
what I had before.

Sometimes, if we were alone in the room together,
as before dinner washing our hands and brushing our
hair, he would talk to me, about nice things.   But the
moment any of the other fellows came up, he always
stopped and went on doing what he was doing in
silence.   I don't mind that either.   I believe he thinks
the other fellows are fools like I do.   At night he never
speaks without some one speaking to him, and then he
won't make a conversation.   Everyone hates him, even
the small boys.

The last few days of that term were very warm.
There was a talk of having cricket and river-bathing:
at any rate rackets began and, I think, some boating
was done.   Football of course had stopped a few weeks
before the Sports, so as to get the field ready: I mean
the Rounds had stopped; but there was always 'little

game' in the Circus field for anyone who cared to go
up. I liked better going walks by the river or about
the fields. I liked to whistle as I went along: sometimes even I hummed tunes. The spring makes one
feel so glad somehow.

One half-holiday, I remember, I got as far up the
river as Morley Mill.

Just past there the bank is very high and thickly
wooded. I began to go up, intending to sit there and
look round a bit: there was not time to go on to the
mill. Up I went by the narrow path, and all at once
came upon Bruce, lying at full length on a piece of
grass with a bundle of flowers and a small microscope-
sort-of-thing, in his hand, through which he was looking
at something. He did not notice me.—Then some
earth rolled away from under my foot and went down
rustling, and he raised his head slowly and saw me,
and said :

'Hullo, Leicester. Is that you?'

I could think of nothing to say but, Yes, and stood
still.

'What brought you out so far as this?' asked he.

'I don't know. I'm fond of walking, especially by
the river.'

'Are you fond of flowers?'

'Yes.—You mean looking at them under microscopes
and things? I have never done that; but I like flowers.
They are so . . . so pleasant somehow.'

His chin flattened on his coat as he looked down,
holding a grass in the fingers of the arm he leant on.

At last I said :

'You have polished that stone nicely, Bruce.'

He looked up.

'I didn't polish it! It is a piece of limestone. Would
you like to look at it?'

'Thank you,' I said, 'I would.'

He held the piece of stone and the microscope for
me to look. I was surprised at the beautiful shapes in-
laid on it. He explained that they were shells.

I asked if I might look at some of the flowers through
the microscope. Certainly, said he: had I never looked
through a microscope before?

'Never, Bruce,' I said, looking up and into his eyes. He turned his onto the dried grass.

Then somehow we began to talk about birds, and he told me about how they paired in the spring.

He was sure birds had a sense of the beautiful. Darwin thinks so.

He paused, and ended, looking up over the tops of the trees below us.

After a little :

Who is Darwin ? ' I said.

He looked round, and then to me :

'The biggest man, maybe, that has ever lived,' he said.

'Do you mean he's the *greatest* man who ever lived?' I asked.

'Yes.'

'I don't think he's as great a man as Sir Walter Scott,' I said.

'What do you know of Sir Walter Scott ? '

'I have read two of his novels, *Ivanhoe* and *The Talisman*, and I am going to read them all. There are thirty-one. I counted them yesterday.'

'Yes ? '

A pause.

Then, after a little, I asked him if he was not leaving this term ? He said, Yes.

'Are you going to Oxford or Cambridge ? '

'To neither. I am going to London.'

'Why don't you go to the 'Varsity ? '

'Because I don't want to. I don't see the good of it.'

Another pause. I sat with my hands clasped round my knees, looking over the river. Suddenly I thought I would ask him something. So I said :

'Bruce.'

'Yes.'

'Would you ever like . . . to be a great man—a big man ? '

He looked at me with a gather in his brows :

'Well,' he said, 'I suppose I might. Why ? '

'Oh, I only wondered. *I* shall be a great man some day, before I die. And I like to think about it when I'm low, low in my spirits I mean. Now yester-

day, as I was standing by my locker, I got hit in the
eye with a board (crust of bread) by a fellow, and
it hurt me very much and almost made me cry with
anger; it seemed so unfair.  But, when I got up into
my room and thought about it a little, I didn't mind
much.  For, when Leslie dies, no one will ever speak
about *him* again or be sorry for him, but, when *I* am
dead, people will often speak about me and be sorry
for me and like me.  It's very nice to think of people
liking you when you're dead, I think. . . .'

I sat looking into the lower sky, not remembering
Bruce.  But all at once I heard him talking in a
strange voice, and started and looked at him.

He saw me looking at him and jumped up, before
I noticed what his face was like.

'You're a rum little beggar!' he said.  Then sat
down again, and went on :

'Do you tell everyone all this sort of thing?'

'No, I've never told anyone of it before, I don't
think.  Why should I ?'

He blew softly through his lips :

'Ph-o-o . . . Fellows do.  Do you know Clayton ?'

'No.'—I shook my head.

'Or . . . Gildea ?'

'Well . . . a few days ago I was writing lines in
my study after second lesson, and he came round for
some ink, and we talked a little then.  That's all I
know of him.'

A pause.

Then he :

'Take my advice, and have nothing to do with
Gildea——'

Another pause.

'Why?' asked I.  'He's rather a nice fellow, isn't he?'

'Because . . . He'll do you no good.'

'I don't twig that, quite.'

'It's no matter,' he said.  'You'll find plenty of
things you can't twig, I expect, before you are a great
man.—Now you had better be starting back,' he
added, getting up, 'or you'll be late for call-over.'

He took out his watch and stood looking at the
face for a little.

I got up, turned away, and began to descend the hill.
He passed me a few fields farther on without
even a nod.

I never talked with him any more. A week or so
after, the term ended, and then, of course, he left.

Those holidays began badly. I went out to Raymond to see Mary the first Monday. When I got to
the farm I found it shut up, and, after I had tried at
every door to find if there was anyone inside, went
away sadly, feeling very lonely. I only walked out
that way once again in the holidays. It was still
shut up. I did not try to discover if there was anyone inside.

Still, these midsummer holidays were, on the whole,
by far the happiest time I had ever spent. I was on
the river almost every moment that I could be, sculling
about in a whiff I got from one of the boat-owners of
the town, with a £5 note sent to me by Colonel James
at the end of July. I bathed a great deal. I see
myself swimming down the red-brown river between
the thickly-wooded banks on either side : down past
'the snag,' to where the river grows shallower and the
sunlight filters through into the water-grasses. Can
see myself dive, and go with large arm-strides over the
pebbly weedy bottom : now rolling over a luxuriant
wavy head of soft green, now turning to face the
current; and all in the fairy light of flowing water
that the sun shines upon. Again, can see myself
driving my light boat down the twilight stream, or,
resting on my oars, drifting slowly with soft har-
monious-moving thoughts.

## III

THE next midsummer holidays, to which I had looked
forward eagerly, were a disappointment. The weather
was bad, chill, windy, and rainy. I forsook my boating at last: took to long walks over the wet fields,
with sadness through all my thoughts. In the end,
dreams became almost nightly, fantastic dreams, never
quite nightmares, although the shadow of nightmare

was often in them like a polyp in a dim submarine water.  I wrote odd things about this, fragments, half-understood by myself, almost always torn up after a few lines had been put down, and then I sat bent over the table, the end of the pen or pencil in my mouth and my eyes staring at nothing, till the fit passed.  The dull or rainy weather held on almost uninterruptedly. I was somewhat relieved when the holidays were over.

With the new term came finer weather.  September, the end of it, and half October were soft and beautiful. Then two or three wind-gales blew, whirling all the leaves and many twigs, and even boughs off the roaring trees: nay, pulling some trees, and not small ones, to the earth.  These gales past, the 'Challenge Matches' between the several 'houses' began.  I got my School House 'colours' all right, as 'three-quarters back.'  I enjoyed those games.  The excitement of the fellows over the stiff tussles we, School House, had with Gough's and Mason's thrilled me every now and then. A sort of viciousness and devilry came into me.  I re member well how once, when Harper, after a grand run down the left side of the Mere field (we had the wall goal), got past first one back and then the other and came on at full speed, the ball not two yards before him, hurrying to pass me—the short run I took, so as to poise myself, and then how I went straight as an arrow for the ball and him.  We met violently.  I, half spun round: tottered: recovered myself: saw the ball, just turning, a yard or so to the right: leaped to it: kicked: saw it go right up, round, through the air, on over the heads of the yelling crowd of fellows a quarter way up the field, and then turned, to see Harper get up off his knee and move away.  I could have given a shout of delight.  That swift rush and violent meeting had gone into my heart and head like strong wine.

Just for the two weeks we wanted fine cold dry weather (for the Challenge Matches I mean), we had it.  Then it broke up: rain took the place of the sun and warm damp the place of the cold dry.  The effect upon me was evil.  The sadness through all my thoughts was with me again.

One night, hot, feverish even, unable to work, I

could not get myself and present sayings and doings out of dream-land. My throat was sore too, as if I had an inflammation there. Preparation and prayers over, I went up to the bedroom; undressed, and lay in the cool sheets, thinking in a vague way about death coming to me sometime soon. The thought was, like everything this evening, in dream-land. I spent a hot sleepless night.

Next morning I went from bad to worse. It was a Saturday. I felt like what I thought a melancholy bird felt, moping with a malady. I went up to my room and lay on my bed till, after about an hour, being thirsty and getting up for some water, I saw my face in the glass over the washing-stand, a scarlet patch upon my right forehead; so bright a scarlet that I wondered a little. I had scarcely lain down again when there was a knock at the door. 'Come in,' I said, and entered—Clayton. I made a dissatisfied noise to myself.

Then he began to ask if I didn't feel well? could he do anything for me? would I like any books from the library? (he could easily get the key from 'monitors' room,' you know), and the rest of it. In the end he went off, and I thought that that was the end of him.

I was dozing when there came a knock again. 'Come in,' angrily from me, and there was Clayton with a pile of books in one hand and a bulging paper-bag in the other.

'I thought you might like some oranges,' he said, putting the books down on the next bed and opening the bag's mouth. I wished him at the devil.—Why can't people leave you alone when you're moping?

After a little:

'You'd better skip first lesson to-morow,' he said, 'and go æger. You look as though you were sickening for something or other. There's a lot of measles about in the town.'

Another pause. Then up he rose, and saying: 'Well I see you're tired, I won't stay any longer'—had passed the second bed, going for the door, before I got out:

'Thank you for the oranges, but I don't want them, thank you; and for the books too.' I forget the rest of it. Somehow he came back for the bag, and took it away, and the door shut, and I turned round to the wall and fell into a doze.

The next morning I lay still. When Mother McCarthy came her rounds at about half-past eight to see who'd skipped 'first lesson,' she recognised the fact that I had scarlet fever. I didn't care much.

I was put into hospital, and the days passed dimly. But, on the seventh or eighth morning, when the rash was all but gone, Mother McCarthy told me as she brought in my breakfast, that 'Mr. Clayton had taken it.' That set me off laughing: not that I wanted him to have it (I did not care a jot about him one way or the other), but it struck me as not bad sport in the abstract, that Clayton should have it and be cooped up here with me.

They soon got him into bed, wrapped up in flannels and the rest of it. I couldn't help laughing to see his face, so elongated, as solemn as if at the celebration of a rite. The idea of what he would look like later on, red all over and his tongue like a white strawberry, quite overcame me. I believe he thought he was not far from death. He closed his eyes with a resignation that was not without sweetness and his lips moved, as if in prayer, I thought. Such a fit of laughter came into me that I had to stuff a piece of the sheet into my mouth. I ended by being rather ashamed of myself.

But later on he cheered up amazingly. His attack was a slight one. Despite my eight days' start he was convalescent before me; for one night I, impatient at my itching hide, got out of bed and took to stalking up and down the length of the room in my nightshirt, despite his assurances that I should catch cold and have dropsy and inflammation of the kidneys and the brain, with convulsions, and God knows what besides. Sure enough I *did* get something rheumatic in my joints and I was told by the doctor that some inflammation of the eyes I had had not been improved by a chill I must have taken somehow. I kept silence, and made the best of it.

Later on, one day when my eyes were still too weak to see to read well, Clayton insisted on reading aloud

to me, and a half week's insisting turned it almost into
a habit.    The fact was I had rather begun to like the
fellow.

At last he was well enough to bear the journey
home.    I remember that last evening, or rather afternoon, we spent together well.

We had been playing draughts by the window, while
the sun set in veins of gold and red-hued light, visible
to us as we looked out in the pauses of the game.    Then
it had become too dark for my weak eyes to see well,
and we did not care to have the gas lit.    We went and
sat by the fire, I lying back in the large, cane easy-
chair, he beside me bent forward with his hand twirling
a little piece of paper in the fingers resting on the
wicker arm.    We had been talking about different
things that had taken place in the school and gradually
dropped into silence.

All at once:

'Leicester,' he said, making a movement.

'Well.'

'Why are you such an *odd* sort of fellow?'

I answered nothing.

'Now don't scowl,' he said.    'You *are*, you know. . . .
Do you know, I think you're very unjust to yourself?
almost as unjust to yourself as you are to other people.'

'Yes?' I said.

'You're such a porcupine!    You're always putting
up your quills at people.    Why do you do it?'

'Do I?' I said.

'Now you know quite well you do.'

I answered nothing.

He went on:

'If I were you, I'd give it up: I would indeed!
Where's the fun in living day and night with your own
sulky self?    Don't you ever feel as if you'd give a great
deal to laugh and— and amuse yourself (you know
what I mean) like other fellows? . . . Instead of brood-
ing over your wrongs in a corner . . . Eh?'

I kept silence.

'Now answer me, do! . . . Come, now *don't* you often
feel as if you'd very much like to have friends like
other fellows have?'

'No,' I said, 'not like other fellows have.'

Another pause.

Then he, with a loud sigh :

' Friends, then ?  You'd like to have friends, wouldn't you ? '

' One 'ud be enough,' I said.

Another pause and another loud sigh as he said :

' You 're in one of your bad humours to-night.'

Then he burst out :

' Upon my word, Leicester, you're a confounded fool! There you sit, like a miserable old cynic, hugging your conceit, as full of morbid nonsense as you can well hold, a fool . . . a . . . a . . .'  He stammered.

' Well ? '

Then he came to a full stop : made another movement in his chair, and began again, with some resolution :

' Now look here.  There you are : a fellow who might be as liked as any one in the school, if you only cared. —Instead of that, you 're the most *disliked* in the school, and all on account of your confounded conceit ! You think everyone else is a fool but yourself : and you think *you* think it doesn't matter in the least what *they* think,—about you or anything else either !  Now that's rot ! '

' I don't see it,' I said.  'In two years, who *will* know whether I was liked or disliked at a school called Glastonbury ?  Of course I don't care about it !  Who *would* ? '

' You *do* care, you care a great deal ! '

' Yes, Clayton ? '

' I know it.  If you *didn't* care, would you take the trouble to tell yourself so a hundred times a day like you do, and make yourself miserable about it ? . . . Pooh-h !  You *do* care, right enough.'

I kept silence.

He proceeded :

' Leicester, you 're a fool.  And it 's all the worse because you needn't be one without you liked.  You might be a very nice fellow.  You *can* be—when you like.'

A pause.

' Well ? ' asked he.

'Well,' I said.

'Then I hope it may do you good then!' he cried, 'I am only saying it in that hope. I think too well of you to believe that you're blind to your own faults: and it may do you some good to see yourself as others see you.—And that's all I've got to say.'

A pause.

At last he, slowly and not unsoftly:

'I'm going away this evening. . . . Mother McCarthy told you p'r'aps? . . . For good. . . . I shall be sorry to go. . . . My father is a silk merchant, and he wants me to enter his office. He's come up here to take me home. . . . The dear old dad! . . . Well (he gave his shoulders a little shrug) . . . I suppose I shall be going abroad soon. There's a branch out in China he wants me to go to . . . or something like that.'

Another pause.

Then:

'Do you want to go?' I said.

'No,' he said. 'No, I don't.' (He made a movement in his chair.) 'It's the last thing I should choose myself. But only one man in a thousand in this world can choose the profession he likes. . . . I'm my father's only son, you see,' he added.

'Well?' I said.

'Well, the long and the short of it is . . . that I wish you wouldn't . . . You know what I mean, Leicester. I don't want to preach to you, but I somehow think you really might . . . might do so much better, if you liked. You'll be a great man some day . . . if you live, that is, and God wills it.'

'What?' said I.

'——Did you ever know a man called Blake?' he asked.

'Yes,' I said, 'I did. Why?'

'Did you know he was dead?'

I was startled. I looked at him sharply.

'Dead?' I said.

'Yes. He died a little while ago.'

'How?'

'It was an accident. He fell off a ladder somehow, and his head struck upon a stone, and it gashed a great

hole into the brain. A piece of the brain was hanging
out over his eye when they found him. It was in his
garden. He had been training up a rose-tree that had
been blown down by the wind. That about the piece
of the brain hanging out over his eye has haunted me
ever since I heard it. . . . Those clear steadfast eyes !
It is horrible !'

I kept silence, scarcely thinking.

He went on in a low voice :

'. . . The night before he left I was in his rooms,
talking with him. He was heavy about leaving the
old place. He said he felt somehow as if he were
going away from the grave of some one he loved. I
remembered that—afterwards. Well, among other
things he spoke about you. He had seen you at some
school he had been to examine, I forget the name now.
You had recited a poem of Longfellow's, " The Psalm
of Life," I think. He seemed very much struck with
you. He said he thought you would be a great man
some day. He said some other things about you, and
asked me to look after you when you came here. He
told me you were coming here soon . . . Well, so I did,
as much as I thought I ought to, for, don't you see, it's
not good for a fellow high up in the school to do much
for a small boy. It's not good for the small boy. It's
better for him to fight out his battles alone. And I
didn't think I was likely to leave—for some time at
any rate. But my brother died : and my father, whose
whole heart's in his business, asked me to—to give up
my plan, and help him with it. So—I did.'

' What did you want to be, Clayton ? ' I said.

' Oh I'd a foolish idea of my own ' (with a smile),
' about going up to the 'Varsity and studying Hebrew
and science and all sorts of things and then going out
to Palestine. You see I should have liked to have
helped Blake if I could, and, when he died—why, the
idea came into my head of trying to do what *he* hadn't
been able to do. You know he was poor . . . And he
gave such a lot of what he had away. I believe he kept
his mother and sister, too. I always thought so.—Any
how (with another smile), there's an end to all those
ideas of mine !'

'Will you tell me what you wanted to do?' I said.

'Oh!' he said, 'it wasn't so much me: it was Blake. He put the idea into my head. He thought that the great need that the Church has at this present moment is some man who would devote his life to a real patient study of the origins of Christianity; so that it might be shown forth, once and for all, that Christianity has for its foundation no vain legend, but events as historically true, and as capable of being shown to be historically true, as anything that has happened within the boasted ages of science. That this might be done, could be done, and would be done, he felt sure, and so do I. But you see, at present, they all seem so taken up with themselves, with their miserable grains of sectarian sand I mean, that such a man is not to be found, or if he is to be found . . . Well, God only understands these things! It *does* seem hard, at times, that all should be so against us!—They all seem to think it's not worth the trouble! or it can't be done! or that there's no need for it! O fools! fools! fools! Can't you see by the shore of what flood we are standing? Can't you read the signs of the times? Can't you see an Art that becomes day by day more and more of a drug, less and less of a food for men's souls. A misty dream floating around it, a faint reek of the east and strange unnatural scents breathing from it; but underneath mud, filth, the abomination of desolation, the horror of sin and of death! O my God, sometimes, thinking of it, my brain turns and I fear I shall go mad. And to be able to do nothing! To see these devils in human shape——'

Suddenly he stopped short: swallowed: put the back of his fingers to his lips, and with a smile said quietly:

'Nay, he was right! There is no need for me, or God would let me go, in such a crisis as this is. Yet there come these moments when I seem to hear his voice as from behind, coming down through the thick clouds, saying to me: ' *Go forth.*' It may be delusion. I'm not sure. I don't know. It is terrible to be so tossed in opinion!' (He was beginning to grow troubled: paused a little, and then with the same smile, his eyes all the while looking brightly before him, went on.) 'Nay he *was* right! And what should I have learnt

from him if I could not . . . To leave my post ! . . .'
(Smiling again.   Then, after a moment's rest :) '. . . I
remember it so well !  I can hear his voice now.  *"Where-
ever any man shall take his place, either because he has
thought it better that he should be there, or because his
captain has put him there*—there, *as it seems to me, should
he remain to face the danger, and take no account of death
or of anything else in comparison with disgrace !"*—And
my captain is God,' he said.    And with that he bent
forward a little with a faint light in his face and
round his lips as of a bright smile that seemed to grow
deeper and deeper in a dim dream that lacked not
sweetness.   I sat for a time watching him; till I too
grew into a dream, a dim one, but it had no forms or
shapes nor any sweetness.

Suddenly I started up and out of it.   Looking at him,
and perceiving no gap in our talk :

' Who says that?' I said.

He answered slowly as if unaware of me :

' Plato makes Sokrates say it. . . . But I was thinking
of a particular occasion.'

—The door was unlatched : opened, and Mother
McCarthy put in her head, tô say that the doctor had
come up to say good-bye and shake hands with Mr.
Clayton.

' It's very good of him !' cried Clayton, jumping up.
' Isn't he afraid ?   Although,' he added, turning back a
little to me from half-way down the room, ' there's not
much fear of us two, anyway.   I 'll be back in a sec. !'

He nodded : turned, and went out.   The door closed:
up went the latch : fell : steps crossed the planks :
another door opened, and closed.   Silence.

I sat thinking vaguely about what he had been saying : vaguely, till my eyelids began to droop, and head
to nod, and at last I must have fallen fast asleep.

I woke up with a start.   The fire was almost out.   I
was full of sleep : got off my things somehow : dropped
into bed, the cool clean sheets : into sleep again, and
slept soundly till morning.

Mother McCarthy woke me bringing in breakfast.
The gold sunshine was pouring through the window.
Her tongue was stirring already.—Mr. Clayton came in

last night, but found I was asleep and wouldn't have me woke.   But he left a note for me.

I got it and opened it at once :

'8.30. P.M.

'Good-bye, my dear fellow !   I am sorry our conversation was interrupted, or rather, I should say my monologue: *your* part of it would have come in later p'r'aps !   Write to me at 21 Norfolk Square, London, whenever you care to.   I shall always be glad to hear from you.   Indeed I do hope we shan't lose sight of one another altogether.   At present my plans are vague in the extreme.   I'll write again soon.   I'm afraid I must have seemed rather a fool to you an hour ago ?   at any rate, very confused and peculiar ?   I was stirred, you see.   I feel strongly about those things.   And believe me, my dear fellow, those things are the only things in the world worth feeling strongly about.   You'll think so too some day.—But I must dry up now.   Excuse paper, also almost illegible pencil, also this final scribble into a corner.   And believe me that I am now, as always, truly yours,

'ARCHIBALD CLAYTON.

'*P.S.—Don't be a porcupine !*'

---

.IV

EARLY in the next term I received another letter from Clayton.   There wasn't much in it, I thought.   'He was really about to leave old England, going to learn his occupation in life, where every man should learn it—under fire, and in the smoke of the battle.'

I put the letter into my pocket, intending to answer it that evening at preparation: indeed, did begin upon it, but, after the first seven lines or so, tore the sheet up and went on with my work.   I didn't care about the fellow enough to write to him any of my thoughts, and, if I couldn't write them, I didn't want to write anything.

I believe he said or wrote things about me to one or two of his friends, especially Scott.   For Scott is every now and then polite to me, when the chance occurs, as Clayton himself used to be ; but that sort of politeness has no relish.

That midsummer term I remember well enough—by its dreariness.   Dull skies and rain, and our wretched

School House 'crew,' pulling up the river, and down again, and on home mostly sulky. Once or twice I almost gave it up; but the thought of the good the exercise did me restrained me. Then the Bumping Races came. On the fourth night we bumped Gough's, and kept our place as head of the river for the remaining four nights.

As I was passing through the hall after the last night's races, I saw two or three letters on the end table and, stopping, I don't know quite why, to glance at them, saw one was for me. I recognised Colonel James's handwriting at once. He wrote to me usually in the first week of August enclosing a £5 note, for which I as usually thanked him, in a jerked letter which invariably caused me not a little impatience; for, as I have already said, when I didn't care about people enough to write to them any of my thoughts, I didn't care about writing to them at all. His letter was somewhat after this fashion :

'JUNIOR UNITED SERVICE CLUB,
*July 21st*, 18—.

'DEAR LEICESTER,—A communication has been forwarded to me from my lawyer's, purporting to come from Mr. Charles Cholmeley, of the Myrtles, Seabay, Isle of Wight, who, I am thereby informed, is the only brother of the late Mrs. Leicester your mother. He has I believe been residing for some time abroad, owing to the weak state of his health, and is, as he is good enough to inform me, by birth an American. He has received from me what information I thought fit to give him about your affairs, and you may shortly expect to receive a direct communication from him yourself. He desires that you should be allowed to pass the first fortnight of your midsummer vacation with him at the Myrtles, Seabay, Isle of Wight, and I at present see no objection to your accepting his invitation ; but you are, as far as I am concerned, at liberty to please yourself in the matter. He is, I understand, likely to go abroad again very shortly, having only come to England, as he informs me, in order to transact some urgent business which requires his presence in England; so that, as there need be no further acquaintance between you, beyond perhaps some small correspondence, I have not, as I have said, seen any objection to your accepting his invitation to pass the first fortnight of your midsummer vacation with him. At the same time I desire you to understand, that, as long as you are under my care, I must insist that your acquaintance with any of the late Mrs. Leicester's, your mother's, relations be nothing beyond what ordinary courtesy to them shall require.  Any intimacy with them was strongly deprecated by the late Major Leicester, your father, during his lifetime, and both as his friend and as your guardian I feel myself bound to follow out his wishes on the subject, even if my own did not coincide with them, as, I may add, they do most completely.

'I enclose my accustomary allowance of £5 to you for the year's pocket-money.  You can apply to the Rev. Dr. Craven for the necessary funds for your travelling expenses, an account of which I shall expect you to forward to me.—I remain, truly yours,                          THOS. R. JAMES.

'BERTRAM LEICESTER.'

As I stripped myself, ran down to the wash-room, took my place behind the last fellow on the stairs, and as I was washing in the wash-room before I went under the tap, I thought in a half-dreamy way about this uncle of mine, and then about my mother and Colonel James, and then about my father.  But going under the tap and standing there with the cool water gushing all over my chest and down my body, my thoughts, arrested, took another turn, and it was not till I was in bed that night that they reverted to the matter.  Who was my mother?  My father was a major in the army, a 'friend' of Colonel James: something like Colonel James seems to me, perhaps: a stiff-bodied, stiff-kneed, steel-grey-headed old gentleman modelled upon Thackeray's Major Pendennis. . . . Was my mother the woman up in one of the berths of that second darker vision, the woman up in one of the berths, soothing and giving suck to the child fractious with sleep and misery?  The baby-boy, then, was my brother or sister?  Had I a brother or sister?  I felt somehow that I had not.  Had I a mother?  I felt that, on the other side of some broad, shelved and dim atmosphere, I had.  Sometimes she stood still, turned towards me; but neither of us made any great effort to see the other.  'My father lies dead in the close dark coffin in the ground with a frown on his face. . . . And my thoughts of them,' I said to myself, 'are this much worth : that my mother is dead, "the late Mrs. Leicester," and my father's face probably past all frowning now.    Nay, they probably are semi-dissolved bodies together !'    On which thought I fell asleep, and had a horrible dream of propping up the body of my father, great, naked, flabby, which would come upon me.    This dream disturbed me for the whole of the next day with a feeling of flabby death near and not near me, by and not by me, my father and not my father.

The morning after that, at breakfast, Armstrong, who sat next me, getting up to look at the letters when they were brought in, returned and threw one on to my plate.    It was addressed to *B. Leicester, Esq.*, in a thin scratchy hand, and the envelope was large and oblong and of glazed white paper.    In a little I opened it, supposing it to be from Mr. Cholmeley, and rightly.    It ran like this :

'THE MYRTLES, SEABAY, ISLE OF WIGHT,
'*22nd July* 18—.

'DEAR MR. LEICESTER,—I daresay that by this time, my name, Cholmeley, will convey some impression to your mind ; for I must suppose that your guardian, Colonel James, has not left you in complete ignorance of the correspondence that has been passing between us.

'I prefer coming at once to the point, or rather one of the points ; for there are two.    The first is, some explanation of what you must suppose to have been nothing short of absolute neglect of yourself on my part ; the second is, as you are probably aware, to ask you to confer upon me the pleasure of your society here for the first fortnight in August. I should, indeed, have been happy to have given you a somewhat larger invitation ; but, as my health requires me to hasten south again to those parts which alone seem able to make my wretched old body an endurable habitation, you will see that this is impossible.

' I now return to the first point.    I saw but very little of my sister, Isabel, your mother ; for having very early shown a decided inclination for the study of the classics, that chiefest *laborum dulce lenimen*, and my grandfather, having himself been a scholar of no despicable pretensions (although of a somewhat more artificial, if sounder, character, than those at present in vogue), and moreover money not being a want to us, I naturally desired, and at last gained, my father's

permission to return to England, ultimately proceeding to
Cambridge, where I obtained the distinction of Chancellor's
Medallist and Second Classic, terms doubtless familiar to you,
a member of a school in which, I believe, the old classical tradi-
tion is still handed down unsullied by the barbaric bar-sinister
of either Science or, what they call, a 'Modern Side!' Shortly
after my matriculation I had heard that my father's health
was a little shaken by a severe chill caught at some festal
gathering, but the evil effects were, apparently, eradicated
by care and a good doctor, and I had given up any anxious
thought about the matter.   Indeed, the account I had of him
for the next few years was encouraging in the extreme.   You
may, then, imagine my consternation and grief when, shortly
after my last University success, I received intelligence of his
sudden death and of my sister's desire to come to England as
soon as possible, in order that she might take up her residence
with an aunt of ours at that time residing near Manchester.
This voyage was actually performed, and I myself stayed for
a few days at my aunt's house, from the experience of which
few days I formed that estimate of, what appeared to me to
be, your mother's natural disposition, which, despite all subsequent events, I have seen no proper reason to cease to hold
as being, in the main, a correct one.   I can say with the
most absolute sincerity, that I believe that the greatest of
her faults was thoughtlessness, and that I have so far considered, and shall in all probability continue to consider to
the end of my life, that all attempts to make her out as,
either naturally or by her early training, depraved are as
unfounded as they are ungenerous and unjust.   I make no
doubt that you already know at any rate the general outline
of your unhappy mother's subsequent career, and I shall,
therefore, make no further allusion to it than that which I
have already made.
  'You will I think easily perceive, that her marriage with
your father and their instantaneous departure for Cork, where
his regiment was then quartered, and my scholastic labours
and ultimately my own marriage, to say nothing of our most
opposed spheres of life, made any close intimacy between the
two families all but impossible.   After a short, too short!
period of happiness I was left to face life with the motherless
pledge of mutual affection and a frame shattered by an, alas
useless, attendance on the sick bed of my beloved wife and
companion.   I felt that change of scene and change of
climate were absolutely necessary to me.   I left England
therefore; and so it came about that, unhonoured by the
confidence of my sister, I remained for long in ignorance of
anything more than the general facts of her history.   It was
only through inquiries, instituted by me shortly after I had

received intelligence of her death, that I learnt of your existence at all, and then, being informed that you were well cared for, and being myself at the time engaged upon a most laborious and absorbing undertaking, I thought it no great neglect of you to wait till, that undertaking completed, however unworthily, and my presence in England being from the nature of the thing (I need not scruple to inform you that I refer to my forth-coming edition of the plays of Sophocles) an absolute necessity, at any rate for a short season, I could make your acquaintance personally, instead of being compelled to know you and be known of you through nothing more intimate than the post !

'There are other things which I desired to say to you, but, for the present, I must forbear, for my exertions of the last few days have so worn out these wretchedly shattered nerves of mine, that I find both energy and acumen to be pitiably lacking. Let this, I pray you, be some excuse for the paltriness of this letter : and more especially for the abrupt ending which I am now about to give to it. I hope to hear from you shortly, and, in the meantime, ask you to believe me, dear Mr. Leicester, to be your affectionate uncle,
CHARLES K. CHOLMELEY.'

The letter made no impression upon me at the time; for it did not seem to have much, if any, concern with me. I had read it with half-absent thoughts : then I put it into my breast-coat pocket : finished my breakfast : got up to my locker : took out one or two books, and went off to my study to look through some Cicero, the *Pro Milone*, which we had for exam. at second lesson. It was not till, the exam. paper over, I stood at my locker in the hall again, putting away my pen and blotting-paper, that my mind recurred to Mr. Cholmeley and his invitation. I shut-to the locker door : took my hat off one of the pegs, and went out into the quad. with my hands in my pockets, thinking : 'I suppose I may as well go down there. . . . And yet I don't know. There's the boating, and I reckoned on a happy time by myself. Well, it's only for three weeks at the worst : and I suppose, as he's my uncle, I . . . And—*he might tell me something about my mother.*' (I lifted up my head). ' I *have* just enough care about her, or her history, or whatever it is, to call it curiosity.' It was on some doubt consequent on this thought that I went in to see Craven.

I found him in the study taking off his gown.   He received me affably.   Yes, he had received a letter (this was it!) from Mr. —— Mr. Cholmeley, yes Mr. Cholmeley—My uncle?   Ah yes, my uncle!—asking permission from him to allow me to spend the first fortnight of my midsummer vacation with him at Seabay in the Isle of Wight.   Colonel James had been good enough to make his (Craven's) permission a requisite? Well (looking up from his inspection of the letter), *he* had no objection to my going: no objection:   No. Mr. Cholmeley was my uncle?   Did I know if he was any relation of . . .  Ah, it must be the same, he saw: *Charles K. Cholmeley.*—He had not noticed the initials.

'Are you aware, Leicester,' he said with his foolish blinking smile, 'that Mr. Cholmeley is one of the greatest authorities on the Greek tragedians that we have? What, what?   You *weren't* aware of it? . . . Now I hope you'll be careful not to . . .'   And so on.   The end of it being that he informed me, after a pause, that he thought a fortnight at Seabay would do me good. I was not to forget to warn Mrs. Jones of the change in my plans.   There were some charming pieces of scenery in the neighbourhood of Seabay.

'—— That is,' he said with another of his silly grins, 'if you care for charming pieces of scenery, Leicester? What, what?'

I thought that it would be purposeless to say to him that I did or how much I did: so kept silence with my eyes on the ground, waiting for the old fool to finish.

'Well, well!' he said.   'Perhaps that will come later on!—You may go, Leicester.'

I went out and up into my study, and sat down in a chair, tilting it back and putting my feet against the table by the window looking out on to the quad., and began to think whether I really wanted to go and see my uncle, or wasn't it foolish to give up the pleasure of an extra fortnight alone on the river?   'Well,' I said, getting up, 'I shall go now I suppose.'

The remaining week passed with imperceptible fleetness.   I read a good deal: stalked out and over the fields to the bathing-place twice or three times, and sculled a little up the river.

I remember, the last night, going in to Mother McCarthy to get my hat from the cupboard—how I came along the dark passage : opened the door, with Gordon (the monitor) under the gas, leaning against the iron-work of Armstrong's bed, reading a book and biting his nails : went on to by my bed; threw the hat on to it : turned to the opened window and looked out —through the branches of two of the dark deep trees, into the quad. all there in the moonlight with the shadowed houses and, beyond, the opened heaven paley blue, lit with some self-containing radiance.

And a feeling of soft peace grew in me, something which was unspeakable and which could not be left, to turn round to the bright gas-light, and the bedded, jugged room and the fellows ; so that the thought of them left me, trailing and fading away as some half-pulsing sort of tentacle in a dream, and I remained with the fulness of that soft peace unspeakable : until there was a start, my attention taken backward, a book snapped up, and I knew the butler had been in and put out the gas.

I went from the window into the space between the two beds, and undressed in silence, thinking.

# II

## I

ARMSTRONG lived in London. As we were getting up
in the early morning he found out that I too had to
go to London, and asked me to have breakfast with
him at Miller's, where they give you a decent tuck-in
for 1/6, and besides Knight's is so dirty, and he hadn't
paid his tick there yet for last term. I agreed to go
with him, though in a glum sort of a way; for I was
in an irresolute humour, half dissatisfied with everything and everybody, particularly myself. Well, into
Miller's we went together—through the shop into a
small poky gaslit room where, round a table, sat some
four or five fellows 'tucking in' at coffee, bread, eggs
and bacon, and jam. In a little, I got a seat next
Tolby-Jenkins, a fat monitorial fool of ignoble sort.

Armstrong and I were coming down the grey-
morning hill to the station before I returned to myself
again. And then there was an entry into a tobacconist's
just opened and a purchase by Armstrong of bird's-eye
and some cigarettes.

'Aren't you going to *get* anything?' asked he, half-
turning to look at me who was looking out of the door
across the station yard to the station steps and doorway. I turned and met his look.

'Very well,' I said, 'give me a box of cigarettes.'
And took out a shilling and 'lifted' it from where I
was on to the counter.

We crossed into the station. A good many fellows
were about. Armstrong had talk with some, and, in
the end, I got into one of the London carriages after
him and sat down next the fellow at the far end facing
the engine. Directly opposite me was Norris our
stroke, of the School House I mean, and in the corner

Davidson. In the other corner of that side, friend
Leslie on his last journey home from Glastonbury
School. Armstrong next Leslie, Jones junior on my
right, and Jacobson next him in the corner.

For the first hour we had a loud time of it. Norris
sang solos of popular songs and the rest joined in
deafening choruses, enlivened by occasional horse-play.
I was set off almost smiling more than once at the
thought of my solemn self sitting there, drawing every
now and then from a desultory cigarette, and sending
out a faint whiff of smoke into the rush of air that
passed through one window rollingly out of the other.
It wasn't that I didn't care for mirth, I thought; for
there have been times when I have felt ready for a
witch's sabbath over the hills, or any laughter-devilry
you please; not to recall other times, when the
readiness for a gibe at some young woman of the
Beatrice stamp was all but irresistible, and prompted
shouting and mirthfulness only ended by sheer ex-
haustion. But what was there in these ' earthy ' fools
(I mean, as if they were not unlike fat, half-lousy
Flemish revellers among the barrels of a cellar : and
yet not quite that !) to inspire mirth, or even laughter ?
—So I sat thinking, till, all at once, Norris set up a
ringing sea-song that, after a little listening, made a
cold shiver go down my back, and my eyes light up,
and the necessity for a loud shout in the chorus a
simple half-conscious satisfaction.

The rest of the journey was peaceful,—by comparison perhaps. Norris and Leslie left us at Bridge-
town : Davidson got out soon after. We could hear
the other London fellows in the next carriage singing
for a little after that ; but those in here grew quieter,
reading or talking, while I sat still thinking. And so
the time went.

At London there was a general shaking of hands all
round and quick parting, and I changed to my second
train.

At Portsmouth I went on board the boat. It was a
heavenly afternoon ; a mild sky streamed with tender
colours, and the air mild, not hot or cool. I stood
leaning against the rigging forward by the bowsprit,

while the gentle scene went by. Faint unreality was with me and something dreamy.

'Altogether,' I said to myself, sitting in the engine-side corner of the waiting train with my hand in my cheek and my elbow in the window-ledge, 'to-day has been a day of dreamy changes: one unlike any one I know, save perhaps three or four of my fever days.' What I remember next was looking forth at *Seabay* on a long board we were passing. Then we stopped. I put my hand out of the door; turned the handle; shoved open the door with my knee; and got out. It was a hot late-afternoon, though a gentle sea-breeze was blowing. The sky was full of rare colours. A porter pulled my box out of the luggage van and landed it, over the stone border, on the brick-red gravel.

I stood by the box and the train went on and away: stood for some little, reflecting that I had forgotten Mr. Cholmeley's address and had neither his letter nor Colonel James's to refer to. It didn't trouble me. I stood still, thinking about things in a vague way. Then took to looking at the station and a tall grass bank opposite. There seemed no one in the station now. A hen fluttered out of some furze a little farther on into the line. Some ducks came paddling their bills along in a broad rut on the other side of it. I could hear a telegraph clock tick-tick-tick-ticking.

As my slow gaze went to the doorway and a small book-stall towards the other end of my side of the station, an old gentleman's head, bent shoulders, and black-clothed body came from just past the book-stall. He had a white stock round his neck. And then, between him and the book-stall, stepped a fair young girl.—They came on slowly along the brick-red gravel.

I observed them with a new feeling: them, neither the old gentleman particularly nor the girl. All at once, he stopped. Then she stopped.

He said:

'My dear, I don't see him.'

The girl raised her head, and looked towards me. Our eyes met. Everything in me stood still, effortlessly though. Then she looked down to him: lifted her hand to his arm, and said in a low tone:

'I expect that is Mr. Leicester there, father.' Up
went his head; out came two horned glasses on to his
nose, and he had a look at me.   I smiled.

'God bless my soul,' he said, 'of course, of course!
My dear, I'm as blind as a bat.'   And on that we all
were together, and he had shaken my hand with his
two; and with 'This is my daughter Rayne,' she and
I had shaken hands.   Then we all turned together
and went on our way over the gravel to the other end
of the station.

'You see,' he was saying, 'it was my fault that we
weren't up here to meet the train.—Yes, my dear,' he
proceeded, 'it *was* my fault, I acknowledge it.'

'But where's your luggage?' said the girl, staying.

Mr. Cholmeley was seized with a sudden and violent
fit of coughing.

'There is my box,' I said, turning and looking towards
it; and, at that moment seeing a porter come out of
a small room we had just passed, called to him.
I turned back to them:

'Shall I tell him to . . . How?   Are there cabs
. . . or . . .'

'Well,' said Rayne, with the light of laughter in her
eyes, there's the pony carriage outside, but . . . I'm
afraid your box will be—rather too much for it!'

I laughed.

'Eh?' said Mr. Cholmeley, 'What?   Eh?   The
box, my dear? you said it was too big?'   He turned
also: adjusted the two horned glasses, and took a look
at it.   The porter was waiting by us.

'Well,' I said, turning and speaking to him, 'will
you manage to bring it up?'

'Yes, sir.   I'll see it's brought up.   Where to, sir?'

I paused: looked at Rayne: again laughed: and said:

'I don't know!—You see, sir,' I went on to Mr.
Cholmeley, 'I forgot the address of the house I was
going to, and I hadn't either your letter or Colonel
James's in my pocket to refresh my memory with.'

'The Myrtles,' said Rayne to the porter: 'Well,'
she added to me (he had gone with a queer comical
look and a 'Yes, miss'), 'it was lucky we came to
meet you then!'

'Very,' I said. Mr. Cholmeley had started slowly on in the original direction. We came up to him in a few steps, one on each side.

'I can't make out,' I went on, 'what could have made me so forgetful.'

'In the over-wrought condition of our nerves nowadays,' said Mr. Cholmeley, 'the wonder is that we remember anything.'

And with that we went out of the station to a small pony-carriage and a small brown fat pony, waiting by the kerb. Rayne drew back. Mr. Cholmeley got in, and made a motion to sit down in the front seat. I ran round to the other side to stop him, and succeeded. In a moment Rayne had jumped in : taken the reins : touched up the pony, and we were off at a smart trot.

Mr. Cholmeley was leaning back with his eyes closed.

Then Rayne asked something about my journey. And I answered in sort : till Mr. Cholmeley came into the conversation, and it drifted to Glastonbury. He asked me a good many questions about the school : the system of teaching the classics in use, the subjects taught in each form, the amount taught, and other things, I answering as I best could.

All at once :

'I do not care for Latin,' said Rayne. 'It is dry.'

Mr. Cholmeley lay back again with his eyes closed, smiling serenely.

'Nor do I, Miss Cholmeley,' I said, 'I can't understand Latin properly. It seems all so lifeless to me, as if they had all sat down and written it to pass away the wet afternoons. But Greek!—Homer, or even Xenophon. You remember that bit in the seventh book, I think, where they see the sea——'

Mr. Cholmeley murmured :

'Καὶ τάχα δὴ ἀκούουσι βοώντων τῶν στρατιώτων, θάλαττα, θάλαττα, καὶ παρεγγυώντων. — A beautiful little touch, that παρεγγυώντων.'

'What does it mean ?' she asked.

I, looking at Mr. Cholmeley and perceiving his eyes still closed, answered rather diffidently :

'It means, passing the cry on to one another like the watchword, I think.'

'Yes,' said Rayne, 'but *I* never got as far as that! I read some Xenophon last January,' she added to me, 'but it was frightfully uninteresting, *I* thought. Nothing but: *Thence he marches nineteen stages, twenty-seven parasangs to—*some place or other; *a city populous, prosperous and great.   And the river Scamander* (or Menander, or whatever it is), *flows close to it, and there is a park and a palace in the middle of the city!*'

'My *dear!*' said Mr. Cholmeley, smiling with still closed eyes, ' *Menander!*'

'I don't think I shall ever want to read any other Greek but Homer,' she went on, flicking with the whip-lash.

In a little:

'Perhaps, Miss Cholmeley,' I said, 'you'll like to read Plato some day, like Lady Jane Grey did.   I have only read part of the Apology and the Crito; but it seemed to me that it was fine.'

'Eh? hey?' said Mr. Cholmeley, opening his eyes and erecting his head and body, 'Why, here we are!'

I gave a glance at the house.   It was a small house at the other end of a garden pretty with bright flowers. There was a faint noise heard, like the wind in a row of tree-tops.   Looking on, as I got down, I saw a line, about a quarter way up the house, with a pale blue band: *the sea!*  The breeze came up softly.   There was a boy waiting just by the gate for the pony, whose rein close by the mouth he now held.

I stretched my hand for Mr. Cholmeley.   He rested on it, and getting down:

'It's a beautiful day for August—in Seabay,' he said, 'That is to say if I may believe what they tell me about it.   An antiquarian friend of mine at Newport describes the place as a bed in a cucumber-frame, in summer.   Myself I am inclined to doubt it—for reasons.'

Rayne was already down and on to open the gate; but I was there first, and unlatched and threw it inwards wide.   Mr. Cholmeley passed in slowly, she following with a look at me like that of when she said: 'Well, there's the pony-carriage outside, but . . . I'm afraid your box will be rather too much for it.'   I went in last, with an arriving thought that I had seen her eyes somewhere before, and perhaps her face.

We went in, through a small green-covered porch,
to a small hall : then to the right, down a passage that
met the little hall at right-angles; down a staircase;
along a little hall again with an open door at the end
and green garden and bluey sea-view; then to the
right into a large light room, in the middle of which
was a laid table and, for the far-side, a large half-bay
window with the two central flaps opened outwards.

Mr. Cholmeley sank down sighing in an armchair
that Rayne turned a little to the window.

'Ah-h,' he said, ' I'm very soon tired out *now*!'

Then, in a little, recovering himself, and looking up
at me standing by the window to his left :

' But perhaps Mr. Leicester is hungry' (turning his
look up to Rayne above the right arm of the armchair).
'We forget that.—And dinner is not till half-past
seven.'

' No,' I said, ' I am not hungry at all, thank you.'

' Are you sure ?'

' Certain,' I said, ' I had some things on the way.'

A pause.

'Then I think,' he said, 'that the best thing to be
done, will be for Rayne and you to go for a ramble
along the shore together, and leave me here. I'm
afraid I should be but poor company just at present.
In fact, I confess that I should like a little nap before
dinner. You remember, my dear, I had no siesta this
afternoon, and I'm tired.' His voice fell.

We left him rather lingeringly, more particularly
Rayne. We went down over the first plot of grass, the
gravelled walk, and the lawn in silence. Then she led
me round a clump of bushes, and on to a path whose
front was a low sea-wall. There was a break of a yard
therein a little farther on. Arrived there, I saw a
ladder, like those from bathing-machines, that touched
the sand.

We stayed a moment. Then I jumped down and
held my hand up for her. She jumped past it alighting
well, and stepped seawards, I following.

' I hope you didn't mind my father going to sleep,'
she said as we moved off together through the dry
loose sand tuneful to our heels. ' He usually takes his

nap after lunch, but to-day your coming disturbed him
so, that he couldn't take it, and he is easily exhausted
. . . now.' Her voice too fell.

'I am sorry,' I said.

'Why should you be sorry?'

'To have disturbed him.'

'I didn't mean that! I meant that it had excited
him, thinking you were coming, and so he couldn't get
to sleep after lunch. But that wasn't *your* fault.'

We moved on in silence for a little. Then she said :
'How beautiful the sea is now, and the sky.'

We stopped a moment to look at them.

'I have never,' I said, 'seen the sea before that I
can remember : and, I cannot tell you why, but it seems
to make me wish now to laugh and then to cry.'

We walked on in silence again for some twenty steps
Then :

'It is so,' she said, 'sometimes, early in the morning,
when I have come out, and the sun was shining, and
everything seemed so happy, I have run down to the
sea dancing and singing. But when I saw how it lifted
itself up, and threw out its arms once—twice—over and
over again—on to the sand ; and it seemed so tired, so
tired . . . I have stood and pitied it : till I felt the
tears all coming out of my eyes.—I think it is God who
makes you pity the sea.'

I laughed, and we moved on together again.

Then we talked of Greek, and how we both loved it,
and of Homer. And I could have cried out with pleasure when she said straight off the line :

βη δ' ἀκεων παρα θινα πολυφλοισβοιο θαλασσης,

which I had thought one of the most beautiful 'ideas'
that I knew : the old man going in silence down by
the loud-sounding sea. And then we traced the words
with a stick on the clean smooth sand, and she said
that she wished she knew how to put the accents on
the words, for they didn't look quite right without them,
and I said that the general rules for marking the
accents were very simple, and explained about oxyton,
paroxyton, proparoxyton, perispomen, properispomen,
and other matters connected therewith.

D

From that, in some way or other, we went to French, of which I knew next to nothing; but, when I asked her and she spoke some of it, it pleased me to listen to it as it came from her lips,—some poetry she had learnt, and lastly a little song. I was sorry when the song was over, and went on by her without a word, for a little, as if the music would continue of itself. Then I remembered, and said that I liked to hear her sing. This led us somehow to Italian, and she repeated some Italian too for me.

'It must give you pleasure,' I said, looking at her 'to know these beautiful languages.'

'Well,' she answered, 'it *does* please me sometimes; but I've known them ever since I was quite small, and so they seem somehow natural to me.'

'I have never been out of England,' I said, 'I should like to see Italy. I think I should like to die in Italy, where the sun shines always, and there is no cold wind and rain, and the fields are full of flowers.'

'But the wind *does* blow,' she said, 'horribly sometimes. The sirocco in the autumn is terrible, and so are the spring winds in Florence—so piercing and cold. All the people wrap themselves up in great cloaks.'

'Ah but,' I said, looking at her, 'that's not the time I was thinking of.'

Then she began to tell me about Italy and their life there. I asked particularly about the pictures and statues, telling her that the only pictures I had ever seen were in the Painted Chamber at Greenwich, and described the one of Nelson rushing wounded on deck, and the other of him being taken up, a pale dead body, into heaven.

At that point we stopped (for walking on the bank of stones and shingle on which we were was toilsome) and she looked aside and up under the cliff, and I also. It was a sort of plateau a few yards higher than the bank, covered with thick grass, and having small trees here and there. She was looking at one part of it. There were two small streams, the one larger a little than the other, which made two small cascades flowing down from a higher elevation through the grass, gathered tufts of which and weeds guided the flow into the

round earthen basin below. There was a gentle mur-
mur, and by the right side, a tree, with a faint shadow
against the earthen wall behind.

We climbed up.

It was a pretty place. Clear streaks of colour, all
hues of red, on the earthen wall that was sheeted with
the ruffled water: then, from an arched break up above,
came the main stream, dividing, to cross and flow down
the swaying grass and weeds into the round earthen
basin.

Rayne sat down on a thick clump of grass under the
tree; and I leant against the wall with the line of
water just by me. We were both quite happy, I think.

All at once she jumped up, looking along the shore
to the brown cliff that ended the bay. I looked also.

'We're caught!' she said.

There was a play of foam, as she spoke, at the foot
of the brown cliff behind which was the sun now almost,
or altogether, set. She rose: crossed the plateau:
jumped down on to the shingle, and started off at a run.
I was up and after her in a moment. She ran well, for
a girl. But the shingle, giving with each footfall, was
tiring to the limbs, and then there were her petticoats. She began to flag a little. We were still quite
a hundred yards from the point.

'Will you take my hand?' I said, passing her, 'let
me help you. The stones!'

She would not. I fell back.

We ran on as before.

Looking down as we came on to some smooth half-
hard sand, I saw the 'Βη δ' ἀκεων' which we had
written; the rest was washed out.

At last we came to the point. The waves were
dashing up foamingly all round. She went straight to
a boulder; jumped on to it, and, with her hand against
the brown earthen side, was about to step to another,
when up had come a large swelled sideward wave,
swirled over the first ring of rocks, and the next moment
she was in a shower of spray. I stepped to try the
boulder on which she was; caught firm hold of her
round the hips, and, lifting her up, made straight on-
ward. Up came another wave, but smaller; swept

past and through my legs up to the knees, but I kept
to both her and the ground.   She did not move, one
arm holding me firmly round the shoulders.   I looked
aside.   There was a large wave just off shore coming
in swiftly.   ' *Now !* '

The wave went back.   I dashed on; stumbled over
a stone; recovered myself; a small leap, a run, and
we were in the light of the setting sun, and she was
standing on the sand before me.   The billow struck
through the first ring of rocks, and burst full upon the
cliff into a lit cloak-like shower of rainbow drops flying
through the soft sunny air.   Then I looked at her.
Laughter was in her eyes, and on her lips, and in her face.

' I will never forgive you for not letting me get a
ducking,' she said, ' I had set my heart on it ! '

She turned, and we hurried on, not saying much.
I never had felt so happy in all my life.

So we reached the garden wall, and she went up the
ladder, and then I : along the path : round the bushes
and out on to the lawn.   There we saw Mr. Cholmeley
looking through a pair of lorgnettes along the other
shore.

She came up to him quietly, I following, and put
her left arm round him and said :

' Here we are, daddy ! I hope we haven't kept you
waiting for dinner ? '

' Eh ? hey ? ' he said, smiling at her, with the lorgnettes lowered.   Then, looking at me : ' Why, I thought
you would be sure to go along the shore towards Crem-
lin, child ! '

And we went over the grass together and up into
the dining-room laughing and talking.

## II

The fortnight I was at Seabay went like a spell of fair
weather in November.

When I awoke one morning and informed myself
that this was the last day I should be here with them,
it seemed to me that I thought foolishly.   Not even
that evening, when we three were in the open air, Mr.
Cholmeley in the arm-chair in the middle of the out-

flung bay window, Rayne on a stool at his feet, touching him with her dear beautiful hand from time to time,
and I half lying on and over the edge of the terrace—
not even then, with the certain quiet and sadness with
us that was of a last evening together, could I realise
that I was going away from the beauty and the life here
with them, not to see either again for long, perhaps ever.

We began to talk a little,—of work, its length and
weariness and the final rest when it was over: or
rather Mr. Cholmeley spoke of it, and every now and
then she or I asked him of the things he told or of
other thoughts thereby.

Then she left us for a moment to go to speak to Mrs.
Jacques about our breakfast, and I came up and sat in
her place.

For a little there was silence, and I knew, somehow,
that he wished to speak to me about my mother. I
waited quite calmly. He was trembling. But at last
the words came.

He had felt that he had not done all he might have
done for her. He ought to have remembered that he was
the only person she had in the world of whom she had
a right to expect care and affection. But he had not
thought of it in that way then. As he had told me,
they had seen so little of one another, that she did not
seem to him to be his sister, and so ‘ sister ’ had meant
but a name that was not as near to him even as ‘ friend.’
He was so full of other things then, his studies, his
work ; and she seemed happy and contented with her
aunt. And then they both married, and she seemed
happy and contented with her husband. He knew
that he had done wrong. It was clearly his duty, both
as a man and her brother, to have befriended her.
Perhaps if he had done so, she might never . . . God
only knew !

He was so moved, that all I saw good to do was to
quieten him.

I said, as I thought, that he had acted for the best,
and that he could not be blamed. The questions that
I would like to have asked him—what my mother had
done, and when and why she had done it—were not, I
saw, to be asked then. I was once almost afraid that

he would do himself some harm, and, as I tried to
soothe him, I felt in some strange way that the pulse
of life beat but faintly here, and, feeling it, grew sad.

And so at last Rayne came back, and we talked of
other things.

The next morning she went with me down to the
station to see me off.  When I had got my ticket and
seen that the box was all right in the luggage van, we
walked up and down the gravel platform talking a
little,—of her father and of their going abroad and
when we might meet again.  She seemed to have no
idea that he was very ill, and mine, of the faint-pulsing
life, having passed away, there was no certainty in me
to tell her of what might after all have been no more
than fancy.

She would write to me once every month, she said :
that was better than promising to write often and not
writing ; for it is so difficult to know what to tell a person if you write often, and it is much nicer to have the
whole month and write to them when you feel inclined
to ; didn't I think so?  Then I reminded her of her
promise to learn hard at Latin and of mine to learn
hard at French, so that we might both know the same
languages and compare our thoughts upon them.
'And,' I said, 'I shall set upon Italian soon, and see
what I can make of it, and write and tell you.'

And a little after that the train came up, and we
went stepping down it, till we saw an empty carriage.
And then I got into it, and put my coat on the seat,
and got down again by her ; but we said little, standing
together, and I now and then looking at her, and knowing a tremble in me and the lump, and would have held
her and kissed her on the lips and said 'Rayne' and never
let her go.  But the last carriage-door banged to, and
the porter was by mine, and there was a hurry to get
in and in the hurry somehow I touched her hand, and
she rose on her toes with her cheek for me to kiss, and
I kissed it, and then was I up in the moving train and
not able to see her for the tears, till we were past the
end of the station, when I saw her standing and
waving her hand with a smile on her dear sweet face.
*Oh, Rayne, Rayne ! Oh, Rayne, Rayne ! . . .'*

Glastonbury seemed very dull to me when I first came back from Seabay. I roamed about the fields in search of consolation for something I had lost, but could find little or none. It was a relief when the term began.

I had determined to work hard. I did work hard, and this term I got my remove into the sixth, and was under Craven, but it seemed that the moments of tastelessness, as Mr. Cholmeley had once said, were more frequent as the autumn grew more damp and decaying and the moments of hopeful delight more rare : and all the while no letter from Rayne.

At last, late on in September that is, the letter came. She was sorry not to have written to me quite within the month, as she had said she would, but her father ('father' simply, as she wrote) had been very ill, and she could not settle down to write me a long letter about some things she had been thinking about, and she did not care to send to me 'a scribble.' They had returned to Paris for a few weeks to see a doctor there about father, and then back again to Switzerland, Thun, which he was very fond of. What she had been thinking about was her neglect of religious study.—I can remember that some one had brought this home to her, and that she was reading the New Testament in the original, and a general idea of mine that she had a fit of religious seriousness upon her that puzzled me in a vague sort of way. I didn't think about religion myself. I never had thought about it, somehow.

I answered her at some length, giving a summary of the authors I had read and the impressions I had formed therefrom, with occasional allusions to events or things that interested me, afterwards noticing to myself that I really wasn't thinking very much about her in connection with what I had written. I directed the letter, as she told me, to a *poste restante*, somewhere in Italy, where they were going shortly.

Late in October her second letter came. I give it entire.

'MY DEAR BERTRAM,—It is a wet and tempestuous afternoon, and therefore I consider it a fitting occasion to answer your long and with difficulty decipherable epistle. Yesterday was one of the hottest days I remember here, my thermometer

going up to over 100 in the shade, and so I knew we should
have thunder and lightning.  We did have, of a sort, but
utterly disappointing.  Of course I went out of doors to see
what would happen, but, beyond two livid sickly green
flashes, all was thick pitchy darkness.  So I returned a sadder
and wiser woman, dripping wet.  We have been enjoying the
most glorious weltering simmering heat, and I am out of
doors reading or rambling alone through the "lustrous wood-
land," or else ;lazily boating, the whole day.  You would
never have got this letter written, if it had not been for the
wet day.  I don't believe this place can be matched for pure
natural beauty anywhere.  Yesterday I went out in a boat,
with two damsels.  It was rough, and they were both sick
and very afraid ; but there was a kind of new glory over
everything, the air marvellously clear, in preparation for the
storm in the night I suppose : the hills all a perfect indigo
blue, and masses of cloud entangled in the ' misty mountain
tops.'  It was a

> "Glory beyond all glory ever seen
> By waking sense or by the dreaming soul."

And I stood upright in the boat with my head bared, and
revelled in it all—much to the disgust of the damsels in
question.  They shouldn't have plagued me to take them
out ! . . . I have got through two volumes of Carlyle's French
Revolution, as you desired, and am much impressed and
edified.  There is rather a tempest going on outside, and so
I am going to try to dodge my dear old daddy and Sir James,
and get out my boat and enjoy it.—By-the-by, I had forgotten
to tell you that an old friend and favourite of ours, Sir James
Gwatkin, has been staying with us this last week.  He is a
most amusing *mondain en villégiature*, with a marvellous
French and Italian accent, and altogether a very amusing
companion to father, and myself at times.  He knows what
seems to me a great deal about Art, the Old Masters particularly.  Father is far from well.  The spitting is very
troublesome, and now often tinged with blood.  Three days
ago he sent my heart into my throat and made me quite
restless for the night, by breaking a blood-vessel ; but he
has felt far better since, he says, more *free* and *relieved*.  The
doctor says too that it has done him good.—But I really *must*
go out now !  Excuse this final scrawl.  I have hopes of a
storm to-night.  Love of course from the daddy.  In haste,
dear Bertram,—Truly yours,      RAYNE CHOLMELEY.
   ' P.S.—As we 're on the move I 'll send you an address to
send your answer to in a little.      R. C.'

   (The part about her standing up bare-headed in the
boat thrilled me : the rest was almost interestless.)

One day at the end of second lesson Craven came upon a piece of Italian in one of his books of reference, and could not translate it all.   He half-smilingly asked if any of us knew Italian ?  No one did.   But I recalled some words of mine to Rayne, and determined that I would learn Italian.   After second lesson, then, I went down to the school bookseller, and bought of him a little Italian dictionary and grammar.   The man knew nothing of Italian literature, nor did I : I could not even remember any of the names Rayne had quoted, except Dante, Petrarca and Boccaccio.   But all at once I thought of Macaulay's Essay on Machiavelli and of some words therein, and asked the man if he had a Machiavelli.   After some search he found a little red-paper covered edition of the *Principe*.   I said that would do, and bought it.

I took it up to the school with me and sat at it for the remaining half-hour before dinner.   Puzzled out six lines and a half, and came up to wash my hands for dinner, pleased.   And after that I gave an hour per day to Italian, at first only to learning the grammar, but, up to the irregular verbs mastered, turned at last joyfully to my book, and found it fairly easy and extremely interesting.   It set me about thinking somewhat in this fashion : ' Most things are this or that, because they are *made* this or that, that is to say, there are certain laws by observing which you can bring about certain results.   It is surprising that the world, which I had somehow or other always supposed to be one great witness to the justice of God, seems to be after all rather more like a great stage on which the drama of Might over Right is perpetually being played.   Now does pure Right *ever* come off best ? that is, does pure Right ever win by its own unadulterated purity ?   I rather doubt it.   For, surely, when Right is crowned victor, there are certain laws which, having been observed, have brought this about, and consequently Wrong, if it only knows how to observe these laws, is crowned victor also.   Honesty is the best policy : rogues can be honest.'

But in a little came a certain disgust with the whole matter, and I determined not to think about it any more.  But determination was wasted.  This brought it about that, on more than one occasion, suddenly catching myself at the old thoughts which then bled me I gave vent to a sharp impatient 'Damn !' to the surprise of those who happened to hear me.  I remember once in second lesson so losing patience with myself that, unconscious of the presence of anyone, I let fly with my foot at a form in front of me, which went over with a loud bang on to the boards in a small dust-cloud, and as I sat motionless frowning at my book, and answered nothing to the questions Craven asked me about the matter, was given the lesson to write out twice, and afterwards was called up and spoken to on the subject.  I preserved complete silence, for what was the good of telling a fool of this sort, who grew furious over a false quantity and preached invertebrate sermons, the truth ?  I would as soon have thought of telling him a lie !  Well, I wrote out the lesson twice, and there that part of the affair ended.

The Christmas holidays were an evil time.  I gave myself up to, as it were, an entirely new consideration of affairs.  A week's close thought, out on my walks, in bed at night, often till after twelve or one o'clock, made me look upon the Bible as a fairy tale.  Then came a fortnight or so of utter confusion, inexplicable to myself: excitement of body and soul, wild dreams, visions or half-visions, a purgatory !  Finally I emerged with a certain calmness to wonder at that time, wonder that it had belonged to me.  It seemed so dimly far away now, and as if belonging to someone else, and yet not to someone else, and yet not to me.

The opening of the term wrought a change.  A new form of the thing which had once done duty to me as woman came to me, producing an amount of longing for her and her love that frequently found vent in emotion and even tears over pencilled poetry sheets.  Then Christ was introduced, as a sweet tender friend who consoled me for her present absence by telling me of her future coming.  But, after a time, this too passed, and I returned to my old doubtful state, deciding that happiness was undoubtedly the end of life, and that happiness to me meant having written certain quietly de-

lightful books, while I stayed alone apart in a dim place
that had little to do with life and nothing with death.
My old idea of greatness *en bloc* was childish, absurd !
My new trouble about God and the world was useless,
absurd !   My ideas about everything were hopelessly
vague !   Happiness and selfishness are synonymous
terms.   Everybody is selfish.   Good men are good,
because they couldn't be happy bad.   Bad men are
bad because they couldn't be happy good.   Men who are
the most unselfish are the most selfish : the very pain
that their unselfishness causes them is their pleasure.
Therefore when I intend to be happy I am simply intending what everybody intends.—It was surprising
how calm I grew upon this and other thoughts ; how
quietly assured of my uninterrupted course towards the
cultured happiness that I now began to look upon as
mine.

Then suddenly an incident occurred.

Some way on in February, one Saturday afternoon
just after dinner, to me, sitting up in the bedroom
looking through some of the *De Oratore* for 'third
lesson,' enter Armstrong, who throws me a letter and
exit.   I pick it up : recognise Colonel James's handwriting : open and read it.   He must request my presence
in London immediately on important matters.   I could
apply to Dr. Craven for the necessary funds.   There was
a train arrived in London to-morrow about one.   (The
letter was addressed from a street adjoining Piccadilly.
I forget its name.)   He hoped I should not be later
than that.   He had something of the greatest importance to communicate to me.   I must excuse a hasty
letter, but the state of his health at present made every
unusual effort very painful to him.

I at once went in to see Craven about it.

I came out from the short interview a little puzzled.
He had heard from Colonel James, he said.   He gave
me enough money for my fare second-class to London
and a few shillings over.   I might start when I liked.
I told him (I don't know why) that I thought I should
take the early morning train, as Colonel James had
mentioned it as one that would do.

As I was dressing for tea, it suddenly occurred to me

that I had heard somewhere about a train which left Glastonbury about six and got into London pretty late that night.—Why not go by it? As well as not!

When I had dressed I went into Mother McCarthy's to see if she had a time-table. She had. I found that there was a train left Glastonbury at 5.55 or so, and got into London at about eight. I looked at the clock. It was twenty minutes to six now. I would try it!

I had bought a glazed black bag last holidays, as being a useful sort of thing for a peripatetic to have. I got a clean night-gown, a clean shirt, a couple of collars, a pair of socks, and some handkerchiefs out of my linen locker: went back into my room: fished the black bag from under my bed: packed in the things I wanted: took my great-coat off the peg, and started away.

I swung into the station at four or five minutes after the train was due to start. I had a sharp cut and run on to and down the platform and got into an empty carriage just as it moved off. The liveliness of the whole affair delighted me. I felt for a little something like an excited child.

The journey did not seem long to me; for I slowly fell into my dim thought-world, and only came out of it for a moment when (about half-way I think) a fat old gentleman got into the carriage with a bulged old carpet-bag which he put on to the seat beside him: then took a newspaper from his inside breast-pocket: put on a pair of black horn pince-nez, and began to read. Just before London they collected the tickets, and I became aware that I felt empty internally: I had had no tea. But I went back into my old dim thought-world again, and was not out of it when we glided down a long gas-lit platform, and it was borne in on me that we were in London.

I got into a hansom and gave Colonel James's address to the driver. We drove through many streets, mostly having little traffic in them, till we drew up suddenly before a house, above the door of which was an oblong of glass lit by a gas-lamp, and in the middle, in black figures, 15, Colonel James's number. I got out; paid the driver, and rang at the bell. The door was opened almost immediately by a man in evening dress with a

napkin in his hand.  I asked did Colonel James live
here?  He said, Yes, he did.  I said:

'Can I see him?'

The Curling wasn't very well this evening, sir, he
said.  He was upstairs there with his cawfee just now,
sir.  He (the man in evening dress with a napkin)
didn't think he'd like to be disturbed.  But I might
give him (the man) my card, and he'd take it up to him.

'I have no card,' I said.  'My name is Leicester.
Will you tell Colonel James that I came to-night, instead of to-morrow, and want to know if I can see him?'

The man turned and went slowly up the first few
staircase steps: then half-turned, and said:

'Leicester was the name you said?'

'Yes,' I said, 'Leicester.'

I leant against the glazed-paper wall, looking at a
large print of Wellington meeting Blucher after Waterloo.  A clock ticked in an adjacent room.  I heard the
man from the top of the stairs say:

'Will you step up, please?'

I put bag and hat on to a dark-red mahogany chair
by an umbrella stand, and went up.  The man ushered
me in through an open door to the right.  I entered.

The first thing I saw was the part of a large low red-
clothed table under the light of a red-shaded lamp:
then, a rather thin old gentleman standing on the right
side of the hearthrug with his back to the fire.  He
raised his head.  There was a light-flash on his glasses.

He spoke.

'Mr. Leicester?' he said.

'Yes, sir,' I answered.

'Ah yes—exactly so.'

He paused, looking aside.  Then again raised his
head with the light-flash on his glasses.

'Will you please sit down?' he said.  'Perhaps you
would like to take your coat off?  It is very warm in
here, I dare say—after the street.'

I slowly took off my greatcoat, and then sat down in
a chair by the table facing him, he remaining standing.

After a pause:

'You have rather taken me by surprise, Mr. Leicester,'
he said, 'I, ah, did not expect you till to-morrow morn-

ing : as you have said, as you have said.—Did Dr. Craven
give you any information about the, ah, reason for your
journey ? ' (Looking up at me as before.) ' No ? he did
not ?—Very well. He acted wisely. I have every
possible reason to believe that Dr. Craven is a man of
distinguished, ah, fore-thought.' (He kept on inserting
' ah's ' in that way all the while.)

Another pause. Then :

' I have a very bad piece of news to give you, Mr.
Leicester,' he said, ' I am much afraid so ; I am much
afraid so. But I think that I had better give it you at
once, and without, ah, preamble. Your father's small
personal fortune, amounting to, ah, from £120 to £130
a year, was invested in—given up to (I am not quite
sure about the correct expression ; but it is, ah, im-
material)—to a bank in which he had every confidence.
I constantly, during his later years, did my best to
prevail upon him to—ah, make some other investment
with his money : as, ah, I had myself seen a very sad—
ah, incident in my own family in connection with—
banks. You may have heard that the Great Southern
Bank has recently, ah, become insolvent, or whatever
it is ? No ? Well, ah, it is so, and every hour is bringing
in worse information on the, ah, matter. It is, you may
perhaps see, Mr. Leicester, quite impossible for you to
continue your career at—Glastonbury. Every penny
of your father's money has—gone. I, ah, have, I am
glad to say, absolutely nothing to—to do with it myself
personally. . . . Have you any, ah, designs yourself as
to a future, ah, career ? '

I put my hand to my mouth, looking steadily at him.
He glanced aside and back again, as before :

' —I am not to return to Glastonbury ? ' I asked.

' Ah, surely not.'

I spoke rather to myself than to him :

' Not to work any more ? not to be able to read my
books ? not to learn ?—Why, all my books are there
with all the notes I have taken such trouble to write
out—and I here. . . . What must I do ? '

There was a pause.

I rose, and said :

' I can only think of one thing, sir. I have, I believe,

some brains, and, I believe, of that sort which can be turned to use. I have more than once desired to write. If I only had time, I am confident that I could make my livelihood——'

'Good heavens, sir!' he exclaimed, 'You are not thinking of becoming a—a writer.—Ah! Why, it is, ah, another word for starvation!'

'Men have made their fortune with nothing but their pens to help them before now,' I said, 'and I am not afraid.'

I noticed a thick blue vein swelling out on his forehead. He threw up his hands, and exclaimed vehemently: 'It is madness, madness, sheer, ah, insanity! I will not hear of it! I will give you no help! (He seemed suddenly to collapse.) 'You must go away. I must ring for Salmon, to show you out. You must go away. You are agitating me—dreadfully! I am not to be agitated. Doctor Astley says so. I am not to be agitated.'

At first I was startled : then amused : then saddened : last angered, by this unexpected outburst. I moved a step nearer to him. He looked at me for a moment, and then dropped into the arm-chair by him to the right of the fire.

'Oh, don't touch me!' he cried, 'Don't look at me like that! I will not have it! I will not endure it! Salmon, Salmon, take him away. He agitates me. . . . Please go away, sir. I am dreadfully agitated.' (I was looking at him frowning. He cried out, almost in a scream)—'For God's sake, don't look at me like that! My God, my God, my God! . . . *She* used to look.' . . . (Then he suddenly started up, exclaiming) —'I say I won't *endure* it! Do you hear? I won't endure it. Don't act at *me*, sir! I know it's in your blood, but, if you think you're going to browbeat *me*, you're mistaken!' (Then he began to fail.) 'Salmon, he is going to act at me. No, no—you're not as careful of me as Edgar used to be. Why did I ever let him go? Why did I ever let him go?' (Ending in a wail.)

I began to grow a little weary of it, and looked aside. He went on maundering about her having killed him, yes, killed him, and other things which I did not notice.

At last came a pause. I determined to go : then thought of some questions I would care to ask him, and said :

'I cannot understand, sir, why you have spoken to me like this. I know nothing of my father or my mother. You say you were my father's friend——'

'So I· was,' he wailed, 'so I was—till she came between us !'

I gave my teeth an impatient clench : then bit my lip and closed my right hand with all my strength, determined not to say what was now on my tongue. What good could it do?

I said :

'I have nothing left then, absolutely nothing?'

He stared at me half vacantly.

'Absolutely nothing,' he repeated.

A new resolution came to me: to leave the questions unasked and go—go at once.

'Good-night, sir, I said, 'I will leave you now.'

He stared at me as before.

'You are not, ah, *going*?' he said.

'Yes, sir, I am going,' I said ; 'good-night.'

As I was turning away, he started up convulsively and burst out :

'But it is insanity ! I will not hear of it ! I will not endure it ! I am your guardian. Do you hear, sir, that I am your guardian? Salmon ! Damn the man ! Salmon, I say !——'

I was out of the door and had closed it to. I could hear his voice now wailing as I went to the head of the stairs. Then it died away. I found my bag and hat in the hall. My coat was over my arm : I do not remember either having taken it up or put it there. I went on to the hall-door : opened it, after a little trouble with the latch : went out : pulled it to, by its big round brass handle in the middle, once, twice, and passed over the step and on to the pavement. It was raining.

I walked on into a main street, and then, turning to the right, walked on down it. The perpetual movement of people and horses and things about me brought a feeling into me that I had never felt before. I forgot about myself and my own affairs and my hunger

in considering them all. So I went on, till I came to
a corner where the main street ended. There I somewhat mechanically crossed. As I reached the pavement
on the other side, I heard a man call out twice :
' Kil-burn ! Kil-burn !' and looked at him standing,
keeping on by a strap with one hand and holding out
the other, on an omnibus perch.

' Kilburn,' I thought, ' is the farthest place he goes
to. Probably, then, it 's a suburb. I may as well go
there as anywhere, for what I intend to do. At any
rate, I 'll see.'

And with that went straight to the omnibus step
and clambered up by the ladder on to the top, where
I found myself exchanging looks with a man sitting
on another omnibus that just then passed by. I laid
the bag down and put on my coat, when the conductor
got up, crossed to my side, and began removing the
tarpaulin from the seat. I thanked him and sat down
with the bag beside me, and took to half-absently
watching the people passing in and out of the light
from the shop windows as we drove on. We drove on
for some time.

At last we turned into a long straight rather dark
street—Edgware Road, I heard the driver say. As
we were some way up it, I noticed what seemed
torches or something of the sort flaring by the right
side, at the top, just above where it bifurcated. I
determined to get down there.

We stopped on the left side just below them. I let
myself down with my bag in my teeth, and paid the
conductor my fare, 2d. or 3d., I forget which. Then
I turned from him, crossed the street, and sauntered
on looking at the stalls. There were not many people
along the pavement : the hawkers cried their cries
rather plaintively : one old man, sitting in front of an
oven with a small steam-jet, cried out every now and
then sharply : ''Ot! 'Ot!'

It was still raining and it seemed colder. I sauntered
on. A tall girl, with a singularly well-made body and
well-poised head, moved with a long swinging step in
front of me. She stopped in a moment, to buy some
nuts, and I saw her face. It was pleasant to look at

E

it, so pure and clear-cut, with crystal eyes and red
rarified lips and large regular white teeth. I followed
her slowly, thinking of her dear face: I felt sure she
would love me if she knew me.

She stopped to listen to a man addressing a few
gaunt, shivering children whose faces formed a line
along the far side of his stall. I went up close to her
and looked at her. She was eating nuts, and every
now and then let the shell-bits fall out of her mouth
down her black coat to the ground. At last she turned
her eyes to mine: then exclaimed in an undertone:

'Oh my! I hope you'll know me next time you see
me, young man.'

I turned away and crossed the road. I faced a
pawnbroker's. An idea came to me. I went in—
into a dusky clothes-hung place where a man was
sprawling over the counter, under a large gas-jet,
with a cigar in his mouth. I said:

'I want to sell this greatcoat. What will you give
me for it?'

'Let's see it, sir,' he said.

I took it off.

In the end he gave me fifteen shillings for it. It
was quite new.

I went out and counted my money before the next,
a jeweller's shop window which was brightly lit up.
I had one shilling and sevenpence halfpenny in my
pocket. That left me fourteen shillings and ninepence
for myself; for I owed Colonel James threepence for
my omnibus fare. This and the rest he should have at
once. Some day (I hoped soon) he should have to
the last farthing I owed him. I turned away, putting
his money into one trouser-pocket and my own into
the other, and went on for a little. Then feeling the
rain and the air colder, and under some unnoticed
impulse turning up my coat-collar, I re-crossed the
road and wandered on. I did not remark particularly
where I went, only that I turned down the narrowest
streets I happened to see.

All at once my eye was caught by a card in a small
window I was passing. I stopped to look at it. The
window, or rather, a linen-blind, was lit-up from within,

the card marking a small oblong on the ledge of one of the upper panes. I looked closer, to read the actual letters: *Apartments.*

Not seeing either bell or knocker, I rapped at the door with my knuckles.

An old woman holding up a guttering candle half-opened it. I said:

' Do you let apartments ? '

' I 've a room. Yes.'

' How much is it a week ? '

' Five shillings a week, sir.'

' Oh ! '

A pause. I turned away considering.

'—But I think I could take four, sir, perhaps ? ' she said.

' Will you let me see it ? ' I asked.

' Please step upstairs, sir.—Mind the wall, sir, it comes off.'

I followed her upstairs.

I took the room, and paid for two weeks in advance.

The furniture consisted of a bed, a washing-stand, a table, a chair, and two ragged scraps of carpet, one under the table, one by the side of the bed. There was a looking-glass over the chimney-piece, and three photographs in faded violet frames of velvet, worn out: Napoleon iii., the Empress Eugénie, and the Prince Imperial as a boy. She had left a gas-jet turned full on.

I bolted the door, and began pulling off my coat, when I felt the emptiness inside me again. I sat down on the unsteady chair, and began thinking about what had occurred to me to-day; but I soon gave it up: rose and, for a moment, stood irresolute whether to go out and get some food, or to ask this woman, Mrs. Smith, for some, or to get into bed without any ? At last I thought I would get into bed. Sleep, cool quiet sleep, would calm and refresh me.

I threw my waistcoat on to the top of the coat, and stood irresolute again, stretching my arms up and down. Then an impulse came to me. I fell down on to my knees and, leaning my arms on the bed, leant my head on my arms. I began in a half whisper:

' *If there be a God——* '

After a pause, of thought almost as much as of words,
I said :

'I ask You, God, if You are, to have pity on me if I
am blindly wandering, and to lead me to know You
some day before I die. I don't know how I am going,
but I know where I desire to go : and yet I don't know
more than that it is somewhere.' Then the feeling of
light and shadow, dream and reality, an eclipsed sun
and moon, came to me so strongly that I got up again,
slowly, with the intention of saying no more prayers
that night. The things around me were all in a sort
of noise above my ears. I went and turned out the
gas; and then slowly undressed, in the dark save for
the light that came from a gas-lamp in the street,
through the far window.

I pulled down the upper-clothes; got into bed; sank
into enclosing coolness, and very soon sleep.

---

### III

WHEN I first woke up, I thought I was back in my room
at Glastonbury : then recalled, but slowly, all that had
happened the day before.—That next-day awakening
was a dreary thing : everything that I had done seemed
so purposeless ! It would be better to marry a red-
cheeked woman, with untidy gold hair and a brown
homely dress, and smoke a pipe in the sun all day
while she brushed out the house. The picture I con-
jured up made me laugh aloud. I leaped out of bed.
The sun was shining.

I went to the other far window : pulled down the
upper part, and looked out. The air clear and rather
sharp, but not cold : as something almost corporal, to
my inhaling lungs. I had no watch. It was about half-
past seven or eight, I thought. A man came with sounding steps down the street and passed invisibly below
me. I pulled up the window again ; stripped, and prepared to wash. Such a little jug and such a little basin!
And no sponge !—What *was* I to do without a sponge ?

I made the best of it : dried myself on the one flabby
towel, and began to dress. Dressed quickly, and then
taking up my hat, went slowly downstairs.

At the house door, I met Mrs. Smith coming out of the room on the left, where I had seen the card. I said 'Good morning,' and she said 'Good morning, sir,' and I asked if there was a park anywhere near? (I had an idea that there were parks all about London.) She told me that it was about ten minutes sharp walk to the Regent's Park, and gave me some confused directions how to get there. I bought a half-pound of dates and a large brown loaf at a shop close by, and with these under my arm, asked my way, which was a very simple one; passed out of a somewhat dirty road, through some lodge gates, and so over two bridges into the Park itself. I sauntered along the side of the lake, looking at the swans and ducks.

It was a glorious morning. The sun breathed a gentle heat upon me, and warmed me gratefully. The dew was still on the grass: a few people hurried across by the pathways: every now and then a duck whirred through the air. I reached another bridge, went on to it, and stood and watched a flight of sparrows bathing themselves wantonly in the shallows of a small bay on the far shore.

'It is beautiful,' I said.

I ate my dates and loaf on a seat beside a tree on an elevation that runs up there parallel to the curve of the lake. The loaf was of good thick crumby bread, and satisfied without satiating me; the dates, a half-pound, 4d., gave the bread a flavour. The only thing that seemed lacking was a crystal stream from which I might drink a pure cool draught. My breakfast done, I rose almost readily, and went back again to the bridge that leads to the gates. For, the fight is begun and loitering looks like laggardness.

Finding myself in the road that led to my street, Maitland Street, and opposite a small newspaper-stationer's, I went in and invested in a pen, nibs, ink and paper. These were my weapons. Then I proceeded on home: went upstairs: found my bed already made (which was pleasing): put my weapons on the table, myself into the chair and, tilted back, began to consider.

I had seen somewhere or other that Byron received £500 or so for his shorter pieces, 'The Bride of Abydos,'

'Giaour,' etc.  There is, then, surely a good chance
of my getting at least £10, or perhaps £20 if my book
sells well, for two pieces, each of (say) 600 lines.  On
that I could subsist for a long time and a long time
meant more poems and more money.  You see, if you
only live as economically as I am going to . . . Well,
many things may be done.

After a little preliminary thought, I came to this : I
had had these almost two years two tales in my head,
that is, connected narratives with a definite beginning
and end ; a story, a fact : not the embodiment of a
passing humour that, being exalted, has to be climbed
up to, but a narrative, to be clothed in the best clothes
I could put on it, and then sent on a journey with the
reader to amuse and try to instruct him, if only in a
lesson of pathos, on the road.—I at once set upon the
first of my ' tales.'

By the time it grew dusk, I had finished over two
hundred lines of it.  I was not at all satisfied.  I had
not, I thought, twined the melody of the rhythm
enough into the sense : that is, had lost some of the
scent, in transplanting my flower.  I was afraid of
becoming a mere painter, and losing the scent altogether.  Still, I reflected, the less subtle I try to be,
the more likely am I to please those who are likely to
read this poem of mine.  One must live prose, before
one lives poetry : prose is paying for your cake, and
poetry is eating it.  Get something to support your
body first : the body is the keystone.  It is no good
having your brain full and your belly empty, for at that
rate you soon die, and look foolish.

For all such thoughts, I was a little ashamed of what
I had done.  My muse had not moved me : she dwelt
but in the suburbs of my good pleasure.  'Well, well,
it cannot be helped.'—So I left her there, and went out
into the streets to buy stamps and return Colonel James
his money.

I wandered far that night.  At last to the Serpentine,
where I stood, some little time, trying to explain the
lamp reflections across the water—two together, large
space, two together.  Then I must have gone down
Piccadilly, and through Leicester Square : then into

the Strand, I think, and so down by Charing Cross
station, for I went under a bridge and ended on the
Embankment.

I came home with an 'aerial breathlessness' upon me:
sat down to my poem and finished it.  It had indeed
moved me this time: two tears had fallen from my eyes.
But, what I had heard called 'mysticism' by some people
(meaning, as I supposed, that it seemed so to them) had
run riot, and I knew that I had not written what I meant
to write.—I lost patience.  It seemed very hard, that I
should not be allowed to try to do my best.  I thought,
not unbitterly, of the thousands of silly men and women,
who squandered on luxury for mere luxury's sake, or
hoarded for mere hoarding's sake, that which would en-
able me . . . Then it struck me that sometimes men
*starved.*—The thought seemed like a cruel being of
darkness.  I looked up sharply, almost hearing a sort of
clang of its departing wings.  And there arose a circling
black cloud, from the outer dark-smokiness of which
many, many eyes looked at me, the eyes of the many,
many men who had struggled and perished.  I glanced
up sharply again, almost hearing my own mental reply:
' *Ay, but* great men *never struggled and perished : they
always struggle and win !* '  But still that circling black
cloud stayed, with the many, many eyes looking at me
from the outer dark-smokiness, the eyes of the many,
many men who had struggled and perished.

For four days I worked at my two poems : finished
them and, sauntering out that night, looked into a
newspaper-shop's window by chance, and there noted
a publisher's name and address on a board below, and
sent him the poems next day.  I had said nothing more
to him than that I begged to submit them for his inspection, enclosing stamps for their return in case of
rejection.  I was sure that he would take them.

I spent most of my time in my room, either writing
more poetry, or reading and studying a Shakespeare,
which I had bought for a few pence in the Edgware
Road market one Saturday night from an amusing man
who was selling off a cartload of books to the stolid
people as he best could.  Generally in the late after-

noon I went out for a walk into the Regent's Park, feeling as if I were away from the streets and the life-worn people there. Many happy hours were spent by me wandering whistling over the middle grass plateau (it seemed to me like a plateau), thinking of my work and, sometimes, of the dear woman to whom some day I should tell all of this; for she had come back to me now, and not quite what she had ever been before, more real because more gentle, more loving, more true, knowing what was in my heart and soul and having much in her own heart and soul that mine would be glad to know of. Often I watched the sun setting in the cloud banks, and once saw him in the dim, slatey, sky-layer, hanging like a blood-red spider, gradually covered with a sort of dusty smokiness and darkened till he was wrapped invisible from me.

I lived all the time on bread, with an occasional relish of fruit or a glass of milk.

I soon learnt my way about, at any rate in one great block that was between Regent's Park and the Thames by Charing Cross. I was very fond of wandering by night : especially to the top of Primrose Hill, to look out over the great city, and the rings of light closer to, as in a vestibule-court of an almost boundless palace-building : especially, too, I loved the populous streets like Oxford Street and the Strand.

One night I had wandered along Oxford Street past the Circus, and then turned down on the right into the block of buildings that is between Seven Dials and Regent Street; had wandered on and on, till I found myself in dim streets, in which every now and then shadows as of women moved with a certain inspiration of fear. I passed close to some of them, drawn as by some latent power of fascination on the ground and in them, but not looking at their faces: till at last, passing somewhat quickly into an alley, I met one face to face under a protruding shadowed lamp. For a moment I stood breathless, with my eyes in the mad wolfishness and glitter of hers, and then, like a lightning flash that fills the whole air, terror of her filled me quite. I leaped aside and then past her : plunged into a dark-covered way that was behind and beyond her, and hurried on, past two silver-ornamented women who stood laughing and talking at a corner shop-door, out into a city street again, not streets of this city of horrible shadowiness! But the impression of that place, its shadowed air, its shadowed women, and the mad wolfishness and glitter of their eyes, was upon me all that night, turning my sleep into a nightmare. It was several days before that impression left me.

It was about this time that a vague idea came to me that I had caught some fever. My hands were so hot at nights, and cheeks and ears. I grew so impatient too. One evening I tilted over the table; and the ink-bottle was in the middle of my scattered blacked sheets on the floor, and I was almost crying, and had scarcely heart to pick the things up again.

This was the evening I determined to go down to Norfolk Square and see the house in which Clayton lived. I rose from the table where I had been reading with the light of a coffin-wicked dip-candle (the gas was an extra shilling a week), took up my hat, and set out. It was a long walk. At last I entered Norfolk Square, a long dark oblong, with a long black thin-railed garden in the middle. And, when I found out No. 21, I was facing a lampless eyeless house, up from the area rails of which protruded a towering *To Let* board. In a few moments, standing, I realised this, and turned away sick at heart. I was quite alone in this city, this careless, cruel London, and, if I were to lie down there in the hollow under the garden rails, and sleep, and never wake again, there would be no one, not a man, not a woman, not a child who . . . I gave up the thought as I began walking. I had never realised that I was quite alone here before this. The realisation seemed to deaden the soul in me. My later weary wandering of that night saw nothing of what was around me. I reached home somehow, and bed, and sleep.

The next morning I went for a long walk out to Hendon, and when I got there, lying on the grass, felt too languid to move : till at last, I summoned enough resolution to set off home again. It was two when I got there, hungry and yet not hungry; thirsty and yet not thirsty, hot and yet shivering. I sat down: lounged

over the table, and began to read at the opened
Shakespeare. I read on till it grew a little dusk. All
at once a few of the letters seemed to disappear or to
have disappeared. I strained my eyes. More went.
I peered closer. Two atmospheric circles almost invisible were out-turning on either side of my sight.
In a little I could make out nothing but a blurred mass
where the two small printed pages had been. I closed
them up; then leant my face in my arms over the
table and closed my eyes; but the two atmospheric
circles almost invisible still were out-turning on either
side of my sightlessness. I felt dimly that I had made
that movement somewhere before: perhaps in a dream?
No, it was not in a dream. I remember now. It was
once when a boy (and that is why it may have seemed
at first like a dream to me) went to the bench and, half
upon it, leant his face in his arms on the cool table-
cover. . . . And could not weep soft tears: the tears
were dried behind his eyes.

I started up impatiently. I was crying, my hands
were wet with my tears. This was all accursed folly!
Hysteria: like a woman! What was the matter with
me? Was I ill? Or going to be ill? Or what? . . .
I was tired. That was all. It was nothing more.—
But my eyes! . . . *O God, if I break down!* 'Nay!'
I cried aloud, smiling through my tears. '*I'm*
the boy who says there is *no* God!' "*The fool hath
said in his heart——*" Cha! That's David's opinion.
If ever *I* write Psalms, I'll put it the other way on.
David was the man who never saw the righteous
deserted nor the righteous man begging his bread.
*There's* "inspiration" for you! You blind old driveller
you! into the ditch, I say! There'll be plenty of your
tribe to follow.' I smiled again, but differently:
'Still Kebes: always hunting out something!'

I had waited for thirteen days now.
It happened that, the afternoon after I had the affair
with the eyes, coming home from Hampstead Heath
by the Grove End Road with my eyes as usual on the
ground, I saw what looked like a small part of a silver
coin in a heap of dust by a lamp-post. I stopped;

bent; stretched down my hand, and found a two-shilling piece. I looked up. I could see no one in the road: no one behind me. I might take it then; for how could I possibly find its owner? And to have found it, I, who had never found anything in my life before! It seemed quite strange.—I had three shillings now. That meant another fortnight. On the force of it, I got a glass of milk, as I went down the Edgware Road.

I came home almost buoyant, and had run up the two first steps before I saw someone was descending. I drew down and back. It was a petticoated being, a girl, but of what sort, the dark of the place and the duskiness of the hour combined to hide. Anyhow, she said 'Thank you,' and went on: and I up and, as I went to my door, I thought that the one on the left must be hers; but perhaps she sleeps up in the attics like a clay-homed swallow? Then I remembered to have heard muffled stirring in that room by mine, and concluded it must indeed be hers, and proceeded to forget all about the matter.

The next day was chilly and rainy. I set out for a walk to Hampstead; for I must, I felt, take exercise to keep 'breakdown' at a fit distance. I had some trouble with my heel which had become sore, till, at last, by the time I was three-quarters there, economical pain-shirking foot positions had made every step painful. None the less I was determined to get as far as the Hampstead Pond. It began to drizzle. I toiled on. I found once that deep thoughts made me forget the pain of movement: so I kept trying this plan, with short-timed success, till (now a quarter way back again, and the rain thicker) a desperate attempt to separate body and soul by resolution proved fruitless. Then an utter despair came upon me. I stood still. It was at a corner in front of the rails of the dingy garden of a lampless house. I could have sunk down upon the shining pavement there; covered my face with my arms, and sobbed myself like a tired child to sleep, but oh! a sleep that should know no waking, no waking to misery and despair! At that moment a light leaped up and out from the big window on the left of the

door.  I saw it, but did not move.  Then I leant
against the nearer hard, cemented gate-post in that
dreary rain of half-darkness, and my body seemed all
bloodless.  A girl, with her dress huddled up all round
her, showing dainty white petticoats and dark-coloured
stockings, and with a nice umbrella spread over her,
came hurrying up to me.  I looked at her slowly.  She
gave me a quick glance, and hurried more.  A devil
rose in me.  I made a short half-step after her.  I
would seize her: tear that thing from her hand: rip
and rend her laced clothes: rip and rend them off her,
till she stood tattered, naked, there in the rain of the
half-darkness with me!  And all I would desire more,
would be to take mud and bespatter and befoul her,
and then turn and go on my way with wild laughter.
The thoughts were lightning swift.  I gave a cry of
fierce-suppressed delight : stepped : and halted.  Was
I mad ?—I turned, and went back, and on.

When I got home I set upon a poem by the light
of a new dip.  If I had had to die for it, alone and in
the early grey morning, I could not have kept out my
mysticism now.  I *must* speak to some one now! it
could not *always* be silence !  I had need to speak to
some one.  I thought my heart was breaking.  And
I could not fall asleep till I had told my death-tale.

But I was too weary to finish it.  I gave it up at
last.  I was in an evil plight, I knew : burning and
shivering and with an empty stomach.  I undressed
slowly, as usual, in the dark, save for the light that
came from the gas-lamp in the street through the far-
window.  As I got into bed I determined that the next
day I would seek some work, even manual ; for I did
not, after all, care to die till I had heard about my
poems (it was ridiculous !  I smiled, but in a strange,
sad way), and I should have to pay four shillings at
the end of the week, rent, and I had only three left
for food.  'Wherefore, work must be done if money is
to be earned : work, even manual, and why not ?'  At
last I fell asleep.

But in the morning I lay in a half-dreamy, half-
exhausted state of heat, from which I had not will
enough for long to rouse myself.  This grew into a

dull, languorous lethargy, not unsweet, and in my very bones, making me altogether indifferent to everything save a sort of aching hunger, which at last drove me out of bed to the table for the half-pound of dates and the loaf I had bought last afternoon. I got them : went back into bed again, and, I suppose, ate them. When I awoke it was evening, the gas-lamp lighting up a part of the far end of the room. I felt flushed with the hunger still in me, and became aware of many troublous crumbs in the sheets and some date-stones, but of neither bread nor dates. In a little I got up, and washed and dressed slowly and listlessly, with the dull hunger ever in me. Now I would go out, I thought. I went to the door, opened it, and heard a voice say :

'Well, I can't help it, you must go!' It was Mrs. Smith's voice, harder and drier than usual.

Another answered some soft, pleading words. I leant against the door-post, rather exhausted, scarcely knowing why I stayed there.

A pause. Then :

'You know it's the second week owing,' pursued Mrs. Smith, 'I can't do it any more, and what's more, I won't! So there! . . . You must give me something, or you must go, that's all.'

'I've only got a shilling,' said the other voice, 'I gave it you. Won't you wait till the end of the week, Mrs. Smith? I shall have my wages then?'

'You said that *last* week! No, not I! Tick's not nat'ral to me, I say. I'm a lone widdy woman, *I* am, but I pays my way, and why don't every one, I want to know? . . . Why didn't you pay me last week, then?'

'I was ill. I had to pay for the medicine.'

'Drat the medicine! You shouldn't be ill. . . . Come now, what are you going to do? Look sharp. Don't go and be blubbering now. It's no go with me, young woman—that!'

Another pause.

'I've never blubbered to you, Mrs. Smith. I asked you to wait a bit, that's all. I'm down on my luck, that's what I am. A lady took a piece of work I did out of hours, a week ago; but she won't pay for it till the end of the month, she says.'

'O my eye, that's likely, ain't it now? It's all fudge—*that's* what it is! Now look here. You pay me to-night or you go! So there, plain and straight! I've got to live like the rest of you, I suppose? Will you give it me now? What's more, let me tell you, I'm reg'lar hard up, meeself. . . . You've given me a shilling already. Now come! give us the rest, and I'll let you go tick for the other week till Saturday.'

Another pause.

'—You know you can get it, if you like, you *know* you can.' Mrs. Smith's voice too was soft now, but hoarsely.

'I can't! How can I? Or else I would give it you.'

'O you can—if you like.'

'*How* can I?'

'Oh, come! *You* know well enough! . . . *You ain't so bad looking as all that.*'

I put my hands behind me; my breath went from me. My fingers scraped lightly on the wood and paper. I was trembling all over. I did not know whether to cry out, or, keeping silence, to see what would be the end.

I waited, the blood pulsing through my head, and whirring in my ears, till I was nigh blinded and deafened.

It seemed to me that it was half an hour before either of them spoke again.

Then:

'O do wait, do wait, Mrs. Smith,' pleaded the other, 'I really will pay you on Saturday night. I will really. I've been ill. I will——'

Her voice maddened me. I pulled-to my door somehow and threw myself on to the bed, shivering and clutching myself, muttering into the pillow: 'O, there cannot be a God in heaven, who is just and good and will let such things be!'

At last I stopped.—*What would she do?* The thought stayed me all into listening for a moment.

Then I began to struggle again, and again stopped and listened. It seemed I was so for hours.

As I listened the fourth or fifth time, I heard Mrs. Smith's voice almost at the door: then there came

silence: a door closed: I heard slow heavy footsteps
with clamping heels go down the stairs. My door was
ajar.—I got up, and closed and carefully latched it.
'*What would she do?*'

'What is the girl to me?' I thought. 'There are
hundreds like—what she will be, in this city. And
one more: "What is one among so many?" All soul-
less things too—like me! And *useless* things too, who
will try to do no more than live in the sun, breed
maggots, and perish. Whereas I ——*What will she do?*'

I came to my bed and lay, face downwards, on it.

'. . . That three shillings perhaps means life,' I
thought again, 'who knows if I can get any work? and
how to live in the meantime? And I'm so frightfully
weak. . . . Means *life*: means *hope*, and all my dreams!
means *everything*! *That* is its *meaning*. And, if I give it
up. . . . No; I *won't* give it up! I *won't* give up my life!
It is the only thing here: the rest is but hope and fancy.'

I heard a board creak.

Some one went down the stairs quietly but quickly.
. . . Who was it?—Along the passage. The door
closed. It was just beneath my head. I seemed to see
it, and her. I got on to my knees on the bed: pulled
up the piece of linen, that hung half across the window,
and looked out.—She was hurrying across the road,
with her head bent down, and her hands hanging beside her.

'Let her go?' I thought, 'what is she to me? Let
her go. Let her go.—Why, see: if I had gone out in
the morning, as I had intended, I might very well
never have known anything about it. I will not do it.
Why, now——' I stopped.

'You *coward*!' I cried, 'you miserable *coward*!'

I covered my face with my hands, pressing my elbows
against my body and tightening every muscle in my body.

At last I moaned:

'If I only thought there was a God—who saw us!
both!—A good God—who would not leave us die—
despairing—I *would* give it her!—But—as it is—I—.
I——'

'*Coward!*' I cried, almost choking. '*Coward!* . . .
You *cannot* let her go!'

I got up on to the carpeted plank : dragged open the door : and went quickly down the steps. At the foot, with my hand on the latch, I cried out : 'Mrs. Smith ! Mrs. Smith !' And, when she came from the room on the left just by me, put the three shillings into her hand, the florin and one shilling, and said :

'There is the money for her.'

I had the door open as her fingers closed. She was staring at me stupidly enough ; but I saw that she understood what I meant. Then I stepped out quickly : ran across the road, and stopped for a moment, looking ahead to see if I could see her. . . . *If she escaped me after all !*

Three great gas-jets flared some fifty yards down, on the opposite side, in front of a fish-shop. I saw her pass by it, casting an irresolute shadow, her head bent down as before, her hands evidently holding one another in front. A few people were moving to and fro.

I walked quickly along the pavement, till I came opposite her.

She hesitated for a moment at the corner of a street. I crossed over, just behind her. As she made her first step forward, I touched her arm, and said :

'Stop.'

She started, turned round sharply, and seemed to recognise me. For a moment we stood facing one another.

'You must not go,' I said, 'I have persuaded Mrs. Smith. She will let you—she will wait till the end of the week.'

She answered nothing. Then I turned from her, and walked away.

I had gone some ten yards, when I heard her running after me. She laid her hand for a moment on my arm, and said, panting :

'You are very kind, sir : very kind. You're very good——'

'I am neither kind, nor good. I have done nothing,' I said.

'You have paid Mrs. Smith for me,' she said, 'I *know* you have. She would not wait else.—But I *will* pay you back, sir, for *sure*, on Saturday.'

'You need not trouble about it—' (Looking at her face, I added smiling :) 'Child.'

'Indeed, sir, I am very grateful to you,' she said.

I could not bear to listen to her any more.

'It is nothing,' I said. 'I am very glad to have been of any use to you.—Good-night.'

And left her.

Near the end of the street I passed a man who stopped and stared at me, till I noticed it and stopped also, wondering what was the matter. I had no hat on ; that was it. I proceeded a little : then, almost as if recollecting something, turned back and came home.

I found my hat up in my room : put it on, and went out again. I felt as if I must go, as if I was going, somewhere.

Wandered out towards the Park and then, up-skirting it, on to Primrose Hill, up which I climbed slowly. It seemed to me that I would not much care whether I lived or died. I would seek for no work. No, not I ! It was nothing to me what happened, or to anyone else, or to God. I was glad the girl had not been driven to prostitute herself in these hellish London streets. When the barrier of the first time you do a thing is broken through, the second time is easier, and the third easier still. I am only sorry that this miserable carcase of mine should have so conquered me as to give the tyranny of its thoughts to my soul. These last few days have unmade me.'

I stood by a bench not far from the top, and turned, and looked out over the darkness from which came the cool breeze fanning my feverish face. All at once I cried out passionately :

'I *will* know, I *will* know !'          .

Then my head fell down on to my breast, and I said :

'Oh fool, fool ! Dost thou think, then, that thou art the first, and wilt be the last, to cry that cry ? They have not known, they will never know !—Ay, they are all wise, and they none of them find out anything ! They beat the air with heavy flails, proving each other fools and us slaves and beasts, and then they also die, and rot, and are eaten. Behold, I here, a starving beggar-boy, know all that they know, and that is—

F

*Nothing!* Ay, you foolish Wisdoms, that spend your days in spinning clothes of air with which to clothe the long procession of Humanity, behold I here, a starving beggar-boy, *laugh* at you and say to you what you know : ' *Why, you go naked,—naked, as when you came from your mother's womb !*' Oh, oh, oh ! we are all fools together. And there's a consolation in that; but not much, if you happen to be starving.—*Starving ?  I, starving,*' I cried fiercely, 'with a better head on my shoulders than all these damned . . . Come, come, we mustn't boast—even now !'

Laughing a sad, short laugh, I stepped out and down, and began to descend.

Half way, or so, down, some impulse made me stop and look up.  And I saw what I took for a small woman, coming down also, just above the seat where I had been standing.  Seeing her, I laughed again.—The poor girl! (For, of course, it was my girl, following me.)  She thought me, *me !* a good, kind, heaven-sent saviour, perhaps ?

I burst out into a keen short laugh and went on : went on in home, with the wings of a shadowy bird-thing or moth-thing fluttering in my inner ear.—Up these weary old stairs with an up-pulling arm.—The landing at last.—My door open.—My room.

I took the match-box off its mantelpiece corner; found the candle ; struck a light ; lit it, and looked.  Then I saw a large envelope lying on the table, and started.

I looked at the candle-light, one long half-vacant look, and turned and went to the table, and took up the letter and slowly opened it and read :

' DEAR SIR,—Our reader thinks very well of your Poems ; but as there is little sale in poetry now-a-days, he does not, on that account, think the work would command a remunerative sale.  The following is an extract from the report which we have received on the MS.  "There is evidence of power in his book which, with due care and cultivation, may ripen into ability to achieve real and lasting poetic work."

' If it were not for the poor attention poetry attracts in these days, we would gladly have made you an offer for a little work which contains so much beauty and melody.— Yours faithfully,          PARKER, INNES, & Co.'

' We are sending the MS. to you per book-post.'

I put it down with a short laugh, and smiling, shrugged my shoulders.

'Very well. There is nothing left for me now, I suppose, but to write my will after Chatterton, and invest in——arsenic and water, was it? But I forget; I have no money! I must go out into the streets, even at *this* hour then, and beg a few pence to be able to kill myself, since in London, too, one can't die for nothing! There is the river. My old river at Glastonbury. If I could roll over and over in the long green weeds, why, it wouldn't matter much whether I was able to come back to the brown earth again, would it? And to look up through the dusky, jewelled lightshafts of the currents! Ha, there are flocks down there! I read about it in a story book once, and a man went down in a sack to find them. But he was drownded. No, drowned. *Drownded* is bad grammar; but what's the odds, I say? These idiotic wordmongers here talk about nothing but grammar . . . "For a good knowledge of the classics (especially of Cicero) is the foundation of all that is worth knowing in the *humani*. . . ." —You think so, my good fellow? You think Art's growing more and more of a drug, do you? And you think, too, that I shall be great—some day? But I've no ambition to be great, I tell you. Fools are great. When they die they rot and are eaten. We all shall die some day, and rot, and be eaten. I wish I were a worm. . . . Hush! Hush! What was that? Who's there? hi! who's there? Rayne? You, Rayne!—No, I assure you! Not starving! Only——But take care, or you'll have the boat over. Why are women done up like mummies? If ever *I* have a wife, Rayne, she shall wear knickerbockers, and race up Taygetus. . . . Hush, hush! Here's Christ come to see me. O dear Christ, O sweet Christ, give me your soft hand! I'll tell *you* all about it. I seem to know you so much better than God. And I haven't a friend in the world. ——I'm afraid they won't understand them . . . Poor little poems! Too mystic; too mystic! I must keep out my mysticism; but how can I, when my heart's breaking? breaking, breaking. . . . Chut, chut, there! You mustn't sit down on the bed like that. *Why, you're*

*a woman!* These are clothes, and here's . . . your soft
breast? And your face? and your hair? O you dear
woman, why are you holding me so with your soft arms,
and laying my face on your soft breast? Let's go to
sleep like that—together. Will you? Come close to
me, I will tell you something. Do you know, I've been
longing for you to come to me . . . to come to me,
ever since . . . But let's rest, now you *are* come, dear.
I saw a woman with a sweet face to-night. She passed
me on the pavement in the crowd: but not so sweet as
yours. I love to . . . Closer, closer! Let me feel you,
I am beginning to be afraid! Don't let these wasp-
waisted waterspouts touch me! . . . How dark it grows.
—The waterspouts! the waterspouts! Ashtaroth, the
terrible woman! A star over her brow, driving in
the midst, under the shadows.—They are on to me!
over me! I am sinking! . . . —Up! up! Hold me
up! . . . Catch me by the hair. . . . Rayne! . . . Rayne!'

-----

## IV

I AWOKE in the dusk.

Up leaped a core of light at the far end of the room:
then grew steady and lived. Some one had lit the gas-
lamp at the street-corner below. I turned over in my
bed. I thought that it was lazy of me to be lying
warm here: to-day, when I had, I remembered, intended
seeking work. *Work!* Work for what? Well, it was lazy
of me to be lying warm here. Where had I been? . . .

Some one came in softly (the door had opened).
And why didn't they knock?

Turning round I saw a girl on her way to the table
with a paper-bag in her hand.

'Hullo!' I said.

She dropped the bag on to the floor with a start:
sharply picked it up, and, looking with round shadowed
eyes at me:

'Good *gracious*, how you *did* frighten me!—Why,
he's *better*!' she said.

'Certainly, he is,' I answered, turning aside my eyes.
'There was never anything the matter with him that
he is aware of.'

She stood, with her hands joined in front of her, holding the bag, and looked down at me.

'You've been very ill, sir,' she said, and gave her head a shake.

'I assure you, madam, that you are mistaken. I have just woken up.—"*Abou ben Adhem, may his tribe increase*," and so on.'

'You have been insensible for on two days,' she said.

I stared at her round shadowed eyes. She nodded her head, and, I saw, smiled at me.

'—Insensible? . . . Why I have never fainted in my life.' I saw an open letter on the table-cloth in that dusky light.

I let my head sink on to the pillow with a sigh and shut my eyes. Memory had flowed back on to me.

'I have brought you some grapes,' she said, 'I thought you might like them.'

I raised my head again, and opened my eyes in the room, now full of light. I had not noticed that she had lit the gas.

'You are kind; but——'

'You will not take them?'

'No, thank you.'

'Oh very well! I shall throw them out of the window then!—Why *shouldn't* you take a present from me? . . . I haven't paid you back the four shillings I owed you yet: but I can—now.'

She took out a purse: unhasped it: opened the leaves: put in two of her fingers, and then, with a quick lift-up of her head and a bright smile came towards me, holding two florins in her extended palm.

'I only lent you three,' I said.

'And I have got no change! Think of that! Only gold and silver. Isn't it ri-diculous? Will you eat some of the grapes? . . . *Please!*'

A pause.

'It was kind of you to bring me them,' I said, 'and I am—afraid I must have been giving you a great deal of trouble . . . Miss——'

'Oh no! none! You *will* eat them then?'

I was silent.

'Oh, Miss——'

'Do you want to know my name?' she asked with a drop in her voice.

'Only if you care to tell me,' I answered, a little sorry for my first attempt at some sort of formality or other.

''Owlet is my name: I'm from Rutland. Rosy's my *Christian* name.—But I hope you won't call me Miss 'Owlet.'

'Why do you hope not?'

'Oh, Howlet is such a *horrid* name!'

I could not help laughing. Then she laughed.

'But what *shall* I call you?' I asked.

'You called me "child" once. I'm not a child. I'm seventeen.'

I smiled at her. She at once caught up the bag of grapes, undid the mouth, and offered it to me.

'Then I beg your pardon,' I said.

She pouted:

'—But you have not *taken* any!'

And our eyes met, and the bag was once more offered, and I dipped two fingers into it and lifted a big bunch half out (she looking at me all the time, and I at the bag-mouth), and stretched out my other hand to break off a portion of the bunch, and had broken off a portion, and was about to drop the remains of the original bunch into the bag again, when she drew back her arm quickly and said:

'That's not *fair*!'

Then she took out another bunch: squashed up the bag in her hands: threw it on to the floor, and came to me holding it up with two fingers in the air. Our eyes met again, and I stretched up my hand and took it. She smiled at me. A small thin black kitten ran out and began chasing the paper-bag.

She turned, saw it, and cried out:

'Minnie, Minnie!—Oh, you *silly* thing! Let it alone, can't you?'

She turned to me again:

'That's my cat Minnie. Isn't she a beauty?'

'Well . . . yes,' I said.

'Why, I should think so!—Now I must go. I oughtn't to have let you talk so much: it's not good for you. I hope you're feeling better?—Here, Minnie, Minnie, Minnie, Min, Min! Oh, she's after that piece of paper. Silly thing! . . .' (Turning to me again.) 'I'll let her *stop* with you . . . if you like.'

'Thank you,' I said, 'that's kind of you. I *should* like.'

'Good-bye,' she said.

'Good-bye,' I answered to her slowly going, 'and thank you for all your goodness to me, Miss' (she stopped)—'Rosebud.'

'I shall see you soon again,' she said; and, at the door, 'If you wouldn't mind going into my room in a little—that's this one here,' (opening the door and pointing to the right), 'we'd get your bed done very quickly, and you could come back again. I don't think you ought to dress and go out yet.'

'Very well,' I said, 'thank you. I will.'

She went out; but looking in again.

'Put on your coat or something,' she said, 'for fear you catch cold.' And withdrew her head, and the door closed, and she was gone.

I sat up in bed, and threw out my arms.

'Oh you Rosebud!' I said, laughing, 'you Rosebud!'

We had a short conversation together that evening as I ate my tea in bed, and then we said good-night, and she left me. And I set about thinking what I had best do now. The failure of my attempt to earn my livelihood by my pen was a heavy blow to me, and the heavier that it was unexpected.—But I gave up further consideration of the matter for the present: I must have some means of support, and immediately. And what was the good of thinking of poetry, after what Parker, Innes & Co. had said about it?

All at once the idea of becoming a schoolmaster flashed upon me. Why not? I was sure I was quite as capable of teaching as poor Currie, the undermaster at Whittaker's.—Or a private secretaryship?—I let my thoughts go, and had planned out my life as under-master, or private secretary, or tutor, before I fell into a sweet dreamless sleep.

The next day, in the morning, although I was, I

found, uncommonly weak, I managed to get into the
Edgware Road as far as a stationer's, where I inquired
in a general sort of a way about such things as under-
masterships and tutorships, of the genteel middle-aged
party who was in the shop.   She took a great interest
in me, I considered, for a complete stranger; but
could not help me in the least.

In the afternoon I made three more attempts at
stationers', and at the last one was so far successful
that I learnt the name and address of the people
whom, it seemed, I wanted.

I set off for Grenvil Street at once (a weary walk of
toil to weak me), and interviewed a respectful clerk a
good deal better dressed and, doubtless, fed than
myself.   He thought he might possibly get me an
ushership in some small school pretty soon; but I
must observe that it was not the time for such (that is
to say, instant) engagements now, half way through
the term.   I told him the sooner the better, for I was
in straits.   He had an equally discouraging account to
give of tutorships and secretaryships.   All these things
required time.   I said that speed was the one necessity.
And on this understanding we parted : I, I cannot say
how forlorn,—nay, once or twice on my walk home,
even wearier and more toilsome, near to tears.   Indeed
I felt more like drowning myself than making any
further fight for existence.

When I reached Maitland Street, I scarcely knew
what I had said or done down at the agent's.   Everything was a muddle, and a jumble, from beginning to
end.   I cast myself down on my bed, and the long-
suppressed tears came.   O why had I not died in that
strange, sweet, terrible dream after the reading of the
letter?   I lay sighing to myself till I dozed.

From this half-sleep of despondency the Rosebud
roused me in the early evening, and took me out for a
short walk.   I don't know what we talked about.
Everything was still a muddle and a jumble, from
beginning to end.   I was glad to get back, and creep
into bed, and sleep.

I was better in the morning: inclined, it seemed, to
feel cheerful, and began, as I lay with closed eyes

thinking, to put the events of yesterday into something like connection and *tout ensemble*; but with no great success.   The one comforting thought seemed to be, that the clerk had said he would send me up anything that came.   Surely something *must* come!   I could not believe I was destined to die here like a rat in a hole.—I played upon my inclination to be cheerful, till it had brought me to cheerfulness: and, getting up briskly, perceived a letter on the chair by my bedside.   The agent, of course!

'Ha,' I said, 'the tide's on the turn! . . . What's in here?' I hesitated.   The sun was shining in through the window upon the envelope.

I ripped it open; took out the letter, and scanned it.

'DEAR SIR,—Please call early to-morrow on Alexander Brooke, Esq., 5 Dunraven Place, Piccadilly, W., who wishes to engage *at once* a secretary to go abroad with him. The engagement would be at least for a year, if not more.

'Terms between £100 and £150 per annum.

'Please inform us of the result of your interview.—And oblige, Yours faithfully,

LINKLATER, PEMBRIDGE AND BLENKINSOP.'

I threw the letter on to the table with new life in me, and began to wash, whistling to myself.   As I was folding on my necktie I noticed how dirty my collar was, and then my shirt, and more particularly the cuffs.   I put on a clean,—the last,—collar in the bag. And that set me off thinking for a moment about my clothes.   'Well, well!' I said, 'I shall have to tell the man the truth I suppose: and why not?'   For I did not doubt but that he would have me.

Rosy was of course off to her work these three hours. This, and what she would think about the secretary-ship, came to me as I passed her door and went down the dark stuffy old wooden staircase.   What would the Rosebud think?   'Well, well!' I said as before, 'it'll be time enough to think about what *she* thinks when I've got it.'   And yet did not doubt for one moment but that I *should* get it.

I knew my way to Piccadilly.   It was a crisp clear morning: the stir of the breezy air and of the life brighter than usual elated me a little.   I went along down the Edgware Road, eating my brown bread and dates with some cheerfulness. Then I had a refreshing glass of milk. And, by the time I was half way across the Park by the path that leads from the Marble Arch up to the Gates at Hyde Park Corner, I seemed to have regained something of my former self: something of my Glastonbury character of will and self-reliance. The last three weeks seemed a dream; almost a bad dream, a nightmare, for a little: then only a dream, save for something of the Rosebud that seemed to reach out half-weakly into the present light. I asked the policeman at the Gates where Dunraven Place was, and he directed me. Then I arrived at No. 5, and was shown into a beautifully furnished room.

Waiting, I began to examine a book-shelf that was full of beautifully bound books that harmonised with the room. They made me think how I should like to be rich and have all the books I wanted. I had my eye particularly on a large Gervinus's Shakespeare in half-calf, and my fingers began to feel as if they ought to take it down, and run away with it to a convenient arm-chair, and begin upon it at once. As I stood so, I heard a step behind me and turned.

'You are looking at my books, I see,' he said.

'Yes, sir,' I answered, 'it was a Gervinus's Shakespeare. I hope——'

'Oh, not in the least! Please sit down.'

He motioned me into a large red leather chair on one side of the fire-place.

'You come from Messrs. . . . The name is rather confusing,' he said. '. . . . I want a secretary to help me with——to make himself generally useful as I may direct. Another young gentleman has been here this morning already: I mean from Messrs. . . . .' He smiled.—'He objected to going out to Africa. Do you?'

'No.'

'You see—shortly—I want some one to help me to get together my things, write letters, and so on.—You understand me?'

'I think so.'

'The young friend who was going with me has suddenly been taken ill, and, as it is important that I should be out of England in under a month—you follow me?'

'I think so.'

'Good. Now tell me. Can you shoot? No. Ride? No. Um! You are strongly made. Where were you at school?'

'At Glastonbury.'

'Ah, so was I! With Craven, I suppose?'

'Yes, sir.'

'Did you go in for sports—much?'

'I was in the first football fifteen, and rowed in my house-boat.'

'School House?'

'Yes.'

'So did I. It was head of the river in my year.'

'And in mine too.'

'—Tell me something about yourself.'

I paused for a moment. Then I said:

'I have been at Glastonbury five years. My father, who is dead, had placed all his fortune in the Southern Bank. My guardian called me up to London about three weeks ago, to inform me of this. I determined then to try to make my livelihood by my pen, and . . . failed. That is, shortly, why I am here.'

'Tried to make your livelihood by your pen, and failed? Did not your guardian help you? How did you——'

'I angered my guardian by refusing to try for a clerkship. I thought that I had something here——' (Lifting my finger.)

'" Quelque chose là "—Yes. Well.'

'I wrote two poems, which I sent to a publisher, hoping——'

'Why all, or nearly all, poetry has to be paid for now-a-days, my poor boy.—Of course they sent it back again?'

'They did.'

'Well? And may I ask how you lived in the interim? You had funds?'

'I sold my greatcoat.'

'Excuse me. I am not asking from mere curiosity. . . . Would you care to tell me more? I will' (looking

for a moment in my eyes), 'if you will allow me, write
to Dr. Craven about you.—Not that I doubt what you
say; but you must see. . . . You understand?'

'Perfectly.—You have no guarantee that I am not
a rogue.'

'Aha! I think you are wrong there! However,'
(suddenly), 'how much did you get for your coat?'

'Fifteen shillings.'

'And you have lived on that for nearly three weeks?'

'Just three weeks.'

'Impossible! You are joking!'

'No, sir, since I did. My room only cost me four
shillings a week, and I——'

'Then you must have lived on a shilling a week?'

'No. I have not paid my rent for this third week yet.'

'And how are you going to?'

'I cannot say. Perhaps, I may get an ushership in
some school, within the next few days. I should
anticipate my pay.'

He stood up; we looked for some little in one
another's eyes. Then he stretched out his arm, and
let his hand fall on my shoulder.

'You are a brave fellow,' he said, 'and I believe you
are a true one. I believe what you have told me.
There, there, now.' (For my eyes were suddenly full
of tears)—'There, there, there, there, there! It's all
right now.' And he turned away and let his arm drop.

Then:

'Stop,' said he, 'did you know Blake at Glastonbury?'

'He left just before I came; but I met him once. He
came to examine a school at Blackheath, where I was.'

'Ah, I am sorry! He was a dear, dear friend of
mine—an old college chum; but I had known him
before then. He was a Wykehamist.'

'Yes; so I remember.'

'It would have been enough to me that he had
thought well of anyone. He would have liked you,
I am sure.'

He smiled, and added:

'You see that I have let slip how well I think of
you, and what you have said to me.'

'Thank you, sir. Some day, perhaps, I may be able

to show you that I deserved your belief in me.—Mr.
Blake was kind to me when he came to my old school.
He was pleased, I think, with some verses I had to
recite, and so . . .' He had snapped his fingers impatiently, and made a sharp noise with his lips.

I stopped speaking.  He cried out with a smiling
mouth :

'You are not the boy who recited Longfellow's
" Psalm of Life ? " '

'I am,' I said.

'Immediately after that visit he came and stopped
with me here in London for a few days.'

His face grew sadder.  He went on slowly :

'It was the last time I saw him.  You know of his
terrible death, not so long after?  All that he said in
those few days has been treasured up by me, and lives
for ever in my memory.  The first night he came, after
dinner, as we were sitting here by this very fire over
our cigars and wine, he told me about the little boy he
had seen that afternoon ! '

He caught himself up :

' Well, and how old are you now ? '

' Eighteen.'

'You strange boy !  Eighteen.—Why, it is ridiculous!  (I really must read some of those Rejected
Addresses of yours some day.)—You are very tall for
your age, and look very old for eighteen.'

I smiled :

'This fortnight has made me older by five years, I
think.  Years are no test of age, sir.'

We talked together for almost an hour—of many things.
Then he looked at his watch and jumped up, saying :

' You have made me forget that I have a very great
deal to do this morning, young man.'

'I am sorry, sir.'

'—But very pleasantly.'

'Then I am glad.'

I smiled, and so did he.  He touched me on the
shoulder.

As I was going, he spoke of Mr. Blake again—how that
he was a truly great and good man, one who was without
the cant of the two words, a Christian gentleman.

A pause.—Then I :

'I think I ought to tell you something, sir, that I have not told you yet.'

'Aha ?' he said.

'I am not a Christian, and . . . I do not say that I do *not* believe in a God, but I do not *think* that I believe in one.'

He put his hand on my shoulder again, and smiled :

'It will pass, it will pass ! We most of us go in a circle now-a-days : most of us, that is, who are worth anything. Christian, or perhaps nothing at all, till seventeen : Atheist till twenty : Materialist till twenty-one (we soon get tired of *that* !) : Deist till thirty, (though some of the wilder sort go in for a course of that nonsense called Pantheism) : and then, either the old original Christianity again on to the end, or some slight modification of it. Take my word for it, boy, there is no religion worth calling a religion that does not take Christ and Christ's teaching as its original. And how much better is it to lift up your eyes from considering the shadow on the ground, to consider the One that casts the shadow, even Christ Jesus, who is as the standing figure that watches this our on-rolling earth, yearning for it as a mother for her wandering child, waiting for the hour when He shall take it to His bosom and for ever ?' He paused. I kept silence.

We shook hands. I turned to go.

He called to me : I turned again :

'I shall not write to Craven.'

'Thank you, sir.'

We again shook hands, and I had my hand on the door, when he said :

'Stay a moment. You are my secretary—for a year. It is so agreed ?'

'Yes, sir : as far as I am concerned.'

'Then allow me to give you your first quarter in advance. It is always—I always manage it in that way. You may be in want of a little ready money. And . . . as regards Messrs.—Messrs. X. Y. and Z., you will of course allow me to settle that with them myself.'

I stood irresolute.

'Come, come!' he said.—'Now don't be foolish, Leicester. If you are going to . . .'

I stepped to him suddenly, saying :

'Sir, sir, you are very good to me!'

He took my hand in his and pressed it.

'Yes, yes, yes, yes! that's all right now!—Now you really must run away! You said that you would like to come to me to-morrow morning, didn't you?—Very well. I will tell you about what you will have to do, then. So good-bye, or rather *au revoir*, or rather (when I think of it) both.'

I was at the door, when he called :

'O you dreadful boy, you haven't taken all your belongings away with you! Here is your first quarter on the table yet. You are inclined to be careless, I see. Look to it. It is an evil, evil vice—carelessness!'

I found that I could scarcely see the folded pieces of paper that he had put down on the edge of the table.

When I had it safely in my hand, I gave one look at him and a bright smile, and went out as quickly as I could ; for my eyes were full of tears, and I feared some might drop out.

Riding up on the outside of an omnibus to Praed Street, I felt as I had felt in some of the days at Glastonbury when I had longed to leap and give a shout and move onwards towards something. And then I grew a little sad, if it is possible to call joy sad, and began to say to myself :

'Well, well, pray that there *is* a God; for you long to thank Him for this! And see, it is very sweet to you to think, that perhaps, perhaps, He has but afflicted you and chastened you by this your suffering so that, in the end, He might lead you nearer and nearer to Himself. . . . It is a sweet thought!'

I spent that afternoon happily. First of all I had a good dinner at a restaurant in Oxford Street, and that gave me an insight into what a healthy pleasure in food meant : and then (the day continuing sunny and almost warm) I went for a long walk in Hyde Park, stopping to look at the men and women riding or driving by, and not one of whom I, in this bright day's dawn of a

new life, could possibly envy.   Their wealth might give
me the chance of leading another life which would not
be without its charm, nay, its delight; yet how much
nobler this one that I was entering upon now, this one
that had work to do, work for others, that is, which
would require self-sacrifice—*conquest of self!*

And after that I came up home, buying on the way
fruit and cakes and other things, for a tea I had in my
mind with the Rosebud in my room.   Then I set about
making it all ready, so that, by the time she came in,
half-past seven, the room, lit up with gas and fire and
well-laid table, was most cheerful.

But the tea was not.   For Rosy took my good news
most gravely, and did not laugh once the whole time.

After tea we went out for a walk together, and, when
we had gone a little way, I said, smiling, that I intended to get her a bonnet to wear as a memory of me.
But she would not see anything to laugh at in that, and
refused the bonnet with dignity.   Then I tried a coat,
but she suddenly exclaimed :

'And do you *think* I would *keep* it all rags and
tatters?'   Dismissing the idea.

I tried a locket as a last resource.

After some persuasion she at last agreed.   We went
into a jeweller's (the very jeweller's under whose window I had counted my money on the first night I was
in London) in the Edgware Road together, and she
chose a small round silver locket, and relented a little.

'No,' she said, as we were walking slowly away.
'For the bonnet and the jacket would wear out, and I
couldn't very well keep them *then*—eh?   And they
wouldn't look nice, all in rags and tatters, *would* they?
But I shall *always* be able to keep the locket, you
know : and when I look at it I shall think of you and
give a sigh ; for you've been very *nice* to me.'

'Ah,' I said, 'who's talking nonsense now?'  And proceeded to demonstrate that, if anybody had been 'nice'
to anybody, it was she to me.   To which she answered
that she liked to hear me talk so,—and for a moment
I felt rather foolish, and proposed that we should go up
to the top of Primrose Hill, and she agreeing, we set off.

I began to question her a little about herself, and she

answered readily, nay, entered upon a regular discourse, to which I played the accompaniment with some plea-sure of amusement and otherwise, till we were half way up Primrose Hill : when I all at once remembered a certain bench not far from the top, by which I had on a certain night stood and looked out over the darkness from which came the cool breeze fanning my feverish cheek. Could it have indeed been *me*, this living, moving, thinking me here, who lived and moved and thought that certain night as memory silently told me that I had ? Poor me !

I led her a little round and then up to it. And we sat down upon it together and talked softly.

What thousands and thousands of stars were in the sky ! And what millions and millions of people had looked up at the thousands and thousands of stars, and yet would look up, and when would it all ever come to an end ?

'Rosy,' I said again, 'does it never seem to you, as if you were here alone in the world, quite alone ? I mean, as if nobody else belonged to you somehow ; and they are all here, and they live and they die, and you can't tell where they go to : and you can't tell where *you* will go to, but you don't think you really ever *will* die, although you know you will ; but when you do die, that you will go to somewhere else, where you will be quite alone again and nobody else will belong to you somehow, and they will be all there, and they will all live there, and then die, and you can't tell where they go to, and then *you* will die. . . . And it goes on like that for ever !—Did you never think of it in that way ?'

'I never thought about it at all,' she said, 'but I like to hear you talk like that. . . . Go *on*.'

I started and laughed, and then said :

'Now I'll tell you a little piece of poetry, a merry little piece, and then we must be going home ; for it's getting late.'

She composed herself to listen.

'It's in Greek,' I said, 'but, you'll be able to under-stand it. I'll tell you about it, first. It's called a Swallow Song. The little boys sang it in Greece when the swallows came back after the winter. They used to go

G

round to all the houses and sing it, just like boys sing
carols at Christmas.   This is it :

> " She comes, she comes, the swallow,
> bringing beautiful hours,
> beautiful seasons,
> white on the belly,
> black on the back.
>
> Do thou roll forth a fruit-cake
> out of the rich house,
> and a beaker of wine
> and a basket of cheeses ;
> and wheat-bread the swallow
> and the pulse porridge

does not reject.  Say, shall we go away, or something receive ?
If thou givest—well !   But if not, we won't let you off !
Shall we bear off the door, or else the lintel ?
Or else the wife that is seated within ?
She 's a small body, easily shall we carry her off !—
> But if you give us something,
> something great may you get.
> Open, open the door to the swallow,
> we are not old men, but childerkins here." '

Then I went on to recite to her the Greek, and she
swayed her body a little in sympathy with the rhythm
of the words, so that I, who was pleased with it all,
gradually grew into the humour in which I had been
before when I exclaimed :   ' Oh you Rosebud !' till, at
the words ἡ τὰν γυναῖκα τὰν ἔσω καθημέναν, I gave one
look at her, sitting there, childlike and fairy-like and
dear, and could have caught her up in my arms, and
then . . . I didn't know what I should have done then.'

I sat still, looking out into the night.

After a little :

' I wonder,' said her quiet voice, ' I wonder if you
would *teach* me that ? . . . I think I could soon *learn* it.'

'——You need not wonder any more,' I said slowly,
still looking out into the night, ' I will teach it you.'

And so we began, I to repeat the translated words,
she to say them after me, I still looking out into the
night, she as I knew looking up at my face.   She had
an excellent memory.   She had soon learnt the piece,
and repeated it alone faultlessly.

' You have a good memory,' I said.

'Yes,' she said, 'I always *was* quick at learning things
—when I *liked* them! I *like* that!'          •

A pause. Then:

'Now we must be going,' I said, rising, 'it is getting
late.'

We went slowly down the dark hill-side together.
Then something seemed to grow with and about us,
and I began to feel somehow as if I were leaving a
thing that had closely to do with me in some low, dim,
dull plain, whereas I was going away to mount up into
a rich warm country of gentle sunshine. And then in
half-forgetfulness of this, I would have taken her hand
with mine, and we, two children, would have wandered
on so over the dim fields together for ever and ever, till
we softly faded away. And yet I felt that I was moving
in a dim dreaminess, and she in one parallel to it and
that she would not (perhaps could not) meet. Then
we turned up one of the roads at the back of St. John's
Wood in order to get to Maitland Street. I looked at
her walking along beside me.

'You're very quiet, Rosy,' I said.

'So are you,' she said, looking in front of her. And
then we went on together with the same quietness; for
I had no care to say more, nor she either, it seemed.

As we stopped opposite No. 3, she heaved a sigh. I
stretched out my hand and opened the door. She said:
'Thank you,' and went in, I following.

Up the dark stairs we went together till we reached
her door, the handle of which she had in one hand as
she half turned to me.

'Good-night,' she said.

'Good-night,' I said, finding her other out-held hand,
and holding it half-loosely for a moment. I could not
see her face in that intense blackness.

She opened her door inwards, and a little light came
from the turned-down gas—opened it wider. She went
in slowly, and closed it after her. I unlatched my own
door, and went into the room. The gas there too was
turned down. I went and turned it up.

'Heigh, ho!' I said, with suppressed weariness. I
sat down in the chair: and stretched out my legs, and
tilted the chair back, and lifted the hands of my

stretched arms to my head, and thought.   All at once
I stopped with listening powers like a rock balanced
on the edge, breathless, motionless.

A low knock came at the door.

'Come in,' I said, breathless, motionless.

The latch was lifted and the door opened a little.

'It's me,' said Rosy's low voice.

Then, the door opening a little, I saw her.   'Rosy,'
she said, 'may I come in?'

I started and sat up straight.

'Yes,' I said. . . 'Yes.'

She came in: her face flushed, her eyes bright, her
hair loosed a little round her head in wavy brown
threads.   I seemed to inhale her fairness like a soft
sweet air.   She said:

'I thought—that as—as you were going away in the
morning—before I come back you know—and as I get
up early—at seven—so as to be down at my work by
eight—I thought . . . —that—that perhaps I—that
perhaps you . . . wouldn't mind if I was to—if I . . .'
She paused with an indrawn breath.   Then I was with
her, and had taken her hands.

'. . . What is it, Rosebud?' I said, with a trembling
in me.

All at once two large tears came out of her eyes and
trickled down her cheeks.

Then she looked at me steadfastly, trying to smile
and not wink her eyelids, whose long lashes had crystal
drops on them.   The trembling passed out of me.   I
thought only of her distress.   I put one arm round her,
and so, holding her small body, stroked her soft brown
hair back softly, saying:

'Why, Rosebud, you mustn't mind like that.   I'll
come back again some day!'

'Oh, you were so *nice* to me,' she said.   'But you
*will* come back again to see me . . . *some* day—*Eh?*'

'Surely I will.—And bring you a bonnet with blue
ribbons and a flower that . . . What is it?'

'. . . I don't *want* a bonnet!'

'—Not a bonnet?'

'. . . No' . . (piteously).   'I want *you!*'

'Very well then: I'll bring you me,' I said, 'some

day : and some grapes, and *bon-bons* to make me go down well.'

Her arms hung listlessly.  She seemed very miserable about it.

I kissed her on the cheek, kissed a tear that was stealing down.—Then the next moment felt her breast heave and shake against mine, and she sobbed out :

'Oh I wish—you weren't going away : I wish you weren't going away !'

I kissed her again, and at last found voice to scold her gently : telling her that this would not do, and that she would be all right again soon.  For we should see one another again soon, and have long walks in the evening again.

'—And learn more Swallow Songs ?' asked she, looking up.

'Yes,' I said, 'and all sorts of other things as well.'

—That *would* be nice : *wouldn't* it ?' she said.

'Yes.—And climb up to the top of Primrose Hill and look at the lights.'

'—Yes, and go up the *River* some day, as you said once.  That would be nice too, *wouldn't* it ?'  She had stopped crying at last.

Then, holding her little upturned face in my hands, I kissed her again, first on one cheek and then on the other.  And then we said good-night.

But at the door she suddenly turned back to me with her arms half-raised, and said piteously :

' Kiss me *again*,—*do* ! . . . I do like you to kiss me so!'

I took her hands and, smiling a little, went and kissed her on the cheek.

' *Kiss me on the lips*,' she whispered, half giving herself to me.

I kissed her on the lips and drew back.

'. . . Good . . . night,' she said.

'Good-night, Rosy, good-night !'

She was gone.

Then trembling came into me again, and I stretched out my arms before me as round something in the air. And then threw them up with an unknown word, and turned away.

' *Good-night, Rosebud, good-night.*'

# III

## I

I BROUGHT a certain amount of enthusiasm to bear upon
my new life.  The idea of working in co-operation with
'the friend of Blake' was a powerful incentive to per-
severance.  I wrote in the Journal, which I began to
keep at this time :

'I have had a great deal to learn and to do in this
swift-flown fortnight.  And I have found both the
learning and the doing very pleasant to me.  It would
seem that my just-past struggle for existence partook,
all along, greatly of the *cul-de-sac*; whereas this new
life is like an open road that leads to a great city : that
city has to be reached : certain things have to be done,
which things constitute a "cause."  There can be no
doubt that a definite aim, object, end is the making of
a man.'

But the next week came a reaction.  I began to
weary of the details of my work, more weary of the
people with whom I was thrown, and there was growing in me a deaf unrecognised notion in connection
with Mr. Brooke that would have partaken, had I let
it, of disillusionment.  Hear the Journal of three days
later, à propos of a dinner at a Mr. Starkie's, a friend of
Mr. Brooke's, where I had met some, what I called,
'travellers' :

'"Travellers" are an aggravating tribe.  They seem
to expect you to know their books better than they do
themselves: to pretend that no one else ever went
where *they* went, or, if some one else undeniably *did*
go,—then that that some one else went the wrong
way, came back the wrong way, and made rather a fool
than otherwise of himself every bit of the way !  People

have no business to be active monomaniacs : passive
ones, as much as you like : I see no harm in that.   I
am a passive monomaniac myself.'
   A little later :
   'Imps have been at me to-day.   The air has been
densely populated with them.   Here is a lugubrious
account for you !   I begin from the beginning.
   'Since the morning I had a longing to write one
particular thing haunting me.   In crowded shops,
before me as the cab cut through the streets, beside
me as I sat at my desk ; wherever I was, whatever I
was doing, I saw the same silent figure, with its hand
to its brow, standing under a tree in the early evening.
I was like an inveterate smoker, robbed of his pipe and
left staring at his full tobacco-jar.   Once or twice I
very nearly went up to my room with paper and pencil
to fill in my imaginary picture : having resisted and
conquered, I was irritable with everything about me
for my own firmness.   How cruel it was that I had no
time ! how badly organised was the world, that so many
other people had time, and wasted it !
   ' Driving down New Bond Street, I saw a young girl,
with a pince-nez and walking-stick, staring into a
jeweller's window.   I at once began to revile her as
frivolity's foolish wasp, and must have done so aloud,
for the coachman opened the trap to inquire if I had
said anything ?   " No," I said, "drive on !"
   ' In the evening (this evening) we had a dinner-party.
The two men who are going with us on the Expedition,
Clarkson and Starkie, were there—with their wives.
Also some other "men of mark" with their wives.   But
the female element was (thank God !) in the minority.
That didn't save me, though.   I sat between a beetle-
browed prude who kept making (bad) eyes at her
husband opposite us (a travelling monomaniac, of
course !), and a big cavalry officer who had cantered
through half a continent, and, as soon as he came home,
sat down and written a book on all its histories, languages and literatures.   The beetle-browed prude told
me about her husband's travels : the cavalry officer
about his own.   (The lady he had taken in to dinner
was a philanthropist, very distinguished, very loquacious,

but unfortunately deaf. She and the cavalry officer soon gave one another up: the cavalry officer, for me, the female philanthropist for a course of lectures to a weak-eyed man on her right—subject, parochial rates, I think.) The officer varied the conversation once, by remarking that Darwin did not appreciate the spirit of Nature, so leading the prude into a disquisition on Eternal Love; but, in the end disagreeing, they called me from my thoughts under the ceiling to give my opinion: found I knew nothing about the points in question, and so repeated them in their entirety for my edification—even to the disagreement.

'After dinner, when we joined the ladies, the prude motioned me to her side by a smile and a gesture. I heard the officer repeating his remark about Darwin to another prude (square-browed: lifeless, combed-back hair, slow eyes, and an altogether suggestiveness of "shoulder arms") just behind us. My own particular prude seemed for some time (that is, till I grew dreamy and inattentive) to have eyes, and I should say a good many tongues, for me only: then she carried me off, tripping over her spasmodic train, to her dear, dear friend Mrs. Basingstoke (to whom she really must introjooce me—a most cul-tivated and highly de-lightful crea-ture, she *assured* me!) and I was presented, as (in a whisper) "a most *in*-ter-esting young man, with de-cidedly marked tastes, my dear Mrs. Basingstoke" (What could I have been saying?)—"and—alas!—a *rare* endowment of young men now-a-days—earnest re-ligious con-victions."—Goats and monkeys!

'But *jam satis*!—After they were all gone, I stood frowning on the hearthrug.—Mr. Brooke came in from the Hall, having seen the last of them off.

'"Aha, Leicester," he said, "and how about those things from Taunton's? I was dressing when you came back. They are all right?"

'"Well, no, sir. The tubes had to be made on purpose——"

'"I ordered them a fortnight ago."

'"And they came. But one of the people in the shop managed to crack one——"

'"And the whole thing will have to be done again.

Bother ! . . . Hoity-toity, I'm very tired ! . . . *You* look tired too."

' " I am."

' " I saw you making yourself very agreeable to Mrs. Napier, and afterwards to Mrs. Basingstoke."

' I curled my lip.—Then, feeling that I should say something foolish in a moment if I stayed, and irritated that I should have to save myself by running away, said :

' I think I will go to bed, sir.—There is nothing more to be done to-night ? '

' " Ah-h-h . . . no ! That is, I don't think so.— Hamilton and Malmesbury sent up everything ?—They are the rudest and most unpunctual people in all London ; but they have the best . . ."

' I made a quick noise with my lips, expressive of impatience and disgust. I had forgotten altogether about Hamilton and Malmesbury.—What business on earth had *I* with running about seeing that Hamiltons and Malmesburies sent up things? Why not use a servant? Or the post? The post is one of the greatest institutions of our country. There was not any need for such frantic haste. Whereas there were creatures, like that girl with the pince-nez and walking stick, who dawdled away their whole lives ! And here was *I* —going out on an expedition into the wilds of Africa, to be killed by fever and eaten by jackals and vultures, or run through with spears and eaten by negroes !— Oh, it was too hard ! I really must write to some Crœsus : state my cruel case, and ask for £100 for three years, offering to refund it out of my first year's earnings.—Nay, a better idea would be, to insert an advertisement in the *Times* agony column : " *An un-appreciated* GENIUS *(male), ætat.* 18, *desirous of benefiting humanity by devoting himself to* HIMSELF, *would be glad to meet with some young woman who would give him the means of pursuing this lofty course of action. Millionairesses with a hankering after (literary) immortality are strongly advised not to let this opportunity slip, as a similar one may never arise again. Apply for further particulars to B.L.,* 5 *Dunraven Place, Piccadilly, W., who* . . ." And I burst out into a laugh, rather a bitter laugh.

' " What 's the matter ? " asked Mr. Brooke.

'I shrugged back my shoulders with a half-sigh, half-groan,

'"I think I am ill," I said.

'He rose from his desk, where he was sitting examining some papers : came across to me and, smiling, put his hand on to my shoulder in his usual kindly unctuous manner. I could almost have struck him.

'"Come, come, come!" he said, "You must not mind now.—It will soon pass, this malaise. You have lived so much in yourself, that you find it very hard to live in other people ?—Ah well, well ! We most of us have that little difficulty to contend with sooner or later." But I, hanging down my head, bit my under-lip with all my might for a moment. The pain made me master of myself. I looked up in his face, with my eyes hedged about with tears, but ready to listen to what he had to say to me.

'He pressed my shoulder with his hand :

'"Don't dream so, my boy," he said, "don't dream so. You're always at it, you know ; and it's *such* a bad habit. It leads to absorption in one's own world, and that means selfishness. Why, I have known in my time at least *three* dreamers, who ruined all their own happiness and their families' as well, simply because they *would* have their dreams. Such are they whom the world calls 'geniuses' and their friends 'brutes,' for no sacrifice is too great for these precious empty dreams of theirs—not excluding the dreamers' lives. It angers me to hear people erecting special codes of morality for such men. Because a man is dubbed 'genius,' is he also to be dubbed demi-god, and allowed to pick and choose from the laws of the land, which he will be so good as to obey and which he won't ?—Give up thinking that you can do anything, and there is a chance of your doing something. Get out of yourself and into other people : they are, probably, better than you are.—You don't mind me speaking like this to you ? Now, do you now ?"

'"No," I said, "it's true what you say. I live too much in myself, and I am impatient of what I think are other people's smallnesses . . . I will try to be more patient.'

'"Very well.   Don't let's talk about it any more.—
*One* moment, though.   Am I to halve the dose ?   Is it
too strong for you ?"

'" No, sir : double it ; but——"

'" Your stomach can't stand it yet?   Never mind.
I only wonder that it has stood so much.   Go on taking
your medicine like a man (I don't mind your pulling
faces now and then : perhaps it *is* rather nasty !) and
. . ." (with a smile).   "Well you shall have some jam
*afterwards* !"

'"Will you tell me the sort?" I asked, but in a purposeless sort of way, for it seemed as if he expected me
to ask for an explanation of his " jam *afterwards.*"

'" You will be more contented, less self-conscious, a
better member of society generally :   I mean, more
ready to put yourself out to talk to ' fools,' less eager
to find fault with wiser people than yourself.   In a word,
more *healthy* !"

' I kept silence ;  for I felt that it would be quite
useless to speak.'

The next day has :

' Mr. Brooke with me to the Riding School.   Nothing
particular.'   And, after a space, the following remark :

' These riding lessons five times a week are not without their pleasure to me.   I am pleased at my complete
freedom from fear.   But, *can* I ever be afraid of anything again ?   For have I not realised how small an
atom I am of things living and dead, how valueless, as
I am, to things as yet uncreated ?   I am a spectator of
existence in general, and of my own in particular.—
How *can* a man who believes in nothing but bare existence and the beauty of Truth, and feels that he is
floating along, weak and not far from helpless, have
*fear* ?   What are a few more seconds to *him* ? '

Here my enthusiasm for a full Journal seems to have
given way.   The rest is made up of simple notifications
of the general events of each day.

This short period of my life is, strangely or not, one
of those about which I remember least.   It may be that
I was too absorbed in what Mr. Brooke dubbed for me
my ' dreams ' to notice even what took place to myself.
It may be.   Perhaps that may account for the long

filing trail of 'society' dressed people that represents
my memory of it all, and for a certain lifeless wanness
that I seem to find in even these conversations between
Mr. Brooke and myself, although written so shortly
after they were spoken.   But as the days wore on, I
with a little astonishment found that I was again beginning to take an interest in my work.   At first, as I
have said, this astonished me, and I half anticipated
that 'it would go off soon.'   But, when it did not, but
rather grew, till it seemed to have achieved some permanent strength, I was led to look upon my early discontent as the momentary humour and this calmer
readiness as the actual individuality.   Something too
of my old adventurous love was rising in me at the
near approach of our departure, and this helped me to
realise that, past denial, there was much in me that
was morbid and self-concentrated, and helped me to
determine to resist these infirmities.   I had begun to
*like* Mr. Brooke better, and this, although I was far
from holding him up to myself as 'the ideal friend,' as
I had done at starting.   No one could help liking the
man's earnestness : an earnestness that had something
of the tenderness-inspiring in it.   It did not matter
that the aim of this earnestness was not altogether apparent to you.   You saw the effect : the effect was
beautiful, earnestness and honesty welded together, and
you 'liked' it.   What matter about the cause ?

It was in a humour of this sort that, some days later,
I sat with him after dinner in the library, he smoking
a cigar, I thinking about things.

We sat in silence.

At last, with a slight yawn :

'We shall be off,' he said, 'before this time next
week.   Oh-h-h ! . . . How delightful it is to think of
it ! '

'Mr. Clarkson is to meet us at Brindisi, isn't he !' I
said.

'Yes.   He does not want to go through Paris, and it
would scarcely do to go through the Continent and he
not go with us.   I do not think so, at least. . . . He
has a perfect monomania about Paris.   He caught
typhoid fever when he was there three years ago, and

almost died of it, up at the top of an hotel, alone. He declared that he would never put his foot inside the place again. It was a very horrible idea, I must confess —death, alone, in a strange hotel, in a strange city.'

'But, if he's afraid of fever, surely it is rather a strange thing to go to ——'

'Yes, yes, it *is*! But men are made up of such inconsistencies. I, for example, am shudderingly afraid of small-pox. Yet I have been through a cholera epidemic : nursed diphtheritic cases ; known cancer, and what not besides.'

' King Alfred used to pray that God's will might be done in all things, but that he should prefer not to die of a loathsome disease. I should perhaps be afraid of such things too, if it wasn't that . . .' I paused.

' Wasn't what ?' he said.

' O, an idea of mine !—I don't believe that ,I shall ever catch anything again, somehow !'

' Fearlessness is half the battle. . . . I too have prayed to God that I may not die of a disease that makes others fearful of me and myself loathe myself.'

' And I do not see why God should not grant your prayer, if——' I left the rest, ' *If He is and can*,' unsaid ; for I had seen his face contract a little.

' I beg your pardon,' I said, ' if I have offended you.'

' Oh no ! I am foolish to notice it. I should not have, but that it recalled to me that the same vile bartering thought had, I am ashamed to say, occurred to me too, as it were despite myself, before now. You see I am trembling ' (he held up his hand) 'like a terrified woman. Upon my word I ought to be ashamed of myself !'

He resumed more slowly :

' I cannot quite account for this hysterical dread of one particular disease. My father died of it just before I was born, and my mother was nigh losing life, and then reason, in giving birth to me. Perhaps that is enough to excuse my poor nerves. . . . But I've not much belief in these things. Hereditaribility, as Herbert Spencer would say, has been done to death now-a-days.'

I remembered a somewhat contrary remark to this of his, and smiled a little to myself.

There was a silence for a few moments.

At last he lifted up his head; looked across at me, and jerked his cigar-end under the grate, saying:

' By-the-by, Leicester, I have something to say to you. . . . It's about my book.' He paused for a moment. Then proceeded:

' You know that it is not yet published?—indeed, it is not fit to be published.—It is like Cæsar's Commentaries—*nudi, recti et venusti* (I think that's the expression all right), *omni ornatu orationis tamquam veste detracto*—' Unadorned, severe and decent, stripped of all the embellishment of expression, like a garment.' But I was carried away from its actual state, *nudus*, into its ideal state, *rectus et venustus.—Decent, comely,* that is the best attribute for a man, his thoughts and his actions, that there can be. But you see *my* poor book never got beyond starkness! It was meant to be as a sort of introduction, or prelude, to a future work, my *magnum opus!* I did not care to tell the tale of my failure—not, at least, till I could tell with it the tale of my success. But . . . if anything happened to me—who can foresee even a moment here?—*Quid humanitus,* as Cicero has it—any of those chances to which humanity is liable——' He paused again. His speech seemed perseveringly jerky.

I waited.—He resumed:

' I should like it brought out—then: supposing, I mean—supposing *aliquid humanitus.* For, you see, it might be of some use to others: more especially to those following on my track. It contains my attempt from the south, and my last journey ending at Injiji.'

' Yes?' I said.

Another pause.

Then he:

' Ah, but I thought I had the bird in my hand *that* time! Only in the bush, only in the bush! And I with no more twine with which to mend broken nets and snare it. I have not told you before, how bitter that moment was to me. To turn back at Mount Nebo, within sight of Canaan, into the sandy desert, so hot and waterless!—And as I turned, verily my anguish shamed me out of my manliness to play the woman. I did restrain myself till they had pitched the tent there,

in the roar and very breath of the mighty waters; but
then I went apart, and sat, and looked at the smoking
columns of the Falls fading into the purpling sky, and
wept.   It seemed to me, as I sat there alone that
evening, that I was not turning back, to come again
with new victorious face and reach to It : but it seemed
to me—I cannot tell you how, or why ; I can only tell
you that so it was.—It seemed to me, I say, that a still
small voice spoke whispering to my heart, and I knew
that I should not see Mount Nebo again ; should not
even cross the desert again, but die far away in the
land of Egypt, in a land of glory and sin.'

Another pause.

He went on :

'Since then, I have tried to persuade myself that I
was mistaken.   Life is so ordinary : it is hard to believe
always in the faith of one's higher moments.—And you
see, my dear boy, in a few days we are off !   What do
you say ?—Well, what I want to tell you is this.   Supposing *aliquid humanitus*.—You follow me ?'

He looked at me, who was a little mystified by it all.

'Yes,' I said, 'to a certain extent.'

He smiled.

'Ah, you've grown deep into my heart, boy? you
cannot know *how* deep !   Perhaps there *is* some selfishness in my love for you : I do not say that there is none.
But I do love you !—I have been rather sharp with you
at times : forget it !   It is, that I cannot bear to see
you with the ideas you have, about this beautiful world
—and God.   It seems to me almost a crime that you
. . . Forgive me !   Now you do, now ?'

He had touched my leg : laid his hand on it, and looked
so fondly into my eyes that I was moved, but not quite
with an answering feeling to what he called his love.   I
turned my look aside.

'You see that I believe in you,' he said, 'Believe in
you even as you are now, a mere boy !   I know that if
you only had some great work cut out for you to *do*,
you would do it, and that there would be no need for
it to be done again—something that would require all
your heart and soul !   At present . . . Why, I am
afraid for you, and that is the truth !   And being

afraid, I am jealous for you, and so—cross with you!
That is my way. . . Can't you understand it?'

'Yes,' I said, 'I think so.'

He went on at last, I was glad, looking away from me.

'I have this presentiment in my mind, and I cannot
shake it off. I shall never reach my heart's desire.
God's will be done!—And I feel it so strongly that
I . . . I am afraid I am very clumsy, beating about the
bush like this! See now. Here it is out straight for
you! I want you to promise me to go on and finish
what I feel *I* shall never be able to do more than begin.
—Every river, every lake of that land shall be mapped
out and known!' (His voice rose and rang) 'Why, I
tell you I dreamt about it as a boy at school. I have
kept it by me all my life. A *grand* idea!—But not
yet, not yet, you understand. That would be foolish.
If we—if they, fail this time, I want you to come back
to England and wait here four or five years, preparing
for it. You will grow apace. Then try again: and
when you do it!—when you do it! then . . . tell them
of my poor old dead book: and of me, just a little, to
say how I dreamt of that hour all my life!—Oh no,
none of the glory! I don't want any of *that*! All that
shall be yours! But—if I could only think that *through*
me, if not *by* me, the thing had been done at last!—if
I could only think *that*, why . . .

He began again deliberately!

'I want you to promise me that, in the event of anything happening to *me*, you will devote yourself to the
Cause.—You see? Study for it: toil for it; do for it
everything; forget nothing! On that condition I
make you my heir.'

There was a pause.

Then I said quite simply:

'I cannot!'

'Yes, yes,' he cried, '*you* can do it, if anyone can;
and it *is* to be done! I am *sure* you can do it! I know
you better than you know yourself. You will grow old
apace: a man by twenty: a—something more than a
man by thirty, if God wills. I pray He may!—No, I say.
Don't be afraid of that. I have no relation whom I can
wrong by making you my heir: be easy on that point.'

He stopped suddenly:
'You answer nothing?'
In a little, I, with my eyes downcast, said:
'You have so completely taken me by surprise——'
'Yes: yes: yes, I know. It was foolish of me. I had intended working up to it slowly: training you into what I wanted you to become.'
He began to drift away:
'Last night I . . . I had a horrible, a horrible dream. . . . Strange, strange how we all are troubled by our dreams! . . . What accursed shadows I saw! shadows of sin; shadows of a tormented universe! Oh my God! . . . My time is short. . . . I know it. I shall not get further than Paris. I know it. . . . "Blake, old fellow: Allan's dead."—"Dead?" he said. —"Yes, *dead*. Renshaw brought me news of it last night. He carried him on his back over a mile through the sands. It was evening when they got to the water-hole. Allan was delirious. I cannot think of his poor parched lips muttering, and his eyes stared so, Renshaw says. But at the last, he grew quite calm, and asked him to hold him up. *Are those the mountains out there?*' he asked.—'*Yes*,' said Renshaw.—'*How peaceful they are!*' Then he closed his eyes for a little; but opened them all of a sudden and cried out: '*Do you see the Cross there?*'—'*No*,'—said Renshaw. '*Where?*'— '*Upon the mountain top, the ridge I mean. Christ is holding it. How sweet His face is. . . . Oh what a light, what a light! It bursts out all round Him. And see, the shadow! There, there on the sand. The shadow of the Cross. Nearer—nearer—nearer, fleet over the golden sand. The shadow of the Cross!*'—And so he died."'
I shook him by the arm:
'Sir, sir—You are ill,' I said.
'No,' he said, 'not ill, only tired.'
All at once he started up:
'I've been talking quickly. . . . My blood's been boiling. But I'm all right now.—You have understood all that I said? No. I see that you don't realise it. Well, well. That is nothing. We'll begin again.— No, I assure you, I'm all right now. Sit down. Draw your chair closer. Now I will go through it again.'

H

It seemed he had quite forgotten the story he had told me of his friend's death. He began to explain the object of the expedition : what was to be done this time: what was to be done next time : lastly, what he wanted me to do. I listened patiently, although I was, as it were, physically wearied of it all.

Dawn was breaking as I stood looking from my bedroom window. I wished that I stood on some Thames bridge, to look at the sleeping town : then turned away sighing, and glad that I was not there—anywhere but where I was, a few yards off my cool, comfortable bed.

As I had one knee on it, getting in, I paused, made half-irresolute by a thought. How long was it since I had prayed ? Had I grown so sure, then, that there was no 'good' in it?—*None! none!* 'If God is, He knows what is in my heart without my telling Him. And yet I haven't given much thought to the subject of late : not had time to go searching for new material with which to build up my belief in disbelief, as I used to do at Glastonbury. Ah, I was a boy then. Now I am . . . a fool to be standing here like this !' I was into bed and had the clothes over me.

'. . . I wonder what Rosy's doing now ? Asleep, of course, like a good little girl. I wish *I* was ! I wish this world had never been made. I wish I had never been born, and then I shouldn't have been plagued with all these things. . . . *No ; this world is not much of a place to be happy in !*

## II

For some time, when I lay half-awake next morning, I was aware of a letter with the usual cup of tea by my bedside. At last I roused myself sufficiently to stretch out my hand and lift the letter into the bed by me. Then I managed to open it, and began, still half-awake, to read it :

'Dear Mr. Leicester,—I have been informed of your appointment as private secretary to Mr. Brooke, and that you are about to accompany him on his expedition to Central Africa, to which I wish all possible success. I have a pro-

found admiration for Mr. Brooke personally.  I once had
the honour of meeting him at the house of my distinguished
friend, Professor Strachan, F.R.S.  I think that you are to
be greatly congratulated on the results of your independent
course of action in having faced the world so boldly on your
own account' (about this point I woke up completely), 'and
I have no doubt that you will always do credit to the name
you bear.  I have to regret and apologise for any little
disagreeableness that may have arisen during our last interview, and to ask you to ascribe it to the very indifferent state
of my health at the time.  I am still, I believe, in rather a
critical condition ; but my doctors give me every hope of the
ultimate recovery of my accustomed vigour.  Thinking that
perhaps you might require some small moneys, cash for your
outfit, etc., I have directed that the sum of one hundred
pounds shall be deposited to your account at my agents',
Messrs. Milnes and Co., Axe Street, which you will do me a
great pleasure by accepting as a small token of my personal
regard.—I remain, Yours truly, Tnos. R. JAMES.
    B. LEICESTER, Esq.
    'P.S.—The £100 will be handed over to you on personal
application.  I have to ask your indulgence for the indifferent
composition of this letter, which you must please to ascribe
to my present condition.  I find any mental effort very painful to me.'

    I lay back, with my head deep in the pillow, staring at
the ceiling : 'Either the man is soft-brained,' I thought,
'or flunkey-hearted, or . . . I don't understand it !
But I certainly shan't waste a quarter of another
minute in trying to.  What's the old hypochondriac
to me ?  Of course, I won't take his money, damn him !'
    Then a crowd of other thoughts came upon me.
There was Rosy, and my books still at Glastonbury, and
the general futility of existence, and particularly of my
own.
    A barrel-organ began playing some way off.  I lay
and listened to it in an arid disgust.  At last it stopped.
Then I got up, and proceeded to my toilet.—'This is
what is generally known as getting, or having got, out
of the wrong side of your bed this morning,' thought I,
going downstairs.
    Mr. Brooke seemed better.  He talked to me quite
naturally at breakfast about things.  Then we parted :
he to go I do not know where, I to see about some

orders that had not been punctually fulfilled, etc.—But
when we met again at luncheon, I thought he had rather a
beaten-out look, a look of extreme weariness.  I ascribed
it to the amount of conventional thought and worry that
he had gone through of late, and perhaps a little to the
unusual excitement of last night.

The next day was quite ordinary and uneventful.
And so the day after.  Everything was done now.  We
were to start early in the morning from Charing Cross.
Consequently, that night we went to bed earlier than
usual at about half-past nine.

I, out in the hall, lit my candle first : said good-night
to him in the library : and was almost up to the top of
the first staircase, where our ways separated, when I
heard him call out.  I stopped and listened.

He called again ;

' Boy ! '

I answered :

' Yes ? '

' Good-night ! '

' Good-night.'

' No : wait.  I will be up in a moment to shake hands
with you.  The night before the campaign opens, eh ? '

He came out : lit his candle (I watched him over the
bannisters.  I see him now) : and came up slowly.  I
stepped back, and stood waiting for him in the dark
entrance of the passage.

Then we shook hands, but he did not let mine go
after he had pressed it.  I turned my eyes from his face
generally to his eyes, and looked into them, puckering
up my mouth a little to one side.

He smiled : smiled a second time, and let fall my
hand.—He meant something by that smile, and I understood something, but I did not, and do not, quite know
what.

Mine was a dreamless sleep that night.

Sitting opposite him in the railway-carriage some five
minutes before we were to start, he caught me glancing
at him in a peculiar way.

' I can tell you what you are thinking of,' he said,
bending towards me and putting his hand on my knee,
' you are half-puzzled, half amused at my "delusion."

Oh yes, that's your word: "Delusion." Very well!
We shall see what we shall see.  My dear boy, _I_ am
not given to morbidity, believe me.—You didn't forget to get some papers?'
    I started up.
    'I am sorry.  I have forgotten all about them.  I
will go at once.—What papers shall I get?'
    'No, I should have got them myself.  Let me go.
I have been doing all the talking and you all the work.
It was very kind of old Gordon to come down to give me
a God-speed and shake o' the hand, wasn't it, Starkie?
—You didn't see him, I thought.  He kept me chattering with him.—Stop! stop! I'll go.  I really insist on
going!'
    'It is only at the end of the platform, sir,' I said, 'let
me——'
    'No, no, I will go myself.'  You stop here.—Is there
any paper you particularly like, Starkie?  Are you a
liberal or a conservative?'
    Mr. Starkie, with his feet upon the cushions, looked
round with his usual beard-twitching smile:
    'Oh, I'm neither.  They're both equally bad.—Get
me a "society" paper.'
    As Mr. Brooke hurried away, Mr. Starkie said some-
thing sarcastic about 'society papers.'  Then, after a
pause (I knew nothing about 'society papers'), I went
on to the platform, and began walking up and down
before the carriage.
    All at once I saw Mr. Brooke, with some papers in
his hand, coming towards the open gate.  A shabbily-
dressed man was slouching along at right-angles to him.
They met.  I saw Mr. Brooke start back: half-loose
and then clutch the papers: let the man pass by, and
then come towards me, but more slowly.
    I thought nothing of it: re-entered the carriage; and
a moment after he was at the door, and threw the
papers on to the seat.  I was arranging some rugs upon
the rack.  Then the guard came to the door to examine our tickets.  I had Mr. Brooke's.  As I gave
it up with mine, I noticed him.  He was sitting staring
in front of him, with his hand supporting his head.  He
was very pale.  I stood in doubt, looking at him.

'Are you ill?' I asked.

He started and laughed.

'Oh, it is nothing.'—We are to have a fine day for our journey. See how the sun is shining through the mist! It must be quite clear out in the country. . . . Do you know what time we get to Dover, Starkie?'

There was a door between Mr. Brooke's room and mine at the Hôtel de Manchester in Paris. We had it opened, and talked as we were dressing for dinner. He was instructing me in the programme that had to be gone through here in Paris. I was at my glass, spoiling a white tie, when I heard him come from his room into mine, but did not turn, thinking he was only continuing the conversation. All at once I saw his face reflected beside mine. I jerked myself round.

His eyes kept opening and shutting. I caught him by the arm. He smiled at me.

'It is as I thought,' he said slowly, 'we must get out of this, boy. . . . That man at the station. I ran against him.'

He shuddered. I heard his teeth click as he closed his jaws.

'You are ill?'

'Yes. That man! It went through me like Weland's sword. Oh, the horrible smell!'

'You think you have caught the small-pox?' I said.

'I do not think: I know. How weak my eyes are. I could almost fancy I saw motes before. . . . What folly!'

'It is the crossing,' I said. 'You will be all right soon.'

'The crossing? An old sailor like me? Pooh! And yet——'

He began to consider to himself:

'And yet . . . how possibly . . .'

I caught him by the arm:

'Stop: stop!' I said. 'You will *give* yourself the small-pox if you go on at that rate.—Have you been vaccinated?'

He moved from me, saying, with great calmness:

'Not I! Nonsense, every bit of it! I never wanted to have all the vile diseases flesh is heir to pumped into my system with bad lymph! See. I will sit down here, on the bed. I don't feel well: that's all—at present. Giddy. Go and tell Starkie. Then go and find a room for me somewhere. A nice room: and flowers. Mind you tell the people what it's for: a case of small-pox.' (He stopped and smiled.) 'Variola confluens, if they are particular. That means something like the certainty of a dead body in the house. You may add that: people like to know. Never mind what you have to pay. A nice room, Leicester. Remember, I shall want to be in it—probably a fortnight —before I die. I used to like Passy: try in Passy.— Now go. No: I am not mad: not in the least!'

'Will you let me fetch a doctor?' I said.

'You will anger me in a moment!—Go and tell Starkie, and find me a nice room. I want to get there while I am sure of myself. We must think of other people as well as of ourselves.—Please go at once.'

I went to Starkie and sent him into my room: then ran downstairs; found out the *maître d'hôtel*, and tried to explain to him that I wanted to know where I should be able to find a house agent. Seeing that I only confused the man, I came up to the room again.

Mr. Starkie was sitting beside Mr. Brooke, speaking to him earnestly—trying, I think to persuade him that he was mistaken in his idea about the small-pox. He stopped speaking as I came in.

I explained how useless it was for me to try to get what was wanted: I did not know a street in Paris, and could not speak French: Mr. Starkie had better go, and leave me here with Mr. Brooke. They both seemed to see this. Mr. Starkie jumped up, saying that of course I was quite right. It would be a dreadful waste of time for me to go, and in the end I might not be successful. Mr. Brooke thanked him.

As the door closed I sat down beside the bed.

After a little :

'I wish you would let me get a doctor,' I said.

'Not yet, not yet, useless! We shall see, boy, in a little while. I hate doctors. They are a blundering race. . . . But I have one or two things to say to you before you go . . . Bertram.'

It was the first time he (or indeed anyone since I was quite a child,) called me by my Christian name. I felt a sort of answering thrill in me.

‘ Before I go ? ’ I said.

‘ Yes.   I shall not allow you to stay, and run the chance of catching it.   That would never do.   Nor must Starkie : he will have to hurry on to Brindisi ; but I’m afraid Clarkson won’t care to go on without me. . . . And *he* wishes to put it off, too.   It is hard : after all these years ! ’

A pause.

‘ I have been speaking to him about you,’ he went on, ‘ he knows all my wishes.   He is one of my executors . . . A brave man : rough and ready : will follow anywhere, but can’t lead.   Clarkson has all the brains of the party.   You *must* have scientific observation to hand, or you can never do any real good.   That is the mistake we have all of us made.   Brave men can plod on and, when there is need, shoot straight (but the less shooting, the better) : but there is something else wanted as well, and that’s perception.   They don’t recognise more than half they see.   There has only been one naturalist in Africa yet—Klesmer, I mean. Think of that !   And he, poor devil, came to grief on the ubiquitous reef of poverty.   I have often regretted I didn’t know of him in time.   But it ’s the old, old story !   When they had muscle, they hadn’t brains : and when they had brains, they hadn’t muscle.   These explorers (especially the French) are a queer lot.   Du Camp’s gorillas are . . . well, let ’s only say exaggerations.   And as for Louis . . . But there, there ! Starkie knows all about it.   He will tell you some day. I have a thousand things in my head, and can only bring you out one.   About yourself.   You would not promise that night to give up your life to the Cause. You said that you believed you had other work to do. I want you to promise *now*.   You must leave me to-night, Bertram—very soon.’

‘ Leave you ?   Here, with strangers ? ’

‘ I want no one but the Sisters.   I have seen them at work before : have worked with them.   They are all I want.   With the small-pox, men die in delirium,

loathsome to everyone.   You could not stay. . . . I am
thinking of going into an hospital instead of taking an
apartment—if it can be managed as I want it.   Starkie
has gone to see.   That was a foolish idea of mine : I am
glad you came back.   It is all right.   Starkie knows all
about it.   If the doctors will only leave me alone. . . .
Oh, boy,' he said, ' if you would but promise to try !   Go
back and study, say, for three years : only three years !
And learn everything, everything !   And then go down
there for another year to learn the life.   And you will
pick up experience very quickly.   I know you.   Starkie
says he will do it ; he will not be too old : a brave fellow !
Ah dear !  ah dear !  I have so many things that I want
to tell you : so many, so many that they confuse me,
and I can scarcely tell you anything.   All one gigantic
jumble, eh ?   But I have not been like myself since
that dream.—You *will* promise ?'

I answered nothing.

He lifted up his head.

' Promise me !   I am so sure you could do it.   If you
only had some beacon-light to steer by !   At times I
have thought that I am infatuated about you.   You did
not know that I was married once ? . . . And God
took away my son from me.   Yet I bore it.   And then
my wife, too.   " *The Lord gave, and the Lord hath taken
away.   Blessed be the name of the Lord.*"   That was
what Blake said to me in the evening when my son
died.   I only saw him dead.   It was very sudden.
Dear child !  dear child ! . . . You have something of
him in you, Bertram, at times. . . . And then Ratcliffe
came and fell ill.   He was not worth much.   Intelli-
gent, and all that ; but had no interest in his work, and
could not have done much for it if he had had.   And then
God sent you to me.   Your struggle in London !—Oh,
you *must* promise me ! . . . Ha !  I am a fond old fool !'

At last :

' You have not answered me,' he said, ' will you not
promise ?   How taciturn you are sometimes !'

' I cannot, sir.   It is as if you asked me to become a
priest, having no vocation.'

' But I have determined that you *shall* promise !   I
have made you my heir.   I am not rich.   Some eight

hundred a-year now; much less than I once had. I
have spent much in the Cause. You will promise?'
 'I cannot, sir. I thank you none the less; but you
must give it to some one else.—To Mr. Starkie. I cannot
promise to give up my life to the pursuit of a thing—
I do not care for: I mean care for, enough for that.'
 After a little he:
 'You will think better of it when you are older.
You are full of dreams now.—Promise me now. In five
years . .. It is not for five years.'
 'I cannot promise. You must not leave me that
money. I could not take it without I did promise,
and I will never promise. How could I—honestly?'
 He sighed:
 'My head is too heavy. I cannot talk any more
now. Remember; I will alter nothing. You will go
some day. Wait till you have been out in the world,
boy. I have seen bees covered with tiny red spiders
innumerable, tickled to death. I will alter nothing.'
 I took his hand gently:
 'I am sorry sir,' I said, 'to seem so ungrateful. It
is not that I am really; but . . I cannot do this: I
cannot give up my life to such a thing! Do not think
that I set great store by my life. I do not. I am not
far from indifferent whether I live or whether I die—
as yet. But, as you have just said, I am full of dreams.
I have scarcely dared to whisper to my own heart
what they are, but, such as they are, I will either climb up
to them or to nothing. Greatness is the only truth.'
 In a little he said:
 'Oh greatness, greatness! what greatness, boy? It
is all vague—visions—dreams—emptiness!'
 'No, no, not to me—now.'
 'I am too weary to talk of it any more. Rest, rest!
This is not the end.'
 I did not say what was upon my tongue. I was
foolish to have said so much. I kept silence for a
little. Then:
 'Can I get you nothing?' I said.
 'Nothing, nothing! . . . Let us wait for Starkie.'
 I rested my elbow on my knee and my chin upon
my hand; and so sat, looking at the floor. Mr. Brooke

lay motionless on his back with his eyes closed. His breathing seemed to me short and heavy.

At last Starkie came. It was all right: Mr. Brooke might go to the hospital.

Just before he went downstairs, he asked Mr. Starkie to leave us alone for a moment. I stood by the large wardrobe mirror, with a certain feeling of almost shame, making me wish to avert my eyes from his face. He came to me—put one hand on to my shoulder in his old way, smiling, and said:

'Well, Starkie knows all about the Book, too. It is to be brought out soon after my death, and you are to be joint editor with him.'

'I, sir? I know nothing about Africa; nothing even of literary matters. How shall I ?'

'I wish it so. You will not refuse me this?'

'But, sir, I am so young.'

'People will laugh. Is that it?'

'What people do or do not do, is nothing to me.'

'You say it with lots of emphasis. Very well.— Then you accept?'

'Yes, sir.—But I hope that neither Mr. Starkle nor I may ever have to touch your book. You may recover.'

He smiled again; less sadly than before, it seemed to me.

'No, no, that is not to be! God has laid his hand upon me; and I am to pay the penalty of my sin. It is just.—May His will be done in all things !'

I answered nothing.

He sighed; let fall his hand from my shoulder listlessly; turned, and was moving to the door. I followed him and touched his arm:

'You have not said good-bye to me, sir,' I said.

I passed in front of him. He raised a hand to either shoulder, feeling up my right sleeve, but not the other: then bent his face forward towards mine, murmuring:

'My eyes are a little weak. I too am a little weak —a little feeble. That is tautological—eh? . . . I did not say good-bye to you? That was careless of me. You were in my thoughts—in the thoughts behind my thoughts, Bertram.—Good-bye, boy, good-

bye ! . . . I have no fear for thee—in the end.   Thou
wilt do it in the end.   Keep a brave heart.   God is
not so far from thee. . . .'

His lips moved after that, but I heard no sound
that came from them.   Then felt the pressure of his
hands moving me aside : caught the door handle :
turned and opened the door, and he went out.

I stood watching him.   Mr. Starkie was at the top
of the stairs.   He offered Mr. Brooke his arm, who
half-absently took it; then started, looked at him, and
smiled.   They went down together slowly.

Mr. Starkie was to go on to Brindisi next day.   I
told him that I would not leave Paris until I had heard
decisive news of Mr. Brooke.   I had still £15 left from
my £25, and had scarcely spent anything, Mr. Brooke
having insisted on paying all my expenses of outfit, etc.

Mr. Starkie told me of a 'pension' in the Avenue
de Fontenoi.   I went there on the same evening that
Mr. Brooke went to the hospital.   The last thing Mr.
Starkie said to me (we were sitting in the courtyard
of the hotel : I was about to leave him for the 'pension'),
was that he had very little doubt but that Clarkson
would agree to give up the expedition, but still, if he
wished to go on, there was nothing left but to go on
with him : in which case I should hear at once, either by
letter or from Mr. Starkie himself.   As for my expenses
at Paris, those would, of course, be defrayed by Mr.
Brooke: but of this, and many other matters, more anon.

It was late in the evening when I arrived at the
Avenue de Fontenoi.   I went straight up to bed and
slept heavily.

In the morning no one appeared for *café au lait* and
*petit pain* in the *salle-à-manger* but Madame Rouff, her
child, and myself.   I learnt from her that there was
a park quite close to us, the Parc Monceau.

I went there at once.   It is a pretty greenery.   I
found a sunlit, bubbling spring at the end of a pool in
what I took to be a sham ruin.   And so, first of all,
sitting watching and playing with the stream : then
sitting watching the passers and some horses being
tried, I was happy enough for the time.   The sense of

it all being in an air and place somewhere between dream and reality was perpetually with me. There were water-jets of pierced hose playing to right and left on the fresh grass: cooings of pigeons, and the flappings of their wings as they took flight: small birds taking baths in the dust: all the morning smiling and soft, and fresh-breathed. I thought of my first morning in Regent's Park, and of others, and that by degrees led me to thinking of Rosy.—What was she doing now? And Minnie? Such a dear beast, but infernally thin!

Later in the day I went to inquire about Mr. Brooke. Nothing new. 'The symptoms of small-pox, you know, sir, advance with order. This does not hurry itself for anyone. You must keep quiet.'—And so, day after day, I went, and it was always the same answer. 'This advances, this goes on advancing.'

I tried once to make myself unhappy by thinking about him. I could not. My sorrow for him was of itself hushed and not untender; but I could not make it into a disturbing gnat buzzing in my ears at all hours. After that one attempt, I let my thoughts wander on at pleasure, as I had always done before, and was contented; for such unceasing misery, producible, it seemed to me, by continued concentration of the mind on one subject, was not 'true.' I instinctively shrank from it.

My old wandering spirit came back upon me in Paris quickly enough. I had nothing to interest me indoors. Perhaps there were few things. that could have taken me out of myself then: I was living for my 'dreams.' I saw many things before me.

So passed ten or twelve weary days, whose only memory to me is unrecorded weariness. At last I received a letter from Starkie, saying that he was back at the Hôtel de Manchester. Clarkson had decided to proceed, but Starkie had refused to do so until Brooke's fate was decided. I went down to him, and we discussed the whole matter together. Then the weary time began again. I spent most of it in wandering about Paris, reading, and talking with Starkie; but that last was only as we went down together to the hospital each morning for news, and sometimes an hour or so in the evenings, he having a good deal of business to do in one shape or another.

On about the thirteenth day (but all accurate record or memory is gone) I lit upon the Louvre, and from that hour forward was in it continually. It gave me much quiet pleasure.

This was broken into by the news of the nineteenth morning. Secondary fever had set in. For the first time, Starkie seemed to give up hope. The effect on me was quite different. I could not realise the fact of Mr. Brooke being in the state I, I almost thought, *knew* he was in. I went into the Parc Monceau, and sat there in a sort of warm, gold dream of wilderment for some time, till, all at once, I caught myself starting up with the exclamation :

'No, no ! If I was right, then, in refusing, I am right in now having refused.'—And I *was* right. For what had I to do with it ? '

I spent the afternoon sculling on the river out at Courbevoi.

After dinner I went for a walk along the boulevards, softly singing or whistling to myself; till, in a dim street by the Opera, I woke up out of vague, sweet thoughts into the perception of something like a breath of fluttering music in me, now melting, now languorous, now fierce, floating up into my brain and pulsing through me, from time to time, with a longing and yearning to stretch out my arms in a happy cry to something. And in this strange, half-ecstatic state I came home; threw off my things, and got into bed as into a white cool haven.

In that night I had a strange and vivid dream. I stood below somewhere, and saw a lady I had known once, in a carriage with a dead child, on a green-lit down by the sea. The carriage had just crossed a bridge. A river rolled down smoothly over golden sands. A boy on the right shore stood watching a ball that the up-cresting sea-waves kept lifting up to and back from him every moment. I rose, and crossed over the stone bridge ; came behind the carriage and began climbing over it from the back. The lady turned, and,

seeing me, put out her brown-gloved hand to me; and
then, when I would have caught and pressed it into
my bosom, touched my chest with her finger-tips: the
carriage moved onwards: the child wailed: I fell back-
wards and down, and awoke trembling and wet with
trickling sweat.

It was the next morning that, when we came together to the hospital, they told us that Mr. Brooke
had died during the night delirious.

In a long moment Starkie turned away. I followed
him.

We went in silence along the pavement with the on-
moving people, till I said to myself half-aloud:

'I cannot realise that it is so.'

'Nor I,' he said in the same way, 'nor I scarcely.
. . . He was a good man.'

Then I said:

'It is a deep thought to think that his soul has gone
out like a candle, and that *that* is the end of him.'

Starkie answered nothing.

'I wish,' I said, 'you would tell me truly and from
the bottom of your soul: do you believe that that *is*
the end of him?'

In a little:

'I believe it,' he said, 'the energy that was in him
has undergone some change. We call that change
death. It is, I believe, the end of us.'

'Do you think that, when that change comes to *you*,
*you* will end, that there will be no more of *you*?'

'I do. Death looses that which grips the gathered
threads of our individualities: the threads fall away,
going to other invisible work, just as the threads of the
body which is left slowly fade into the earth and air,
going for other *visible* work. What death or, to use
what seems to me its proper name, solution may be, I
cannot of course pretend to guess: but our grandchildren may be able to, and their grandchildren,
perhaps, to know. You asked me to tell you my belief:
what I truly and from the bottom of my heart believe.
*That* is my belief.'

'I thank you for it,' I said, 'for from to-day I purpose
beginning my soul's life anew, and I might go far be-

fore I met one who believed what you believe, and
would tell it me as you have told it me. Will you let
me ask you one more question?'

'Twenty, if you care to·ask them.'

'Have you not in you a feeling, a strange unaccount-
able, but nevertheless undeniable feeling, that you, *you*
—your individuality, as you said,—cannot possibly be
destroyed?'

'You mean have I, what is called the instinct of immortality?—No: I have not,—now.  When I first
began to think about these things, my mind was
strongly prepossessed in favour of immortality, and
consequently this instinct soon developed itself from
its passive unconsciousness into active consciousness,
and I held fast to the idea of immortality when everything else, save belief in a deity, had gone.  It was not
till after more than three years of thoughtfulness and
study, that I learnt that my desire for immortality was
only a synonym for my selfishness, and, having learnt
this, I began to see, too, the complete needlessness,
though as complete naturalness, of that desire.  I determined to devote myself to benefiting, as far as I
could, my fellow men.  Whether this was a result
from, or parallel to, my loss of all belief in immortality,
it would be difficult to say.  At any rate, there are the
two facts contemporaneous.'

'And do you not believe in a deity either?'

'I cannot answer you; for I do not know.  I am
content, seeing a world full of ignorance and woe, to
strive to lessen however little of that ignorance,
knowing that thereby I shall lessen a corresponding
amount of that woe.  This seems to me the one undeniable duty of each of us: to make the earth better
for our having been in it.'

I answered nothing.  We walked on together in
silence till we came to the hotel door.  Then, as he
half-turning faced me, I held out my hand for his, and
when it was in mine, pressed it, looking into his eyes
that looked into mine, and I said:

'Thank you.'

We passed to other matters; for what more was to
be said or done as regarded this?

We bought Brooke's grave in Père-Lachaise *à perpétuité*. Upon the tombstone a plain white marble cross was to be put, his name, the dates of his birth and death, and below :

* Thy will be done.'

---

III

ON my way to London, I sketched out something like a plan of action for what I should do when I got there. The first thing, I thought, was the mastering of Mr. Brooke's business affairs,—all (I meant) that was connected with his property and money : the next thing, the editing of the book. I had determined to take as much of the income of one year as would keep me in comfort while I was engaged upon my work for him. Starkie had given me a letter of introduction to Professor Strachan, who would assist me, or rather, who would be assisted by me. Doubtless, after the first few weeks, I should be able to find time to set about the recovery of my books and clothes from Glastonbury. Also, to see Rosy. Also, to meditate as to what I should do when the time of my work for Mr. Brooke was over.

I had a certain amount of trouble about the business affairs, despite both what Starkie had already done to save me from as much of it as possible, and the extreme courtesy, and indeed kindness, of Mr. Brooke's lawyers. Howbeit, at the end of some ten days, I found that it was now time to present the letter of introduction to Professor Strachan.

He received me quite cordially. I had, at a dinner at Mr. Brooke's, seen but not spoken to him, and so he was not altogether a stranger to me : besides which, I had heard a good deal about him from Starkie on our last night together, and he, I could see, was not unacquainted with me. He arranged to come to Dunraven Place the next morning, and we would then proceed to examine the work that was before us.

After we had talked a little on general subjects, he asked me to go up with him and have some tea with

I

Mrs. Strachan in the drawing-room.   Up, then, we
went and into the drawing-room, where we found
three womenkind, one middle-aged and two young,
to whom I was presented : Mrs. and the two Miss
Strachans.   Mrs. Strachan struck me as an ordinary
good-looking middle-aged female, and her two daughters
as two ordinary pretty young females, clothed with
decorous fashionableness and speaking platitudes of
the most irreproachable character : or shortly, as three
'ladies.'   And, this seeming so, it followed that not
even a certain demureness in Miss Connie's face and
manner, not unsuggestive of experience in the art of
flirting, added to what I subsequently was told was a
'grave sweetness' in Miss Isabel, were enough to
entice me out of my shell.   It was far more amusing,
as it seemed to me, to sit and listen to their silly
prattle, which, it was not hard to see, they took for
delightful if not brilliant conversation, than to enter
into the splashing shallows myself; for, if I had been
a talker, I must inevitably have missed over half of the
nature-strokes which as a listener I caught.   The
amusement of hearing Mrs. Strachan and her daughters
talk about 'Culture,' while the Professor sat drinking
his tea and occasionally throwing in a gibe, which they
either did not hear or quite misunderstood, seemed to
give me something of an insight into the meaning of
the word Comedy.   Finally, towards the end of an
almost irrepressible fit of amusement, I rose and said
good-bye to them, and went away down the stairs and
out into the street, hot and a little exhausted.   If I
had stayed much longer, I thought, I must have shown
some sign that perhaps might have offended them, and
that would have been to be regretted.   And then I
was led to think of my last society experiences of
three, it seemed years, but it was only weeks ago,
till I came to Dunraven Place, when it occurred to me
to write to Mother McCarthy about my things at
Glastonbury.

Accordingly I wrote : took out my letter and posted
it ; and went for a walk into the Park, Hyde Park, till
seven, when it was time for supper.   And after supper
came a reading of *Esmond*, highest Thackerayan

art, in the low, red-leathered armchair under the green-shaded lamp; till eleven, dumb-bells, bed and sleep.

The next morning Professor Strachan and I began our work.

My Journal takes out a new lease on that evening. (It seems to have given me pleasure, though no great pleasure, I fancy, to record events or conversations, or to deliver some few of my impressions of present people and things in that way. Perhaps there was some small necessity upon me to write these things. I cannot say.)

Here is from a week later:

'We are often almost in despair over the manuscripts. In the first place the writing is fearful. He seems to have thought it quite enough to write the first three or four letters of a word, for the rest is nearly always comprised in a twirl. Now this is aggravating to the son of man. Then, the Journal is broken off by chance notes, and these notes have references to other note-books, and so on. I never was made for editing other people's books. I lack patience, and the worst of it is, that I don't believe that anyone can do anything worth calling thing *without* patience. The Professor is Job and Griselda put into one.

'After a week's hard work we have arranged the stuff,—I should say materials or notes, I suppose,—into something like chronological order, having separated the whole mass into three almost equal parts: to wit, The Travels in Palestine and parts of Arabia, The Expedition from South Africa upwards, and the last Expedition to Injiji.

'A sheet was pasted on to the inside of the cover of the first note-book of the "Journal through Palestine and parts of Arabia," which we are going, we think, to use as an introduction to the two first expeditions. It is as follows:

'"This Journal through Palestine and parts of Arabia was undertaken by me in 18—, with a view to helping by details, principally geographical, my dear friend the Rev. Charles Blake, in the compilation

of his proposed *History of the Origins of Christianity.*
On returning home, however, in 18—, I learnt that he
had been compelled to abandon his scheme for certain
most satisfactory reasons. I therefore laid aside my
ms., hoping that events might some day make it
possible for him to utilise it as he had originally
intended. With that hope I seal it up now.—In case
of my death, this packet is to be given to him unopened.

'"*February 15th*, 18—.
'" My Journal through parts of Arabia was connected
with the same scheme, Blake proposing to draw a
parallel between the life of the Saviour and that of
Mahomet, as illustrating——" [Last two words erased.]

'It seems in some way a little strange to be sitting
here copying out these words of a dead man. It would
perhaps seem really strange if I *realised* even now,
that he *was* dead. Is he *dead?* It seems rather as if
he had gone a journey into a far land, and now stays
there. I wonder if I shall ever read this after many
years to come, and what shall I think of it then?
'I think I should like to go to Palestine some day.
Nazareth must be a very beautiful place, from what he
says of it, and what so sweet as to wander in that dear
land, thinking of——' [*Cetera desunt*, and this last
scratched out.]

A little lower:
'That sheet may originally have been pasted on the
outside of the packet; at any rate the packet has been
broken open; for the note-books are all mingled with
those of the other two journals in the drawer,' etc., etc.

Another entry:
'Books and things from Glastonbury. My Ruperti's
Juvenal missing, also my Greek Lex., also several
note-books. A distinct nuisance. I have divided my
day off as follows—Breakfast, 8.30: Italian, 9 to 10:
The Book with Strachan, 10 to 1: Walk, 2 to 5:
Greek, 5 to 7: (Supper): Latin, 8 to 10: English, 10
to 11. I find it is the only way to get any real work
done. Now and then I go with the Strachans to the

theatre, or spend afternoons or evenings out at people's
houses. Mrs. Strachan does her best to drag me into
what she calls "society," by introducing me to her
women friends (especially those having daughters), who
send me invitation cards, and the rest of it. I believe
she would like to see me married, or at any rate engaged, to some young woman or other. She seems to
look upon me as lawful prey in the matter of endurance
of female *agacerie*. Sometimes I grow mischievous,
and talk "atheism" to the young women she puts me
with, or who are put with me, or whatever the real
case may be. It is sufficiently amusing. I had great
sport with Miss Isabel's "grave sweetness" last Wednesday afternoon in this way. (Miss Isabel would
marry me, "atheism" and all, I think, if I, after all
proper formalities, asked her to ; which is a tribute to
my personal charms and her belief in my personal
possessions that I appreciate.) Miss Connie, however,
resolutely refuses to be drawn into discussion of anything deeper than flirting, and I respect her for it.
She is a frank little sensualist. Take it all in all, the
womenkind I have so far met with have been of a
most God-forsaken sort. There is not one that has
seemed to me worth more than a mild sort of feeling
that might by some be denominated "lust." The
idea of having to live with one of these things for your
natural life, short though it is ! But the idea is happily
out of the question ; for where could you find one that
would live with you without being your wife with bell,
book, ring, and the rest of it ? And I simply would
not, could not, go through the foolery of the marriage
service for any woman (or so I think) alive. The more
I consider Christianity as compared with humanity—I
mean, that Christianity is the only divinity and all
other than Christians are either damned or at the best
deluded—the more I revolt against it as an accursed
libel on God, if He is, and His justice.'

About three weeks later :

'The first part of our work was finished to-day. I
must say I hope the rest may be a little more interesting. And, indeed, it has at times seemed, perhaps

illogically, that this "Journal through Palestine and
parts of Arabia" has been as it were extra work; at
any rate, it has at times made me feel a little
aggrieved.  Strachan doesn't care for it, either.  I
told him that Mr. Starkie had said nothing to me
about it, nor yet of Blake's proposed "History" in
connection with which Brooke's journey appeared to
have been taken.  He said that he had known of it
through Clarkson, but had thought that the MS. had
been destroyed, he did not quite know why.

‘We should have liked not to have suppressed or
added a single word of it, for obvious reasons; but
this was really quite impossible.  At times we came
upon whole pages of, what I dare say were abbrevia-
tions, but which were to us absolutely meaningless
signs: then there were long extemporary prayers,
coupled with the most childish virulent attacks on
different scientific men of the day and Christians whose
conceptions of Christianity were different to Brooke's
own.  Now all this was neither beautiful nor to the
point, and, besides, we felt sure that he himself would
never have wished them to see the light, at any rate,
in their present form.  Accordingly we eliminated
certain passages that seemed to us to offend: and
were, I think, justified in so doing; for to whom could
they do good?  Certainly not to the future investigator
of the origins of Christianity : certainly not to the people
who would read this book : certainly not to the memory
of Brooke.  None the less, I for my part felt that it was
very delicate work touching anything, and so (apparently) did Strachan.  However, it's done now, and
the best we could do it: so what's the good of troubling?

‘It is astonishing how carelessly he put his materials
together, considering that the object in view was one
apparently so dear to him.  I had to copy it nearly all
out.  The only interesting part was where he debated
upon the sincerity of Mahomet.  This we left intact
in the form of an excursus.’

The next day has :

‘Went to Maitland Street this afternoon, after a
good boring at Mrs. Cunningham's.  Upon my soul

(*Façon de parler!*) I don't think I will ever enter a drawing-room again. The sickening foolery we all talked! And yet—' [a pause expressed on continuing by half a row of dots.] '. . . And yet, how, if I do not go out into the world and talk with people therein, am I ever likely to meet the woman I am to love, nay, love already in my heart?—"O dear woman with sweet clear eyes, standing waiting and looking for me while in my light boat on that, the night of my life, I pass from the shadowiness into the silver-purled moon-track; pass on and on to the grass mingled with the gently-moving wave in which the roses dip. I am there now, and know not of you: see, breathe, only this terrestrial beauty. I step from the boat into the soft grass: the rope is tied, and I turn and come up through the rose-perfumed garden, up through the brushing dew-laden bushes; and look into the blue unspeakable depth, and the stars, and one crystal-rayed star beside the peerless moon, and then look and see *you*, O dear woman mine, with sweet, clear eyes, standing waiting and looking for me, and feeling that I am come at last. And at first it seems that we are there in a dream, parts, unknown parts of it; and I come closer to you, closer and closer, till more than dream's passion grows in me, and at last my eyes are in yours and yours in mine, and my lips can feel your playing breath. Oh the kiss! the kiss! the kiss! the draining of life and love! *" Mine, mine, mine, mine at last! Met in the time of eternity : met, and with a meeting that can never be undone. O thou loved, thou loved, thou art come to me at last! O thou loved, thou loved, take me body and soul to thyself. As river mingles with sea, as moisture with cloud : so let mine mingle with thine; for I am thine, and thou art mine, and we are Love's !"*

'Rosy was out.' [A pause, expressed as before.]

'. . . I do wonder if I ever really shall meet a "dear woman"? It doesn't seem like it somehow. At any rate, I shan't meet her in *that* way. What brought up that sudden vision? I saw it as distinctly as I see that window-curtain there with the red blind behind it.—*This is purposeless.*

'Rosy was out, and, as I didn't feel like waiting, I

scrawled a few lines for her on a leaf of my pocket-book : tore it out, and, giving it to Mrs. Smith, who was wiping her dirty hand on her dirtier apron, asked if anyone had my room now ?

'"Oh yes, sir, Miss 'Owlet 'as it *now*, sir!   Another young lady, Miss Martin, sir, 'as the back room.   Miss Rosy've changed, sir.   She likes the front room best, sir—*she* does!   It's more airy like.' (With a twist of the jaw, and an indescribable tone.)

'"Oh," I said.

'"Miss Martin's a friend of Miss 'Owlet's, sir.   But I don't know anything about her 'istory—nothing about her 'istory, sir."

'"Oh," I said again.   And then :

'"You will give her that when she comes in, Mrs. Smith?"

'"Yes, sir, I'll be sure I will, sir.'

'"Thank you," I said.   "Good-evening."

'"Good-evening, sir. . I'll be sure to give it her."

'*The old she-devil !*'

The next entry is five days later :

'Rosy, not seeing fit to write to me as I asked her (I don't quite know what I expected her to write), I went to No. 3 again yesterday.   She had just gone out.   I was a little angered (having a most ridiculous ,idea that she had done it on purpose): scrawled her another note, "Why hadn't she written to me ?   If she would only tell me some fixed hour, I would be happy to come and see her," etc. : gave it to Mrs. Smith, as servile as usual; and then went for a long walk.—Half round Regent's Park : up Primrose Hill once more, and then back to Dunraven Place.   It was all strangely dim to me, this walk over the old land.

'After my afternoon's walk to-day, I found a letter from Rosy waiting me.

'"DEAR MR. LEICESTER,—I was very happy to see you had not forgotten me.

"I am very sorry that I was out when you called on me the two times.   I hope you are quite well, and have enjoyed yourself in Paris.

"Minnie is quite well, and I am quite well.

"And I have not forgotten the Swallow Song.—Yours truly,—ROSY HOWLET.

"P.S.—I shall be in to-morrow night early by eight.   If
you care to go a walk with me then, I shall be very happy to
go a walk with you.   I hope you have not forgotten Minnie.
—Yours truly,—Rosy Howlet (Rosebud.)"'

The Journal follows:

'The work is much easier now, though not particularly interesting.   Brooke, I must say, seems to
have taken a good deal more pains over his own particular mania than over his friend's.   Great parts of
this second Journal are continuous narrative that (thank
God) require nothing on our part.   Strachan thinks
my old friends Parker, Innes, and Co., will be the best
publishers to send it to when it's done.   Here is a
copy of my preface.—But I can't trouble to do it now.
I only said that all the credit of the editing of the book
was due to Strachan, that I had only, etc., etc., etc.
There was nothing else to be said.

'He calculates finishing it by about the middle of
July.   O Destiny!'

---

## IV.

THE next day after lunch, I went for a walk to Hampstead, and wandered about there, my thoughts alter-
nating between the beautiful sweet nature about me
and the past days of my first London weeks, till half-
past six.   Then I remembered that Rosy would be
waiting for me at eight.   It used to take me something under an hour to get from Maitland Street to
Hampstead.   It was now half-past six.   What to do
with myself for an hour?—from seven to eight, that
was.   Then my thoughts turned off in memory:
memory of the many times I had come marching
along this very pavement in those first London days
whose second half was an age of weariness and woe.
Here was the very corner at which I stood that dreary
day.   Was it all a dream?   'I stand still here to-day,'
I said to myself, 'as I stood still here that day, and
look at the brown cracked concrete of the low wall
and the black sooty rails that top it.   The windows
are lampless too, as they were when I first stood still
here.   Will the left one light up suddenly too as it

did then? No. Lampless yet. Who lives here? God knows? And yet, foolish though it be, will not the thought occur again: '*Is it nothing to you, all ye who pass by, my weariness and my woe.*' Here I put my hand on the nearer cemented gate-post, brown and cracked like the low wall, and think of the figure that leant against it in that dreary rain of half-darkness when my body seemed all bloodless, and the girl hurried by me with her huddled-up dress and umbrella spread over her. I see her now—her quick glance, and that hurry by: the devil that rose in me——'

The door above opened and an old lady came out and, looking at me through the spectacles on her elevated nose, asked:

'Do you want anything, young man?'

I took off my hat and held it off.

'Nothing,' I said, 'madam, I thank you. I hope my stopping a moment to examine your gate-post has not troubled you? I see that the cement is cracked and peeling off. Now I am the patentee of a cement which is warranted——'

'No,' she said sharply, looking at me over the spectacles of her depressed nose, '*I* don't want any of your cement, young man. *Good*-day!'

And was in and viewing me suspiciously through the glass panel of the closed door. If I had not been afraid of disturbing her feelings, I should have given a shout. As it was, I repressed the shout, and marched off quickly, laughing to myself.

It was a little past seven when I reached the canal bridge at the bottom of Maida Vale. I stayed a little there, looking at the flowers, finally buying a rose, and carrying it off with me. This I took to No. 3, and inquired of Mrs. Smith if Miss Howlet was in? She wasn't: as I expected. I left the rose, and went for a prowl about the streets.

All at once I found myself looking at the Marble Arch clock, by which it was five minutes past eight. Away I went up the Edgware Road, and was marching along at full speed, a little past Praed Street on the right side, when, passing before a gas-flaming fruiterer's, my eye took in a girl's form, and by the time I had

gone five or six yards my heart was up in my throat
at the sudden thought of—*Rosy*! I turned back at
once. We met face to face, she smiling up into mine,
I looking with a strange graveness into hers.

'Well,' she said, 'you *were* in a hurry!'

We were walking on together, I taking one stride
to her two. It seemed to me remarkable somehow,
this meeting. We had not shaken hands. I did not
know what to say. We walked on together for a little
in silence. Then I began:

'I am very glad to see you. And I hope you are well.
If you have taken walks, as you told me you would, then
I am sure you are better than you were when I left you.'

We talked of general things that did not interest me
or, I think, her much, till we came to the corner of Maitland Street. Then ensued questions and explanations,
and, in about five minutes, Rosy returned from her visit
to No. 3, full of the beautiful rose I had given her.

'Beautiful rose?' I said. ' . . . How do you know
*I* gave it to you?'

'Because,' she answered, 'who else *would*?'

She was ready for the walk now. We set off at
once, in a half-mechanical way Park-wards, beginning
to talk like two children.

All at once:

'Here's your locket!' she said, taking it from inside
her coat, and holding it out, small and round and silver.

'Nay, yours,' I said, 'not mine.'

'You gave it me, though.'

'I did. That made it yours.'

'But it *was* yours before that, or how could you have
given it *me*?'

I acquiesced, with the reflection that Adam must
have had some trouble to get an authentic account of
the eating of the historic apple.

'What are you laughing at?' said Rosy.

'Have you forgotten the Swallow Song?'

'Forgotten it? O my gracious, no!—

> "She comes, she comes, the swallow,
>     bringing beautiful hours,
>     beautiful seasons,
>     white on her——"

What *are* you laughing at?'

It was no wonder she asked. Peal after peal of laughter, quenchless, re-echoing, came from me. The more I tried to stop it, the more it came. At last I stood still, exhausted, with my hands on my hips. But a glimpse of her face was enough to generate a fit of laughter as violent as the first.

We went on together somehow or other, I still shaking with this second fit, she solemn to a degree. All at once it struck me that she was a little afraid I was mad. And then came the task of appeasing her outraged sense of dignity. I was sorry, I said, to have laughed in this way. I explained that what had made me begin was the way she scampered over the Swallow Song . . , and so on.

Her outraged sense of dignity took a good deal of appeasing, but I managed it in the end. Nay, I pleaded so hard, that I obtained from her a repetition of the Swallow Song, as we sat on that seat not far from the top of Primrose Hill, which I knew so well, so well, and she too remembered perhaps.

We parted at the door of No. 3 at about eleven.

As I marched away down the Edgware Road, I went through the evening I had spent with her, ending at her grave bow of the head as I went back from her at the door with my hat down in my hand; but, going across the Park, other thoughts came to me, and I had lost sight of the evening I had spent with her when I reached home.

Here the Journal has a single entry:

' O Claire, Claire, that we should have met here in the time of eternity, and so parted! Claire, Claire! Oh, it is a vile devil's earth, and good is only in the slave. To have held thee in my arms, and, with my eyes in thine, to have kissed thee once, and died. Death were sweet so.—But it is useless to think. This city is a market where souls are pledged for bodies, and bodies for souls, and wealth buys all. I will go out from it. Useless to think, useless to think ! '

It was a few days after this that Rosy and I went

our second evening walk together. There is no allusion
to it in the Journal, and as I was during most of it in
more or less of a half-dreamy, half-abstracted state, I
cannot remember much of what we said. That walk
was not what might be called a success. We went up
to the top of Primrose Hill again, and I snuffed in the
breeze and was somewhat revived; but (it had been
raining heavily earlier in the day) that made me
appreciate how stickily muddy it was going down, and
I was forthwith driven into a state of utter saplessness
and disgust. Rosy mocked at me as well as she could,
but I took no heed. Finally she declared she wouldn't
walk with me any more. (This was half-way down
the St. John's Wood Road.) I acquiesced. We stood
still, I looking in front of me at nothing in particular,
not thinking of offering my hand. Then she turned
and walked away. I did not look at her. When she
had got some twenty yards, I looked at her with a
comic smile: sighed: hit my iron-tipped stick-end
straight on the pavement: said a little wearily, 'Oh
dear,' and went with large strides after her.

I soon caught her up, and we walked on side by
side in silence; till I observed:

'I'm sorry I was rude—if I *was* rude.'

'Then you *were* rude then!' said Rosy, tossing her
head a little.

'Rudeness implies deliberation,' I said, 'now the
best definition of sin is: the deliberately doing anything that may harm anyone else. Thus, it is sin to
buy a pistol, intending to kill, and then absolutely
killing a man: or, to ruin your body by excess, intending
to beget, and then absolutely begetting, children.'

'You talk great *stuff*!' said Rosy.

'Dear child,' I answered, 'I intended you to apply
my definition of sin to the point at issue, my rudeness
or unrudeness. But this, like so many good intentions,
has gone to the artificial protection of infernal cause-
ways.'

Rosy vouchsafed no reply.

I proceeded:

'Well, be that as it may, considering the inability of
the feminine intellect to comprehend anything of subtle

in the matter of metaphysical psychology,—or anything
else you like,—I shall proceed to admit that I *was* rude ;
and apologise accordingly.'

'*I* never asked you to apologise,' she said.

'*I* never said that you did, my dear—well, something
or other.'

'You're very *aggravating* to-night, *that's* what you
are !'

'Oh, Polyphemus and Abracadabra, did you ever
hear such a libel as that ? '

Rosy began to hum a tune shortly and defiantly.

After a little I said :

'Lady, it seemeth unto mine uncultured ear that
thou warblest the melody of which men say the vene-
rable vaccine one rendered up the ghost. Now——'

'You're very *cruel* !' she suddenly sobbed. 'And I
*hate* you. *Why* do you go on at me like that? . . .
(The rest inarticulate.)

'God bless our souls !' cried I, standing still, 'if——'
And I proceeded in a brotherly way to comfort her.
And so at last got her in a rather limp state to No. 3,
where we said a final good-night after I had promised
to write and tell her when I could get time to go for
another walk.

If it had not been for my recalling friend Horace to
the effect that 'Dulce est desipere in loco,' I should
have been in a most disconsolate humour going home.
As it was, I could not help laughing at the memory of
my fantastic squabble.

The next entry in the Journal is a record of my
having seen, or thought I had seen, at a theatre the
girl of the nuts, her who struck me so on the night of
my interview with Colonel James. (She was playing a
second part in a 'realistic drama,' and not playing it
badly, it seemed to me.)

'I was with the Strachans in a box made for two
people to see comfortably in, and three others to be as
miserable as they disliked. I asked the Professor,
when we two went out for a stroll in the passages
during an entr' acte, if he had seen her before, and he
said that he had not.

'I should like to know her. She might marry me

perhaps, and then I should be properly wretched for the rest of my life,—if I didn't murder her or she me before the honeymoon was over. Well, the original expression holds all right, even then. I wouldn't much mind her murdering me, if I was only sure she'd be hanged afterwards. I have thoughts of proposing to Connie. She is a sweet little cocotte, only wanting development. But it would be better fun to marry Isabel, and see what could be done in the way of ruffling her " grave sweetness " a little.—I'll stop here.'

My feeling towards the book was, at the end, nothing short of positive loathing. Strachan, I think, perceived this; for he did all he could to lighten my share of the work. And I accepted his doing so without remark. I remember his asking me one morning if I hadn't been a little out of sorts of late, and my answering that my bowels were not as they used to be, and that I feared I had trichinosis. I don't know what he thought of my answer. He said nothing.

Late on in June is the next entry in the Journal.

'*Last night.—*

'Something making me come back quickly from the corner of the street, I found that she had not opened the door with her key yet; or even taken the key out of her pocket; but was standing watching me seriously. I took off my hat, and stepped close to her with it in my hand. The moon was shining clear.

'Neither of us spoke. We looked into one another's eyes.

'At last:

'"What made you such a serious Rosebud to-night?' I said.

'She sighed softly:

'". . . I don't *know*. . . ."

'"Good-night, Rosy."

'"Good-night."

'"*Good-night?*" turning, I repeated to myself, and put on my hat, and strode away. . . .

'Round the corner, I drew a breath of relief.—*That was temptation.*

'*I will not see that child again.*'

## IV

### I

It was four days after this, a Wednesday as I see, that
I awoke at about half-past eight in the morning and
found that there was a letter with my cup of tea.
After a while I summoned up sufficient energy to pull the
letter somehow from the table on to the bed, and then
must have fallen off into a dose again; for I remember
that the writing of the envelope that must have been
just under my half-closed eyes, was wound with some
other writing in and out of a fantastic sort of a dream-
space from which I suddenly started, with the recogni-
tion that the letter was *Rayne's.*

With all my soul in my eyes, I stared at it. A large
white glaring envelope with

'B. Leicester, Esq.,
    '*Glastonbury School, Glastonbury.*'

in Rayne's hand, in 'the middle, the last three words
lined through, and below in a thin scrawly hand:

'5, *Dunraven Place,*
    '*Piccadilly, London.*'

These details realised, I took the envelope; ripped
it up at the back; produced the thick white folded
double sheet inside, and opened it. This is something
like what I read:

'22 Balmoral Street, W.
'My dear Bertram,—We are in London for a short time
—three or four weeks, before going north to spend the
summer at Kirkory, my husband's family seat, or I should
say home. I have wondered a little at hearing nothing from
you. You are, at the least, two letters in my debt. I do

not even know where you are, and address this at random. I need not say, dear Bertram, how pleased I should be to see you again ; but I am afraid you have quite forgotten me. Why, it is—how long is it, since you last wrote to me? I last heard from you at Montenotte in the autumn of—! How long ago is that? You ought to be ashamed to think ! But here is time and space and patience all exhausted. I must end, as usual, in a hurry. Write to me and tell me what you are doing. You know that, if for no other reason than because you were loved by what I loved best in the world, you are and always must be dear to me: and so let me write myself down as being what, I trust, I always shall be,—Your friend, .            RAYNE GWATKIN.

I lay still for a time and thought about what I had read, and then re-read it, and thought of the past that concerned all this strange present, and of my whole life. And so at last I got up and went to my small polished-oak box (a small box in which I kept certain things that were, or had once seemed, precious to me), and, having opened it, found a letter, which began :

'MY DEAR BERTRAM,—' It is a wet and tempestuous afternoon, and therefore I consider it a fitting occasion to answer your long and with difficulty decipherable epistle.'

Through this letter I glanced, till I came to words that stopped my glancing and steadied it :

'. . . Rather a tempest going on outside, and so I am going to try to dodge my dear old daddy and Sir James, and get out my boat and enjoy it.—By-the-by, I had forgotten to tell you that an old friend of ours, Sir James Gwatkin, has been staying with us this last week. He is a most amusing mondain en villégiature, with a marvellous French and Italian accent, and altogether a very amusing companion to the father, and myself at times. He knows what seems to me a great deal about . . .'

And I folded up the letter and put it into the box, and relocked the box, went back to bed ; and lay thinking for another half-hour, when I got up and dressed.

At breakfast I reconsidered the matter :

The news amounted to this : Rayne had married the

amusing mondain en villégiature, and was here, in
London, for a short time—three weeks or so, before
going north to spend the summer at Kirkory, her
husband's family seat or home.   Where was Mr. Cholmeley?
   I started:
   '*Dead!*'
   'That could not be. . . . And yet——' I took
out her letter and considered it. '"You know that—
if for no other reason than because you *were loved* by
what I *loved* best——" (Nay, that may be nothing:
or only mean that she *loves* her husband best.   And
there is no black edge on this white sheet.) "by what
I loved best in the world,—you are and always must
be dear to me: and so let me write myself down as
being, etc., etc."'
   All at once I exclaimed:
   '*She oughtn't to have married that man!*'
   '. . . *Why?*' asked the faint voice of the air and the
room.
   I answered to myself: '*I wish she hadn't.*'
   '. . . *Why?*' said the same faint voice.
   I considered a few moments, and then rose, a little
viciously.   Some of the viciousness was expended in the
sharp putting of my chair directly in front of my plate:
the rest in my casting myself into the arm-chair in the
window, my hands at my mouth, scraping my lower lip
with my upper teeth.
   Then:
   'What is the matter with me?' I said to myself;
and, after a pause: 'I don't know!   Is there anything,
then, in the whole world would make me happy?   I
don't know.   I don't think so.   I'm just weary of it
all!   What of that new soul's life of mine, produced
before Starkie, and believed in then?   What have I
done?   What shall I do?   What do I believe in?
What do I doubt about?—Doubt about?   *Everything;
even doubt!*'—I let my thoughts rest for a moment.
   Then once more:
   'If I only *knew* something!   If I only *loved* something!   Oh, is there not a woman in the whole wide
world who would take me as I am, and help me to be

what I want to be? A *woman*—to save *me*? Oh, God, God, God, God, I would I had never been born!—Nay, is it not strange that, in an hour of weakness like this, the only thing I cry out to for help is what I have always thought I despised as being itself incarnate weakness—*woman*! I don't know what 's the matter with me. I'm not myself. Virtue is gone out of me. This must be a passing humour. I shall be strong again, as I used to be. *Or was it that I did not know my weakness?* . . . I don't know!' A complete sense of loneliness and purposelessness seemed suddenly to grow like a great grey-cut chasm in me. I could struggle no more to find out what was the matter with me. I turned and let the current take me where it would.

From that depth of weariness I raised myself a little to take up a book off the table beside me and read it. It was no good staying stretched on the bottom of that dark submarinity in that way. Better kill myself at once; and that most certainly I would not do. . . . Why not? I was *afraid* of death? I didn't know. I had not thought about it. I would not think about it. A piano-organ was playing outside.

I looked out into the sunshiny day; for some little of the sunshine had entered me even then. I would go out for a walk. Nay, I would go and see where Rayne lived. Why not?

Away I went, and out for my walk—out and away to beautiful summer Hampstead, fresh and green from the late showers, in the soft lights of the early day. I did not think much of Rayne. I do not remember what I thought of: probably of hundreds of unconnected things, passing in a fairy-procession in the yellow-gold light before my eyes. I wandered about happily till about one o'clock, when hunger made itself perceptible, and I went off in the pursuit of bread and fruit and milk. Followed a Pythagorean feast on the grass, with delightful half-dreams as in the old time; till it occurred to me to return home and read. Accordingly, after a little trifling with resolution in the shape of dawdling about in hollows, looking at a small stream's meandering water, or the serried grasses and the earth, I fairly set off.

After a little, it occurred to me again to go and take a look at Rayne's house.  So I asked the next policeman I saw where Balmoral Street was, and learnt that that it was on this side of the Park, and, more particularly, close by Lancaster Gate, for which I had better ask.  That was all I wanted at present.  I set off again, and was in Maida Vale before I was aware of it.  I had no idea of going to see Rayne to-day : I only wished to look at the house.

I went on seriously enough, and began to think about Rayne—Where she was now and what she was doing?—somehow as if I had wondered thus about some other woman some time and somewhere; till a faint far-away tremulousness entered into me and was perceived.

I came sharply round an area-railed corner, and beheld . . . a low carriage, two horses, two footmen, the pillars of an exit into the street, a lady just out of the open door—passing to the top step—descending—*Rayne!*  I stood still.

Some one followed.  Rayne was on the pavement, making for the low carriage door, now held open.  She stopped a moment, half turned.  And the some one following was in her view and mine.  It was the mondain en villégiature : I knew him at once.  But Rayne's face was all to me ; and yet I could not see it properly.  Then our eyes met.

Somehow or other I was moving to her with my hat in my hand, and she had said : ' Bertram ! ' and I had stood still again.

Her face seemed to me, as it were worn, but filled with the light of steadfastness, and her eyes were quiet and deep.  I had seen, not her face, but her face's form, and, as it were the light of it, before, and this memory was on me now almost as in the dim low distance.  I cannot say what either she said, or he or I for a little ; not that I was bewildered by their presence and its thoughts within me, but that this memory of the likeness to the light of her face kept me from them.

At last I had shaken hands with the mondain, and she was sitting in the carriage and we two, standing by the low opened carriage door, were talking together.

'It was, indeed, a surprise to see you in London,'
she was saying, 'I thought you were . . . In fact I
did not know what to think, for you did not answer
either of the letters I sent to you——'

'Letters?' I said. 'I received no letter from you,
excepting this morning, since November—two years ago.'

'I am a witness to the writing of at least two,' said
he, looking at me with a little smile round the corners
of his mouth.

'Then you did not know—' she said, 'And I had
wondered why you had not written to me. . .'

'That Mr. Cholmeley was dead—' I said softly,
perceiving that her dress was of black. '. . . I feared
so this morning.' What sorrow was in me for her was
given in the words here.

'And where have you been all this while?' she said,
looking up,—'if I may ask?'

I bowed my head.

'I left Glastonbury last February. I was in London
for a little, and then in Paris for a little, and then in
London again till now.'

'Perhaps,' he said, 'Mr. Leicester would go with
you? You must have a great deal to say to one another
after so long and so silent a separation?' I saw, or
thought I saw, that she did not desire that I should go
with her. Half-hesitation of hers was not enough to
entice me. I said:

'I am afraid that, even if Lady Gwatkin should be
so kind as to think of allowing me to inflict my company upon her, I should be unable to do so.' There
was a surprise in this for him, perhaps for her: pleasure
for me to find my nerves my own, and under the govern-
ment of a Jupiter will in a serene heaven that might
have seemed Olympus, if it hadn't seemed like a
monkey-house on its good behaviour. She with some
few gentle low sentences, bowed to or accepted my
words' meaning, and then it was time for her to be
going, and I drawing back with an apology to Sir James
for being in the way.

Then came preliminaries of movement followed by
movement, and her (and his) expressions of wish to see
me again soon, and she (with him) had passed away,

while I stood bareheaded, watching her as she sat, till the corner was rounded, and she was gone, and I alone with the streets and houses and all the dismal day-time.

The next morning I found a note from her, asking me to dine with them on Monday. I smiled, and, when I had had breakfast, wrote an answering note of acceptance. Then Strachan came in, and had a short talk with me. He had his doubts about the financial success of the Book, considering that I wished to have illustrations. I was in an absent humour, and simply echoed his remark—Yes, I wished it to have illustrations, maps, and everything of that sort.

'Of course,' said he, 'we have abundance of material; but I am rather inclined to doubt Brooke's accuracy in these matters, and, in short . . .'

'Has he taken it?' asked I, 'Parker, I mean.'

'No;' he said, 'he hasn't taken it—yet; but . . . Well, well—we'll talk about that later on! What are you going to do with yourself this morning? A walk; what do you say? I'm just going to the Museum for half an hour or so, to look at some bones Davies has got hold of. Will you come?'

'I'm very sorry,' I said, 'but I do my work in the mornings. I find that if I go out then, it ends in my doing no work at all.'

We made talk of this sort while he was nearing the door and at last had it a little open, when:

'Did you ever,' I said, 'hear of a man called Gwatkin? Sir James Gwatkin, a knight or a baronet, I don't know which.'

'Hum,' he said, Gwatkin? Gwatkin? I know the name somehow.—Oh yes, I know him! I met him down at Oxford at dinner at a don's—two years ago! One of the Culture people. He has written a book about Michelangelo. I remember him quite well now. The next day I stumbled upon him with Sir Horace Gildea——'

'Horace Gildea?' said I, 'I was at school with him. Do you know him?'

The Professor grimaced:

'Yes, a little. He did me the honour of seducing one of my maids.'

I laughed.   The Professor proceeded :
' They 're an odd lot, those Culture fellows.   I don't
believe in them myself.   A—' (turning his eyes to mine)
' I hope they 're not friends of yours, either of these
two ?   If so, of course I——'
  ' Nay,' said I, ' they 're no friends of mine!   I only
wanted to know if you could tell me anything about
Gwatkin—what books he 'd written, and that sort of
thing.   I happen to be dining at his house on Monday,
and one likes to know something about one's host's
particular line of thought, if he happens to have one.'
  ' Ah yes, just so, yes,' said the Professor, turning his
eyes to and then away from mine.   And on that we
parted.
  I came back from the closed hall-door into the library,
and went to the window and stood looking out on the
sunny day.   A feeling of disgust at work rose in me.
I sighed as I took down ' Antigone,' the Greek play I
was then reading, and lexicon and translation, and
bundled myself into the easy chair.   Folly ! and I knew
it.   None the less I intended proving it once more.
  I had last time stopped just before a Chorus.   I began
on the Chorus now.   Such a delightfully corrupt Chorus;
and here (in two nice close-printed note columns) was
what Hermann thought about the first lines, and then
what somebody else thought, and then what the present
Editor thought, damn him !   Finally I gave it up in
disgust : got myself out of the easy chair and the books
into it ; and stood looking disconsolately out of the
window.   Then the idea of taking a steamer down the
fresh breezy river came to me—to Greenwich, and go
into the Park, or, first, to see the Painted Chamber, and
then for a walk over the Heath to look at the old school
day places.   Why not ?
  I went.   It was a fair sweet morning on the river,
somehow as I suppose my Italy to be, with the air so
pure, like wine that had no fieriness in it.   I got out
at Greenwich : I saw the Painted Chamber again, my
heart making its flutter felt as I passed along that
coloured gallery where I had moved and dreamed in
the dim sun-shot air of my boyhood.—Ah, here was
Nelson, and here !   And here the sacred relics of him !

How long, how long ago it was since I stood looking at
that pallid body going with its heroic message of
'*England expects every man to do his duty*' up to . . .
Where ?   Somewhere where the pallid bodies of heroes,
who have fought the fight and done that duty well, are
taken by soft hands and laid in the quiet of the Eternal
Fields.—And how I used to think that, in some simple
way, although it seemed so vague and unreal, that body
was *my* body and that duty well done was *my* duty, and
this small child here, with eyes half-brimmed with tears,
so saw the final requiem of its own manhood, the seal of
death with which it had sealed life, the fight well fought,
the duty well done, and the pallid body taken by soft
hands and laid in the quiet of the Eternal Fields.——
'*It is all changed now !*'

I turned from it with the lump of tears in my throat
and went out into the air, and away.   And I thought
in this wise : that the dreams of boyhood are for boyhood and are sweet, while the sights of manhood are for
manhood and are bitter : and, that it is given to many
to desire the well-fought fight and the well-done duty
and the tender progress to the quiet of the Eternal
Fields, but that few, the dwindling sacred few, achieve
to it : and that it is very hard to learn this simple
lesson, that I, this me, this only real *existence* that I
know in Space and Time and Life, is one of the many.

As I slowly climbed up the hill, I noted the old tree
in the middle of the path, against which I, dizzy and
faint from the pernicious tobacco smoke inhaled in the
shade of a gnarly oak while the small gentle deer fed
round me, leant full of the nausea of this wretchedness,
resolute never to incur it again !   Then I came in sight
of the haunted house, darksome abode of awe and
wonder.   Then there was the field on the brow of
which I had lain with Wallace, playing some game at
'chuck' with clasp-knives, looking at times out over the
dark, silver-twining Thames, and dusky, far-stretching
London ; till one unlucky throw of his spiked my hand
(here is the scar on my right thumb still), and how I
insisted that there was *not* the end of chuck for  the
day !

It is all changed now, the field in which we played

that game or, lying along the grass, talked as we ate
sugared compounds or the satisfying parkin.  Even the
school is changed.  The brass-plate is gone from the
gate.  The house is freshly painted and enlarged, but
empty.  I see the top of the cherry-tree over the wall.

I turned from it and went down the little lane,
passing many remembered spots and things, and down
the hill and to the small boat pier.  And as I stood I
began to think of my future.  There was something of
Capua in my present case : not so much bodily, as
spiritual, Capua, and yet I knew quite well that at the
best it was not in either case a campaigning ground.
It was time I took some steps towards the great
object of supporting myself.  *Time ?* more than time !
Why had I not thought of it before?  This money of
Brooke's—it was not mine.  I had said that I would
not take it : I had said that I could not devote myself
to the Cause.  Oh Jupiter and the other immortals, I
should think not ! . . . And yet, why such a decided
*not?*  Supposing I *did* devote myself?  Well? . . .
No, it would not do.  I don't care about it.  No: I
won't do that.  No !  I couldn't take and keep the
money. . . .  God knows it's a poor earth enough, this
earth ; and where is belief in fire and brimstone being
my reward for doing this—or any thing?  But that's
nothing.  There is the tribunal of my soul—that ideal
of myself, by which I measure the actual of myself,
and do not care to find too great a difference between
them.

'And yet,' I thought, standing up at the bow of the
boat and looking across the river, 'I could wish that I
was sleeping the sleep of death, under the earth—at
rest !'

-------

## II

WHEN I awoke on Monday morning it was into a state
of dreaminess, the shadowy realm that is between the
night's dreams and the day's.  Rayne moved in it,
with Claire, and myself; but all so dim and bodiless
that they could not be called by names whose counter-
parts were realities.  They were not of the night's

dreams : they were not of the day's, but emanations.
Outside this shadowy realm there was some other
emanation, some child's, that was more of the earth
than ours that were of this middle place, and it would
have entered therein, but could not.   And if this was
a distress to anyone, I could not tell, not even if it
was to myself.—The end was that a start shot up
through me, and I awoke fully.   The green blinds
covered the two large windows opposite my bed.   A
little light came in through them and made a submarine atmosphere in the room.   This I had known
before.   I sat up : then raised myself, till I could see
myself in the large dressing-table mirror between the
two green-blind-covered windows.   That made me
smile.

After lunch I went out for a walk.

The knowledge that whatever humour I went out
in was sure to be different from the humour in which
I returned, held to me a momentary trouble now.   For
I was happy enough with the life of the morning, the
mild sunny air and soft heaven, to wish for no better
state in which to face the ordeal of to-night.   'Ordeal ?
Ay; the faint tremor that comes to me at the thought
is surely enough to tell me that to-night *will* be an
ordeal.   *Ordeal ?*   No : what ordeal can there be ? . . .
Of what am I thinking?   I do not know. . . . Ay,
that is the truth: "I do not know."   And yet the
sense of the unknown does not. . . . What ?—Was
ever such confusion ?   No : not confusion.   What
then ?   I don't know.   It's folly trying to be subtle.'
I gave it up.

That day was a day apart.   A day apart is a day in
which the past is pallid : the present pallid : the
future a mist into which the earth-floor goes, not even
unknown : a day of feelings about feelings, of dreams
about dreams.

I came in about five.   I had seen many things,
known nothing.   I felt and realised that I was hungry.
I went to the top of the kitchen-stairs and called to
Mrs. Herbert, asking if I could have some soup and
rice ?   She agreed.   I went into the study again, and
stood in the window, and looked out.

I finished the soup and the rice.

Dinner was at seven. I had not the intention of eating a dinner then. That was why I had eaten the soup and the rice. It was almost six now by the mantelpiece clock. I got up and rang. Then : ' But Mrs. Herbert,' I thought, 'tells me she has varicose veins.'—So off I went down the kitchen-stairs, and got a can of hot water for myself.

Then I came up again and began slowly to mount the hall-staircase.

As my heavy foot struck the soft carpet, and one or two of the rods sounded, I suddenly recalled my going up the staircase that last night of ours in London. After a few steps, I stopped and looked over the broad banister down upon the dark shiny table where my bed-candle was, and where two had used to be then. I went on again : the thought had occurred to me before this. Now, I have always supposed that there would be something of . . . of something or other, in living in a house, and alone too, where you had lived with some one that is dead. The sharp sound that struck your hearing would startle you? The lonely depth of the darkness, or the shadowiness, or the gloom would contain its spectre? I cannot say. Death is so dim a thing, if it is anything at all, to me. What do you mean by death? *You* are not dead. *I* am not dead. *Who* is dead?—And with the thought that this was rather ridiculous, I came into my bedroom with the hot-water can. The gas was low.

I put down the can on the washing-stand, and went and turned up the gas. The room was all light. I took off my coat and threw it on to the bed.

I washed slowly, thinking. There was a little of the tremulousness in me somewhere. I felt it for a moment vaguely. But went on thinking and forgot it. I put on, first one, and then the other dress-boot, with the small steel shoe-horn, and tied their laces tight. Then changed my trousers, and brushed my hair before the mirror. Then put on my white shirt, and found and fastened the studs, and my collar to the top stud. As I was looking for the glass-topped box that held the white ties, I thought the gas seemed burning low,

and looked up at it. It was, confound it! I found
the white tie-box in the shadow of the curtain, and
took out a tie, and began to tie it. My fingers confused. At that instant everything in me contracted.
I stared into the mirror. *Brooke was looking over my
right shoulder.*

My body was all a creeping thrill. I jerked round
like one half-mad, with my fist tightly clenched, in
some way saying:

'*Devil!*'

I would have beaten his pale, cold, corpse's face with
my hard fist. There was not anything—except (I saw)
the shadow of the bed-top on the upper wall-paper.

I paced up and down the room, looking to right and
left.

'Assuredly,' I said aloud in an observer's way, 'I will
never believe in ghosts. It is far too easy to see one.'

In a little I came back and finished my hanging tie.
I had been startled. There was no mistake about that.
If I had really believed that I should have seen him,
I pondered, then I *should* have seen him. And yet I
desired to strike him. And yet I did not believe in
him, somehow.

So, having turned down the gas, I came to the
staircase-head and began to descend. A certain something, not too far from fear, prompted the idea of a
hand reaching on to me from behind. I desired to turn
and look. My will overcame my desire. I descended
slowly, step after step, in an actor's way rather. My
heel sounded on the tesselated floor of the hall. My
eye observed of the big clock that it was a quarter to
seven. I had beaten that something not too far from
fear. I had not looked either round or behind.

I went to the coat-rack; took down my theatre-
coat; felt my latch-key in my right pocket, and went
to the door. Opened it: went out, and drew it to
with a low clang. Yes, I left certain supersensual
things behind in the house—with Mrs. Herbert and
the varicose veins!

I laughed as I drew on my coat; shot open the
gibus, and put it on my head. I had been startled.
There was no mistake about that. But I was wide

awake now, surely.  And I was going to dine at Sir
James Gwatkin's, with Rayne.  I stood on the pave-
ment-edge (in Piccadilly now) and called out:

'Hansom !'

I should be there, with him, with *her* in ten minutes
—in all human probability.

The hansom came up, and I got in, and gave the
address—22 Balmoral Street—through the opened
trap to the man.  We set off quickly, the horse, a
small beast, trotting.  When we had gone a little way,
I knocked up at the trap, two or three times before
the man opened it, the horse's speed slackening.

'Go through the Park,' I said, 'through the Park !'

He shut down the trap, and the horse's speed
quickened again.  The evening was light and cool, the
sun hid behind thick horizon clouds.  We turned through
the gates into the Park.  I bent forward a little, looking
at the carriages and people that we passed.

Then we swept by the Marble Arch into Oxford
Street and by the mouth of the Edgware Road, up
which, some way up which by a by-way to the left,
lay in a small street, Maitland Street, a small house,
No. 3.  She would not be in yet.  She would be still
at her work, sitting sewing probably.  Should I ever
see her again ?  No, best not.  Our paths of life went
on in all but opposite directions.  Poor child!  'Alone
in the world, as if nobody else belonged to her.'  *In
a hundred years, perhaps fifty, perhaps less, it would all
be as if it had never been !*

We drew up sharply.  I looked out.  It was the
house all right.  I threw open the flaps, and jumped
on to the pavement, and went back and paid the man.
Then ascended the steps, and knocked and rang as
the little brass plate bade ; and waited.  A footman
opened the door and ushered me in.  Sir James was
coming along the passage below the stairs, and saw
me.  He at once advanced, saying cordially :

'Ah, Mr. Leicester, how do you do ?'

We went upstairs together slowly, I just a step
behind him : then through a tall doorway with a deep-
red velvet hanging, and along a room that was like a
passage ; and then he had opened a door and we were

together in the soft light of the drawing-room, he just
a step behind me.

I at once saw Rayne and some other woman, a
young woman, seated close together under the pink-
shaded candles, but my look was for Rayne's face, not
for her companion's. How beautiful it was! How
steadfast, and how sweet! And I thought that where
I had before seen, as it were, the light of her face's
form was in the sad wistful face of a child whose body
had been sold to an evil task-master—*Claire!* And,
at the thought, something of tearfulness rose in my
heart and gathered to my eyes; for that sad wistful
child's face had grown so bright for me and mine so
bright for her, and then we had been parted by the
task-master, who was jealous of the soul of the body
that he had bought, and I had never seen her again.

'Rayne,' I thought, 'would to God or Fate or Chance
or what it may be, that I had not found that light on
*your* face too! . . . Your hand is soft.'

We had been speaking to one another with low
tones and movements, and now I was turned from
Rayne, bowing to this young woman her companion,
whose name, his courteous voice had said, was Cholmeley too. And as I looked at her seated there before
and below me, I smiled.

'It is strange,' said I, sinking with the smile into a
chair by her, between her and Rayne, but nearer to
her, 'It is strange how much men and women have in
common.—I mean,' I said, leaning on the elbow next
her, and looking at her, 'how much we have in
common with one another.'

'Yes?' she said, elevating her brows a little, being
a little surprised, I supposed, and wondering what sort
of strange masculinity she had come across.

'I mean,' I said, with narrowing eyes, 'that—
perhaps no one can live a life of his own. Suppose a
man or a woman give themselves up to (say) love of
money, as common a ruling-passion as any other, then
that man or that woman will notice, if they only know
how to, that their love of money generates, as it were,
a subtle odour in their souls, and they will recognise
that subtle odour in the souls of others who have

given themselves up to the same dominion. *La destinée est une !* '

' I do not see *how* destiny is one,' said the young woman.

' Here,' said I, ' is the answer for you in eternal words :

' " We are what sun and winds and waters make us." '

' I do not see yet,' she said.

' We are all what we are made.   Some of us are made by the sun ; and some by the winds ; and some by the waters ; and some by them all.   And that is how, is it not ? we have so much in common with one another.'

' And you think,' said Rayne to me, with something of a smile, ' that the children of the sun recognise one another accordingly ? '

' I suppose I do,' I said, now a little off the direct scent, ' that is, I think that any given passion, as a rule, expresses itself in the same way in different people ; and so one is constantly being struck by resemblances between people, and wondering wherein these resemblances lie.   Am I not clear to you, Miss Cholmeley ? ' I asked.

' You are too subtle for me,' said the young woman, ' I am content to do my duty in that state of life—and the rest : and leave metaphysics to the choice spirits like you, and Sir James, and ' (turning her head) ' you, Rayne.'

But it seemed to me that this young woman did not, for some reason, care to have matter of this sort talked now, and had quietly taken steps to stop it.

We went down to dinner soon after, Rayne and I, and Sir James and Miss Cholmeley : we two so far ahead, that I could say to her, in an odd, unnatural way, that I did not know she had any relation . . . like Miss Cholmeley.

' Miss Cholmondeley is no relation of mine,' she said quietly, as we passed through the dining-room door, ' our names are spelt differently.'

And there the big, liveried dolls stood by.

' C-h-o-l-m-o-n-d——,' said I half to myself, the actor's sense growing in me, ' ah—I beg your pardon ! '

The actor's sense went on growing in me as we took
our places, and culminated in my high slightly-frowning
downward survey of my menu card: *Soup, Turbot and
Lobster Sauce, Quenelles.*—'Damnation!' I said under
my breath.    It was ludicrous!

I shivered: tightened my jaws, and in an instant
thought: 'What foolery is this? I . . . ' I might
have been sitting, as I sat in my place that prize-giving
day at Whittaker's, waiting for my turn, with my lips
rather dry, and every now and then shivering as if a
draught came upon me from an opened door.    But
Blake was *dead*.    And Brooke was *dead*.    And Mr.
Cholmeley was *dead*.—And I raised my eyes and beheld
this vision of fair youthfulness; with dark-gold hair
whose floating outskirts were sunny, and deep slow
eyes, and red lips ripe, and half-transparent teeth-tips,
and soft sweet whiteness of the rounded throat whose
thought was of the soft sweet white cool body.    And
all the while they talked, and ate from their plates,
and I talked and ate from my plate, and the big swift
quiet liveried dolls moved hither and thither and bent,
ministering to us.

'You do not take wine?' he was saying.

'Nay,' I was answering, 'I love wine; wine that is
yellow and foaming!'    I could not, or would not, or
did not see any face but his, bending with a mask's
upward smile to me.

'But you refused to have any champagne just now?'

'My dear Rayne!' she was saying, the beautiful,
voluptuous young woman was saying (Corisande is
her name.    It sounds like a cleft pomegranate), 'but
you really cannot mean . . .'

'I did not notice it,' I said, 'I will have some, if you
please.'

And then from a gold-papered bottle-mouth out
came the clear stream into the large round low glass,
all foaming, but yellow as I lifted it up and drank it.
I sat there, filled with the actor's sense, smiling, and
bending and smiling, and smiling and bending and
smiling and talking, and, in my deeper heart, in a sort
of way, defied this devilry.    I knew what they were
saying, I knew what I was saying, although I have for-

gotten it now.  Once, or twice, or three, or four times,
I could have laughed outright at all this ; but restrained
myself with the feeling that I did well to restrain
myself.  I drank more champagne, and then fell into
a somewhat dreamy state.

They were talking of French literature ; a string of
names and words scarcely comprehended by me, but
there was light laughter in the yellowy air and restrained sadness.  There was no one in the room now
but we.  The footmen had all gone.  I was slowly
twirling my champagne glass round, with my eyes on
it : the light laughter was foaming in the yellowy air,
and the sadness almost withdrawn.

Suddenly she, Rayne, rose.  I started up.  Corisande
rose.  Then they were moving round the table, and I
was with my backward hand on the door-handle, and
my face towards her.  I had opened the door.  She
had passed out, my lovely Rayne !  The young woman
was by me, Corisande, the cleft pomegranate, the
sweet soft harlot body.  I crushed my right hand on
the smooth hardness in it.  I could have gripped that
soft white throat just below the rounded half-shadow of
the apple and throttled her, and, as I cast down the
breathless limp body, softer but less sweet, the harlot
body, been glad with a quiet half-fierce gladness.  I
closed the door softly upon her, and came back to my
place.  Sir James was looking at something just before
and below his eyes, with the little smile round the
corners of his mouth.  I all but loved him, for having
a swift thought of ' *Arise begone,*' I had another of one
sitting in a summer parlour, with *the fat closing upon the
blade.*  I too had a little smile round the corners of
the mouth.

We talked in a quiet orderly way for a little ; and
then went upstairs together.

Rayne was seated in her old place on the sofa,
looking half-absently before her, Miss Cholmondeley
lying back in the easy chair in which I had sat.  She
stopped speaking as we came in ; looked up at us, or
at Sir James, and smiled slightly.

We talked in low half-nonchalant tones.  The night
breeze bulged in the window-curtain behind Rayne

L

and the sofa with a slight rustle. There seemed something of hushed, but withal dreamy in the air : perhaps the quiet after the sunny wind-tempest of dinner-time.

Then Sir James spoke, his words sounding somewhat as a return to one's past humanity.

'I have as good as promised Mr. Leicester, Corisande,' he said, 'that you would give us Retsky's setting of Vivian's " Lullaby." I hope I did not take too much upon myself ? '

She raised her eyebrows a little and the corners of her mouth, as she answered :

'But you forget that I only sang it to you the night before last. Rayne, I am sure, must be quite tired of the very name of Vivian by this time.'

'No,' she said, 'his story is too sad for one to be so soon tired of hearing his name. I should like to hear the Lullaby again.'

'Vivian,' said Sir James, now addressing me, 'was an old school-fellow of mine, and I might add—friend.'

I asked about Vivian. Sir James gave particulars of him :

'He ran away from Eton and came up to London, with the idea of achieving fame and fortune with his poetry. It is needless to say that he achieved neither. His parents were poor and obstinate,—and he, he had the pride of Milton's Satan. He died—starved, rather than ask help from anyone. A volume of his poems has just been published : this is *it*. You were reading it, Rayne ? '

'Yes,' she said ; 'I was reading it this morning.'

'How old was he ? ' I asked.

'A mere boy,' he said, 'eighteen or nineteen. Poor fellow ! There is nothing really remarkable in any of his poems, as poems. Their chief interest lies in the fact of their having been written by one so young.'

I still stood thinking.—'*Poor* fellow ! Nay, but I account him rich ; for the strife of living and the terror of dying are for him both past and over now, and he is at rest.'

Miss Cholmondeley had passed into the other half of the drawing-room through the hanging lace-curtains, to where Sir James was standing fingering the music.

Here was I with my head thrown down like a medita-
tive cow.   I made a few steps towards Rayne, and
standing before her, with my head half-bent, said
something or other purposeless about the Lullaby and
Vivian.  She answered with something of the same sort.
I asked if she liked Retsky's music?  She said she
did not much; but she was afraid she didn't altogether
appreciate it.   I said that Sir James had been talking
about him to me, saying he was the subtlest of modern
composers.   Doubtless he had written many pieces
that were very 'precious,' if not 'entirely' so?  She
took no heed of my smile, but said that doubtless that
was the reason (the subtleness was the reason) that she
did not appreciate him.   She only cared for simple
music, and admitted that most classical music wearied
her.   But this Lullaby was not like any other music of
Retsky's that she had heard.   It was simple, and soft
and sweet.—I was about to say that two of these were
rather necessary qualities in a lullaby, especially if the
baby was teething, when a flow of soft low notes came
and made me think better of it.   Certainly Miss
Cholmondeley knew how to play.

I listened attentively.   The soft low notes flowed
on, flowed on, flowed on, but into their softness was
gradually growing some other sound: more like an
invasion of still dim water by rolling slaty-coloured
volumes than anything else I could then think of.   I
was the song's now: my whole soul filled with it.   A
softer, lower place was heard: softer, far away: lower,
closer to the front of the picture that was in me, the
place in which I felt was a presence, two presences.
They were sleeping; or they were lying together in
rest.   Then one of them roused—himself, for it was a
man, or a boy with something of a man's soul: roused
himself, and his voice began, at first with unrecognisable
words rolling over the low slaty glassiness of the
water, and rolling about, till that first melody of soft
low flowing notes, all but filled with the rolling
volumes, was hidden away.   And another voice, a
woman's, or a girl's with something of a woman's soul,
answered softly and sweetly.   And the other voice
answered softly and deeply, with the depth of passion.

And the rolling slaty-coloured volumes of his first unrecognisable words, which had filled the space between this softer lower place and that first mingled melody, had filled it into peacefulness, were growing disturbed: the volumed column of that first mingled melody was passing down over the slaty glassiness towards this lower place. The voices rose in an unspeakable harmony together, but some of it was losing itself in the slaty-coloured rolling volumes that came over the glassiness of the water of the now back-confused picture, and at last, half-dying, half-fading away, left the whole picture lost in the coloured rolling volumes: from which now came short, sharp notes, like the cracklings of connected and disconnected electric lines: crackle: crackle: crackle. And then the whole thing was whelmed in a full slaty silent flood.

I awoke.

'You remember,' Sir James's voice was saying, 'with what thought Keats closed his sweet, short nightingale's song? that wish to the bright star of steadfastness. There is just the difference between that death-song of Vivian's and this of Keats' that there was between Hylas and Narcissus.'

'Perhaps,' said Miss Cholmondeley, by him with the music in her hand, and looking at it, 'the difference was between their deaths rather than their songs. Do you think *Vivian* would have said: "*Lift me up—I am dying—I shall die easy.*" I don't.'

'No,' said Sir James, 'he would not. He probably would have died in trying to lift *himself* up, as Emily Brontë did. But I was not prepared to have my words pressed home. I only meant to notice the two death-songs as being characteristic of the two singers: the likeness and the difference. Vivian's is a child's dream of a sensuous death, Keats' a man's. Of course, any further comparison than the superficial thoughts suggested by the two death-songs would be ludicrous.'

'Would it?' asked Miss Cholmondeley, looking up, 'personally, I prefer Vivian's.'

I suddenly thought she was teasing him. I thought

he was mocking Rayne and mocking me; so that that she-devil was as the laughter inside the laughter, the aerial merriment that came from Comus under the low horizon clouds. Her song had bewitched me. I had been positively arrayed against Rayne a moment ago. I was bewildered.

I watched Sir James and Miss Cholmondeley cross into the piano-room again, talking about Retsky's conception of the Lullaby. I looked at Rayne. I sat down in the chair I had sat in before going down to dinner. The sensations of being in the chair unsettled my bewilderment. I spoke, scarcely expecting to hear my voice's sounds.

'That was a wonderful song, the Lullaby.'

'Yes,' said Rayne, looking at me.

Her look shot through me. I scarcely realised what it meant: I only felt it,—felt it, it seemed to me, in every part of my body and my soul. A mass of ideas rushed into my mind. My eyes flashed.

We spoke some words together. I do not know what I said. I do not think she knew what she said. Surely some feeling was in her, as it was in me? There was a sense of mystery in this half-sympathy of ours. I went on speaking to her, not knowing what I said (We were in a low soft melody that rose and fell, and rose and fell. *We were alone.*), and not knowing what she said, or what she thought; but she knew, not what I said, but what I thought. My thoughts grew more distinct:

'Rayne, Rayne, I will not leave you! I will rend you from him. He shall not have you. Let him have his soft-bodied harlot there. You are the queen of my soul.'

I knew that they were together in the next room, and that she was playing that soft melody that rose and fell and rose and fell. *We were alone.* There was something of the villain and his chance in my heart.— I looked at her. Ay, she was dazed, a little dazed; not altogether. But how could I get her away? *Get her away?* I clenched my teeth. Take her by the hand, lead her out, away! away! away!

'Rayne!' I said, 'Rayne! Listen to me. It is the

night of our lives, this. It is the night of all eternity
for us. Come! quickly!' (She was looking at me
with dilated, almost sightless eyes, opened breathless
mouth, beatless heart. I did not know where we
were—in heaven, in hell, in the earth, with sea around
us, in life, in death, in eternity.)

'Are you ill, Bertram?' she said. 'What is the
matter?' I half threw myself back in the chair with
something that partook of smile and laugh and was
neither smile nor laugh. She knew nothing! A
phantasy! A pure phantasy!

Then:

'Nothing is the matter with me,' I said, 'now. I
suffer from my eyes occasionally.' I rose. 'Really, I
am afraid I must be saying good-night,' I said, 'I——'
I looked at her.

'Whither away so fast?' I thought; 'are you so
sure, oh wiseacre, that she knew, knows nothing? She
knew! She knows!' Then I thought: 'Shall I pass
it over in silence? Shall I say anything of sorrow for
it? No. I am *not* sorry for it!—*My dream? My
dream in Paris?* . . . "*I rose and crossed over the stone
bridge : came to behind the carriage and began climbing
over it from the back. The lady turned and, seeing me,
put out her brown-gloved hand to me ; and then, when I
would have caught and pressed it into my bosom, touched
my chest with her finger-tips, the carriage moved. . . ."*'

For a moment a superstitious feeling all but possessed
me. Then I cried to myself that, at this rate, I might
as well become a clairvoyant, or an augurer, or a fool.
—I looked at her again. (It was not more than four
seconds perhaps since I had looked at her before.)

I said :

'I did wrong. I ask pardon.'

I left her. I passed across the room and through
the door and down, and, as one in a day-dream does
the things that his body remembers but his soul forgets,
took hat and coat and passed out into the night.

I went on.

Then the thought came :

What, was it done? Was it really done? Was I not
in that room with them and was not this a dream?

No, I answered to myself, it was no dream.  I had left her. . . . *What did it mean?*  I had left her.  I had left her.  I had left her.  I had left her.  I had left her.—*Ay; I knew now!*  That woman was the woman of my heart and soul.  My life had been lived for her since the day I had first dreamt of the dear girl-comrade.  *I had left her.*  The cross-road of my heart's life and soul's was reached.—*I had left her!*

I stopped; then went on again.

'The malice of fate is infinite,' I said, ' It is too late!'

And everywhere was dim.

---

### III

EVERYWHERE was dim.  It seemed as if all the rigging of my soul's bark had turned to calcined semblances that fell, as calcined semblances fall, making no noise.  And then it seemed as if some semblance of myself wandered to and fro, and round about, in this strange dim place, and thought and thought, trying to regain its hue and presence of health, and could not.  Snatches of the music of that lifeful past came to me and grew into deeper colour, bringing hope of permanency—only to be lost again in this strange dim place of noiseless falling calcined semblances.

At last the great dim mass grew pale and receded : my own figure stood darker in the foreground.  I began to think.  I had vaguely felt in the earlier part of my walk that my body was a little weary : perhaps it was but the action of the mind on it; for, now that the mind was in almost healthy activity again, the body was in sympathy with it.  I went on with a springy step, and began whistling, turning my thought into the parallel though less distinct expression of music.

And I had some enjoyment in the fine clear night, its air and its star-sown heaven.  So at last I found myself in Trafalgar Square, where bells had been ringing and the air filled with an aerial swinging merriment; and the clear-soaring moon up above, and here and there stars.  And one particular star twinkling through a slanting downward bank of gauzed clouds.  Then I

was in that road that I knew so well, that road by
which I went to Hampstead. A little higher up on
the left hand side was the concrete pillar ; the memory
of which and its accompaniments made me smile, as,
now moving on, I glanced at it.

Then I stood looking in the Hampstead pool at in-
numerous small up-leaping crescents of moonlight, as
from a rain of moonlight only turning to colour as it
struck. Sadness came to and grew of me, sadness
almost of tears, thoughts of that past that was no more.

I turned and set off homewards. The walking in-
vigorated me.

By the time I had got to Dunraven Place, I was
almost happy. I let myself in, and entered the library
with an elastic step. The lamp was turned low, casting
a tender rose-tinted shadow into the air. My supper
was laid out, fruits and bread. The scene, colour and
scent of it all pleased me. The tender rose-tinted
shadowy light, the mellowed silver of the knives and
forks, the subdued colour of the rich-bound books and
costly ornaments around me. There were two letters
on my plate.

'Two letters ?' I thought, 'Who the devil should
write to *me* ? '

I lay back in the soft chair ; reached to some grapes
(I was a little hungry), and the plate with the letters
on it : put them on the table-cloth just under the
lamp, and, eating grapes, observed them.

'One blue, stiff, and with two stamps. A double
weight of nonsense probably. The other— . . . *Rosy.*
Yes, that's her handwriting. What does the child
want? I have not seen her for . . .' (I took up her
letter and looked closer at the address.) 'How long?
Three weeks? Well, up you go on to the table-cloth !
. . . Good! Scientific, quite ! Miss Rosebud can wait
a little . . . And now for you, my mystery of blue
paper double-stamped. Who the devil are you, and
what the devil do you want? . . . You rip up tena-
ciously. . . . An enclosure. *Two.* What's this ? A
cheque-book. And you, oh foreign-papered——'
A sudden suspense was in me before I knew of it. I
opened the foreign-papered letter of four sheets, and

looked at the end of it—'*Colonel James !*' Then I recognised the writing. I had the other letter open in a
moment, (from my mother, perhaps ! from my father !),
and had glanced at it. '*Dead !*' I glanced on :

'. . . Sunday night . . . sympathy . . . last thing
. . . spoke . . . name . . . reparation . . . heir . . .
in all something more than £1,000 . . . beg to enclose . . .'

I looked up.
' Great God,' I thought, ' what's this ? '
I read the letter : then re-read it, more slowly.
This is what struck me in it. Colonel James had died
on Saturday night : had left me his fortune, and a letter
—this letter enclosed, of the sending of which to me
was almost the last thing he had spoken.
I took up the foreign-papered letter from my knee
and began to skim it :
'. . . I have, after some thought, concluded that . . .
proper and seemly. . . . Your father and mother . . .
the regiment stationed . . . theatre in London . . .
against the advice of all . . . married. [Pause for a
moment.] . . . Quartered . . . Cork . . . unhappiness
owing to religious . . . I . . . and the attentions of a
. . . Captain Melvil . . . exchanged . . . Guards . . .
of whom I frequently warned . . . but in vain . . .
shortly ordered to Dungarvan and subsequently . . .
Guernsey. I regret to have . . . attentions continued,
and I was compelled to speak to your father . . .
neglected warning, and . . . next day . . . scene with
your mother, in which . . . common talk. I . . .
could do no more, and remained. . . . One night . . .
dining at mess with . . . walked home togeth . . .
and . . . silence in the house. She was gone. I could
not have imagined that anything could have made
your father, a man naturally of the most praiseworthy
self restraint, and rendered doubly so by his steadfast
relig . . . sat down and cried like a child. I felt that
I could not leave him in this condition, and accordingly,
after having done all I could to comfort him by religi
. . . so completely prostrated by the blow that I began

to fear lest . . . sofa; lay there with his face . . .
groaning. . . . From that time . . . strange personal
dislike to you . . . till at last . . . almost madness
. . . considering the state of his health . . . did not,
then, think it advisable . . . and as soon as you were
able to bear the . . . village in Derbyshire.  Most of
the rest you know already; for it has been your own
life, I mean your education at Mr. Whittaker's and
subsequently at Glastonbury with Dr. Craven. . . .
Your father . . . while you were with Mr. Whittaker
. . . died . . . Scotland . . . leaving his affairs in a
. . . owing to his fatal confidence in. . . . It remains
for me only to . . . ['What's this?'] . . . Late one
bleak, windy night last March, about a fortnight after
I had seen you, coming from my club in Waterloo
Place . . . Regent's Street . . . lamp-post . . . unhappy woman pestered me, and . . . [A low cry
smothered itself in my throat, my eyes growing to the
paper.] I turned, saying, 'Here is some money for you.
For heaven's sake, go home and . . . on such a night
as this . . .' . . . then suddenly caught me by the
arm, and cried out: 'Captain James, Captain James,
don't you know me?—I'm Isabel Leicester.' I fell
against the lamp-post, and almost . . . The apparently
reliable news of her death, the . . . seemed like a
horrible dream.  At first I could not . . . then she
told me that she had accidentally heard from a friend
that he was dead, and had . . . and then asked about
you. I answered nothing, for reasons which you will,
I think, understand. But on her repeating her
question, and adding that surely she had a right to
know how you were, even if I refused to tell her *where*
you were, I felt constrained to speak.  I told her that
you had been sent, first to a small school, and subsequently to a public school, where you had, I believed,
done satisfactorily: and then proceeded to inform her
of the events that had led up to your interview with
myself about a fortnight ago, blaming myself as much
as I justly considered I could, and you also in the same
manner.  She listened to me very quietly, and, when
I had concluded, asked me if I had any idea where you
had gone to?  I answered that I had none.  Then, as

she remained silently looking in front of her, and as I began to perceive that any further prolongation of the scene could only be very painful and quite useless to both of us, I . . .' [I suddenly slipped a paragraph, catching only the word 'money.'] '. . . reviled me and flung it into my face with mad curses . . . went away. After some moments' thought, I decided that my duty . . . followed her . . . with a policeman I had happened to . . . to an arch under a railway-bridge, where the unhappy creature . . . approached and found that she was sunk in a stupor-like dream . . . and ultimately . . . hospital . . . comforts . . . died.'

*Died.*

I stood up with the letter in my hanging hand.

Nay, what was the meaning of all this?—I turned to the table.

How many apples were there on that plate? One, two, three, four, five, six.—I rent the letter into pieces.

I strode across the room to the opened window: then looked back sharply, viciously, over my shoulder, almost expecting to see some one, some semi-human figure, with a cold smile on his cold face, behind me. Then the idea of Brooke, come from his grave to mock at me, seemed to cut my brain with a lash of madness. Then it was a loin-swathed, emaciate Christ that stood sardonically there in the shadow. I leaped fiercely to the place, and found that light and shade had tricked me.

Tricked me? Everything had tricked me! I was in a cave of trickery.

Then the realisation of what I had been reading came to me again, and with it the frantic suspicion of false play: I began thinking of my mother, taking my sufferings as being the shadow of hers, for she, too, surely had gone through all that I had. Suddenly an idea came to me that almost made me shriek out. '*At last, passing somewhat quickly into an alley, I met one face to face under a protruding shadowed lamp. For a moment I stood breathless, with my eyes in the mad wolfishness and glitter of hers, and then, like a lightning-flash that fills the whole air, terror of her filled me quite. I leaped aside,*

*and then passed her, plunged into a dark-covered way that*
*was behind and beyond her, and hurried on, past. . . .'*
I began to laugh.

Yes, yes, yes, *I* was the cub of the she-wolf that
was driven by hunger into the public way to see what
price her empty, filthy carcase would bring! But she
found no purchasers. Nor shall I !

Then suddenly, turning to the open window :

'Oh, you accursèd city!' I cried, 'If I could sweep
you off the earth with every . . . God!' I cried again,
wheeling round convulsively with clenched fists, 'I
have a few words to say to You, and then I have done.
You have given me sight. The earth that You have
made and the creatures that You have put into it are
foul. You have given me thought. You have no
right, be you God a thousand times, to make your
creatures foul and then damn them for their foulness :
You have no right to make them foul at all! You
have given me love and hatred. With the love You
have given me, I loathe You. With the hatred You
have given me, I hate—I despise and scorn You! I
am but a worm in the earth that is but an atom in your
universe. But I stand here and scorn You! I am in
your hand. You can do with me what You will—all
except this : turn from my heart that scorn I have of
You. Hear my last word to You, God. It is the last
I will ever speak to You. Henceforth I endure your
acts in silence. If I have joy, I will not thank You
for it. If I have grief, I will not curse You for it.
Henceforth, I am a stranger to You. If You are, You
are to me as if You were not. If You are not——' I
smiled.

'Enough of this,' I said : 'perhaps something too
much. I am sorry I railed. And yet the poor cuckold
that we call soul must pour forth the lava of its discovered deception, or it would burst. I have done
now, I think.'

I looked up and saw the other letter lying on the
table-cloth, where I had thrown it past my plate.
This letter was Rosy's.

I stretched across to it : opened it ; and glanced
into it :

' . . . I waited for you on Friday night for an hour and a half. And I really did think you would come some time to me, or you would write and tell me why you hadn't come these three Fridays. And I am very sorry if you are angry with me for writeing to you to tell you of it; but I think you must have forgoten that you told me that evening that you would come again the next Friday, and I thought perhaps I had made a mistake about it, and that is why I wated these three Fridays, and I think you might have written to tell me why you could not come.

'Minnie is dead. A man hit her across the back with a stick Yesterday, Mrs. Smith says, when I was away, and it killed her. I cried about it; which thing I have never had to do before quite like that. Please write to me and explain why you did not come these three Fridays, as you said you would. I hope you will please excuse this long letter and the writeing, but I don't suppose you care enough to mind.—I am, yours truly,          Rosy Howlet.

I re-read some parts of it, and then threw it up on to the plate, and rose and began to pace about the room, thinking.

After a time I stopped at the open window.

' "There is a budding morrow in midnight," ' I said to myself.

I took up the lawyer's letter, and having folded, put it on the plate, and Colonel James' letter, and Rosy's, and put the cheque-book on the top. Then, standing thinking, I ate all the grapes, and drank a glassful of water, and gathered up what was on the plate, and went upstairs into my room.

The gas was low as I had left it. I turned it up. I set about doing what I intended. I changed my clothes and boots quickly: put the papers I had brought up, together with my usual cheque-book and a pocket-book containing bank-notes to the value of twenty-five pounds or so, into my breast-coat-pocket, all the gold I had into my right waistcoat-pocket, and all the silver I had into my right trouser-pocket. I had a sudden thought of packing a portmanteau; or my old black hand-bag. No: I couldn't be troubled with it. · I would get what was wanted on the way.

Then I turned out the gas; went downstairs again, and wrote a short note to Mrs. Herbert, saying what

I wished to be done in this matter. And as I sealed
up the letter (force of habit, I suppose) I thought that
it was lucky Rosy's letter had come in this way.
Perhaps I should not have been doing this if it hadn't.

Luck favoured me again : I lit upon a hansom at
the end of the street. I told the man to drive up the
Edgware Road, and I would tell him where to stop.

The gas-lamps burned faintly. There was a hush in
the place, broken every now and then by distant sounds
of stirring life. We were going quickly. I sat thinking.

We were almost at the turning that has to be taken
for Maitland Street. I thrust my hand out and waved.
We came up a little, as it were, sideways to the pavement. I got out. How much should I give the man?
I stood with two fingers in my waistcoat-pocket, considering a sovereign and an order to wait here for me.
Then I determined no ; and took out some silver, and
gave him five shillings.

I went on alone to the corner of the turn that was
to be taken for Maitland Street, and crossed over into
the deeper shadow of the other side. The horse was
wheeling round : the cab drove away with sounding
hoof-strokes. I went on, but rather slowly. Then an
idea came into my head to run as far as the corner of
Maitland Street. I set off : came to the lamp-post :
crossed over ; knocked with strong knuckles at the
door, and waited.

No sound.

I knocked again as before, but for longer. I listened.
No sound. I knocked a third time. Nothing. This
was foolery !

I went into the road, and bent down to pick up something to throw. There was nothing of the sort there.

I gave up an idea of thrusting my finger down
between the stone-blocks, to jerk out problematical
pebbles, and went into Hill Street, and set about
searching for something to throw. I could find nothing.
I went on looking in the road, in the hope of seeing a
mended place, whence I could take gravel. At last
I found one, and picked up some.

I returned. There was no sign of life in the house :
no sign of life anywhere here apparently. Her head

would be by the left-hand window. I threw up a pebble.
It struck a pane: cracked it, I thought, and, falling
on the pavement, bounded and rolled into the gutter.
I made a step, picked it up, and, standing, threw again.
Same result. But I didn't look for the falling pebble:
I looked steadily at the window. Surely she was awake.

Now for a little soft earth!—Up it went.

I looked steadily at the window.

No—yes! A movement: a movement of the blind.
I stepped back, and, taking off my hat, and turning a
little sideways, so that she might if possible see something of my face, looked up as before.

Another movement of the blind. It was, I thought,
drawn aside a little. I held up my outstretched arms.

All at once I knew the blind ran up; heard a hasp
strike, and the top half of the window came down.
There was something white in the dark space that
had been the top half of the window. I cried out:

'Rosy, it's me!—me! Come down and let me in.'

'O gracious!' said her dear voice, 'how you frightened
me! What's the matter?'

'Let me in! let me in! let me in!' I said,

> ' "Do thou roll forth a fruit-cake
>    out of the rich house,
>    and a beaker of wine
>    and a basket of cheeses;
>    and wheat-bread the swallow
>    and the pulse porridge

does not reject. Say, shall I go away, or something receive!"'

Heaven only knew what the poor child thought of
it all! I began laughing at the idea. Then, suddenly
serious:

'Mrs. Smith is fast asleep,' I said quietly, 'down
here. I want to tell you something—something very
important to us both. Will you come and let me in?'

A pause, then:

'Yes,' she said, 'I will come down.'

Then the window was drawn up, and I stood waiting
for some minutes. At last I heard her coming down
the creaking stairs. A bolt was softly undone at the
top of the door, a lock shot back: the door opened,
and I was standing by her in the narrow passage.

'Don't make a noise,' she said, 'or else you 'll wake——'

'"The baby?"' I said.  She had put on her dress. She closed the door softly.

'What's the matter?' she asked.  I was pleased by her quiet tone.

'Let's go upstairs,' I said, 'and I 'll tell you.'

We went up carefully; she first, stopping once to tell me to be quiet, or Miss Martin would hear.  My fickle thoughts that had become rather pallid (the trouble of going up so carefully, that is so slowly, and the hitting of my head against some damned beam or something), brought me into the shadowy room in no cheerful state.  Why had not she lit a light?  She was groping on the mantelpiece for the matches now.

She found them; struck a light; and then there we were in the yellow full glare of the gas for a moment, before she turned it lower.  I had not anything to say ready.

At last:

'I am tired,' I said, Will you sit down? there'—(pointing to the foot of the bed), 'and I will sit here'—(at the head where the bed-clothes were drawn back).  The child obeyed in silence.  Although I did not look at her, I noticed her.  Her hair was all disordered, and rather matted, her cheeks flushed with what I knew was a hot dry flush.

I put my hat on the chair by me—the old cane-bottomed chair I knew (the same as of old, save that the hole in its bottom was grown larger).  Then I said (she looking at me in a strange way all the time):

'Rosy, I have come to make an offer to you.  I have committed a crime here, in London, to-night.  I must bolt out of England at once.  I have scarcely any money left—in fact, just enough to get out of the place with.  I want to know will you come with me?'

I heard her breath go suddenly sharply inwards, and stop for a moment.

Looking at my booted toes shoving together on the carpet, I proceeded:

'I don't know what I'm going to do—supposing I am not caught, that is.  But I dare say I shall be able to turn my hand to something or other that will do to keep body and soul together, and I dare say you, supposing you would care to come with me, might do the same. It's not a very inviting prospect to offer anyone—and there's worse to come yet. I don't believe in marriage. You would have to come with me as my mistress. I might tire of you. You would have no guarantee but my word that I wouldn't bolt from you there, just as I am bolting from justice now. You know the sort of creature I am.' I looked up at her.

Then, in a moment, she was in my arms, kissing me, laughing, crying, kissing me over and over again, and I her, speaking unintelligible sentences, uttering unknown words. A thrill went through me—the same thrill, it seemed, that had gone through me that winter's evening in the farm-house kitchen where Mary kissed me with her soft red lips, the same thrill that had gone through me when I saw Rayne standing there on the station platform, while I was carried away from her.

I pressed her closely to me, my cheek against hers, the tears welling out of my eyes. The stubborn will seemed broken at last. But I was tired, tired in body and soul. Breathless as she was from my embrace, she yet strained me to her with strength, strained me to her when my embrace relaxed, held me when, all things turning and swimming, I would have fallen. In that place of confused and dreamy sensations, I felt her hold, and had some comfort in it. I think I moaned and muttered things scarcely intelligible to myself. At last I opened my eyes. She was smiling at me as a new-made mother might at her wakened child. For a moment I felt the pleasure of that hold and look. Then I loosed myself from her and said :

'Damn it, I must have been fainting.'

She nodded her head at me in her old half-merry way.

'That's just what you did, then !'

'Dear child,' I said, getting up to my feet, and making some steps, 'I'm a fool. Let me see. What did I say to you just now ?' But, feeling a little dizzy, came back and sat down on the bed before I said any more.

M

Then, looking at my booted toes shoving together on the carpet as before, I began :

'We've both, it seems, been making fools of ourselves, especially I.  Now listen to me.  Did you intend this to mean that you wanted to go with me abroad ?  Yes or no ? '

' Yes,' she said, ' yes !'

' Did you understand what I told you about the crime I'd committed, and the rest of it?  Did you *understand* it, what it *meant* ? '

' I don't mind about it,' she said, ' one bit, so long as they don't catch you.  And I'm sure they *won't* !'

' How do you know that ? '

' It would be so *cruel*!'

' *What* would be so cruel ? '

'Now that I've *got* you, for them to take you straight *away* from me again!'   (She shook her head.) ' I'm *sure* they won't!  I'm *sure* they won't!'

Her tone of voice, almost fierce, made me laugh.

' Rosy,' I said, ' I'm too tired to spend an hour in asking you to consider what a serious question all this is.  Do you understand that our life will be a hard one—perhaps a very hard one ? '

' Yes,' she said ; ' I don't mind one *bit* !'

' Do you understand that I won't marry you—now or ever ? '

No answer.

' Ah,' I said, ' You *didn't* understand that?  You thought I was joking?  I was not.  I am not.  I am in earnest.  I will never marry you, if you come with me : never, O never !'

I rose and stood before her, and looked at her looking fiercely at me.

' Now,' I said, ' answer me simply ; but do not hurry.  Reflect before you answer.  Don't be afraid of saying " No."   Believe I shall not break my heart if you say " No." '

She looked down now, and seemed to be thinking.  What of?  *Did* she believe that I wouldn't break my heart if she said ' No ' ?  If that was her thought, I must answer it.

' This very night,' I said, ' I asked another woman

to come with me, and she wouldn't.   You see the sort
of man you have to deal with.'

I waited.

At last:

'Yes,' she said in a low voice, 'I'll *go* with you.'

'You'll have a hard life of it with me—even supposing the life itself wasn't hard.   You see the sort of
man I am.   I am a little mad.   I care for nobody but
myself.   Then I'm a terrible liar: you can believe
nothing I say.   I have told you bushels of lies to-night.'

She rose, and looked me in the face.

'I don't be-*lieve* you!' she said.   'You're *not* selfish!
you're *not* a liar!'

'But I'm quite mad.'

'How can you talk like that?' she cried out, 'You
*know* I'd go with you wherever you liked in the *whole
world*!   You *know* I would!'

'Very well,' I said, 'very well.'   I sat down on the
bed almost exhausted.

As I sat with my head bowed, looking at the carpet
and not caring to struggle any more, she knelt down
in front of me, looking into my face, and then put her
arms up and round me.   I opened my knees: she put
herself between them.   I closed my eyes.   My head
nodded, and nodded, and nodded.

'Ha!' said I, waking with a start, 'what's the time?
I mustn't forget to wind up my watch.'   I took it out.
A quarter-past three.   Time had gone quickly.

'Let me see,' I said, 'What time's the morning mail
to Paris? . . . Can we get a cab here easily?'

'Yes,' she said, 'there's a mews at the end of the
street.'

'It'll be all right if we start by six, I'm sure.'   I
was thinking what time it was when Brooke and I left
Dunraven Place for the French mail.

The end of it was that I lay down on the bed to
rest myself for a few minutes, while she did something
or other (I did not notice what she said), and then I
fell asleep.   Then I was half-wakened by feeling some
one bending over me, to kiss me on the lips: to which
I objected, and moved my head, but the other lips
came after mine, and almost caught them, despite a

quick move back again.    I awoke after that : and saw
Rosy standing by the door, and the room filled with
light not the gaslight.
  ' Is it time to go ? ' I asked.
  ' *Yes*,' she said.
  I got up.
  'Now, what about the cab?    Where is this mews
place you told me about, Rosy ! '
  ' The cab's downstairs at the door waiting.'
  ' You didn't go and get it, did you ? '
  ' Yes, *I* got it ! '
  A pause.
  ' What's that ? '    I asked, looking at a bundle on
the table.
  ' My things.'
  ' You needn't take them, you know,' I said.
  ' But——'
  ' No ; we'll get everything we want in Paris.'
  ' But——'
  ' There, now ! there, now ! ' said I, putting my arm
round her, and getting her along, expostulating, to
the door and opening it.    ' Don't talk any more about
it !    It's no good talking about it !    Get along ! '
  ' But——' she said, turning at the top of the stairs.
I put my hand on her mouth, whispering :
  ' You'll have Miss Martin up in a moment.    Do
you owe Mrs. Smith anything ? '
  ' No,' she said, ' *Hush !* '
  She went down the dark stairs, I following her.
Mrs. Smith was standing by her door.    She made a
sort of curtsey to me.
  ' Good-morning, sir,' she said.
  ' Good-morning,' I said.
  She had the door open for us in a moment.    Rosy
went out quickly, and was into the cab (a hansom),
and I followed, without a further word or sign to the
old devil.    As I was getting in, I told the man
' Charing Cross,' over the roof, and then sank down
beside her.
  ' I have had rather a hard day of it on the whole,'
I said.
  ' But why did you make me leave——'

I put my hand over her mouth.

'But——'

I pressed my hand closer.

'If,' I said, 'it's your economical soul that's alarmed, know, my pippin, that there's no need for it. I'm not a forger. I'm not a beggar. I *am* an atheist. I *am* a liar. I told you that I had told you bushels of lies to-night, or rather, this morning.' I took down my hand, adding :

'Now don't ask more than twenty questions at a time, and I will do my best to explain matters.'

I looked at her, and seeing her pretty puzzled face, laughed, and gave her a kiss sideways.

'You *are* mad!' she said.

'I am!' I answered, 'everybody's mad. And the maddest people of all are those that are most sane!'

---

## IV

FORTUNE favoured our flitting. We arrived at Charing Cross in good time for the train. I took two first-class tickets and tipped the guard heavily, for the privilege of having the compartment to ourselves. I lay back deep in my seat, with my feet up opposite me, full of thought, unobservant. Then I felt a hand steal into mine, and, looking up at a sweet anxious face, smiled, and said :

'Well, Rosy! Here we are, you see!'

'Yes,' she said, 'Here we are.'

'Are you sorry you came?' I asked.

'No, no! Not *sorry*.'

'Glad then?'

'I would be—if you'd speak to me!'

I drew down her face and kissed the cheek, and laughed a little.

Then she said :

'What were you thinking about all this long time, that you didn't say anything to me?'

'Well,' I said, 'among other things, about where we were to go to.'

'Yes,' she said.

I proceeded :

'I think the best thing for us to do will be to get out at Calais ; not go on to Paris. Suppose we went to some little seaside village in Brittany for a month or so ? It must be very hot in Paris now.'

'I will do what you like,' she said.

'Very well,' I said, 'we'll get out at Calais.'

We had a beautiful crossing, the sea like a mill-pond. Rosy wasn't sick, nor was I. Fortune still favoured us.

At Calais we got out, and I set about making inquiries as to the whereabouts of the desired little seaside village in Brittany. After many difficulties, that ended in—for me at any rate—complete weariness, I found out a place that seemed eligible, Pierlaix.

In Pierlaix we arrived that evening, and found our way to an inn, where we entered, and I demanded two rooms for the night, and something to eat at once. After some trouble, that would have been amusing if it had not been so dreary to us who were tired out, we were shown two rooms, a bedroom and (as we thought) a sitting-room, which I accepted on the spot, and proceeded to iterate my demands for a bath in the morning and something to eat and drink at once. (We were in the sitting-room.) They left us.

I opened the folding-windows wide, and stepped out onto the little balcony, into the noise of the sea and the coolness of the evening breeze from over it. As I leant on the rail I felt Rosy at my side, and turned to her. Poor child, how pale and tired she looked !

'Never mind, Rosebud,' said I, putting my arm round her shoulders and smiling at her. 'Keep your heart up ! You'll be all right in the morning ! I'm afraid the sea disturbed your little stomach. Do you feel ill ?'

'No,' she said ; 'I'm all right, thank you.'

'Then let's go up and wash ourselves. I feel filthy.'

We went up into the bedroom together, and made some discoveries regarding the quantity of water here considered sufficient for the ablutions of two. However, this difficulty also was at last overcome ; but we gave up the soap in despair. It was just after this that the fat hostess reappeared with considerable complacency, producing a species of scrubbing-brush, as being, *à coup sûr*, what monsieur required. (All the English gentlemen had the habit of using it, she explained to the puzzled host beside her.)

When they had gone away :

'I thought you *knew* French,' said Rosy, a little piteously, 'What did she bring that scrubbing-brush up for ?'

Weary and dreary as I was, I exploded into laughter at this, and kept on at it till I fell exhausted backward on to the bed, and lay. From there, having rested a little, while Rosy was trying to wash her face in the bowl that did duty for a basin :

'I was only trying,' I said, 'to make them understand that I should like to have a tub in the morning.'

'I believe the *whole hotel* was on the stairs *listening*,' said Rosy, rather disgustedly. I went off into laughter again.

'I don't see what there's to *laugh* at,' she said : which made me continue even more than before, she drying her face and hands at the window, with dignity.

I suddenly stopped.

'It will be rather fun,' I said, 'seeing us buying new clothes to-morrow ! You can't expect me to do that for *you*, you know !'

'*I* shan't,' said she.

'Very well,' I answered philosophically, 'then . . .' She was crying. I jumped up and came to her.

'Ah child what's the matter ?' I said, taking her in my arms ; 'what is the matter ?'

'It's very *unkind* of you,' she sobbed, 'to go on like that at me, and you *know* it is.'

'Indeed,' I said, 'I'm very sorry. I didn't think you minded my fun. I was only joking. . . . There, there now ! It's all right. Give us a kiss, and let's be friends again.'

'I'm *tired*,' she said, wiping her eyes : 'and *hungry*.'

I continued chattering to her, till I at last succeeded in making her cheerful, and in quite a happy humour we went down together into the sitting-room. But, her hunger somewhat appeased by shrimps and fried sand-eels, the weariness once more began to acquire the ascendant. Before we were half through the

meal, the big brown eyes were blinking fast and frequent, and the little head nodding downwards and
suddenly starting up when it was approaching the
table-cloth, at ever shortening intervals.  I persuaded
her to sit in the arm-chair in front of the window, so
that 'she might look at the sea, since she didn't care
to eat any more,' while I finished the stewed fruit and
three shrivelled apples.

When I had peeled apple number two and cut it
into pieces, I went round to have a look at her.  She
was fast asleep.

I went back and ate the pieces, and then apple
number three, thinking all the while till I became
quite incoherent in my ideas about things.  The end
of this was that I awoke with a start, and, having
realised where I was and with whom, decided that bed
was the best place for both of us.  But when I came
and looked at her breathing asleep, so pale and tired,
I did not care to awaken her.  And going, first opened
and left open the sitting-room door, and then the
bedroom door, and returned, intending to carry her
up to bed.  The dear child let herself be lifted with
no more trouble than a few uneasy sounds and movements of her arms; and then up with her I went, and
laid her softly on the bed.  She sighed, and sank into
unruffled sleep again.  I made her as comfortable as I
could, and shut the door.

Over the door there was a small window.  The walls
of the room were simply boards, polished.  I went to
the other end; opened the window, and leant out.
Below was a garden.  I could hear, but not see, the
sea.  The evening breeze still blew softly and coolly.
I gave a large long yawn, and bethought me of lying
down.  I took off my coat, putting it on the back of a
chair, and came and lay down quietly beside her.  I
must have fallen asleep almost immediately.

When I awoke, the room was half-full of sunlight;
a bird was singing outside, and I saw Rosy, lying half
a yard away, seriously looking at me.

'Good-morning,' I said.

'Good-morning,' she answered.

'. . . I wonder what time it is?'

I got out my watch and looked at it.—Half-past five.
'Stopped!' I said, '. . . How long have you been
awake?'

'Oh, a *long* time.'

'. . . I feel hungry.'

'What time is breakfast going to be?'

'God only knows——or the fat woman! *I* don't
know what even the French for it is. Suppose I get
up and see.'

I got up; and, feeling very dried and not a little
dirty, pulled off my waistcoat and shirt, and entered
upon the best course of ablutions possible with the
basin and neither sponge nor soap.

'This is certain,' I said, drying myself on the small
towel, 'I never knew what it was to be without a
sponge *and* soap before!'

We talked a little about such things, till I was
dressed. Then, on my way to go out, I stopped by
the bedside, and stooped down over her.

'May I have a kiss?' I asked.

She put her arms up round my neck, and drew me
down to her. Our lips would have met, but that I,
avoiding hers, kissed her on the cheek. Then I,
supporting myself by my two arms on either side of
of her (for she still held me), and, looking at her, said:

'If you think you wouldn't be happy with me, Rosy,
it is not too late for you to go back again.'

'Naughty boy!' she said, smiling at me. '*Fancy*
talking like *that*!'

'Nay,' I said, 'I was quite serious. You see what a
weathercock I am: one moment laughing, the next
crying, the next cursing. It is not too late to go back
again to your old life. Nay, it will never be *too* late!
Whenever you are tired of me, you must leave me.
Half of what was mine is yours. That goes without
the saying. You are your own mistress—now, as
always, as far as *I* am concerned.'

'Well,' she said, 'then I'll take you, if you please.'

After a moment:

'That being so,' I said, smiling, 'I am yours—till
you are tired of me, that is. Till when, I will do my
best—what in me lies, to make you happy. So help

me my own poor will and love for you !' I bent down
and kissed her on the lips.

For the first week or so, there was no one in the inn
—or, as they called it, the Hôtel du Midi—but we;
but a good many people came over from the two
adjacent towns of St. Denys and Marny to spend the
day, going back by the diligence in the evening. Then
two Englishmen, evident 'Varsity men or aspirers
thereto, en tour, arrived and stayed for a short time;
but, beyond talking with them a little at dinner (what
I had taken, by-the-by, for our private sitting-room,
turned out to be a public one), we, or rather I, saw
nothing of them.

The following, written later, refers to now :

'I had some things to trouble my peace : to write,
and more than once, to Mr. Sandford, the solicitor who
had informed me of Colonel James' death and of my
inheritance of his fortune, and to Strachan touching
the Book.

- 'I scarcely knew what to say to Mr. Sandford.
Certainly I was not going to explain to him the cause
of my sudden flight, and as certainly I was not going
to lie about the matter.  In the letter in which he
informed me of the burial of Colonel James in Kensal
Green, and of the probable cost of a suitable tombstone,
etc.; he said that he now regretted, after his long, he
might say, personal affection for the deceased, an
affection which, etc., and in which, etc., etc., but he
must request that I would transfer the conduct of my
affairs to, etc., etc., etc.

'I sat frowning over the regular winged writing for
a little, with a vague wonder as to the nature of the
friendship here alluded to, and sorrow that I had
apparently profaned it : then tore the paper across,
and threw it on to the table beside me.  And Rosy
came in with her hat on, ready for a ramble over the
reefs now the tide was out; and that was the end of
the matter—as regarded the friendship, I mean.

'One afternoon, in a fit of despondency, I sat down
and began a letter to Rayne.  I am not quite sure
whether in my inmost mind I absolutely intended

sending it. I think that the chief reason for my
writing, or rather attempting to write it, was the
relief thereby given to my pent-up feelings. Sheet
after sheet was ripped up, and at last I sat still in a
disgust that was almost petulant.

'Suddenly a hot flush stole up to my cheek, and I
looked fixedly at the pile of torn-up paper in front of
me, which contained shameful words: hints of what
I had done. "I could never see her again," I had
said; "I could not forget what had passed between
us. Did she expect me to return and look at her
being consumed alive at the stake of Duty? *I* was
made of flesh and blood. Such a sacrifice as she was
making was a sacrifice to Moloch: sin, not heroism."—
In any case, how purposeless, all this! in every case,
how unmanly! She had to dree her own weird, and I
too, with what light conscience and knowledge could
impart. That was all. All that day I felt I had done
a wrong to Rosy. If there was a victim anywhere, it
was she.

'Then came Strachan.—I told him simply that it
was impossible for me to return to London, at any
rate, at present: I hoped never. I was going on to
Paris in September, and might perhaps take up my
permanent abode there. Could not the proof sheets
be sent to me there, and from me on to him? I
would write to him again from the Hôtel de Manchester,
Rue Faubourg St. Honoré, when I got there. I hoped
Parker, Innes, and Co. had accepted the Book all right.
I should stay at the Hôtel de Manchester till I found
a house to please me. But, more later. I asked him
to excuse haste and confusion. As a matter of fact, I
hated pens, ink, and paper now. To write at all
required an effort. I was thinking of buying a vine-
yard, and eating fruit till I brought on—whatever the
disease was that was induced by a surfeit of grapes. I
hoped Mrs. Strachan and the Miss Strachans were
well. It was rather dull weather here. We had not
had a fine summer for long. I doubted we ever should
have one again. And I remained, etc., etc.'

A few days after this, a small troop of students and
girls who, the fat hostess assured me, were their

brides, arrived, and we had rather noisy times of it at
dinner. Rosy did not like any of them. Me they
amused. I used to talk with the men, or rather boys,
as I best could. (Among other articles I had purchased
at St. Denys, was a French dictionary and a stock of
French novels at which I studied some hours a day.)
But my belief in the brides (I mean in their brideship)
was soon first considerably shaken, and then altogether
demolished. I remember how one evening I was
sitting out on the veranda (in the evenings the sitting-
room was nearly always deserted for the garden or the
country round about), having been reading Balzac's
*Mémoires de Deux Jeunes Mariées* with some pleasure,
when I became aware of one of our young couples at
the bottom of the garden, sporting together somewhat
as I supposed Isaac to have sported with Rebekah
on a certain historic occasion not unconnected with
Abimelech and a window. The idea made me laugh,
and laugh again, till it shook my book down off my
knees : when a hand was put over my eyes and firmly
pressed there. · I threw it off, and beheld Rosy
standing, absolutely glaring at me.

' Hullo,' I said, ' what's the matter ? '

' You were laughing at one of those girls,' she said.

' No,' I said, ' I was laughing at a couple there in
the bushes, playing together.'

' You were *not !* You were laughing at that girl
with the red hair. I saw her go out there a moment
ago on *purpose* ! '

' Are you joking ? ' I said surprisedly, getting up.
I could see she was not. I turned a little. She turned,
so as to keep her eyes on mine. Our eyes met and
stayed together while I spoke :

' Rosy,' I said, ' I do not tell lies, at least of this sort.
When I tell you I have done a thing, I do not expect
you to question the truth of my words.'

' But you *did* ! ' she burst out, ' you *did*. You *know*
you did ! '

' Did what ? '

' *Nod* to her, and *laugh* at her ! I *saw* you ! '

I lost patience. I gave one step to her.

' I warn you never to say such a thing again,' I said,

'there must be trust between us, or nothing. I did
not tell you this before. I thought you understood it.
Now choose. Believe me, or we part—for always. I
will never see you again.'

If I had not caught her, she would have fallen. She
writhed about in my grasp, muttering quickly, her face
and hands working, her eyelids quivering. I held her
and looked at her steadily. I did not know what was
the matter with her ; but was decided that she must
say she believed me, or we would part. Life with a
woman who did not trust you, would be nothing short
of the popular conception of hell.

At last she became coherent enough for me to
gather that I had terrified her. Then she appeared to
recognise me, and covered me with a hundred endear-
ments, beseeching me over and over again not to leave
her, or she would kill herself. I did not *know* how she
loved me ! Indeed, indeed, she couldn't *help* it ! She
always *was* jealous—from a child ! If I would *only*
kiss and be friends again, as we were before, she
would never, *never* be jealous again. But that girl
with the red hair was so forward-like, she didn't care
*what* she did !

Weary of this, I sat her down on the sofa, and stood,
half-turned away, before her. She went on in the
same strain for a little, and then came a pause. Perhaps she was exhausted. I said :

'Well, Rosy, have you considered ? I was not
joking just now. I asked you to choose. Do you
believe what I said to you about those two down there,
or do you not ? You know what your choice implies ?'

'What ?' she asked ; 'what do you mean ?'

I answered :

'I cannot live with anyone who thinks that I have
told them a deliberate lie. If you think I have told
*you* a lie, then I will leave you.'

'I don't think you told a lie. I never said I *thought*
you told a lie.'

'Didn't you say just now you thought I had been
laughing at that red-haired girl ?'

'Yes, I said I thought you did.'

'And didn't I say I had not ?'

'Yes.'

'And didn't you say then that I had?'

'Yes.'

'And didn't I tell you that I had not?'

'Ye—es.'

'And didn't you refuse to believe me?'

'Ye—e—es.'

'And what is that but telling me, straightly and directly, that I had lied to you?'

'I don't *understand* it,' she said, piteously, bewildered.

I walked round the table, with my hands in my pockets.

Then, standing in the middle of the open window, I stared out into the dull evening and my thoughts. I do not know how long I stood so: maybe scarcely two minutes, but it seemed more than two hours. I roused myself with a sigh, turned round, and going to her, knelt down by her knees; put my arms round her, and kissed her.'

How the child smiled, and cried, and laughed, and caressed me!

We came on to Paris in the first week or so of September, to the Hôtel de Manchester. A letter had arrived there for me the night before, from Strachan. He expressed surprise at my flight in the night time, and hoped that there was nothing serious the matter with me? But Mrs. Strachan had been pestering him to take her and the girls to Paris for a fortnight, and as his term at the Queen's College did not begin till the end of October (by-the-by he had not informed me that he had just got the chair of Natural History there, had he?), he thought he might manage it (say) half-way through September. We could talk over matters about the Book then. Parker had agreed to publish it all right; but there was some lumber about plates, etc. He would write again shortly, or, perhaps better, when he arrived in Paris.

I answered this letter at once.

First, as regarded the Book. No expense was to be spared to make it attractive. That was my affair, or rather it was Mr. Brooke's own. I only held his money and property as a guardian till Mr. Starkie returned from Africa, when I should hand it over to him with

the account of what had been expended of the one or
made use of of the other, during his absence. But, I
was quite sure, no possible objection could be raised to
any expense undertaken in behalf of the Book. I
would be responsible for that. For the rest, I need
not say how glad I should be to see him (Strachan)
here in Paris, but it would be, I thought, impossible
for me to see Mrs. Strachan or his daughters. For
this reason : there was with me now one who had given
up all she had for my sake, for which I loved and
reverenced her, and, considering that the only reason
that she was not my wife was because I did not believe
in what was known as 'marriage,' I would go nowhere
where she could not come with me, and be assured of
the same respect as if she *were* my wife. This I knew
was more than I could ask (my first form of the sentence
was : than either I could ask or desire) of Mrs. Strachan,
with the beliefs that I knew she held. I repeated
that I should be indeed glad to see him here, I hoped
in my own house, and have some opportunity of returning him some little of the hospitality which he and
his had given to me while I was in London.

There was, I thought, no more to be said than this.
If he were a true man, it would be enough : if he were
not, then let each go on his separate way. It was as
nothing to me. Only one acquaintance the less. . . .
Should I never have a friend ?

In the morning Rosy and I set out together in pursuit of a house, or rather a flat, to suit us. After some
trouble, I remembered that, when I had been at the
pension in the Avenue de Fontenoi, I had noticed a
flat that was to let, some way up the street, which
had impressed me favourably for some reason or other.
I suggested that we should go there now, and we did.
The place suited us, and we took it.

We, or rather I, began with a delightful scheme of
doing each room (there were seven, not counting the
kitchen, all opening into one another) in some particular style : as, for instance, there was to be a terra-
cotta room, and a brass room, and a silvered room, and
so on. I got through the first two pretty well, I think,
but with some trouble, in the next three or four days.

Then one morning came a letter from Strachan.—He would manage to see me soon somehow, and we could arrange about the Book. He was bound to cross the Channel in any case, he found, before the term began. There were some bones in the Museum of Natural History that he must manage to see somehow before he went on any further with a monograph on the *Elephas Primogenius* he was now working at. Mrs. Strachan and the girls were not coming to Paris this year. I must excuse haste, and, hoping to see me well, he remained, etc., etc.

What a time that was, furnishing the house! As for the idea of doing each room of the house in a particular style—*L'homme propose, les commis disposent!* I really don't know how we ever got the place done at all. However, at the end of a fortnight, we, or rather I, again had made five of the seven rooms habitable. and the two servants I had got had done the same for the kitchen. (The servants of the whole house slept up above in the *grenier*, as they call it, not in the several flats.) I worked like a slave, and rather liked it: hanging all the pictures, deciding where, and generally helping, to put all the things in their places, and so on; for I had my doubts about the Parisian sense of the beautiful in the matter of furniture arrangement.

Rosy's chief anxiety in the matter was as concerned the fate of the things which she had herself ordered, all the linen and the household utensils. She did not care to come up to the place itself, for reasons of her own: not unconnected, I thought, with a small coffin which had happened to be exposed by the door one morning, covered with flowers, a child's coffin. When I had asked her, as we went up the staircase, why she hurried by so quickly, she said in a half-whisper:

' It was a *child*! Don't let 's talk about it.'

It must have been a fine thing in the way of amusement to have seen her ordering her things at the Magasin du Louvre her favourite shop, lists in hand. The composition of those lists in the evenings with pen, ink, paper, and dictionary was delightful; but she would not hear of my going with her to see their fulfilment.

At last all was ready for her, and the next morning we installed ourselves.

I remember that, as we sat together that evening, I looked across to her sitting with far-off eyes with her book, and thought how impossible it was to *know* anything about anyone else. I felt that in her mind a train of ideas existed of which I was absolutely ignorant.

At last:

'Rosy,' I said, getting up, 'I have not welcomed you to your home.'

She rose, and I took her hands, and, looking into her eyes, went on:

'Welcome to it, and may you be happy in it! And here at the beginning of our new life together, let us say that, whatever may happen, one thing shall always be between us—Trust. Believe me,' I said, taking her in my arms and looking closer into her eyes, 'Believe me, child, that without Trust, happiness can never live, let love be as broad and as deep as is the sea. Oh Rosy, give yourself to me, heart and soul! It seems to me, as we are now, that Love is not so far away from us.'

Her arms pressed me with strange strength. Her face grew to mine: our lips met in a kiss that was her full surrender unto mine: a kiss so sweet, so long, so mingling, that I knew not whether this was death or life, or earth or heaven. And then I thought that it was Love.

# V

## I

THE Professor came in upon us after twelve o'clock lunch, one mild October day, when we were standing together, outside the study, leaning over the balcony-rails and watching the aerial manœuvres of two martins.

'I am glad to see you,' I said, holding his hand and looking into his face. Then turning to Rosy, who had drawn back on the sudden appearance of this stranger by my side, I explained :

'This is the friend for whose sake I wished our house to be ready—Professor Strachan.'

Rosy put out a timid hand, and said blushingly and softly :

'I am glad to see you, sir!'

The Professor smiled—who could help it?—and then gave an odd glance at me which I rejected, and that, I think, dismissed some invisible commonplace trouble of ours into the outer air, and he and I were in some way more really friends than we ever had been before.

He stayed in Paris for eight or nine days, during which I had the pleasure of going with the Rosebud and him to see the plays which were the best worth seeing. Those evenings were happy ones. He and the child took to one another, quite remarkably : and therein perhaps lay the happiness of those evenings— at least to me—to sit still and listen to their talk, with a certain half-dreaminess in my thoughts of them, and with a certain half-wonder in the half-dreaminess. I remember how particularly this feeling came to me the last night he was with us (at the Gymnase it was), and how it dominated me all the way home, and how, looking into his eyes, as after supper he said good-

night to me a second time at the street-door, the
sudden thought came that he knew my final thought,
and to where did that final thought tend? As I came
up the dark staircase with my candle-light sending un-
couth shadows about me above and below, I wondered,
in a half-vague way about the meaning of the thing?

When I entered the dining-room, I found Rosy
leaning against the mantelpiece, warming one foot.

'Are you cold?' I said, putting down the candle on
the table and throwing myself into an easy-chair, with
my knuckles up to my mouth and my eyes to her.

'Yes,' she said; 'I *am* cold—a little.'

'Why, it's quite warm.'

She made a little motion with her back expressive
of a shiver. I took up a book. She turned her head:

'Don't read any more to-night,' she said, 'You're
*always* rea-ding.'

'Am I?' I asked, looking at the tops of the leaves;
'perhaps I want to get wise. Now if I were you,
Rosy, I should learn French. I'd be only too glad to
get you a master. And why not music too?'

'I don't seem to care about it,' she said.

'You are lazy?'

A pause.

She came to me.

'Don't sit on the arm of the chair,' I said, 'or you'll
break it.'

She stopped. I continued looking at the tops of the
leaves. Then she drew a stool from underneath the
table to my feet, and sat down upon it and looked at
me. In a little I met her gaze.

'Well?' I said.

'I will learn the French and the music if you *like*!'
she said.

I laughed.

'My dear, the liking must be yours. I don't want
you to do what you *don't* like.'

'You're always *rea*-ding,' she said, 'I don't believe you
ever think about *me*. You don't care *what* I do!—*really.*'

'I don't,' I said, 'You are right.' She seemed
struck speechless.

I opened the book and began reading.

At last:

'You don't—care—what—I *do*?' she repeated in amazement.

'No,' I said 'You may go to the devil as soon as you please.'

Silence. I reading.

At last I said :

'The Professor, you see, came over later than I thought he would.'

A pause.

I felt her hand on my knee.

'Are you *joking*?' she asked.

'Joking?' said I, lowering the book and looking at her with surprise, 'Not the least in the world. I said I didn't care what you did. I don't. You remember my agreement with you? You were to take half the money and leave me the moment you tired of me. I have come to the conclusion that it's only fair for me to be able to do the same with you. I'm tired of you.' I lifted up the book and continued my reading.

In a little she rose and went to the fire-place. I read on. She made no sign of life. A sudden idea came to me that she had fainted—nay, was dead! I lowered my book : saw her gazing over the table into the air : got up, throwing the book on to the table by the candle, and said slowly :

'Well, my dear, let's part good friends at the least. It was a blunder our acquaintance, but there is no ill-feeling on either side ; eh? In token whereof we will spend one more night together, and then—part? . . .'

Silence ; she still gazing over the table into the air. I advanced, and recognised that I desired her, which made me laugh. It was the first time I had recognised the fact. She answered nothing : made no motion. A sudden feeling of the cruelty of my experiment seemed to bite me. I had not thought of it in that way : cruelty. I at once began to undo my sewing :

'Well, Rosebud,' said I, taking her two little still hands in mine, 'You little duffer, what are you thinking about?'

At last she looked at me ; looked in my eyes long, till I laughed.

'You are a *bad man* !' she said.

'You do not mean it?' I said saucily.  You are a *good* wom . . .' She had in a moment smitten me smartly on the cheek with the palm of her hand! I burst out into bright laughter, catching her, as she sat bolt upright with an expression half-startled, half-defiant, in my arms, and smothering her cheeks and lips with kisses. . . .

But the experiment was spoilt.  Perhaps it was premature.

I wondered that night, or rather morning, as I lay awake thinking in the grey light, while she slept gently like a child beside me, why I had attempted that experiment, and what I had quite meant by it?  And wondering, I fell asleep.

The next evening, I met the Professor at the Gare du Nord, as we had arranged, and (he, at the end of our walk up and down in the hall, commending Rosy to my care as a last sudden thought which I felt he hadn't liked to broach as of any other sort) I saw the last of him that was to be seen, and turned away a little sadly.

As I walked home to Rosy, who was waiting for me (to go out a walk she had said, and I had half agreed), I had a feeling that we two, she and I, were going through a somewhat difficult stage of development, and thought of it, as usual now, half vaguely. When I opened our door, I found her seated on the ottoman in the hall, dressed in furs, waiting.

'Dear girl,' I said, drawing out the latchkey, 'it's quite warm out.  How can you expect to walk quickly when you're muffled up like a mummy?  And stays on underneath, I'll be bound.' I was smiling.  She came towards me with a saucy strut, holding up her dress, so to show her small pointed boots and pretty coloured stockings.  I looked at them and said:

'Oh, frightful !'

She caught me by the arm and half-swung there.

'You're in such a *good* temper to-day !' she said, laughing.  'We'll go to a nice café on the boulevard, and drink café noir, in nice china cups, and play at dominoes.  I *do* like dominoes.  We will—*Eh ?*'

'If,' said I, 'you die before me, I will have you
buried in stays and patent-leather boots, and have a
corset cut on your gravestone. You won't find corsets
in heaven when you get there. You will have to
migrate further south. There are plenty of them in
hell. Satan invented them.'

'How shockingly you do talk!' she said.

'How so? tell me that?' I said seriously.

'You shouldn't talk in that way.'

I sat down laughing on the ottoman.

'Shall we go to the café by the Français?' I asked,
'You see, my dear, this earth is, after all, rather an
odd place to live in; and we humans—or rather, we
animals—are really, after all, rather odd things to be
living in it; and this is all the more so on account of
murder and sausages. Shall we go to the café by the
Français?'

'How ri-*diculous* you *are*!' she said, 'very well.'

'My dear,' I said, 'shall we take a cab?'

We took a cab, and I talked like a rational (or
irrational) being for the rest of the evening.

It was late when we got home again, and the concierge apparently deep in his slumbers; for we stood
at the door (I pulling at the bell, Rosy seemingly
tired into the quietness of an implicit acceptance of
things), for over five minutes. At last we got in, and
went slowly up the dark staircase together, I all at
once thinking of last night's experiment till I began
to laugh. Then I found we were standing in front of
our own door; perhaps had been so for some time.
Rosy stood with her hands muff-wise in her sleeves,
and her eyes half-closed, and her pretty little head
sleepily quavering downwards. I chucked her sharply
under the chin.

'It's time to get up and eat sally-luns,' I declared.

'Good gracious, how you *did* startle me!' she said:
'What's the matter?'

I drew the latch-key out of my pocket, and, at the
first shot, drove it into the key-hole, and opened the
door. The ornamented, luxurious passage looked as
if it were warm and almost cosy in the red light of
the hanging oil lamp's little floating red core-flame.

She went in, and I after her, closing and locking the
door behind me, while she passed on into the morning-
room.   There was a small window halfway up the left-
hand wall of the passage, and it looked into the study.
I could see that the curtain, that was usually drawn
right across the window, was only half drawn.  I went
and observed what she was doing.  She was on her
way across the room—to the fire, of course.  Down
she sat on the hearthrug, and doubtless was staring
into the red-ember realm of castles and dreams.  Then
she looked round : 'Why wasn't he coming?'  Then
back again at the red-ember realm.  What a strange
thing for me, here, in Space and Time and Life, so to
be observing her here, too, in Space and Time and
Life.  What were we to one another?  Not only Rosy
to me, and I to Rosy, but each one of us—each one
of us humans to each other one?  The thought grew
broader in me, my eyes still regarding the firelight
picture there, but not comprehending it.  She looked
round again.  The movement recalled me to my
ordinary self.  'Why wasn't he coming?'  I felt a
sudden great tenderness for the poor child waiting for
me there.  Oh, Rosebud, Rosebud !

Then I passed in and through the morning-room,
where, on the sofa, lay her furred coat and hat, and,
parting the curtains of the doorway, stepped into the
study.  She was looking back for me.  I threw my
hat into a chair; pulled off my coat; sent it after the
hat, and came to her.  I threw myself down behind
her on the soft hearthrug, and resting my head, that
was beside her, on my hand, looked into the eyes that
were looking into mine.

'Rosy,' I said, 'do you believe in God?'

'Yes!' adding, her eyes in the red-ember realm,
'of course.'

'Then don't you think you're doing wrong being
with me?'

'Yes.'

'And don't you think you'll be punished for it?'

'I am *sure* I shall,' she said.

A pause.

'Then why do you do it?'

'Because I can't *help* it!'

'What do you mean?'

'I can't *help* it.—Can't you see,' she said, turning full unfathomed eyes on me, 'I can't *help* it! I love every muscle in your body.'

The simplicity of thought, and voice and word made me say, with a suspicion of a small smile round the corners of my mouth: 'That's awkward,' and bring my eyes down to the hearthrug, while I thought for a moment of that last expression of hers and its meaning.

Then, looking up:

'Would you like me to marry you?' I asked.

Her eyes went as unfathomed as before into the red-ember realm again, and became distant. Her lips said slowly:

'I *should* like to have you without the sin; but . . .'

'Well——'

'I shouldn't like you to *marry* me.'

'Why?'

No answer.

I repeated:

'Why?'

'*Can't you see*,' she said, turning her eyes to me, '*why* I shouldn't like you to marry me?'

'No.'

She looked to the red-ember realm once more, but not into it, and her eyes became dreamy.

At last she spoke. 'I don't think,' she said, 'you'd care for me even as much as you do now if you *married* me. No' (she shook her head), 'I wouldn't like you to *marry* me. Besides . . . .'

'Well—— ?'

'You will *want* to marry some one,' she said, suddenly looking at me, 'some day.'

'No,' I said, 'I shall never want to *marry—any* one!'

'Ah,' she said, 'wait till you *love* some one—and then!' She nodded her head.

'Why do you think I didn't marry *you*?' I asked.

'Because you didn't *want* to!' she said.

'No! At least, no to your thought.'

'What do you mean?'

'I don't *believe* in marriage.   If I did, I should have married you.'

'That's sinful, not to believe in marriage.   Don't you believe in God?'

'To the best of my belief, no.   One thing I am sure about: I don't believe in Jesus.   I suppose Jesus and God are one and the same thing, are they not?'

'Yes, Jesus is God.'

'And God is Jesus?'

'Yes.'

'How is that?'

'That's the mystery.   We don't *know*.   You ought to have *faith*, and believe in it.'   I looked down. There was absolutely no good in attempting to say anything serious on these matters to her.   I looked up again.

'Rosy,' I said, 'I don't like you to think what I can see you *do* think about my not having married you.   I would not marry any woman in the world, however much I loved her.   I could not repeat the words of the marriage service with my lips, and laugh at them in my heart.   That would not be true.'

'You *would*, though,' she said, looking at me with a look of experience, 'if you *loved* a person.'

What was the good of contradicting her?   I kept silence, with downcast eyes, for a moment.   Then I said.

'Why, if you believe that you will be punished for all this, don't you ask me to marry you and chance my not caring for you then even as much as I do now—as you say?   What sort of punishment do you think you'll get?'

'I shall be burned in *fire*!   I knew that long ago. . . . I knew quite well it would be like this some day. I used to pray to God not to think about you, but I could not help it: I *did* think about you!   When you went away to Paris, I was ill, and I thought I was going to die; and I promised God I would never think about you any more; but I got well again, and I went on thinking about you more than ever!   I couldn't *help* it!   And at last I felt I couldn't do without you. You've no idea what a way I used to get in sometimes.

I used to feel as if I must get up that very moment,
and go and find you, and hold you in my arms and
love you.   I couldn't *help* it!   I know I shall be
punished for it; I suppose I *must* be!—Then, you see,
you came back, and we had those walks together.   I
knew you didn't care for me; but you were *so much to
me.   I couldn't do without you!*'

To watch the child as she sat, looking with her
dreamy, unfathomed eyes into the fire, and to hear her
telling her story in this way!

I drew myself up beside her, and put my arm round
her shoulders, leaning her body against mine.   She did
not seem to notice my movement, or to feel my arm
round her shoulders.   She was silently gazing before her.

'Rosy,' I said, 'Rosebud,' rubbing my cheek softly
against hers, 'I would do anything, if it were only
true, to make you happy.   I would marry you to-
morrow if it were not for those . . . those words that
would be so false in my mouth, that I could not utter
them.   I could not do that.   But there are other ways
of marrying people, now I think of it.   I will find out
about them.   Then, you see, you would be my wife :
I mean, as far as having my name; so that no one
could think or say anything against you.'   (She was
shaking her head.)   'Nay,' I said, smiling, '*can't you
see* that in this way you would have a greater, a more
*lawful* claim, as you might say, upon me, in case I ever
*did* want to marry any one—with the marriage-service
and the rest of it?'   I was smiling.

'No,' she said; 'I wouldn't care about that.   Not
one bit!'

'But suppose,' I said, 'suppose I ever *did* fall in love
with any one, and *did* want to marry them? . . . What
then?'

'Then you'd *have* to, that's all!' she said.

'But what would *you* do?'

'I'd go *away*, and never see you again!'

'I hope you wouldn't, Rosy!   I hope you never
would, whatever comes or goes.   You would always
let me be your friend.'

'While some other woman *had* you?   That's likely!
Oh, *you* don't know what love is!'

'I don't,' I said, 'but you know quite well that I never would leave you, however much I loved any one else.'

'But *I* would leave *you*, if I thought you loved any one else.'

'But I wouldn't let you know.'

'But you couldn't help it.'

'But I never *shall* love any one.'

'How do you know that? *I* thought *I* never should love any one; but, you see, I do. I hope you'll love some one some day who doesn't love *you*, and then you'll know what *I* have to suffer.'

A pause.

'Supposing,' said I, 'that I loved you, and you didn't love me.'

'Yes.'

'Well, supposing you loved somebody else, and left me, I shouldn't mind always being your friend.'

She gave a short laugh.

'Wouldn't you! Oh no! I tell you: if I ever found out that you touched any woman besides *me*, I would go away from you! I would never see you again! You never should touch *me* again! The idea of being your—*friend*, as you call it! Do you think I could look at any woman, and know that she had you, and . . . and not *kill* her?'

She stopped: then began shaking her head and laughing to herself. I eyed her from under gathered brows: I suspected the actor's sense in her as well as in myself. I turned her head round to me and kissed her full and long on the lips. The effect was strange.— It was a new child this, here with me in a new place of early day's air and light. I could scarcely think of the old self of hers that was now gone, gone I knew not where.

'Kiss me again,' she said in a low, half-breathless voice, bringing her mouth towards mine, 'kiss me!'

A certain devil's light of mirth came into my eyes: I laughed at her, and drew sharply back with back-spread arms.

'No, no, no,' I said, 'you little green-eyed monster you! You shall chase me for another kiss, if you want it. I . . .' I had stopped.

She bent to me with her hands half-up, frightened a little at the look in my face:

'What is it?' she said.   'What's the matter?'

She came close to me anxiously.

'What is it, dear?' she said, 'Oh, *do* tell me! What's the mat-ter with you, dear?   Are you *ill*?'

'Nothing's the matter with me,' I said. It's time we were going to bed . . . There, there!   It's all right, I tell you.   Now, off you go to bed!   You're tired out.'

I took her hand and patted it between my two; and then led her, strutting with fantastic, playful gallantry, to the door-way and held up one curtain for her to pass.   Just through it, she turned her head and shoulders back and asked prettily:

'But *you* will come, *too—soon*?'

'Yes,' I said, smiling at her, 'I have something that I must do, that will take me a few minutes, and then I will come.'

I let fall the curtain.   In a moment I heard her step go on.

Then I sat down in the easy-chair and began to think: to think of all this and what it meant, and then of the events of that far night of supreme folly at Rayne's, or best say madness at once.

Something which I had to do was now done—done well, as it seemed to me, and that something was the final and complete clearing away of all the clouding illusion that had blackened the sight of that strange time of devilry, had dimmed the sight of the time that had followed upon the other as an oblivious summer upon an intoxicated spring.   I was at last free.   I saw things as they were, not as they seemed to be.   It might well be that illusion would play its part in my future's wilder hours; but it never could be what it had been to the daily hours of my past.   *I was free.* And that, I thought, *meant* something.

I blew out the candles and drew back the hearthrug (for fear of some hot coals falling out of Rosy's specially procured English grate, and burning her and me and the house, and my so significant freedom in the night), and then went in to her.

She was already in bed, lying on her side, looking to

the door-way curtains.  A deep-shaded candle on the reading-table by the bedside threw a light over the lower part of her face, and on one out-stretched arm in its long white-worked frill, and on the hand with up-held fingers on the white rounded edge of the bed. All the rest was shadowed.

' Well ? ' I said, smiling, and standing for a moment with the curtains in my backward hands.

She smiled back to me.  I crossed over to her, and sat down beside the outstretched arm of the long white-worked frill and the hand of the upheld fingers on the rounded edge of the bed.  And I took the hand of the upheld fingers, while her two eyes looked quietly in mine ; and bent, and softly kissed her two soft red lips ; and she murmured :

' You *see*, I hadn't to *chase* you for it, after *all*!'

' No,' I answered, ' I cheerfully do what the dilly-ducks would *not* do : I come to be killed.  Death 's too sweet to be fearful.'

'. . . What do you mean ? '

I kissed her, again, smiling :

' That I love you.'

'. . . Then I hope you will *always* mean that ; for I love *you*—oh, I *do* love you,—*ever* so much !'

' More than you love yourself? '

' I don't think I have any self left to love.  It 's *all* yours !'

Then, in loving myself, I shall but be loving you ? '

' Yes !'

' Love *must* be unselfish, then, whether it like it or no.  For, in loving itself, it only succeeds in loving somebody else. . . . Do you understand it all ? '

And seeing she did not, all of it, I once more bent again, and once more kissed her two soft red lips ; and she once more murmured, laughing low :

' I understand *that* part ! . . . But—I *seem to think* you might do it over a-gain !'

---

## II

I HAD divided the day off in this way : My books from ten to one ; then lunch ; then generally somewhere with Rosy till four or five; then two cups of tea and slices of thin bread and butter in the study, with the accompaniment of quiet talk, till talk died away in the inspection and desultory reading of desultory books and newspapers; then, at half-past six, dinner; then either somewhere with Rosy again, or a less desultory reading of less desultory books and newspapers, till, at ten o'clock, bed. The only real work I did was my morning reading. I devoted three hours each day of the week to Homer, Sophocles, Plato, Vergil, Horace, Juvenal, and Dante severally. I do not think I had any definite aim in view then for this study. I was content to do it, as I did all things, and be still.

Walks with Rosy were not successes at first, for she walked both slowly and badly; but I soon grew accustomed to the slowness, and the badness was remedied by occasional rides on the way. I liked to listen to her; and she, if she was in good spirits, indulged me to the top of my bent. The childlike and seemingly endless interest that she took in things amused me. Her whimsical likes and dislikes of people she had never spoken to used once to put me out: now I listened to her expositions of their faults with a curious pleasure. Her alternations of passion and quiet, of tears and laughter were an endless April day, and, though sometimes her unreasonableness made me impatient, and at others I could not help teasing her to see the pretty results, on the whole I found it a real pleasure and comfort to be with her.

One evening, when we were in her favourite position—she between my knees talking to me as I sat in the armchair:

'Rosy,' I said, 'I will tell you what you are.'

'Well,' she said, 'what?'

'You are a *loving* girl—one who squeezes softly, and kisses, and tries to steal away breath. I will tell you who was your prototype: a certain Shunamite. '*And let her cherish him and lie in thy bosom.*' And moreover: '*A bundle of myrrh is my well-beloved unto me; he shall lie all night betwixt my breasts.*' And: '*I charge you, O ye daughters of Jerusalem, by the roes and by the hinds of the field, that ye stir not up nor awake my love till he please."* '

'Yes,' she said, '*that's* me.'

The mild autumn perished in rain-storms and the weather grew colder; bracing and invigorating to me, enervating to her—the veritable traditional winter. At last we had keen frost. She spent most of her time by the fire, generally sitting with her knees gathered up on the hearthrug, reading a book or thinking—heaven knows what about!

My walks were nearly always alone now. Consequently they ceased to be semi-rides and became pure peripatetics. With them came also thought again, to oust its poor substitute of dreaming. The frost continued. We had a little snow. At first I tried to get her to take more exercise; but being out of doors in such weather was only misery to her, and so I let her alone.

'We will go to Italy next winter,' said I one evening, having been for a tramp in the falling snow, changed my clothes, and stopped by and above her (she on the hearthrug, that is). 'To Italy! to Italy! Italy was the dream of my boyhood. I am a real northman. I have the migratory instinct in me. Oh Italy, Italy——'

I stopped, and sat down in the easy-chair, and thought about Italy and about my past dream of Italy, and about some one with me in Italy.

At last:

'You must be so cold,' she said.

'Not I!' I answered, with a sudden look to her, 'I'm as warm as a toast. By Jove!' I added, 'I must do something to-night.' (The something being a something in my head that seemed to wish for written expression.) My remark was a sort of outwork designed to stop any advancing objections on Rosy's part.

None came. She sat silent on the hearthrug, with her chin on her up-gathered knees, and her eyes in the fire. I wished her away in bed—the best place for her. I disliked writing with anyone in the room. As I was settling my desk and paper on the table, I suggested it to her.

'What?' she said, looking round at me.

'You seem tired,' I said, bringing a chair to my place. 'Hadn't you better go to bed?'

'. . . Is it very cold outside?'

'Very. The snow is freezing.'

'How long do you think it will last?'

'The snow?'

'No; the cold.—I do *hate* it so!'

'How can I tell? I . . .' (I had begun writing something) 'don't know.'

'Why do you talk in that way?'

'What way?'

Ultimately, after some annoying attempts at interruption, she went off to bed, in an injured frame of mind, and I was left alone with my work. An opening scene of a story had occurred to me, and I was interested in expressing it: a not too unfrequent occurrence at that time, so far unfailingly accompanied by gradual loss of interest as the story proceeded till, quite disgusted, I either burnt or cast it into an MS. drawer of mine, and troubled myself no more about it.

I finished my opening scene in the first heat of emotion, and then, after a pause, re-read what I had done. What seemed to me my grip on, my mastery over the characters I had created, pleased me; not because it was mine, but because it was there, and in harmony with my mood. Then I sat for long thinking. It was early: I was beginning to feel both tired and hungry. Yes, it was impossible for me to sink into mere sensuousness. I had a work to do in the world and I intended to do it. This work would require patient preparation and I was determined that I would give it. I had been unhappy in London: 'Society' was not enough for me. I had been unhappy with Rosy: Love was not enough with me. I had been unhappy with my dreams: My self was not enough for me. I had lived for 'society,' for Love, for myself, and had found that they did not satisfy me. It was time that I lived for something else—for something higher, and broader, and deeper! . . .

I spent the next three or four days in the same way outwardly as any others, that is to say, did my classics in the mornings; took my 'constitutional' in the afternoons; and read in the evenings; but inwardly I spent them in a different way from any others of my life. I reviewed my past in order that I might see what causes lay there, that were likely to have an influence on my future. I faced all these causes, good or evil, fearlessly, quietly resolved to encourage those that were good, and do all that lay in me to eradicate those that were evil. The one idea that I kept constantly before me was the idea of Strength : I must be *Strong.*

Rosy looked upon what was already apparent as my new intercourse with her, with a somewhat suspicious eye. I believe she would far sooner have had even the old state of things with her back again. For, if my caprice leaped in evil-humoured moments far away from her ; in happy-humoured moments it leaped close to her; whereas, now her line of life and mine seemed parallel ; and parallel lines are those which are always the same distance from one another, that is to say, which never meet. Rosy, like the true woman she was (so it appeared to me), was quite ready to offer herself up on the altar of my happiness. It troubled her that now, instead of being, as I ought to have been, capricious, that is to say, selfish, I preserved a uniform cheerfulness of demeanour towards her ; was always ready to do her little services ; was always ready to prevent her doing me little services. It is true that I had in our happy period of 'lotus-eating,' as I had once called it to myself, devoted myself to her *en bloc*; but, as she had said, or as I had said, in so devoting myself to her *en bloc* ('loving' was our term) I was but devoting myself to myself *en bloc,* and vice versa. *Then* all the little services had been hers. I had been capricious; I had been selfish ; and she had delighted in my capriciousness, in my selfishness—whereas, now ! . . . Now I was the highest sinner that is arraigned by Love, the sinless one ! What right had *I* to the preserving of an uniform cheerfulness of demeanour towards *her*? What right had *I* to the perpetual readiness to do *her* little services, the perpetual readiness to prevent *her* doing *me* little services? 'Ah !' thought Rosy, 'that old time was the better time; for if it knew the depth of hell, it knew also the height of heaven ; whereas, this new time knows only the dead level of purgatory.'

o

I remember how I sat one evening, in the after-dinner hour when we were together in the study, observing her and translating her thoughts into my words, somewhat as above : and how at last, smiling at her for a poor dear child, I got up, and went and chucked her under the chin, and in a serious way that made her eyes looking at me brighten up at the antici-pation of one of the old erratic hours, the old erratic hours so often full of the golden atmosphere of heaven. And indeed there was a temptation in the air for me to enjoy one of those hours again. Why not? I com-menced.

But it soon made itself apparent to me that I had set myself, not to be, but to act.

And Rosy showed that she too perceived, perhaps more clearly than I gave her credit for, that it was not the doer but rather the actor that was wooing her. She was up and away in a pet : I, tickled by the idea of energetic desire in my Rosebud, laughing consumedly, careless how she took it. Then all at once I realised that I had once more been cruel to her : nay, but the word should be stronger, brutal. I was serious at once, and away to her to try and soothe her. And succeeded, and we had, as she said, a happy time again.

Nevertheless her discontent with the new intercourse, as I now called it to myself, and to which I promptly returned, seemed to increase. And at last I found out that the more cheerful and obliging I was, the more uncheerful and disobliging was she, and this discovery having come to a head during the course of a whole evening, erupted in the bedroom in the shape of what is usually (I believe) called a 'scene,' reproaches and tears versus sarcasm and silence. After a few minutes of Tears, Silence betook itself out of the bedroom and the house for a long ramble about the streets, and at last joining itself to Thought in preference to Irritation, with which it had set out, I began to draw a sort of picture of what life would have been with a woman—like Rayne, a *strong* woman ! Rayne had, I felt, been for some time an elevation to me, and now it seemed that she was growing into an ideal. After all, was she not the outward and visible sign of that inward and

spiritual Strength which I worshipped? It was right
that she should become an ideal to me; she was a
*strong* woman. Then I came back home and the storm
flew over in April showery kisses. But this made no
difference about the new intercourse which was
promptly and unquestioningly persisted in.

Meanwhile she was, I found, apparently in persistent
readiness to be suspicious. It occurred to me once or
twice that she beheld that there was a woman in the
case, and so kept on the look out for proofs. The idea
amused me, and once led me to demonstrations of
my feeling somewhat in the manner of that factitious
chucking under the chin. She seemed to recognise
something ungenuine; for she would have nothing to
say to me at that rate, and so I determined to do without the demonstrations in future, and did. I do not
know if she was happy at this time. She took a
greater interest in her household affairs than before,
going out shopping with Amélie (the cook) in the
mornings, drawing up lists of things, and so on. I was
pleased to see this; for it gave her something to do.

In this way it came about in a remarkably short
time that we two grew more like acquaintances or
friends than lovers. Then I realised this, and was
rather troubled by it; for I felt that the reason for it
was mine, and that she could not like the present condition of affairs. But what was to be done? An inch
with a child like Rosy meant, not an ell, but the whole
article. If I suddenly softened, she would take it as
a sign of repentance, and that meant trouble of all
sorts! At present I was working away at my classics
and what composition suggested itself; with occasional
fits of disgust, it is true, but avoiding the depths and
getting out of the shallows as soon as possible. And
I bore these occasional fits with a good deal of philosophy now, ascribing them to some internal derange-
ment, such as of liver, kidneys, or stomach, and as
such to be endured in patience and silence. Weather,
I found, affected me considerably.

March came round, but a March more like the
traditional May. I took long walks each day, ten
miles as a rule: once out to Père-Lachaise, to look at

Brooke's grave with its *'Thy will be done,'* and saw
Balzac's bust, and de Morny's tomb (de Morny being
a gilded rascal that interested me) and others, and
stood and looked thoughtfully over the city that
seemed like a great parasite that had driven its claws
into the earth.   Then there was the Louvre, and the
Luxembourg, and, sometimes, theatres in the evenings
with Rosy.   A quietly happy time for me, made
happier as the days stole on and found me still un-
shaken in my scheme of life.

One evening, Rosy having a headache and not caring
to go out anywhere, I went for a ramble about the
streets, observing the stirring multitude in a most
delightfully philosophic way.   The conviction of the
general poorness of life was the deepest, but serenely
deepest, conviction in me.   My view of the matter
was that, since I was alive and in certain circumstances,
the only thing that was to be done was to make the
best of them.

The dawn was breaking as I pulled at the concierge's
bell.   I was a little tired, mentally and bodily.   I came
upstairs; let myself in, and went into the study.   All
at once not only the general poorness, but also the
general, and also the particular purposelessness of all
life and of my own life came over me.   I did not care
to go to bed, I did not care to do anything.   My eyes
fell on my easy-chair: I went and lay back in it, in a
state that kept, every now and then, rising to a level,
over the edge of which lay disgust, and even despair.
At last, I rose, with an impatient curse.   Was there
*never* to be an end of this foolery?   was I *never* to have
rest, peace, comfort, self-sufficiency, call it what you
please,—that spiritual sailing with spread canvas before
a full and unvarying wind?   *Why* was it, *why?*   Was
it really because the strange shadow of Purposelessness played the perpetual-rising Banquo at Life's feast
for me?   Or was it that I was one who could not lack
the Personal Deity with impunity?   I didn't know,
I didn't know!   I wished that I were dead.   I wished
that I had never been born.   What Personal Deity
had I *ever* had? . . . My thoughts stood still.   I saw
a small child go to the bed and slip down on his knees

and tell God about it; but then, remembering that *He* was up in the sky, clasp his two hands together, and look up to *Him*; and say:

'Dear God, You are a long, long way away from me: right up in the deep, blue sky, farther away than even the sun, perhaps, and the moon and the stars.—But I love You, I love You! because You know everything I think about and everything that I want to do! And I pray that You won't let me die till I am very old and have done all the things I want to do. But please help me to be a great man. Through Jesus Christ our blessèd Lord, Amen.'

I threw up my face with my hands behind my head, the sob rising to my lips, the tears to my eyes. 'Oh God, God, why shouldn't I pray to You now? Is there no one to hear me? Is there no one to——*What?* Rayne!—Rayne! you here!'* Everything in me stood still. She was looking at me through the curtains.

I made a sharp stride and opened them. It was Rosy.

'You startled me,' I said, 'I took you for a ghost.'

'Took me for a—*ghost*,' she said slowly, advancing slowly, till her eyes were close to mine.

'You *called* me—*Rayne*!' she said.

'No;' I said; 'not you—the ghost.'

Fury seemed suddenly to possess her.

'I *hate* her!' she cried discordantly.

I took her in my arms, in a half-unconscious way that meant quiet.

'Don't be a fool,' I said, 'why did you get up?' She was struggling a little to get free.

I let her go; and, turning, walked away to the hearthrug, and stood collecting my thoughts. I felt her hand touch my arm. I looked aside and down, at her face.

'Don't be un-*kind* to me,' she said. 'You're not *kind* to me!'

'Then,' I said unaffectedly; 'I'm sorry.' I turned again, and, putting my hands on her shoulders, looked at her; 'As for that "Don't be a fool," of mine, you mustn't look upon it, or the things I say like it, as unkindness.' The expression of her full, half-dreamy unfathomed eyes was pleading, pleading all but pitiful. I did not know what to do, what to say.

At last :

'Dear girl,' I said seriously ; ' I 'm afraid you 're still in love with me.'

She answered nothing.

'I wish you weren't,' I said. 'If you only knew what folly it is—love, everything ! In ten years, you may be a worm-eaten piece of carrion : in less, perhaps. I too. Where do you think you 'll be then ? Where shall *I* be ? What 'll be the good of your having loved me ? or of my having loved you ? '

'You *don't* love me,' she murmured, with eyes far away.

'By Love,' I said, 'I don't know if I love you or not !. Do *you* love *me* ? '

She smiled a little.

'Ah !' said I, 'I wish to goodness you didn't then !'

'Why shouldn't I if I *like* ? ' she murmured, with eyes still far away and something of a little smile round her lips. I slipped my arm round her shoulders, and led her gently towards the door.

'Come,' I said, 'we have talked enough. Let us go to bed, and sleep. If so be that——'

At the door curtains, I turned a little, saying :

'I have forgotten to blow out the candles.'

I went back and blew them out. She waited for me. We went on together, I with my arm round her shoulders as before, through the dark dining-room, and salon just lit with the light from the open door-frame, and into the lighter morning-room, where I said :

'Are you afraid of death, Rosy ? '

'No,' she said ; 'I 'm not *afraid* of it.'

(We had passed through the curtains into the bed-room, lit with two unshaded candles.)

She said no more, nor did I. And we went on to the bed : where I sat her down, and myself close beside her. Her hands she put together in her lap.

'Would you be afraid to die *to-night* ? ' I said softly in her ear, ' Rosy.'

'No,' she said.

' *Will* you die to-night?' I asked, a little evilly.

'What do you *mean*?' she said, looking at me. The same expression was still on my face, nor did I change it.

'Will you die with *me*—to-night?' I said; 'I am ready to die with *you*: although, my dear, as the saying goes, I don't love you.'

'You are very *wicked*!' she said, her eyes rounding, 'That would be wrong.'

'No:' (shaking my head a little); 'only tired of it—. only tired of it!'

Then I looked at her:

'And so,' I said, 'that would be *wrong*?'

I took down my hand from her shoulder and stretched out my arms backward and yawned.

'Be it so,' I said, 'That would be wrong!'

I lay awake by her in the dark for a little, thinking about my work, and whether I would go on with it, and whether I would go on with anything. By degrees, my thoughts grew to present occurrences, to to-night's; and then, without thinking whether she was asleep or not, I asked—her, I suppose:

'Why did you get up?'

'Because I wanted to see you.'

I fell into my thoughts again; till at last, 'Ah!' I said to myself, 'if I were but some some poor, striving, struggling devil in some country town, and she my brave little wife—some poor, striving, struggling devil of a man of letters, with hopes of some day forcing a callous English world to know him as its teacher, and she the brave little wife that believed in me! Ah, why have I not had to strive and struggle? Perhaps I should have become a great man some day, then. Life would have been self-sufficing for me. I have almost a mind—a mind to throw away all these disgust-bearing, despair-bearing golden grains, and go out and struggle and strive again. Surely, I was happier as a boy in London than . . .' But there was little good in talking in this way now, to-night.—I did not ask myself why. I left the question alone: and dozed; and fell asleep.

I was awakened by being kissed on the lips. I opened my eyes and looked at Rosy. She was a little

sleepy, a little languorous, lying with her pretty face
deep in the soft pillow, and her escaped hair flowing
—brown-gold tresses—round about her head.    The
sun was on our feet.    A little canary she had bought
yesterday was singing snatches of song in the morning-
room.    The idea of her solemn bestowal of that half-
awakened kiss made me smile brightly at her.    The
little canary was singing snatches of song.    The sun
was on our feet.

-----

### III

THAT was the morning of the evening on which I received a book and a letter from Mrs. Herbert, enclosing
another—from Starkie, at last !    I read Mrs. Herbert's
first, in order to be able to better give myself up to
Starkie's and the book, which I guessed was Brooke's.
There was nothing of any interest in hers ; a mere report
of the satisfactory condition of things at Dunraven Place.
Then I opened Starkie's, and began reading it slowly.
He had caught up Clarkson at Zanzibar.    Things were
not going as well as they might.    Two months frittered
away in taking great pains about doing nothing !    But
they had at last started, and here they were on the
Continent.    Clarkson wanted to turn down to Lake
Intangweolo, instead of making for Lake Eugénie, to
explore that block, which was comparatively unknown ;
whereas the other place was both known and interestless, save for the fact that poor old Osbaldistone died
there.    He, Starkie, should like to know what the
devil was Clarkson going to do in *that* galère ?    Get
fever or dysentery and manure a patch of sand ?    He
could not possibly say when they might be back ;
perhaps not at all.    He had a faint hope that it might
possibly be before next year was out.    But he couldn't
write any more of this stuff.    He was out of sorts—in
the *blues*.    Clarkson seemed determined to give his
name to a new species of beast, or bird, or die in the
attempt.    They 'd do no good this time.    Only another
instance of wasted time, and wasted treasure, and
perhaps wasted—life.    But here was the end, or he

would be tearing up this miserable stuff.—Mine disgustedly, but truly,          OLIVER S. STARKIE.

I began to consider this letter till it struck me that
it was odd I had not received it sooner. Then I examined the post-marks, and found that it had arrived
in England in early February.

'Damn the old woman!' I said, and pulled the
paper covering off what as I had rightly guessed was
Brooke's book, the Book! Rosy asked what was the
matter? I explained, and, after a little small-talk,
took to examining the thing. When I had satisfied
myself, feeling in a sociable humour, I began babbling
with her, and she, soon brightening, came to me gladly.
We had a quiet talk about past things, one of the, if
not the best talks I had ever had with her. We went
over how she had made me eat the grapes and had
made me call her Rosy (*Miss* Rosebud, I insisted. She
had not had *all* her own way from the first!), and how
Minnie (poor Minnie!) had chased the piece of paper
under the table: and how we had gone out for our
first walk together when I was so weak—and stupid
(Where was the respectful clerk a good deal better
dressed and, doubtless, fed, than myself, now?) and
how we had tea together that other evening in my
room, with the fruit and the cakes and all the other
things, including a sweet solemn little owl who wouldn't
laugh properly once the whole time, and then the
walk together afterwards. And so on.

And then afterwards, in the bedroom we had a look
at a certain little round silver locket (chosen in a
jeweller's in Edgware Road), of which there had been
some mention in the study, and I repeated dramatically:

'*But I shall always be able to keep the locket, you know ;
and, when I look at it, I shall think of you and give a sigh ;*'
(and I gave one) '*for—you've been——*'

'Don't *tease* me!' cried Rosy, with puckered brow
and a slap on my arm. And I didn't.

The next day after breakfast I set upon my work
again, but could make nothing of it. I felt I had
better go out. I went out: down to the Seine and
frittered away half an hour or so looking at books in

the book-boxes on the river walls. It was a dull grey day, with a certain amount of wind, north-east wind I thought: altogether quite like a half-bred London day in early March, before Boreas has grown boisterous.

I lit upon an ill-used copy of a book by an English writer whose name I had heard spoken (evilly spoken) of in my later London days. I was in the humour for buying the book of such a writer, so I bought it and came home with it and straightway began to read it. The subject was an author whom I had been of late accustomed to read both rather frequently and rather carefully. I was struck by the number of my own thoughts that I found. Then there began to creep over me the sense that I had done nothing yet, written nothing yet, that is: a displeasing enough sense when coupled with another—that I never *should* do anything, write anything; anything, that is, worth the doing or reading. I envied this man who wrote with such assurance of work done.—About which point Rosy came in from her afternoon walk and we had tea.

It often happened that I was silent at meals and she content to let me so, but this evening, apparently because she saw that I particularly did not care to talk, she kept on asking me questions and chattering ceaselessly. For some time my sense of duty kept successful guard over my patience and I answered her quietly; but at last I sent my sense of duty packing and began to answer her rather irritably: then, gradually worked into an aggrieved state by her nervous babblement, at last kept a frowning silence. She was defiant: went on gibbering and laughing with flushed cheeks and sparkling eyes, and at last proceeded to tease me. I was not in a humour to be teased. I said so. She was excited now and not to be stopped, despite that Marie (the maid) was in the room clearing away the things for dessert. I kept my frowning silence till Marie was gone, and then said, as playfully as I could, that I was rather tired of hearing her little tongue wagging and wished it would stop still for a while. Then came an indignant flare up, to which I made no answer, only looking at the grapes I was eating and my plate: then a second indignant flare

up, spiced with hot reproaches. I expected wet
reproaches to follow ; and expected rightly. She was
getting tired of them when, having finished my grapes,
I got up and went into the study.

I made an attempt to work, but failed : made another
attempt, and failed again. I determined I would go
out. Then, under the influence of a collapsing sense
of tiredness and sleepiness, thought of bed : but bed
meant Rosy, and I could not stand her just at present.
I went into the dining-room. She was sitting knitting,
in a chair. I told her that I was going out, and might
not be in till late : to which she deigned no answer.
I went into the hall and, taking my hat and stick,
down and out. Which way to go ? where to go to ?
I stood, whirling my stick about, considering. It was
a beautiful night, clear and cool—no moon, with the
heavens star-sown.

There was evil in me. I felt it in a little : and did
not care to combat it. I walked to the right, a little
jerkily like an actor. It was not now, 'Which way
to go ?' but, 'Where to ?'

I began to think of piquant pictures of Grévin's—
dumpy, strutting little cocottes of undeniable chic,
and smiled at the thought. There was evil in me, and
I did not care to combat it. Names I knew of the
supposed haunts of said dumpy, strutting little cocottes
—Rue Blanche, 'le Skating Théâtre' (the pronuncia-
tion of which, 'le Skatting Théâtre,' made me laugh)
and the Folies-Bergères.

I took a cab to the Rue Blanche.

When I entered the hall there was a certain tremulousness in me, chiefly the result of an imperfect sense
of wrong-doing, and a little, perhaps, of the music and
the bright scene. I stalked round the rink, not quite
daring to openly regard anyone : in fact, very self-
conscious. At last I sat down at a table, and, having
ordered a bock, began to argue with myself for a perfect
fool. Here was I, who had pondered on Life and Death
and Time and Space and God, and God knows what
not, absolutely nervous in a hall filled with harlots
and harlot-mongers ! What more ludicrous ? I paid the
waiter ; drank a little of my bock, and looked about me.

In five or six minutes I was master of myself: in ten I was stalking round the rink again, observing the people with interest. I thought I would speak to one of *ces dames*, and see what she had to say for herself. Variety is pleasing. But *ces dames* had such uninteresting faces, and such puffed out breasts and contracted waists, that I found I had no real inclination to speak to any of them. I wandered about for half an hour or so without seeing any face that attracted me; and then went out and (not analysing my motives) took a cab to the Folies-Bergères.

At first sight, I liked the place better than the Rue Blanche: the fountains pleased me, and the verdured seats. Then I was attracted by a *vendeuse* of somethings or other, who had a finely developed bust and pair of whiskers, quite bushy. I stood and began imagining her point of view of life and things generally, till, catching my eye, she smilingly proffered one of her somethings or other, addressing me. This made me laugh and, laughingly declining, pass on. I wandered about once more. The faces of the women seemed to me a little more interesting than those at the Rue Blanche, but not interesting enough to be spoken to.

Once, coming down a staircase, I found myself faced by myself in a huge mirror. I paused in my descent for a moment, in which I saw my solemn face set above my shoulders, squared by my hands being clasped together behind my back. The idea of this figure and face stalking about among these people made me grin to myself.

At last I grew wearied of it, and went away for a long walk about the streets.

When I came home I found Rosy sitting in the study, in the easy-chair, looking as if she had kept herself awake by means of some sort of emotion: I soon perceived, jealousy. In a little she began questioning. Where had I been? why was I so late? I answered her simply. First, I had been to the Skating Theatre, in the Rue Blanche, then to the Folies-Bergères: and then for a walk.

Those were *bad* places: *bad* women were *there*! I

needn't have kept her up all *this* time, and then come and told her *that* !

How did she mean that I had kept her up? Since when had she taken to sitting up for me when I went out at night?

She believed that I had been talking with a lot of *those women* ! And why hadn't I gone home with one and never come back here again? She (Rosy) had always thought it would be like this ! she knew quite well when I went away this evening that I was going after some . . . some one else (Tears): I was a horrid . . .

I thought the child was ill, and tried to comfort her. She would take no comfort. I came to her, intending to try more personal comfort. She was up and, with an intense: ' I *hate* you ! . . . Go away !' herself went away.

After a little pondering, I decided that it would be best to let her alone, and composed myself to sleep in the arm-chair and another chair for my feet.

Next morning, Marie, entering to dust the room, was apparently the instrument of wakening me from bad dreams. For a little I did not know whether to grin, or pull a face at myself, or take Rosy's quarrel with me seriously: then, observing the sunshine in the room, determined to go out and get rid of all these spiritual cobwebs. Dried and somewhat dirty as I felt, I would not go into the bedroom and wash myself, with the chance of awakening her. I passed into the hall and, taking up my stick, out on to the the landing. I was going down the first flight of steps, with my mind full of thought, when, all at once, there was a stumble; a fall; a clutching at and a missing of the bannister, and I was lying, half-stunned and dazed, on the broad step at the foot of the flight.

Then wrath rose in and burst forth as I got up in a keen:

' Blast !'

This foolery was past all endurance !—I suddenly dropped down again. My foot had failed me. The anguish in it, in my ankle particularly, was almost intolerable. It turned me sick. I rolled on to my stomach and face, stiffening my muscles so as to bear it without the threatening childish collapse, or, at least, moan. After a little I determined I would get up—up the flight, into the house.

With great pain, aided by my stick, I reached the door; opened it; went on into the study, and let myself down in the easy-chair.

There I began to reflect.

Presently in came Rosy, dressed, but still in the sulks. I did not speak to her. I was wondering now whether I would send for a doctor for my foot, or no; deciding no. Rosy pretended she had come to look for something, and, not being able to find it, went out again without a word.

I got up and made my way to the dining-room doorway; then through the dining-room to the salon doorway. She was in the salon. I had only a moment's hesitation. I crossed half the salon as ordinarily as I could; but I knew I limped a little, and this rather angered me. Then I suddenly thought: *Why* should I care to disguise from her the fact that I am hurt? and limped altogether. She said nothing. Once in the bedroom, I rang the bell and went and sat down on the bed.

I got my boot off myself, and Amélie, following my directions, bandaged my ankle up in a wet napkin. Her final adjusting touch of the bandage extorted a sound of some sort from me, and I looked up. Rosy was standing by the doorway, watching. I looked down again. She went away.

I ordered my breakfast in the study, whither I proceeded, passing by Rosy in the dining-room. My foot was ceaselessly painful.

I ordered a bed to be put up in, what we called, the bath-room for me. Rosy came into the study at about five; found a book of hers on the mantelpiece just above my head, and went out without a word.

At half-past Marie brought in the tea, Rosy following her. Then she poured out a cup; put sugar and milk into it, and, taking a piece of cake, retired to the chair in the far-window, where she began to drink the one and eat the other in silence. As I wished for my cup of tea, I got up and poured it out, and, taking a piece of cake, retired to my seat again. I determined that I would have dinner in here, in the shape of some fruit and bread and milk.

When she had done her cup of tea and piece of cake, she renewed them : I, after some thought as to whether the pain of getting them was worth the candle of partaking of them, and the supposed display of my feeling toward her in this matter, did not. When she had finished, she put her cup and saucer on the table and went out of the room. I rang and told Marie what I wished about my dinner. I was not angry or even piqued by Rosy's proceedings ; I was too indifferent to be either. The reason why I did not make advances towards reconciliation with her was, that I did not care to trouble myself so far.

During the course of the day she contrived what little annoyances she could for me ; but with no other effect than making me rather amused at her simplicity. ' If you quarrel with a woman,' I thought, ' you must expect this sort of thing.'

Then, when I was in bed, I considered what was the real condition of my feelings towards her. Without doubt, they were those of complete callousness and, perhaps, something more. There was no ' imperfect sense of wrong-doing ' in the thought. It seemed to me to be something little short of folly to stay here and be troubled with her. I ought to go out into the world and see its ways, so as to prepare myself for my work ; that work which was nothing else than, having by self-culture and observation got an impression of things generally, to put down that impression on paper. Truth was the object of my work, and, by the very fact that I was a quite unprejudiced viewer of the phenomena of what is called Life, I did not see why I should not produce such an impression of things generally ' as posterity should not willingly let die.' The idea of telling the truth about things was a pleasing one. I could almost believe that some day that idea might be of itself a sufficient incentive to a love of existence. Meantime the connection with Rosy was passably stupid and tiresome, and perhaps even harmful.

IV

FOUR days passed. Then it seemed to me to be best
to put an end to this.

The reconciliation with Rosy was therefore effected,
and then there came a flow of gentle tears, soft em-
bracements, and the rest of it; all of which I endured
in an actively passive sort of way, as being to the
female mind the necessary sequence of a ' quarrel.'

The days sped on again. I was for the present
content. Once or twice, I thought to myself that I
should, perhaps, have been more content if I had *not*
been content; for indifference was, I held, to be
avoided. But there was always this inevitably unde-
cided position of Rosy's and my relations towards one
another. One interesting particular I one day learned,
as it were, parenthetically, from Rosy. Her departure
from No. 3 on that memorable evening, with head bent
down and hands holding one another in front, was not,
as I had supposed, to the streets, but to the house of a
Mrs. Vincent, who owed her money for some work she
had done. It was some sign of my philosophy (or
indifference) that, on realising that the whole of this
luckless connection of ours rested on a mistake, I did
no more than remark to myself that it was a pity, and,
after thinking about it for a few moments, dismissed it
from my mind. Nevertheless it came back to me
later on, and my philosophy was more dubious.

One afternoon we were having tea together in the
study, both of us reading or skimming the last batch of
illustrated boulevard newspapers, when I, hearing a
ring at the bell, looked up, and said :

' What's that, I wonder ? '

She suggested that it might be some things which
she had got at the Bon Marché Magasins in the
morning, and proceeded to explain that she had transferred her custom from the Louvre to the Bon Marché
for some reason or other which I did not remark.
There came a knock at the door. She said, *Entrez !*
and Amélie came in with a letter on the letter-tray
and towards me, saying that it was a letter for monsieur.

Rosy inquired who had brought it up? As I had my upward hand on it, Amélie was answering that it was 'monsieur the concierge' who had brought it up that very moment, and had said that he was sorry to have overlooked it in the morning. A glance at the re-directed address had shown me that it was Rayne's handwriting. My heart went up to the bottom of my throat.

'Is it from Professor Strachan?' asked Rosy as Amélie was going out.

'No,' I said, striving to be full master of myself.

She refrained from further question, and I slowly opened the letter :

'DEAR BERTRAM,—I should not have written to you, but that many things have come upon me. My little son is dead. God, in His great Love, saw fit to give him to me, as I thought, for my consoling ; and He has seen fit, in His great Wisdom, to take him away from me again. God's ways are not as our ways.

'I do not say that my affliction is not hard, very hard to bear. At times I have doubted that I should ever see the good of it. I do not deny this. But I pray always for Faith in His Goodness, and Faith full and perfect, I am sure, will be given to me before the end. Yes, I am dying ! Perhaps it is better so. And yet, I do not mean that. My head, you see, is not quite clear now. There is something I should like to say to you. Will you come to me? But yet do as you think you ought to, and remember, that any wish of mine is as nothing in comparison with your duty. I have written too much already. But you will understand. For my head is not clear now.

'My husband sends this. He has been very good to me. Remember about your duty. If I do not see you again, I ask God to bless and keep you and make you His at last, as I know He will.'

'Brave heart,' I said to myself, 'brave heart !'

My eyes stayed fixed on her name for a little : then I thought ; till my thoughts turned to confusion.

I half crumpled up the letter in my hands. Some one touched me on the arm. I had risen : was standing up, here, in the room. It was Rosy. I did not know she was here too.

I looked aside at her ; her cheeks flushed red, a

P

star-gleam in her eyes, her brows knit. A vixen.—
What did she want?

'It is from *her*! I know . . . it is from *her*!—She
wants you to *go* to her?' (She was panting out her
words.)

'Yes,' I said.

'You *will* go?'

'Yes.'

'You shall *not* go! Oh, you shall *not* go!—I will not
*let* you go!'

I passed slowly by her clenched, upraised hand:
then, turning, found her close beside me.

'. . . My dear girl,' I said, smiling a little evilly,
'she is dying!'

I stood, thinking of Rayne.

'. . . Won't you say *anything* to me?' she cried,
'what does she *want* with you? What *right* has she
with you? You are not *hers*!—She wants to take you
away from me. I know her.—But she *shall* not!'

Suddenly she stepped to me and caught me by the
arm, crying:

'I *won't* let you go to her! I *will* not! you *shall* not
go! I will not *let* you go!'

'Hey?' I said, 'what are you talking about?'—and
looked at her.

Realising her to be there,—her, the tool demoniac
Circumstance had chosen to undo me with, the plague
of a mistake,—her, the red rag flaunted in my face by
the thing that fleered and jeered because I could not
gore horse or man again,—I concentrated, sudden,
unutterable hate in my look at her. She shrank back.

'Ah,' she whispered, shivering, 'don't! Don't
Don't. I will let you go. Yes: really, truly, indeed,
now, now! Only don't look like that, or I shall shriek.'

I turned away my face, indifferent: and thought
again.

'. . . But you *will* come back?' pleaded she.

'I have told you,' I said, 'yes.'

'You have told me nothing! *Promise* me that you
will come back. *Swear* to me——'

I went to the paper-cupboard; opened it, and stood
looking for the time-table. She touched me on the

arm.  She had come after me.  I turned to her and said :

'I tell you that I will come back.  Now, do not trouble me.  You see that I don't want to be troubled.'

'Oh, *what* shall I do, *what* shall I do?  You will leave me!  And I shall never see you again!  You will never be the same to me again.—I *hate* her !'

'She is dying,' I said, smiling again, 'you won't have to hate her long.'

'You *love* her !'

'I do not.'

'You *do*, you *know* you do !'  (She caught my hand in hers up to her lips.)  'I *can't* let you go ?' she sobbed.

I comforted her in a quiet way, stroking her hair back :

'Come,' I said, 'Come, come !'  And went on, till all at once it occurred to me that I ought to have looked out the time the night-mail went, and paused.  The clock struck six.

I turned and began rummaging in the cup-board till I had found the time-table.  I opened and began to study it.

A pause.

'I am . . . very sorry,' said her soft voice by me.  'I didn't mean to *vex* you.  Will you for-*give* me ?'

'I have nothing to forgive you for.'

'And may I pack your things ?'

'You are kind.'

'Don't say that,' she pleaded, don't say that !  Will you give me a kiss, and be friends again ?'

I turned round and, with my arm about her back, gave her a kiss on the cheek.  I was surprised at her child's woebegone face.  Then, leaving her, I went to the window and at last found out the time of the night-mail.  I took to walking up and down the room in front of the fire.  I saw the envelope of the letter with the newspapers on the floor at the foot of the easy-chair.  I picked it up and considered it.  A horrible thought came to me : *She might be dead !*

I looked at the postmarks.  The letter had taken four days to get to me.  I cursed Mrs. Herbert to hell.  Where was the letter?

I found it it my waistcoat pocket, put there I did not know when.

Marie opened the door. I told her to tell Amélie to be as quick with dinner as possible, as I wanted to catch a train. Marie agreed and went back, closing the door. ' I have found your small port-*manteau*,' said Rosy, coming into the dining-room doorway with a noise of the opening curtain-rings. ' Will you come and choose the things you *want*, because I'm not *sure* ?

We went together.

When we, or rather I, had finished packing the portmanteau, we returned to dinner. The portmanteau was to be taken down by the back staircase.

' I forgot the flask. Do you know where it is ? You'd like to take the flask with some cognac in it ? It's such a *pretty* flask, and you've never used it !' (She had given it me.)

' Yes,' I said, ' to be sure.' And told Marie to go and bring it.

Marie brought it, and then came the question of the cognac. There was none in the house; which had not struck any of us before. I was for not minding about it, till I saw that Rosy would be hurt if her flask was not used : so Marie was sent down to get some cognac, while Rosy and I went into the study again, not caring for more dinner.

Then Marie returned with the flask filled, which Rosy took from me, and reaching, put on the table. It was not yet time to start. We sat in silence, till I turned my head to look at her seated there with large upward eyes whose gaze was far away somewhere.

' Are you all right now ?' I asked.

' Yes,' she said, ' I'm all right.'

I was sorry for her : somehow as I had been sorry for her sitting on the hearth-rug in the fire-lit room waiting for me who stood at the small window. I could not help thinking of the pity of it, that that mistake had been made to give me to her and her to me.

I put my arm round her neck and drew her cheek to meet my lips :

' Rosebud,' I said, ' Rosebud !'

Then I felt the tears coming soft from her eyes: and the memory of a scene rose before me, when I said:

'Why, little Rosebud, you mustn't mind like that! I'll come back again some day!'

Ah, I *had* come back again, and had brought her, not a bonnet with blue ribbons and a flower that should look so real that the butterflies should settle on it, but what she wanted—myself; and also what I had promised with myself, some grapes and bon-bons; and also what I had not promised with myself, some thorns and nettles. Alas, alas, was she not indeed 'alone in the world, quite alone, as if nobody else belonged to her. . . .' 'Good-night Rosebud. Good-night!'

Well, I said to myself, there is no good in this.——

> 'The cocks they crew, and the horns blew,
> And the lions took the hill;
> And Willie he gaed hame again,
> To his hard task and till.

—I must be off, pippin,' I said aloud, 'or I shall miss the train.' And got up and went across the room and turned, looking at her.

She rose and, saying 'I will fetch your coat,' went out through the doorway, leaving me with my mental stretching and rubbing of limbs that had been asleep and wakened up to the feeling that their blood was sluggish.

Presently she returned with my greatcoat, which I took with thanks from her, and then I felt that she felt that the final embrace was coming. In a moment it was come. She was in my arms, pressing up with a poor little tearful face for the soft lips' kiss. None other kiss than that now, none other kiss than that! Oh Rosebud, Rosebud! Then our beings, scarce met, parted again; and I had left her.

I went down.

As I got into the cab opposite the door, I looked up at our balcony half hoping to see her there. No. Nor at the window.

Once more, as we drove away, I looked up at balcony and window. No. I was a fool.

I thought much on my way to the Gare du Nord.

When I arrived there I found that I had abundance
of time. I began to walk up and down the hall, still
thinking profoundly. At last this came: 'The next
evening I met the Professor at the Gare du Nord as
we had arranged, and (*he, at the end of our walk up and
down in the hall*——There we turned, there he began
to speak—*commending Rosy to my care as a last sudden
thought that* . . .'

Sudden thoughts came quickly now. I paced up
and down. A porter with my portmanteau came to
me to remind me that it was time to be getting my
luggage weighed and myself on to the platform. We
went up the hall together. I looked at the clock. He
was right. I made one big step forward, and stopped.
He passed me, and stopped too, but not as I had done.

'Thanks,' I said, ' I shall not go to-night.'

' Good, sir,' he said.

' If you will put that into a cab,' I said, 'I will be
back in a moment.'

'Very well, sir,' he said.

' I went off to the telegraph office, where I wrote on
a form: *Lady Gwatkin, 22 Balmoral Street, London,* and
*B. Leicester, Paris,* and (in French) *I cannot come.*
Then, when the clerk had shown me that he understood
it aright, I returned to my porter and the portmanteau
in the cab.

When I arrived at the Avenue de Fontenoi, I did
not look up at either balcony or window, but got down
with my portmanteau and, having paid the man, went
slowly in. As the impulse to look up had been denied,
so was that to ask at the concierge's if she had gone
out. But the concierge came forth to proffer carrying
up the portmanteau; and I surrendered it to him. Up,
then, I went slowly, deliberately, with mechanical
limping foot. At the second story some one came
out, a man, and descended upon me: when, through
the mutual choosing of first one side and then the other,
there was a moment's delay. I cared not. Up I went
again slowly, deliberately, with mechanical limping
foot; till I reached our third story, and the door, and
had unlocked it, and gone in, and drawn it to quietly.
What then? The passage in the red light of the

hanging oil lamp's little floating redder core-flame. . . .
No: not to look in at the small window !—In here, into
the study.   Almost dark: no one here.

Now into the salon.   Almost dark too: no one here.
Don't call for her, or your voice will unnerve you as a
concession to ghostliness.

In the morning-room.   Almost dark: no one.

In the bedroom : no one.

Will you go into the bath-room ?   Yes.   No one.—
Stand and think a little.

Now go back through all those almost dark and
empty rooms, restraining that cry that is in the top of
your beating heart.   And, going back, *what an emptiness
there is in the place !*

It is foolish to feel the presence of the ghostly or
something visibly unseen here.   The matches are on
the mantelpiece behind the jar.   Don't knock it over,
groper . . . Light?   No: darkness !   These thin con-
traband matches are better than the stinking sulphers,
but still . . . Out again.   *Damn !*

Now be careful this time.   Light the candle.

It is lit.

What is the time?   A quarter to nine.   Now——
*A letter on the table.*

*She is gone !*

Open and read the letter.   Here :

'Mr. LEICESTER,—I see it all now.   I told you I would go
away when it came.   The last thing I ask from you is for me
never to see you again.   You will find everything in the
house.   I have only taken the clothes I have on and £2 7s.,
which I had when I went with you.   You are not to try to
find me.   If you do, you are a coward and no gentleman.   I
pray God will forgive me for my wickedness ; He knows I
did not do it for gain, but for pure love for you ; that is the
only comfort I have within myself.   I loved you, but what is
love and how strong when through suffering hate takes the
place of that love.   I hate you and I always shall.
                                                    'R. H.'

I sat down and, with my elbows on my knees and
my head between my hands, tried vainly to understand
it all.

## V

DESPITE every effort that was made to discover her, Rosy remained undiscovered. At the end of a week I made my arrangements and crossed over to London, where I felt sure I should ultimately have news of her. I had been informed by a chief of the Parisian police that either she had got off by the very train which I had intended to take, or else she was dead. I felt a strong conviction that neither had she got off by that train (how was it possible?), nor yet was she dead; but at times a horrible idea came over me that she might be being detained in some infamous den. This the chief of police had confidently assured me was not so: I had, myself, wandered about filthy back-streets enough in the forlorn hope of finding her: had at last, thinking of Marina, visited infamous dens enough, places of hot air and bright light and tawdrily-rich ornament, filled with fat and ghastly painted naked women who had at first almost terrified me, thinking of that awful breathless picture of Juvenal's Agrippina, and then made me sorrowful past tears. And, here in this London, where my own poor mother had offered her body for sale in the public way, what a thought was it to think, that perhaps I had not persevered enough in that search; that perhaps if I had stayed another week, another *day*, I might have found her! I could do no work. As day followed day, and still no news either from Parisian or London police, I became so feverish at nights that I could not sleep. And I knew then in my dread and anguish and horrible reproachful longing, how dear she was to me—how inexpressibly dear—dearer than anything, my darling of love!

At last, one evening about a fortnight after she had left me, sitting in my easy-chair in the study window, trying to read a book, I began to think about the little canary (up there now, the little pet, asleep in his cage), singing snatches of song, while the sun was on our feet, and, realising once more that all this was not done in a dream, but that she was indeed gone from me, might at this moment be in misery, might die

without my ever seeing her again!—the tears came,
and then, bowing my head down between my hands,
I sobbed and wept.    These were the first tears I had
shed.    They were a relief to me.    I began to think of
it as I had not yet thought of it, quietly and fully,
recognising the great love I had for her and resolute to
win the radiant future.

That night, for the first time since she had left me,
I had a dreamless refreshing sleep.    In the morning
I went down the river to Greenwich again, and up
on to the Heath, thinking of Rosy and Rayne together,
as I had so many times this last fortnight.    The place
seemed somewhat strange to me now: stranger than
it had seemed before.    I did not go to the school and
the field where Wallace and I had lain and played at
'chuck,' looking out at times over the dark, silver-
twining Thames and dusky, far-reaching London.—I
determined that I would find out about Rayne when I
got back.

I went to Balmoral Street, and, seeing no assuring
sign in No. 22 of life or death, rang, and inquired of
a maid who opened the door, if Lady Gwatkin was
any better?    There was no surprise in her face.    *Rayne
was not dead.*    My breath flowed out almost in a sigh.
—Lady Gwatkin was a good deal better.    She had
gone with Sir James into the country.

It was enough.    Further words I did not hear.    I
went away almost joyfully.    She could be dead to me
henceforth without a troubling thought.

A few days later, I saw Strachan, and spoke about
the Expedition, Starkie, Clarkson and Brooke, again.
Worked with a will at my classics, and at my spiritual
classics as well : struggled against despondent and not-
to-be-dismissed terrors and horrors about Rosy : was
once almost setting out for Paris, with a notion (il-
logical enough) that she was there, but a little reflection
showed me that my arrangement of things was best.
She was in London I was sure.    She would probably
write to me in Paris (perhaps not knowing my London
address).    My man would telegraph at once : I would
be with her at once.    But a sudden idea that my man
might, after all, be negligent, unsettled me.

The afternoon after my consideration of the matter in this light I spent in a long walk and debate with myself.

When I returned home, looking as usual on the hall table for the longed-for telegram, I saw one. (My heart started). I picked it up; came quietly into the study and, at the window, opened it.

*She was found.*

I threw up my face and laughed. *Found ! found ! found ! found at last.*

A letter from her. This:

*' I cannot give you up. I am ill. Do come to me. I am sorry for it. It was wrong of me. Will you forgive me and come?*

*' R. H.'*

'Forgive you? Come?' I said, laughing: 'Oh, little Rosebud, I will forgive you for forgiving me! I will come to you, and keep you, and——' Ending in laughter and tears.

To have found her again! To know that I had not . . . Nay, I knew nothing yet! And she was ill.

How long it took for the gold-incited hansom to get to the place! How long the Anglicised Italian woman took to tell me where she was! But upstairs I went at last: up, up, to the very top of the house, the dusty, dingy attic. She was there.

I knocked softly at the door and, on *her* voice saying that I was to come in, went in, and stood for a moment looking. I had but seen her pale worn face on the pillow before she had started up with a wild cry. And then I was holding her in my arms, and she me, silently.

In a little I felt how she squeezed me in her old dear child's way, so quietly, pulling me in to her, and I bent back my head so as to look at her face. But she would not let me: turning round her head and pressing it to my neck, in her old dear child's way. It seemed a dream that we had ever been away from one another. And then all at once she kissed me on the lips, such a long kiss; and hid her face again, and sighed contentedly. And so we remained in one another's arms some time—in perfect silence.

At last I began to think; but had no more than
begun, when her breast heaved, all her body heaved,
before the sound of the cough came as a relief to it.
I feared that my holding her might increase the effort,
and made a little move to loosen from her, but she
would not. *Feared* indeed : there was fear in me still.

' Rosebud,' I said, when I was sitting by her on the
bed, stroking her hand, she lying back on the pillow
looking at me, ' you 've got a very bad cold.'

' Yes,' she said, ' I——' And went off into another
fit of coughing, the third she had had since I came in.

' How did you get it ?' I asked.

' *Got* it !' she said with a smile, ' *Caught* it !'

' Well——' I began; and stopped. I was deter-
mining that she should be out of London before that
night.

And so she was.—We went down together to Mickle-
hurst, a place I had once heard of as sunny and with
a deep blue sky. The child seemed very contented,
quietly contented, dreamily contented, somehow contented as I did not quite like her to be. The patience
with which she bore her convulsive fits of coughing
seemed to me strange. Once I caught myself thinking of a dying monkey I had seen in the Paris streets.

Arrived in the hotel, albeit I hesitated a little, I
determined that I would go and bring a doctor to see
her at once. And, having made her comfortable in
the window of a room that looked over the blue winding sea-y river, with its girdling darkened mountains,
over which the sun was setting in mellow golden
warmth, I went down and inquired the name and
address of some doctor. I seemed to be drinking in
the clear, pure air as I walked along.

I found the doctor's house, and the doctor; and
brought him to see her. He reported a bad cold,
cautiously adding that he would come again and see
her on Saturday. (This was Wednesday). I accompanied him down to the hotel door. I rather liked
his face : he had a little gold light in his eyes somewhere, perhaps only something to do with the sun
there. I asked him one or two questions about her
which he answered simply. She had caught a bad

cold : that was clear. Perhaps it was nothing more :
perhaps again it was ; perhaps even it might develop
into congestion of the lungs. She seemed in rather
a low state of health ; but he would see her again in
a few days, on Saturday, and then he should be able
to tell me if there was anything. I said :

'Thank you ; very well, be it so. My name is
Leicester. We shall probably be staying here for
some little time.'

And so we parted.

Rosy spent a bad night with the coughing. She
did not care to go out, although the day was delightfully sunnily warm, but stayed in an easy-chair by the
open window looking over the blue winding sea-y river
and the girdling mountains, all set in the deep blue
enamelled firmament. I left her with a book for an
hour in the morning and went down on to the shore ;
and again, late in the afternoon. Her cough grew
worse towards evening, and at last it struck me to go
out and get her some sweets to suck to try and stop
it. I brought in a large packet of divers sorts, which
pleased her : and we sat by the fire, which she had
wished should be lit, and talked quietly and happily
about ourselves in the past.

This night was worse than the last, and the next
day than that which preceded it ; and so with the
next night. Two or three times during this last
after a long fit of convulsive coughing, she brought up
some sticky, rusty-coloured stuff, with thin streaks of
blood in it, that I examined in the candle-light, and
having examined, felt a renewal of that indefinable
fear that had entered me when all her body heaved
before the sound of the cough came as a relief to it.
As I lay back, wondering about this, she all at once
said :

' I think, dear, I'm going to *die.*'

I was startled.

After a pause :

' What makes you think that ? ' I said.

After another pause :

' I *wanted* to die ! I knew I was catching it all the
while, and I *didn't care*: I didn't stop it a bit ! That

was because I wanted to die. But when I found how
. . I think God is going to *punish* me for it.'

I turned over, and kissed her on the cheek.

'Serious,' she said, moving her head a little and
looking at me, ' *Serious !* '

'Quite serious,' said I, beginning to smile. 'Quite
serious,' and kissed her again and was silent.

That inspection of the handkerchief ultimately decided me at breakfast to go and find the doctor again :
which I did, but he could not come till later.

Then Rosy was informed that she would have to go
to bed again, and perhaps have to stop there a little.
I at once suspected congestion of the lungs, whatever
that precisely meant.

As the doctor and I went down stairs together I
catechised him. He said that she had pneumonia. I
inquired the precise meaning of pneumonia.

' Inflammation of the substance of the lungs.'

' Was it dangerous ? '

' Sometimes.'

' Fatal ? '

' Sometimes.'

' How long did it last ? '

'Three or four days, in good cases ; more generally
a fortnight or so.'

'I asked him a few more questions, and then he
took up the word, and told me what would and what
might be required to be done. And so we parted
again.

I came upstairs to Rosy with a feeling as if there
was going to be a species of campaign undertaken.
The first thing to do was to find out if she minded
leaving the hotel. She did not. Then I went out to
observe the house that the doctor had recommended
to me.

It was rather a cottage than a house. I liked it.
It had a small garden, bright with flowers, in front of
the dining-room, a long thin room with two garden-
windows opening on to a little lawn. I came back
with a description of it, which, having pleased her,
sent me off to take the place at once ; and back to
bring her to it.

By lunch-time we, I and the landlady and the servant, that is, had the dining-room turned into a bed-room—light, airy, and comfortable.

The doctor came in the afternoon again. Further directions were given, and he left us, saying that he would leave the prescriptions at the chemist's as he went home. By tea-time everything was ready. Rosy had throughout remained quiescent, except that, as she was coming into the house, she noticed some red daisies in the bed under the window, and plucked one, saying : ' A *pretty* thing !' and for a moment stood looking at it, while I stood looking at her.

I had everything to hand — inhaler, medicines, milk, beef-tea; and the kettle, with a long brown-paper spout to it, so as to keep the atmosphere moist with the steam, on the fire, from whose immediate heat and light she was sheltered by the bed-curtain drawn out and tucked under the mattress. I felt no fear now. The sense of her lying there as she was, seemed to admit of no feeling but calm tenderness.

The cough was very troublesome : more violent, more as it were ineffectual. She was very thirsty, and complained of the warm milk and beef-tea. Orders had been left that it was to be warm, and so of course she would have to drink it warm. I had to coax her to it like a child. The same with the inhalation. At first she, half sleepy, would not inhale, but kept moaning, and turning her mouth away from the pipe, till I bantered her into taking twenty pulls to show she was not afraid of it, and then turned the twenty into thirty, and the thirty into fifty, and so on up to a hundred, and far over (I deceiving her by dropping back the number several times). So the requisite ten minutes inhalation was achieved. The poor child could get no sleep. She kept up a low moaning all the while, occasionally sitting up with her chin on her knees, and the lower part of her hands turned round in her eyes. Once she suddenly looked up at me and said :

' Don't you *believe* I got this as a punishment for wanting to die ? '

'No,' I answered 'I don't.   I think you got it as the result of catching a severe cold.'

'But I *did* it—I did it on *purpose*!'

'The cold wouldn't know anything about that.   And you mustn't talk any more.'

She had a violent fit of coughing.   When it was done she said:

'I do wish you'd talk to me.   I can't get to sleep. I *like* to hear you talking!'

'Very well,' I said, 'I'll tell you a story.   Will that do?'

'Yes,' she said, 'but lie down there.   I don't like you *sitting up*.'

I lay down on the extreme edge of the bed, with my head on the bolster, and began my story.   It was the story of Undine.   Often I had to stop on account of her coughing.   Once the story was so broken into by a fit of it, that I hoped she would forget or not care to hear any more and would try to go to sleep.   Not so. She began to talk about what had happened to her in London, and would not.brook interruption.   At last, I let her say what she had to say.   She told me of her life at Wiltshire Crescent.   Then, suddenly, after a pause:

'I was *glad* when you came,' she said slowly, 'I had a most horrid dream of you.   I dreamed you were dead, and that I saw your coffin carried by men to the ceme-tery.   I thought I was in such grief about parting with you in anger, that I would have given half my life to have parted with you friendly. . . . I know I have been very wicked in doing what I have, but I do believe God will forgive me.   I *did* love you! I was also in trouble as to whether you were safe in heaven, and I thought I wept so bitterly, and my grief was so great that, while I was following to see where you were buried, I was obliged to kneel down to pray God to take you to heaven, and to forgive all, at the same time promising I would be good all the rest of my life, in hope to see you there—when I awoke and found it all a dream.   And I was pleased, but it upset me for days, and at last I made up my mind to write to you, as I could not rest.'

She had another fit of coughing, and I got up to give her some milk. After that I thought she had forgotten the story, but she requested its continuance, and so I continued it, with the necessary breaks, till four in the morning, when she fell asleep.

Not even the orders of the doctor prevailed over my disinclination to awakening her at five for her medicine. She herself awoke a little later: the medicine was given; and at her request the story continued; but only for a little, for we could not get on with it 'one little *bit*,' as she said, owing to the growing frequency of her fits of coughing. She was quite exhausted by the time the sun came into the room over the top of the hedge; that is, about seven o'clock. I was tired, but not sleepy: and less tired when I had washed myself. Then she fell asleep again.

The doctor came about eleven. He sanctioned her drinking her milk and beef-tea cold if she really did not like to drink it warm; and Rosy's silence said that she did not like. I went with him to the door and into the garden, where I asked him if he could not give her some opiate? He shook his head. I said that she was being torn to pieces by the cough, and that I could not help thinking that it was dangerous to let her get as exhausted as she had been a few hours ago, and was yet. He said:

'I *dare* not give her anything.'

The words and their tone settled the matter. I asked again if it was possible to give her any stimulants now? He said:

'No; best not. Go on just the same as yesterday with the inhaler and the poultices, and the milk and beef-tea. That is all.'

I said that as fast as I gave it her, she brought it all up again: purposelessly. Then, after a proposal about a nurse, which I refused, he left me. I thought no more of him.

At about five she would have me lie down on the edge of the bed and try to get some sleep; and, with the promise from her that she would awaken me in an hour, when it would be time for her to inhale again, I closed my eyes. She deceived me. It was seven when I awoke : was awakened by what was, probably, an unusually violent fit of coughing.  I scolded her, my thin-faced little darling, as I got the inhaler ready : she, between her coughings, smiling at me.

After tea—I sitting by the bedside, holding her hand and thinking—she all at once quite opened her eyes and looked at me.

'Where do people *go* to when they die?' she said.

I looked at her dear child's eyes, but did not answer her.

'Do *tell* me,' she said, in a child's aggrieved tone, rumpling her brow, 'Don't *tease* me!  Tell me true!'

After a pause, I answered her :

'I believe that they go into the earth and the air from which they came.'

'Yes,' she said, 'but that's not their *spirits*.  What do their *spirits* do?'

'Their spirits, too, go into the earth and the air.'

She shook her head :

'No,' she said, 'their spirits go up '—(looking up)— 'up into heaven!'

I lifted her hand, and bent my head, and kissed her hand softly.

'But don't *you* think so too?' she said.

'No,' I said, still bent over her hand, 'But' (looking up at her and smiling), 'what does it matter *what* I think, dear?'

She began to cough, and went on for a little.  Then :

'Don't you think,' she said, 'that *good* people go up to heaven when they die?'

'Don't talk any more in this way!' I said, getting up and sitting on the bed by her, 'or I shall—Well, I shall have to stop you some way.'  And I put my arm round her shoulders, and drew her head to mine.

'Ah,' she said, drawing her head back so as to look at me, 'but *don't* you?'

'Don't I what?'

Her brow rumpled.

'Don't *tease* me!' she said, 'You *must tell* me!'

'Very well,' I said, 'I will tell you, then.  'I don't think anyone goes up to heaven, dear, however good

Q

they are, for I don't believe there's any heaven to
go to.'

'But what be-*comes* of them, then?'

'They go into the earth and the air from whence
they came.'

'That's *horrid*!' she said, 'I don't——' and began
to cough again.

I put my arm round her shoulders, and leant my
cheek to hers that was wet.

'What is it?' I said, 'Why are you crying?'

In a little:

'I was thinking,' she said, 'that God wouldn't let
us see one another then, perhaps, because we had
been so sinful, and because you—because you talked
in that way. If you didn't talk in that way, perhaps
He would, you know; because I *did* love you so!'
(She had turned and thrown her arms round my neck.)
'Oh, *I couldn't do without you!* I *did* try, I *did* try!
But you were so much to me!' Her trembling lips
could scarcely finish it.

At last:

'Oh, Rosy,' I said, with a low, choking voice, 'My
little Rosebud!'

'Hush!' she said, 'hush, dear. Don't trouble about
it afterwards. I don't think God'll be so hard upon
us; I don't *think* He will! And it wasn't *your* fault,
this. It was all *my* fault; *I* did it! I *knew* I did!
But I don't mind now. Kiss me, dear; kiss me. It
wasn't *your* fault.'

I kissed her, and straightway the cough caught and
shook her poor body through and through; but she
would not have me take my arms from round her.
And as I felt all this, the thought in me turned to
utter fierceness.

We talked no more of these things, except that
Rosy told me that last night she had dreamt of being
smothered by wreaths of smoke, and could not wake
me. We talked of the dear hours in the past, and of
the dearer that were to be in the future—by snatches;
for her cough was almost ceaseless, and, it seemed to
me, more violent than last night. She had, apparently,
forgotten about the story.

But, as the night wore on, she became worse. I had great trouble to get her to take the inhalation. She kept up the low moaning all the time, as she had done on the first night; occasionally, too, sitting up as before, with her chin on her knees, and the lower parts of her hands turned round in her eyes. I did not leave the bed-side for a moment. Now and then she fell asleep, but 'the low moaning did not cease, except when she muttered incoherently.

The slow hours passed. I must have dozed. I awoke with a start. She was struggling violently. I saw that, and her swollen, livid face, and eyes strangely prominent with strange, clear brightness. Then I knew that she wanted me, and, in a moment, was across the bed, with one arm round her body and the other loosening her nightdress at the throat; but she had caught it, as it were, by chance, and rent it down wide open, just as the button was coming undone. I held her steadily up, despite her violent, downward struggles. She knew I was holding her. She could not get breath; she was suffocating. Her chest seemed rigid. I looked at her livid face again, her bright eyes, her stretched nostrils.

Then, before I scarcely knew what had happened, except a tightened effort of her body in my arms, she had ceased struggling.

I looked at her face: looked long, and at last, wildly. I shook her gently; lowered my arm to shake her again. Her head fell back with upward, staring eyes. I thought, *She is dead, she is dead.* What did it mean? No . . . No . . .

I gathered her close in my arms, kissing her warm, pure throat, talking to myself; and let both of us lie back in the soft pillows, I with my cheek on her warm, pure breast. Ah, better to sleep now without more words; better to sleep! Think no more of that phantasy. I was ever given to such. As a boy, I could not quite tell sometimes whether I was in a dream or awake; I could not quite tell sometimes whether I had seen things in dreams or in the vital air: So now! But that was enough of speaking. Better to sleep now without more words; better to sleep!

'*A bundle of myrrh is my well-beloved unto me; she shall lie all night betwixt my breasts. I charge you, O ye daughters of Jerusalem, by the roes and by the hinds of the field, that ye stir not up nor awake my love till she please.*'

**THE END.**

Printed by T. and A. CONSTABLE, Printers to Her Majesty
at the Edinburgh University Press

# BOOKS BY FRANCIS ADAMS.

Essays in Modernity. 5s. net.

A Child of the Age. 3s. 6d. net.

*Published by* JOHN LANE.

The Australians. 10s. 6d.

The New Egypt. 5s.

Tiberius. 10s. 6d.

*Published by* T. FISHER UNWIN.

John Webb's End. 2s.

The Melbournians. 3s. 6d.

*Published by* REMINGTON & CO.

Australian Life. 3s. 6d.

*Published by* CHAPMAN & HALL.

Songs of the Army of the Night. 1s.

Poetical Works. 2s.

Australian Essays. 1s.

*Published by* WILLIAM REEVES.

*Fifth Edition, just ready.*

KEYNOTES.   By GEORGE EGERTON.   With Title-page by
AUBREY BEARDSLEY.   Crown 8vo, cloth, 3s. 6d. net.

'Emboldened, doubtless, by the success of "Dodo," the author of "Keynotes" offers us a set of stories written with the least amount of literary
skill and in the worst literary taste.   We have refrained from quotation,
for fear of giving to this book an importance which it does not merit.'—*Pall
Mall Gazette.*

'The sirens sing in it from the first page to the last.   It may, perhaps,
shock you with disregard of conventionality and reticencies, but you will
all the same have to admit its fascination.   There can be no doubt that in
Mr. George Egerton his publishers have discovered a story-teller of genius.'
—*Star.*

'This is a collection of eight of the prettiest short stories that have appeared for many a day.   They turn for the most part on feminine traits of
character; in fact, the book is a little psychological study of woman under
various circumstances.   The characters are so admirably drawn, and the
scenes and landscapes are described with so much and so rare vividness,
that one cannot help being almost spell-bound by their perusal.'—*St. James's
Gazette.*

'A rich, passionate temperament vibrates through every line. . . . We
have met nothing so lovely in its tenderness since Mr. Kipling's "Without
Benefit of Clergy."'—*Daily Chronicle.*

'For any one who cares more for truth than for orthodox mummery, and
for the real flood of the human heart than for the tepid negus which stirs
the veins of respectability, this little book deserves a hearty welcome.'
—*Sketch.*

'Singularly artistic in its brilliant suggestiveness.'—*Daily News.*

'This is a book which is a portentous sign of our times.   The wildness,
the fierceness, the animality that underlie the soft, smooth surface of
woman's pretty and subdued face—this is the theme to which she again and
again recurs.'—T. P. in *Weekly Sun.*

'To credit a new writer with the possession of genius is a serious matter,
but it is nevertheless a verdict which Mr. George Egerton can hardly
avoid at the hands of those who read his delightful sketches.'—*Liverpool
Post.*

'These lovely sketches are informed by such throbbing feeling, such insight into complex woman, that we with all speed and warmth advise those
who are in search of splendid literature to procure "Keynotes" without
delay.'—*Literary World.*

'These very clever stories of Mr. Egerton's.'—*Black and White.*

'The reading of it is an adventure, and, once begun, it is hard to tear
yourself from the book till you have devoured every line.   There is im-
pulsive life in every word of it.   It has passion, ardour, vehement romance.
It is full of youth; often enough the revolt and despair of youth.'—*Irish
Independent.*

'Every line of the book gives the impression that here some woman has
crystallised her life's drama; has written down her soul upon the page.'—
*Review of Reviews.*

'The work of a woman who has lived every hour of her life, be she young
or old. . . . She allows us, like the great artists of old, Shakespeare and
Goethe, to draw our own moral from the stories she tells, and it is with no
uncertain touch or faltering hand that she pulls aside the curtain of conventional hypocrisy which hundreds of women hang between the world and
their own hearts. . . . The insight of the writer into the curious and com-
plicated nature of women is almost miraculous.'—*Lady's Pictorial.*

'She is a writer with a profound understanding of the human heart. She understands men; and, more than this, she understands women. . . . For those who weary of the conventional fiction, and who long for something out of the ordinary run of things, these are tales that carry the zest of living.'—*Boston Beacon.*

'It is not a book for babes and sucklings, since it cuts deep into rather dangerous soil; but it is refined and skilful . . . strikes a very true and touching note of pathos.'—*Westminster Gazette.*

'The author of these able word sketches is manifestly a close observer of Nature's moods, and one, moreover, who carefully takes stock of the up-to-date thoughts that shake mankind.'—*Daily Telegraph.*

'Not since the "Story of an African Farm" was written has any woman delivered herself of so strong, so forcible a book.'—*Queen.*

'Powerful pictures of human beings living to-day, full of burning pain, and thought, and passion.'—*Bookman.*

'A work of genius. There is upon the whole thing a stamp of down-right inevitableness as of things which must be written, and written exactly in that way.'—*Speaker.*

'"Keynotes' is a singularly clever book.'—*Truth.*

## THE DANCING FAUN. By FLORENCE FARR. With Title-page and Cover Design by AUBREY BEARDSLEY. Crown 8vo, 3s. 6d. net.

'We welcome the light and merry pen of Miss Farr as one of the deftest that has been wielded in the style of to-day. She has written the cleverest and the most cynical sensation story of the season.'—*Liverpool Daily Post.*

'Slight as it is, the story is, in its way, strong.'—*Literary World.*

'Full of bright paradox, and paradox which is no mere topsy-turvy play upon words, but the product of serious thinking upon life. One of the cleverest of recent novels.'—*Star.*

'It is full of epigrammatic effects, and it has a certain thread of pathos calculated to win our sympathy.'—*Queen.*

'The story is subtle and psychological after the fashion of modern psychology; it is undeniably clever and smartly written.'—*Gentlewoman.*

'No one can deny its freshness and wit. Indeed there are things in it here and there which John Oliver Hobbes herself might have signed without loss of reputation.'—*Woman.*

'There is a lurid power in the very unreality of the story. One does not quite understand how Lady Geraldine worked herself up to shooting her lover, but when she has done it, the description of what passes through her mind is magnificent.'—*Athenæum.*

'Written by an obviously clever woman.'—*Black and White.*

'Miss Farr has talent. "The Dancing Faun" contains writing that is distinctively good. Doubtless it is only a prelude to something much stronger.'—*Academy.*

'As a work of art the book has the merit of brevity and smart writing; while the *dénouement* is skilfully prepared, and comes as a surprise. If the book had been intended as a satire on the "new woman" sort of literature, it would have been most brilliant; but assuming it to be written in earnest, we can heartily praise the form of its construction without agreeing with the sentiments expressed.'—*St. James's Gazette.*

'Shows considerable power and aptitude.'—*Saturday Review.*

A

POOR FOLK. Translated from the Russian of FEDOR
DOSTOIEVSKY. By LENA MILMAN. With an Intro-
duction by GEORGE MOORE, and a Title-page and Cover
Design by AUBREY BEARDSLEY. Crown 8vo, 3s. 6d. net.

'The book is cleverly translated. "Poor Folk" gains in reality and pathos
by the very means that in less skilful hands would be tedious and commonplace.'—*Spectator.*

'A charming story of the love of a Charles Lamb kind of old bachelor
for a young work-girl. Full of quiet humour and still more full of the
*lachrymæ rerum.*'—*Star.*

'Scenes of poignant realism, described with so admirable a blending of
humour and pathos that they haunt the memory.'—*Daily News.*

'No one will read it attentively without feeling both its power and its
pathos.'—*Scotsman.*

'The book is one of great pathos and absorbing interest. Miss Milman
has given us an admirable version of it which will commend itself to every
one who cares for good literature.'—*Glasgow Herald.*

'These things seem small, but in the hands of Dostoievsky they make
a work of genius.'—*Black and White.*

'One of the most pathetic things in all literature, heartrending just
because its tragedy is so repressed.'—*Bookman.*

'As to novels, the very finest I have read of late or for long is "Poor Folk,"
by Fedor Dostoievsky, translated by Miss Lena Milman.'—*Truth.*

'A book to be read for the merits of its execution. The translator by
the way has turned it into excellent English.'—*Pall Mall Gazette.*

'The narrative vibrates with feeling, and these few unstudied letters convey to us a cry from the depths of a famished human soul. As far as we
can judge, the English rendering, though simple, retains that ring of
emotion which must distinguish the original.'—*Westminster Review.*

'One of the most striking studies in plain and simple realism which was
ever written.'—*Daily Telegraph.*

'"Poor Folk" is certainly a vivid and pathetic story.'—*Globe.*

'A triumph of realistic art—a masterpiece of a great writer.'—*Morning
Post.*

'Dostoievsky's novel has met with that rare advantage, a really good
translator.'—*Queen.*

'This admirable translation of a great author.'—*Liverpool Mercury.*

'"Poor Folk" Englished does not read like a translation—indubitably a
masterpiece.'—*Literary World.*

'Told with a gradually deepening intensity and force, a pathetic truth-
fulness which lives in the memory.'—*Leeds Mercury.*

'What Charles Dickens in his attempts to reproduce the sentiment and
pathos of the humble deceived himself and others into thinking that he did,
that Fedor Dostoievsky actually does.'—*Manchester Guardian.*

'It is a story that leaves the reader almost stunned. Miss Milman's
translation is admirable.'—*Gentlewoman.*

'The translation appears to be well done so far as we have compared it
with the original.'—W. R. MORFILL in *The Academy.*

'A most impressive and characteristic specimen of Russian fiction.
Those to whom Russian is a sealed book will be duly grateful to the translator (who has acquitted herself excellently), to Mr. Moore, and to the
publisher for this presentment of Dostoievsky's remarkable novel.'—*Times.*

# List of Books

in

# Belles Lettres

ALL BOOKS IN THIS CATALOGUE
ARE PUBLISHED AT NET PRICES

*1894*

*Telegraphic Address—*
' BODLEIAN, LONDON '

# ·A FEW PRESS NOTES

### GALLIENNE (RICHARD LE).

PROSE FANCIES. Third Edition. Crown 8vo. 5s. net.

' The sentiment rings true, and the quaint conceits which abound have a dainty prettiness which gives distinction to the prose.'—*Athenæum.*

' A more delightful collection of essays has not issued from the press since the time of Charles Lamb.'—*Weekly Sun.*

' They deserve to rank forthwith among the gems of English prose. And why? Because they could have been written only by a poet.'—*Daily Chronicle.*

### DAVIDSON (JOHN).

PLAYS. Small 4to. 7s. 6d. net.

' Mr. Davidson is in many ways one of the most remarkable of the younger poets, and in many respects the most richly endowed of all.'— Mr. QUILLER COUCH in *Speaker.*

' A very singular dramatist indeed, and, as a poet, so full of curious and varied power that we have conceived the greatest interest as to his personality and his plans.'—*Spectator.*

' There is no truer poet in England to-day than Mr. John Davidson.'— *Westminster Gazette.*

### EGERTON (GEORGE).

KEYNOTES. Fifth Edition. Crown 8vo. 3s. 6d. net.

' Singularly artistic in its brilliant suggestiveness.'—*Daily News.*

' Eight of the prettiest short stories that have appeared for many a day.' —*St. James's Gazette.*

' We have met with nothing so lovely in its tenderness since Mr. Kipling's "Without Benefit of Clergy."'—*Daily Chronicle.*

' Not since "The Story of an African Farm" was written has any woman delivered herself of so strong, so forcible a book.'—*Queen.*

### STREET (G. S.).

THE AUTOBIOGRAPHY OF A BOY. Second Edition. Fcap. 8vo. 3s. 6d. net.

' A creation in which there appears to be no flaw.'—*Pall Mall Gazette.*

' A quite priceless treasure. Tubby is indeed a new immortal.'— *Academy.*

' There is more observation and art of presentment in this little book than in a wilderness of three-volume novels, even by eminent hands.'— *Athenæum.*

' It is admirably done throughout, full of delicate strokes of ironical wit.' —*Daily Telegraph.*

1894.

# List of Books

IN

## *BELLES LETTRES*

*(Including some Transfers)*

# Published by John Lane

𝔗𝔥𝔢 𝔅𝔬𝔡𝔩𝔢𝔶 𝔥𝔢𝔞𝔡

VIGO STREET, LONDON, W.

*N.B.—The Authors and Publisher reserve the right of reprinting any book in this list if a new edition is called for, except in cases where a stipulation has been made to the contrary, and of printing a separate edition of any of the books for America irrespective of the numbers to which the English editions are limited. The numbers mentioned do not include copies sent to the public libraries, nor those sent for review.*

*Most of the books are published simultaneously in England and America, and in many instances the names of the American Publishers are appended.*

———◆———

ADAMS (FRANCIS).
ESSAYS IN MODERNITY. Crown 8vo. 5s. net. [*Shortly.*
Chicago : Stone & Kimball.

ADAMS (FRANCIS).
A CHILD OF THE AGE. Crown 8vo. 3s. 6d. net.
(*See* KEYNOTES SERIES.)
Boston : Roberts Bros.

ALLEN (GRANT).

    THE LOWER SLOPES : A Volume of Verse.  With Title-page and Cover Design by J. ILLINGWORTH KAY. 600 copies.   Crown 8vo.   5s. net.

    Chicago : Stone & Kimball.

ALLEN (GRANT).

    THE WOMAN WHO DID.   Crown 8vo.   3s. 6d. net. (*See* KEYNOTES SERIES.)        [*In rapid preparation.*

    Boston : Roberts Bros.

BEARDSLEY (AUBREY).

    THE STORY OF VENUS AND TANNHÄUSER, in which is set forth an exact account of the Manner of State held by Madam Venus, Goddess and Meretrix, under the famous Hörselberg, and containing the adventures of Tannhäuser in that place, his repentance, his journeying to Rome, and return to the loving mountain. By AUBREY BEARDSLEY.    With 20 full-page illustrations, numerous ornaments, and a cover from the same hand.  Sq. 16mo.  10s. 6d. net.  [*In preparation.*

BEECHING (REV. H. C.).

    IN A GARDEN : Poems.   With a specially-designed Title-page.   Crown 8vo.   5s. net.            [*In preparation.*

BENSON (ARTHUR CHRISTOPHER).

    A NEW VOLUME OF POEMS.   Fcap. 8vo.   5s. net.
                                  [*In rapid preparation.*

BROTHERTON (MARY).

    ROSEMARY FOR REMEMBRANCE.    With Title-page and Cover Design by WALTER WEST.   Fcap. 8vo.   5s. net.
                                  [*In rapid preparation.*

DALMON (C. W.).

    SONG FAVOURS.   With a specially-designed Title-page. Sq. 16mo.   4s. 6d. net.            [*In preparation.*

D'ARCY (ELLA).
> A VOLUME OF STORIES. Crown 8vo. 3s. 6d. net.
> (*See* KEYNOTES SERIES.) [*In preparation.*
> Boston : Roberts Bros.

DAVIDSON (JOHN).
> PLAYS : An Unhistorical Pastoral ; A Romantic Farce ;
> Bruce, a Chronicle Play ; Smith, a Tragic Farce ;
> Scaramouch in Naxos, a Pantomime, with a Frontis-
> piece and Cover Design by AUBREY BEARDSLEY.
> Printed at the Ballantyne Press. 500 copies. Small
> 4to. 7s. 6d. net.
> Chicago : Stone & Kimball.

DAVIDSON (JOHN).
> FLEET STREET ECLOGUES. Second Edition. Fcap. 8vo,
> buckram. 5s. net.

DAVIDSON (JOHN).
> A RANDOM ITINERARY AND A BALLAD. With a Fron-
> tispiece and Title-page by LAURENCE HOUSMAN.
> 600 copies. Fcap. 8vo, Irish Linen. 5s. net.
> Boston : Copeland & Day.

DAVIDSON (JOHN).
> THE NORTH WALL. Fcap. 8vo. 2s. 6d. net.
> *The few remaining copies transferred by the Author*
> *to the present Publisher.*

DAVIDSON (JOHN).
> BALLADS AND SONGS. Fcap. 8vo. 5s. net.
> [*In preparation.*

DE TABLEY (LORD).
> POEMS, DRAMATIC AND LYRICAL. By JOHN LEICESTER
> WARREN (Lord De Tabley). Illustrations and Cover
> Design by C. S. RICKETTS. Second Edition.
> Crown 8vo. 7s. 6d. net.

DE TABLEY (LORD).
> A NEW VOLUME OF POEMS. Crown 8vo. 5s. net.
> [*In preparation.*

EGERTON (GEORGE).
> KEYNOTES. Fifth Edition. Crown 8vo. 3s. 6d. net.
> (*See* KEYNOTES SERIES.)
> Boston: Roberts Bros.

EGERTON (GEORGE).
> DISCORDS. Crown 8vo. 3s. 6d. net.
> (*See* KEYNOTES SERIES.)     [*In rapid preparation.*
> Boston: Roberts Bros.

EGERTON (GEORGE).
> YOUNG OFEG'S DITTIES. A translation from the Swedish
> of OLA HANSSON. Crown 8vo. 3s. 6d. net.
> [*In preparation.*

FARR (FLORENCE).
> THE DANCING FAUN. Crown 8vo. 3s. 6d. net.
> (*See* KEYNOTES SERIES.)
> Boston: Roberts Bros.

FLETCHER (J. S.).
> THE WONDERFUL WAPENTAKE. By 'A SON OF THE
> SOIL.' With 18 full-page Illustrations on Japanese
> vellum, by J. A. SYMINGTON. Crown 8vo. 5s. 6d.
> net.                          [*In rapid preparation.*

GALE (NORMAN).
> ORCHARD SONGS. With Title-page and Cover Design
> by J. ILLINGWORTH KAY. Fcap. 8vo, Irish Linen.
> 5s. net.
> Also a Special Edition limited in number on hand-made paper
>   bound in English vellum. £1, 1s. net.
> New York: G. P. Putnam's Sons.

GARNETT (RICHARD).
> POEMS. With Title-page by J. ILLINGWORTH KAY.
> 350 copies. Crown 8vo. 5s. net.
> Boston: Copeland & Day.

GOSSE (EDMUND).
THE LETTERS OF THOMAS LOVELL BEDDOES. Now
first edited. Pott 8vo. 5s. net.
New York : Macmillan & Co.

GRAHAME (KENNETH).
PAGAN PAPERS : A Volume of Essays. With Title-
page by AUBREY BEARDSLEY. Fcap. 8vo. 5s. net.
Chicago : Stone & Kimball.

GREENE (G. A.).
ITALIAN LYRISTS OF TO-DAY. Translations in the
original metres from about thirty-five living Italian
poets, with bibliographical and biographical notes.
Crown 8vo. 5s. net.
New York : Macmillan & Co.

GREENWOOD (FREDERICK).
IMAGINATION IN DREAMS. Crown 8vo. 5s. net.
[*In rapid preparation.*

HAKE (T. GORDON).
A SELECTION FROM HIS POEMS. Edited by Mrs.
MEYNELL. With a Portrait after D. G. ROSSETTI,
and a Cover Design by GLEESON WHITE. Crown
8vo. 5s. net.
Chicago : Stone & Kimball.

HARLAND (HENRY).
THE BOHEMIAN GIRL AND OTHER STORIES. Crown
8vo. 3s. 6d. net. (*See* KEYNOTES SERIES.)
Boston : Roberts Bros. [*In preparation.*

HAYES (ALFRED).
THE VALE OF ARDEN AND OTHER POEMS. With a
Title-page designed by E. H. NEW. Fcap. 8vo.
3s. 6d. net. [*In preparation.*

HOPPER (NORA).
BALLADS IN PROSE. With a Title-page and Cover by
WALTER WEST. Sq. 16mo. 5s. net.
[*In rapid preparation.*

IRVING (LAURENCE).
GODEFROI AND YOLANDE: A Play. With three Illus-
trations by AUBREY BEARDSLEY. Sm. 4to. 5s. net.
*[In preparation.*

JAMES (W. P.).
ROMANTIC PROFESSIONS: A Volume of Essays. With
Title-page designed by J. ILLINGWORTH KAY.
Crown 8vo. 5s. net.
New York: Macmillan & Co.

JOHNSON (LIONEL).
THE ART OF THOMAS HARDY: Six Essays. With
Etched Portrait by WM. STRANG, and Bibliography
by JOHN LANE. Crown 8vo. 5s. 6d. net.
Also 150 copies, large paper, with proofs of the portrait. £1, 1s.
net.    *[Just published.*
New York: Dodd, Mead & Co.

JOHNSON (PAULINE).
WHITE WAMPUM: Poems. Crown 8vo. 5s. net.
*[In preparation.*

KEYNOTES SERIES.
Each volume with specially designed Title-page by AUBREY
BEARDSLEY. Crown 8vo, cloth. 3s. 6d. net.
Vol.    I. KEYNOTES. By GEORGE EGERTON.
*[Fifth edition now ready.*
Vol.    II. THE DANCING FAUN. By FLORENCE FARR.
Vol.    III. POOR FOLK. Translated from the Russian of
F. Dostoievsky by LENA MILMAN. With
a Preface by GEORGE MOORE.
Vol.    IV. A CHILD OF THE AGE. By FRANCIS ADAMS.
Vol.    V. THE GREAT GOD PAN AND THE INMOST
LIGHT. By ARTHUR MACHEN.
*[In October.*

KEYNOTES SERIES—*continued.*
Vol. VI. DISCORDS. By GEORGE EGERTON.
[*In November.*
Vol. VII. PRINCE ZALESKI. By M. P. SHIEL.
[*In November.*
Vol. VIII. THE WOMAN WHO DID. By GRANT ALLEN.
[*In November.*
Vol. IX. WOMEN'S TRAGEDIES. By H. D. LOWRY.
Vol. X. THE BOHEMIAN GIRL AND OTHER STORIES.
By HENRY HARLAND.
Vol. XI. A VOLUME OF STORIES. By H. B. MARRIOTT
WATSON.
Vol. XII. A VOLUME OF STORIES. By ELLA D'ARCY.
Boston : Roberts Bros.

LEATHER (R. K.).
VERSES. 250 copies. Fcap. 8vo. 3s. net.
*Transferred by the Author to the present Publisher.*

LE GALLIENNE (RICHARD).
PROSE FANCIES. With Portrait of the Author by
WILSON STEER. Third Edition. Crown 8vo. Purple
cloth, uniform with ' The Religion of a Literary Man.'
5s. net.
Also a limited large paper edition. 12s. 6d. net.
New York : G. P. Putnam's Sons.

LE GALLIENNE (RICHARD).
THE BOOK BILLS OF NARCISSUS. An Account rendered
by RICHARD LE GALLIENNE. Third Edition.
Crown 8vo. Purple cloth, uniform with 'The Re-
ligion of a Literary Man.' 3s. 6d. net.
[*In rapid preparation.*

LE GALLIENNE (RICHARD).
ENGLISH POEMS. Third Edition. Crown 8vo. Purple
cloth, uniform with 'The Religion of a Literary Man.'
5s. net.
Boston : Copeland & Day.

LE GALLIENNE (RICHARD).
GEORGE MEREDITH: Some Characteristics. With a Bibliography (much enlarged) by JOHN LANE, portrait, etc. Fourth Edition. Crown 8vo. Purple cloth, uniform with 'The Religion of a Literary Man.' 5s. 6d. net.

LE GALLIENNE (RICHARD).
THE RELIGION OF A LITERARY MAN. 5th thousand. Crown 8vo. Purple cloth. 3s. 6d. net.
Also a special rubricated edition on hand-made paper. 8vo. 10s. 6d. net.
New York : G. P. Putnam's Sons.

LOWRY (H. D.).
WOMEN'S TRAGEDIES. Crown 8vo.    3s. 6d. net.
(*See* KEYNOTES SERIES.)          [*In preparation.*
Boston : Roberts Bros.

LUCAS (WINIFRED).
A VOLUME OF POEMS. Fcap. 8vo.    4s. 6d. net.
                                  [*In preparation.*

MACHEN (ARTHUR).
THE GREAT GOD PAN AND THE INMOST LIGHT. Crown 8vo.  3s. 6d. net.
(*See* KEYNOTES SERIES.)        [*In rapid preparation.*
Boston : Roberts Bros.

MARZIALS (THEO.).
THE GALLERY OF PIGEONS AND OTHER POEMS.    Post 8vo.   4s. 6d. net.       [*Very few remain.*
*Transferred by the Author to the present Publisher.*

MEREDITH (GEORGE).
THE FIRST PUBLISHED PORTRAIT OF THIS AUTHOR, engraved on the wood by W. BISCOMBE GARDNER, after the painting by G. F. WATTS. Proof copies on Japanese vellum, signed by painter and engraver. £1, 1s. net.

MEYNELL (MRS.), (ALICE C. THOMPSON).
POEMS. Second Edition. Fcap. 8vo. 3s. 6d. net. A few of the 50 large paper copies (First Edition) remain. 12s. 6d. net.

MEYNELL (MRS.).
THE RHYTHM OF LIFE AND OTHER ESSAYS. Second
Edition. Fcap. 8vo. 3s. 6d. net. A few of the 50
large paper copies (First Edition) remain. 12s. 6d. net.

MILLER (JOAQUIN).
THE BUILDING OF THE CITY BEAUTIFUL. Fcap 8vo.
With a Decorated Cover. 5s. net. [*Just published.*
Chicago: Stone & Kimball.

MILMAN (LENA).
POOR FOLK. Translated from the Russian of F. DOS-
TOIEVSKY. Crown 8vo. 3s. 6d. net.
(*See* KEYNOTES SERIES.)
Boston: Roberts Bros.

MONKHOUSE (ALLAN).
BOOKS AND PLAYS: A Volume of Essays on Meredith,
Borrow, Ibsen, and others. 400 copies. Crown 8vo.
5s. net.
Philadelphia: J. B. Lippincott Co.

NESBIT (E.).
A VOLUME OF POEMS. Cr. 8vo. 5s. net. [*In preparation.*

NETTLESHIP (J. T.).
ROBERT BROWNING: Essays and Thoughts. Third
Edition. With a Portrait. Crown 8vo. 5s. 6d. net.
New York: Chas. Scribner's Sons. [*In rapid preparation.*

NOBLE (JAS. ASHCROFT).
THE SONNET IN ENGLAND AND OTHER ESSAYS. Title-
page and Cover Design by AUSTIN YOUNG. 600
copies. Crown 8vo. 5s. net.
Also 50 copies large paper. 12s. 6d. net.

O'SHAUGHNESSY (ARTHUR).
HIS LIFE AND HIS WORK. With Selections from his
Poems. By LOUISE CHANDLER MOULTON. Por-
trait and Cover Design. Fcap. 8vo. 5s. net.
Chicago: Stone & Kimball. [*Just published.*

OXFORD CHARACTERS.
A series of lithographed portraits by WILL ROTHENSTEIN, with text by F. YORK POWELL and others. To be issued monthly in term. Each number will contain two portraits. Parts I. to V. ready. 200 sets only, folio, wrapper, 5s. net per part; 25 special large paper sets containing proof impressions of the portraits signed by the artist, 10s. 6d. net per part.

PETERS (WM. THEODORE).
POSIES OUT OF RINGS. Sq. 16mo. 3s. 6d. net.
[*In preparation.*

PLARR (VICTOR).
A VOLUME OF POEMS. Crown 8vo. 5s. net.
[*In preparation.*

RICKETTS (C. S.) AND C. H. SHANNON.
HERO AND LEANDER. By CHRISTOPHER MARLOWE and GEORGE CHAPMAN. With Borders, Initials, and Illustrations designed and engraved on the wood by C. S. RICKETTS and C. H. SHANNON. Bound in English vellum and gold. 200 copies only. 35s. net.
Boston : Copeland & Day.

RHYS (ERNEST).
A LONDON ROSE AND OTHER RHYMES. With Title-page designed by SELWYN IMAGE. 350 copies. Crown 8vo. 5s. net.
New York : Dodd, Mead & Co.

SHIEL (M. P.).
PRINCE ZALESKI. Crown 8vo. 3s. 6d. net.
(*See* KEYNOTES SERIES.) [*In preparation.*
Boston : Roberts Bros.

STREET (G. S.).
THE AUTOBIOGRAPHY OF A BOY. Passages selected by his friend G. S. S. With Title-page designed by C. W. FURSE. Fcap. 8vo. 3s. 6d. net.
[*Second Edition now ready.*
Philadelphia : J. B. Lippincott Co.

SYMONS (ARTHUR).
A New Volume of Poems.  Crown 8vo.  5s. net.
[*In preparation.*

THOMPSON (FRANCIS).
A Volume of Poems.  With Frontispiece, Title-page, and Cover Design by Laurence Housman.  Fourth Edition.  Pott 4to.  5s. net.
Boston : Copeland & Day.

TREE (H. BEERBOHM).
The Imaginative Faculty : A Lecture delivered at the Royal Institution.  With portrait of Mr. Tree from an unpublished drawing by the Marchioness of Granby.  Fcap. 8vo, boards.  2s. 6d. net.

TYNAN HINKSON (KATHARINE).
Cuckoo Songs.  With Title-page and Cover Design by Laurence Housman.  Fcap. 8vo.  5s. net.
Boston : Copeland & Day.

TYNAN HINKSON (KATHARINE).
Miracle Plays.                    [*In preparation.*

WATSON (H. B. MARRIOTT).
A Volume of Stories.  Crown 8vo.  3s. 6d. net.
(*See* Keynotes Series.)           [*In preparation.*
Boston : Roberts Bros.

WATSON (WILLIAM).
Odes and Other Poems.  Fcap. 8vo.  4s. 6d. net.
[*Early in December.*

WATSON (WILLIAM).
The Eloping Angels : A Caprice.  Second Edition.  Square 16mo, buckram.  3s. 6d. net.
New York : Macmillan & Co.

WATSON (WILLIAM).

    EXCURSIONS IN CRITICISM : being some Prose Recrea-
      tions of a Rhymer. Second Edition. Cr. 8vo. 5s. net.
New York : Macmillan & Co.


WATSON (WILLIAM).

    THE PRINCE'S QUEST AND OTHER POEMS.   With a
      Bibliographical Note added.  Second Edition.  Fcap.
      8vo.  4s. 6d. net.


WATTS (THEODORE).

    POEMS.  Crown 8vo.  5s. net.       .  [*In preparation.*
    *There will also be an* Edition de Luxe *of this volume printed at
      the Kelmscott Press.*


WHARTON (H. T.).

    SAPPHO.  Memoir, Text, Selected Renderings, and a
      Literal Translation by HENRY THORNTON WHARTON.
      With three Illustrations.  Fcap. 8vo.  7s. 6d. net.
                         [*In preparation.*


WILDE (OSCAR).

    THE SPHINX.  A poem decorated throughout in line and
      colour, and bound in a design by CHARLES RICKETTS.
      250 copies.  £2, 2s. net.   25 copies large paper.
      £5, 5s. net.
Boston : Copeland & Day.


WILDE (OSCAR).

    The incomparable and ingenious history of Mr. W. H.,
      being the true secret of Shakespear's Sonnets now for
      the first time here fully set forth, with Initial Letters
      and Cover Design by CHARLES RICKETTS.  500 copies.
      10s. 6d. net.
    Also 50 copies large paper.  21s. net.       [*In preparation.*

WILDE (OSCAR).

DRAMATIC WORKS, now printed for the first time. With a specially-designed binding to each volume, by CHAS. SHANNON. 500 copies. Sm. 4to. 7s. 6d. net per vol.

Also 50 copies large paper. 15s. net per vol.

Vol. I. LADY WINDERMERE'S FAN : A Comedy in Four Acts. [Out of print.

Vol. II. A WOMAN OF NO IMPORTANCE : A Comedy in Four Acts. [Just published.

Vol. III. THE DUCHESS OF PADUA : A Blank Verse Tragedy in Five Acts. [Very shortly. Boston : Copeland & Day.

WILDE (OSCAR).

SALOMÉ : A Tragedy in One Act done into English. With 10 Illustrations, Title-page, Tail-piece, and Cover Design by AUBREY BEARDSLEY. 500 copies. Small 4to. 15s. net.

Also 100 copies large paper. 30s. net.

Boston : Copeland & Day.

# THE YELLOW BOOK

## An Illustrated Quarterly

Vol. I. Fourth Edition, 272 pages, 15 Illustrations, Title-page, and a Cover Design. Cloth. Price 5s. net. Pott 4to.

The Literary Contributions by MAX BEERBOHM, A. C. BENSON, HUBERT CRACKANTHORPE, ELLA D'ARCY, JOHN DAVIDSON, GEORGE EGERTON, RICHARD GARNETT, EDMUND GOSSE, HENRY HARLAND, JOHN OLIVER HOBBES, HENRY JAMES, RICHARD LE GALLIENNE, GEORGE MOORE, GEORGE SAINTSBURY, FRED. M. SIMPSON, ARTHUR SYMONS, WILLIAM WATSON, ARTHUR WAUGH.

The Art Contributions by Sir FREDERIC LEIGHTON, P.R.A., AUBREY BEARDSLEY, R. ANNING BELL, CHARLES W. FURSE, LAURENCE HOUSMAN, J. T. NETTLESHIP, JOSEPH PENNELL, WILL ROTHENSTEIN, WALTER SICKERT.

*Vol. II.  Third Edition.  Pott 4to, 364 pages, 23 Illustrations, and a New Title-page and Cover Design.  Cloth.  Price 5s. net.*
The Literary Contributions by FREDERICK GREENWOOD, ELLA D'ARCY, CHARLES WILLEBY, JOHN DAVIDSON, HENRY HARLAND, DOLLIE RADFORD, CHARLOTTE M. MEW, AUSTIN DOBSON, V., O., C. S., KATHARINE DE MATTOS, PHILIP GILBERT HAMERTON, RONALD CAMPBELL MACFIE, DAUPHIN MEUNIER, KENNETH GRAHAME, NORMAN GALE, NETTA SYRETT, HUBERT CRACKANTHORPE, ALFRED HAYES, MAX BEERBOHM, WILLIAM WATSON, and HENRY JAMES.
The Art Contributions by WALTER CRANE, A. S. HARTRICK, AUBREY BEARDSLEY, ALFRED THORNTON, P. WILSON STEER, JOHN S. SARGENT, A.R.A., SYDNEY ADAMSON, WALTER SICKERT, W. BROWN MacDOUGAL, E. J. SULLIVAN, FRANCIS FORSTER, BERNHARD SICKERT, and AYMER VALLANCE.
A Special Feature of Volume II. is a frank criticism of the Literature and Art of Volume I. by PHILIP GILBERT HAMERTON.

*Vol. III.  Now Ready.  Pott 4to, 280 pages, 15 Illustrations, and a New Title-page and Cover Design.  Cloth.  Price 5s. net.*
The Literary Contributions by WILLIAM WATSON, KENNETH GRAHAME, ARTHUR SYMONS, ELLA D'ARCY, JOSÉ MARIA DE HÉRÉDIA, ELLEN M. CLERKE, HENRY HARLAND, THEO MARZIALS, ERNEST DOWSON, THEODORE WRATISLAW, ARTHUR MOORE, OLIVE CUSTANCE, LIONEL JOHNSON, ANNIE MACDONELL, C. S., NORA HOPPER, S. CORNISH WATKINS, HUBERT CRACKANTHORPE, MORTON FULLERTON, LEILA MACDONALD, C. W. DALMON, MAX BEERBOHM, and JOHN DAVIDSON.
The Art Contributions by PHILIP BROUGHTON, GEORGE THOMSON, AUBREY BEARDSLEY, ALBERT FOSCHTER, WALTER SICKERT, P. WILSON STEER, WILLIAM HYDE, and MAX BEERBOHM.

*Prospectuses Post Free on Application.*
LONDON : JOHN LANE
BOSTON : COPELAND & DAY

www.ingramcontent.com/pod-product-compliance
Lightning Source LLC
Chambersburg PA
CBHW021059030726
47496CB00006B/1913